Kandy Shepherd swa for a life writing roma the Blue Mountains n husband, daughter, and at first sight and real-life they worked for her! Kandy loves to hear from her readers. Visit her at kandyshepherd.com

Since 1988, nationally bestselling author **Rochelle Alers** has written more than eighty books and short stories. She has earned numerous honours, including the Zora Neale Hurston Award, the Vivian Stephens Award for Excellence in Romance Writing and a Career Achievement Award from *RT Book Reviews*. She is a member of Zeta Phi Beta Sorority, Inc., Iota Theta Zeta Chapter. A full-time writer, she lives in a charming hamlet on Long Island. Rochelle can be contacted through her website, www.rochellealers.org

FROM BRIDAL DESIGNER TO BRIDE

KANDY SHEPHERD

A NEW FOUNDATION

ROCHELLE ALERS

MILLS & BOON

First Published in Great Britain 2021
by Mills & Boon, an imprint of HarperCollins*Publishers* Ltd
1 London Bridge Street, London, SE1 9GF

www.harpercollins.co.uk

HarperCollins*Publishers*
1st Floor, Watermarque Building,
Ringsend Road, Dublin 4, Ireland

From Bridal Designer to Bride © 2021 Kandy Shepherd
A New Foundation © 2021 Rochelle Alers

ISBN: 978-0-263-29954-0

0321

MIX
Paper from
responsible sources
FSC™ C007454

This book is produced from independently certified FSC™ paper to ensure responsible forest management.

For more information visit: www.harpercollins.co.uk/green

Printed and bound in Spain
by CPI, Barcelona

FROM BRIDAL DESIGNER TO BRIDE

KANDY SHEPHERD

In memory of my wonderful long-time friend
Jan Herbert, taken recently by ovarian cancer.
Jan enjoyed my books and had her own real-life
romance in a long and very happy marriage to Ric.
When she became unable to read, he read my stories
to her. 'Your books gave her pleasure and that was
a wonderful gift,' he told me.

Vale, Jan, you are so missed.

PROLOGUE

JOSH TAYLOR WATCHED the expressions of disbelief and amazement flash across his friend Tori Preston's face as she scrutinised the images of the woman in the glossy magazine.

'Can you see the resemblance?' Josh asked.

Tori continued to stare at the image of the beautiful blue-eyed woman with the dark hair that tumbled around her shoulders. His friend looked back up at Josh, a frown pleating her forehead. 'Except that my hair is cut so short and we have a different way of dressing we…we're identical. How can this be?'

'Immediately I thought she must be related to you. A cousin maybe. Out of curiosity I looked her up,' Josh said. 'She's an Australian fashion designer named Eloise Evans.'

He wasn't going to admit it to Tori but, while he had only ever seen Tori as a strictly platonic friend, there was something about Eloise Evans that fascinated him. He'd read through the article about her several times as he debated whether or not he should point out the uncanny resemblance to Tori.

'Not only is she twenty-eight, like you, but she also has the same birthdate.'

Tori paled. 'You're kidding me?'

Josh shook his head. 'There's more. While she lives in Sydney, Australia now, she was born here in Boston. In this interview, she makes no secret of the fact she was adopted as a two-year-old toddler.'

Tori drew a sharp intake of breath. She looked up at Josh, her cornflower-blue eyes troubled. 'I've always known I was adopted when I was two years old, after my birth mother died.'

'I know,' he said.

She peered harder at the image on the page, the woman smiling a smile so very like Tori's own. 'You know, I feel I've seen her before.'

Josh laughed. 'Seems you might see her every time you look in the mirror.'

Tori shook her head. 'It's not that. My memory of someone like this is of a little girl. My imaginary friend, my mum used to call her, when I spoke about her. But I stubbornly insisted she was real.'

'It could all be a coincidence,' said Josh, knowing it seemed like one coincidence too many.

Tori looked up at him. 'What if it isn't? What if… what if there were two babies?'

Josh paused. 'Adopted to different families, you mean?'

'Twins,' Tori said.

'Twins?' he echoed.

'I need to meet her, see if there could be any truth in this. Oh, my goodness, Josh, what if…? But Australia. It's so far away and it's such a busy time for me at work with the spring wedding season in full swing.' Tori was the wedding cake baker of choice to the elite of Boston.

Josh paused. 'Why don't you let me scout her out first? I have to visit Australia for business next week. Why don't I look this Eloise Evans up for you?'

Tori's eyes widened. 'You'd do that?'

Tori and her brothers had been so supportive of him when his own sibling had disowned him. He could never repay her enough for her friendship. 'Of course. In the meantime, why don't you talk to your parents and see if they know anything about the circumstances of your adoption? This could be a crazy coincidence, or...'

'Or... I might have a twin sister,' Tori breathed.

CHAPTER ONE

JOSH TAYLOR WAS a highly successful entrepreneur; a billionaire at age twenty-nine. He possessed multiple effective business skills, but it seemed engineering a face-to-face meeting with his friend Tori's possible twin sister, Eloise Evans, wasn't one of them.

Tori had discovered there had indeed been twin baby girls put up for adoption, and there was a very good chance the Australian woman was her birth sister. 'Just get close enough so you can see for yourself if she really does look just like me in real life,' Tori had asked.

Within a day of arriving in Sydney, Josh had tracked down Eloise Evans. He'd learned that her high-end bridal wear business was considered among the best in the country and had a growing international reputation. He had scoped out her elegant Eloise Evans Atelier headquarters in the exclusive inner eastern suburb of Double Bay in the hope of catching sight of her. But days later he still had not seen even a glimpse of the elusive bridal designer.

On Saturday morning, his last day in Sydney, he'd switched track and was looking out for her near her apartment in Rushcutters Bay. The nineteen-thirties-style apartment building faced a park and he sat in the balmy autumn sunshine on a bench near the low sandstone sea wall that separated the park from the sparkling blue waters of Sydney Harbour.

His seat was carefully chosen for the unimpeded view of Eloise's building, but still there was no sight of her. He bent his head to text Tori the news that unfortunately he hadn't been able to make contact.

But then something made him look up. A peal of feminine laughter. The barking of an excited dog. And there she was. Eloise Evans emerged from the shade of the large trees that formed the perimeter of the park. She had a dog on a lead and was heading across the park towards the water—and him. He recognised Eloise instantly, even from this distance, this woman who'd grabbed his attention on the pages of that magazine. There could be no doubt she was Tori's doppelganger.

As she crossed the grass and came closer, Josh got up from the park bench and started to head towards her. Thoughts of how to engineer an 'accidental' meeting pushed insistently through his mind. Tori might think it a good idea to bump into Eloise but he realised it was a very bad idea. She would take him for, at best, a mugger, at worst, a groper. It would be better to stroll by and take a quick sideways glance at her face to confirm, and then continue on his way.

As she and her dog got closer his heart started to thud and his mouth went dry. It was uncanny. Not only was there a remarkable facial similarity but the Australian designer was also the same height, around five feet seven, and had the same slim build as his friend Tori. They *must* be related.

But the more he looked, the more he noticed the differences rather than the similarities. Ms Evans seemed to waft rather than walk along the pathway, whereas Tori would stride. Her black hair fell to her shoulders in a thick, glossy mass—the opposite of Tori's spikey crop. When Tori walked her dogs, she wore jeans or gym pants. Eloise Evans was dressed in a narrow calf-length skirt made of some kind of lacy fabric in a rich cinnamon colour with a cream top that was tied to show off her narrow waist and high, round breasts. To tell the truth, he had scarcely ever noticed Tori's curves—she was more like the sister he'd never had than a girl whose figure he noticed in any way other than the abstract.

As Eloise Evans walked, the skirt split to reveal tantalising glimpses of long, slender legs, and he noticed them—*man, did he notice*. Josh took a short, sharp breath. That was the main difference between this woman and his friend back home in Boston—he found this woman *hot* in an ultra-feminine, sensual way. He didn't want to get caught ogling her but it was difficult not to stare—she was utterly gorgeous.

As she got closer she veered away, heading for the nearby off-lead dog play area, by the look of the bright yellow dog ball launcher she carried. He should leave it at that.

But he had made a deal with Tori that he would observe her possible sister as closely as he could. He'd also promised, if he actually made contact with her, that he would not say anything about Tori.

And when Josh gave his word he did his best to honour it. He had spent his first sixteen years living his mother's lie—turned out the man he'd thought his father wasn't his father at all. The discovery of her secret, and his subsequent abandonment by his family, had seared a hatred of lies and dishonesty onto his soul. He didn't give or take trust easily.

Eloise Evans's dog was somewhat at odds with her glamorous appearance. Pure mutt, by the look of it. Small, with a mess of black, ginger and white fur. Josh took note, as he knew Tori would want to know all about the dog. As it neared the dog park the mutt started to prance with excitement, pulling at its lead, and yapping.

'Okay, okay,' Ms Evans said, laughing as she bent down to unfasten the lead from its harness. Josh froze. Her laugh. It was like Tori's but not like Tori's. This woman's laugh was low, musical and immediately he wanted to hear it again. She ruffled the fur around the dog's neck in a casual caress. *That lucky, lucky dog.*

Now she was dangerously close. Close enough to affirm there was a very good chance this woman could be Tori's twin. His time here was done. He'd got what he came for. Mission accomplished. He should walk away in the opposite direction. And yet he lingered, taking slow steps, unable to take his eyes off the beautiful woman who only had eyes for her dog.

Eloise Evans launched a green tennis ball and the little dog took off, grabbed it in its mouth, scampered back to her and proudly dropped the ball at her feet. 'Good girl, Daisy,' she crooned, her voice husky and sweet and warm with affection.

Josh paused to savour the sound of her voice. It reminded him of a time before he'd locked up his heart against hurt and betrayal. She scooped up the ball and launched it again. The dog rushed to catch it, but this time the ball bounced off its nose and shot towards the water—and Josh. Instinctively he reached up and caught it—smack—hard in his hand.

He was about to throw it back when Eloise Evans hurried up to him, the dog at her heels. 'Well caught. Thank you.'

Josh shrugged with feigned nonchalance to cover his shock at her sudden close proximity. He caught a tantalising drift of her sweet, floral scent. 'An easy catch.' When he was twelve years old he had dreamed of playing baseball for Boston's Red Sox. All the practice had paid off today.

'Seriously, that's her favourite ball. She'd have tried to swim after it if it had gone into the water. And then we'd be in trouble.' Her accent was Australian, while Tori's was pure Boston. But the voice was uncannily similar.

This close, Josh could tell Eloise had the same blue eyes as Tori, the same full, curving mouth, the same small, straight nose. Like Tori's, her beauty wasn't one of vapid prettiness. There was strength in the set of her chin, intelligence in the intensity of her gaze. He could readily believe they were identical twins. But she was also very different from Tori in ways too subtle for him to articulate. More of a feeling than anything substantial. There was something about her he found extraordinarily appealing—had done so from when he'd first spotted her image in that magazine. In real life the impact of her presence knocked the breath out of him. But, lovely as he found her, Ms Evans could only be the subject of his investigation on behalf of his friend.

He forced his voice to sound normal. 'You're so welcome,' he said. 'Glad to be of help.'

He knew he should hand the ball over immediately. But the longer he held on to it, the longer he had the opportunity to enjoy being closer to Eloise Evans. Unexpectedly, the little dog ran up and stood up straight to put both front paws on Josh's knees. She looked up at him with gentle brown eyes, pink tongue lolling, and he swore she was smiling.

'Hi there,' he said, bemused when the dog made no move to remove her paws. She wagged her plumed tail in response.

'Daisy!' Eloise admonished.

'She's okay,' he said. 'I guess she wants her ball back.'

'Thank you for not objecting to her jumping up on you. I've never seen her do anything like that before. She's usually scared of men. It's awesome she trusts you.'

Josh looked down into the little dog's sweet face. He wanted to reach down and stroke her but didn't want to risk frightening her.

'Did someone hurt her?'

'Undoubtedly. She was found dumped on the side of a busy road. Just skin and bone, an injured leg. No ID, no microchip. Just abandoned when someone tired of her.' Eloise's voice hitched. 'Thankfully a good person from a dog rescue centre was able to catch her.'

Josh swore under his breath. 'Surely there's a special place in hell reserved for people who hurt animals.'

'I certainly hope so,' she said vehemently.

'So you adopted her?'

She shook her head. The sun picked up blueish glints in her black hair. The kind of thick, luxuriant hair he would like to run his fingers through. Not that he'd ever get the chance with lovely Eloise Evans. Not when his promise to Tori stood in the way. Not when Eloise lived on the other side of the world. Especially not when he had goals to achieve by the time he reached thirty that didn't allow for distraction.

'I love dogs but I can't have one full-time right now,' she said. 'I have to travel for work too often and…'

She stopped, perhaps aware she'd revealed too much to a stranger. The rest of her words came out in a rush. 'So I foster rescue dogs and keep them with me until they're ready to go to a forever home.'

Just like Tori did. Tori was passionate about dog rescue, and they both worked in the wedding business. The similarities between them were more than skin deep. The thought crossed his mind that if the two women ever met they'd find a lot in common.

'It's great Daisy is safe with you,' he said. 'She seems a very nice dog.'

'She's a sweetheart. When I first got her she would cower with her tail between her legs if she ever got near to a man. For her to have taken to you is a huge step forward.'

If it were Tori, Josh would joke it was purely because of his natural charisma and she would slap him down in a sisterly manner. Instead with Eloise he was serious. 'I'm glad to hear that,' he said. 'Shall I throw her ball for her?'

'Oh, my gosh, you've still got it in your hand. Is it horrible? I mean, covered in doggy slobber?' She looked at him, and he could tell she was trying not to laugh at his dilemma. *She was enchanting.*

'It is a tad on the damp side, but what do you expect from a well-loved dog ball?' He didn't think wiping his hand down the side of his trousers in disgust was the way to impress Ms Evans.

'I'm glad you understand.' Her lips curved into a smile that lit her blue eyes. 'I'm sure Daisy would love you to throw her ball for her.'

Josh had grown up with dogs. He donated substantial sums to dog rescue organisations. But he didn't want the responsibility of owning one himself. He never wanted to be tied down by anything or anyone. Not even a dog. Certainly not a woman. He'd been driven to prove himself to people who didn't believe in him and that had left no room for emotional entanglements that might have hindered his race for his first million, then the next and the next.

Eloise handed him the launcher. He looked down at Daisy. 'Do you want your ball?' The dog yapped her assent, her eyes following the ball. Josh was determined to throw it as far and fast as he could. For the dog's enjoyment, of course. Not just to impress Eloise with a testosterone-fuelled show of strength.

The ball flew across the width of the park and Daisy scampered after it. 'She's loving it,' said Eloise, clapping her hands in enthusiasm. 'I could never throw the ball that far.'

The little dog ran back, ball triumphantly in her mouth. She paused, her eyes going from Josh to her foster mother. Then she deposited it at Josh's feet, sat and looked up at him. He felt curiously moved by the gesture. Eloise's eyes were misty and her voice unsteady. 'That's really something. Thank you. I never thought she'd trust a man with her precious ball.'

He had to clear his throat. 'Shall I throw it again?'

'Please,' she said.

Josh threw the ball and again the little dog brought it back to him. Only this time she came back via the muddy area around the doggy watering station. Her paws were dark with mud, and before Josh could stop her she jumped up and streaked mud on his biscuit-coloured linen trousers.

'Daisy! No!' Eloise took hold of her dog's harness and gently tugged her down. 'I'm sorry. She didn't mean to make that mess,' she said to Josh.

'Of course she didn't,' he said. He patted Daisy to show there were no hard feelings. She smiled her doggy smile.

'I hope she hasn't ruined your trousers.' Eloise had a small handbag crossed over her shoulder. She burrowed into it and pulled out a handful of tissues. 'Take these. They're clean. Might get the worst off. You can't use a wet cloth on mud; water makes it worse.'

He took the tissues and wiped the surface dirt off his trousers. 'It's okay,' he said. 'It's just mud.'

'I know about fabrics. That's very good linen. Mud can stain. Of course, I'll pay for your trousers to be dry cleaned. Or replaced if you can't get the stain out.'

'There's no need. Really. I have other trousers.' He'd have them dry cleaned at the hotel. If the mud stained, he'd throw them out. It would be worth it for the story he'd tell Tori. She loved a good dog story.

'I insist.'

'I refuse.'

'So we've reached an impasse,' she said, a smile tugging at the corners of her mouth.

'It appears so,' he said.

'Can I at least buy you a coffee? Daisy and I usually go for coffee at a dog-friendly café further up in the park and we're heading that way now. Would you like to join us?'

Josh didn't hesitate. The dog had decided this course of action and this was a better way to make contact with Eloise than he could ever have engineered himself. *Thank you, Daisy.*

'I'd like that very much,' he said.

CHAPTER TWO

ELOISE WOULD NORMALLY never invite a man she'd just met in the park for a coffee. The words had just slipped out of her mouth, much to her own astonishment. However, strictly speaking, it was Daisy who had made the approach. Eloise could still hardly believe the little dog had displayed such trust in the tall American when she was normally so wary of men. It was a huge step forward in her rehabilitation. *Dogs could be very good judges of character.*

She looked up at the man. With his thick brown hair, lean face and hazel eyes he was strikingly handsome. Probably around her age, she figured. He'd been so kind to Daisy, a little survivor who was in such need of kindness. And he'd been so good about the mud on his very expensive-looking trousers when he was quite within his rights to be cranky. The least she could do was offer him a coffee. He was a stranger and she should be cautious but there was actually very little risk to her in doing so—she was a regular at the café and she could always find a table out in the open for Daisy or the other dogs she had fostered.

'I'm glad you can join us. However, if you change

your mind about letting me pay for your dry cleaning just say so.'

'I won't change my mind and I'm looking forward to the coffee. I'm Josh Taylor, by the way.'

'Eloise Evans,' she said. 'And you've met Daisy, of course. Let me put her lead back on. The café is further down the park.'

They started to stroll along the waterfront path towards the café. She never tired of the sight of myriad yachts moored near the yacht club, the distant view of the Sydney Harbour Bridge. This was one of the most elite areas of the city.

Eloise appreciated the way Josh Taylor slowed his long stride to accommodate Daisy trotting happily along between them. This was a man who genuinely liked dogs.

'You're American. Do you live here? Or are you visiting Sydney?'

'I'm visiting for a few days.'

'Business or pleasure?' she asked.

'A business trip,' he said. 'Although it's always a pleasure to visit Australia.'

'Let me guess,' she said. 'You're from Boston.'

'Correct,' he said. 'I'm told we have a distinctive accent, although I don't hear it myself, of course.'

'My dad was from Boston,' she said. 'Your accent is like his. It's nice to hear it again. Brings back happy memories.'

'Was?'

'He died thirteen years ago when I was fifteen. I adored him and still miss him.'

'I'm sorry,' he said.

She made a dismissive gesture. 'It was a long time ago.' She didn't want a gloomy conversation, although her heart still spasmed with grief every time she thought about her father.

At the café, she and Josh were quickly shown to her favourite table outside, in the shade of an awning and near to the doggy water bowl. She noticed the little dog's tail went down at the friendly male waiter's greeting but wagged when Josh showed her attention. 'You've certainly won her heart,' she said.

He grinned. 'Could be my magnetic personality, but she can probably sense I like dogs. My dog was my best friend when I was a kid. Sadly, I travel a lot and—like you—I'm not in a position to have my own dog right now.'

Daisy had taken a shine to Josh Taylor and Eloise found herself drawn to him too. In her experience it wasn't often you got both outrageously handsome and personable in one man. These were only first impressions of course, and she couldn't always trust them. But she could trust her dog's instincts. 'It gives me hope we can get her over her nervousness with men. Though she'll probably do better rehomed with a woman.'

Josh looked into her face and she saw compassion in his hazel eyes. 'It must be hard to let a foster dog go when you've put so much care into them.'

'I fall in love with them every time. Saying goodbye is hard. But I have to force myself not to get too attached. The work I put into them helps them get a forever home, then frees me up to socialise another traumatised dog. Most of the dogs' new owners keep in touch and send me photos.' She reached down to pet Daisy, who sat between them.

'She's a lucky little dog to be cared for so well by a kind person like you.'

Eloise surprised herself by blushing. 'Thank you.'

Their coffees arrived. An espresso for him, a cappuccino for her, and a 'puppuccino' for Daisy, served in a shot-sized paper cup. 'It's just frothed lactose-free milk, no harmful chocolate or caffeine,' she explained.

'What's life without an occasional treat?' Josh said, smiling.

'I like your philosophy,' she said with an answering smile.

She liked *him*. It was a long time since she'd felt so at ease in a man's company. He was easy to chat to and she had no trouble opening up to strangers. It was one of the reasons her business did so well. Apart from the superb design, craftsmanship and sheer beauty of her couture wedding gowns, her clients also had a warm, friendly shopping experience. Eloise had a gift for drawing them out, particularly the shy brides, and to do that she had to sometimes share some of her own life.

'You must be enjoying the glorious weather we're having here,' she said. 'I imagine it's getting chilly back in Boston now.' Weather was always a safe topic for conversation.

'Mild one day and back to winter the next. That's typical. You said your dad came from Boston. Have you visited there?'

'I was actually born in Boston,' she said.

'Really?' he said.

'I left there when I was eight years old.'

'So you're an Aussie now?'

'I have dual citizenship. My mother is Australian and my father was American.'

'Best of both worlds,' he said.

'I think of it that way.'

'What brought your family back here?'

'My dad used to joke it was the relatively mild winters we have in Sydney.'

'I can see the appeal,' he said. 'Boston winters are bitterly cold.'

'I remember.' She pretended to shiver and wrapped her arms around herself, which made him smile. 'But seriously, my mother got homesick. Her family was here. When he was alive we used to go "home" to Boston to visit my grandparents.'

She didn't want to tell him that conflicting loyalties between Australia and the United States had put stresses on their family. Her grandparents had never forgiven her mother for taking her father away and she'd lost touch with them after he'd died. That was only part of it, though. The more painful truth was that they didn't consider her their 'real' grandchild. Not when she was adopted and not her father's 'real' child. Not that her father had thought that. Not at all. *'My darling daughter,'* he'd used to call her. DD for short.

Which had made it all the more painful when she'd discovered, quite by accident, at age thirteen, that she was adopted. She'd needed a vaccination certificate for school and had burrowed through where she knew her parents kept the family medical records. And there it was, proof she'd been born to a Boston woman who had died when Eloise was two, and then adopted to the people she'd believed she'd been born to. There was a notation on the document that the family history of both parents was unknown.

She'd been too stricken by shock to move. Just stood there with the document in her hand for heaven knew how long. How hurt and angry she'd been, how betrayed she'd felt, how humiliated that everyone knew the secret of her birth but herself. When she'd confronted her parents she'd lashed out at them, too hurt to listen when they'd said they'd intended to tell her but had never found the right time. She'd screamed at them that she could never trust anyone again if she couldn't trust them. Only their obvious devastation at her words had tempered her anger.

Her parents had worked hard to win her trust back, to seek forgiveness, to assure her everything they'd done had been out of love for her. Eventually they had won her around. She was so glad she'd forgiven them, as her beloved father had died two years later of an unexpected heart attack. But she sometimes felt she was like a cracked vase that had been repaired but was never quite the same. There was a weaker seam running along that crack that had left her with a nagging distrust because the people closest to her had lied to her—and conspired to make sure she was oblivious to it.

When their waiter asked if they wanted another coffee, Eloise looked to Josh. He nodded. 'And another puppuccino for Daisy?' he asked.

'But of course,' she said, smiling. She was glad she'd have some more time with this thoughtful man. 'What line of business are you in?' she asked, to change the subject from the personal.

'Tech entrepreneur just about covers it. As a teenager I started developing apps and trading gaming codes and went from there.'

'Clever you,' she said.

So he was smart as well as handsome. He wore a very expensive watch and his jacket and trousers were tailor-made from Italian fabrics. She figured he was about her age, so she could add *successful* to the list of his attributes.

'What about you?' he said.

'I'm a dress designer. Bridal wear mostly.'

'Always a market for that, I guess,' he said.

'Indeed,' she said.

But not for her. She made her living ensuring her clients' dreams of fairy-tale weddings came true. However, she had no intention of walking up the aisle herself any time soon.

Once, she'd been idealistic about the concept of romance, of falling in love at first sight the way her parents had—the story of their meeting at summer school had become family mythology—but those illusions had long been shattered. Perhaps because she had gone into her early relationships too ready to fall in love, and got too easily hurt and disillusioned as a result. These days she seemed to attract controlling men who hid behind superficial charm. Just because her business was 'girly'—their word—and she liked dressing in a feminine, vintage-inspired style didn't mean she wanted to be submissive. She'd escaped a difficult relationship a year ago and wasn't looking for another one.

'My gowns are exclusive and unique. I say without boasting that I have a long waiting list. Women in the know put their names down as soon as they think there's a chance of their guy proposing. Or their girl in the case of a same-sex couple.'

'It sounds a romantic way to make a living.'

She laughed. 'People often say that. Most of the time it is romantic and beautiful. To create an exquisite gown for a bride is a truly joyous thing. But have you heard the term Bridezilla?'

'Yes,' he said quickly. Too quickly. 'I…uh…have a friend who works in catering in Boston. She knows all about demanding Bridezillas.'

Eloise wondered how serious the 'friend' was and noted that he didn't wear a wedding band. It was just coffee, she reminded herself.

'The stress of organising a wedding can bring out the worst in people. Dream weddings can turn into nightmares.' She stopped herself. Okay, so she could get a touch cynical about happy-ever-afters that went wrong. But she would be wise to keep that level of detail to herself when she was chatting to a stranger.

Since she'd gone to Los Angeles and dressed the bride and eight attendants for the extravagant wedding of mega American pop star Roxee—the diva used only the one name—Eloise had been pestered for interviews. And learned how easy it was to be misquoted. She was very careful what she said now and never revealed anything confidential about a client.

'Thankfully Bridezillas are the exception,' she continued. 'Most brides are awesome and it's lovely to work with people at such a happy time of their lives. There's nothing I love more than being invited to their weddings. I go to mush and cry my eyes out every time.'

'Do you have a retail outlet? A factory?' She noticed he kept the conversation business-focused, which she liked. No disparaging 'girly' comments here, which she appreciated.

'Yes, to the store—no, to the factory. I have a storefront. In the window I display just one perfect dress that changes weekly. There are fitting rooms at that level. Upstairs is my atelier, which is a fancy name for a designer's workroom. But the French sounds classier, doesn't it?' She'd learned the term during her internship at a Paris couture bridal house.

'Branding is everything,' he said seriously.

'Eloise Evans Atelier works for me,' she said lightly. Her last boyfriend had been pushing her towards marriage. And expected that she would change her surname to his and her business name to reflect the change. *As if!*

She had worked too hard to build up her business, to make sure it was hers and hers alone, and no one would be allowed to take it from her.

'How long are you in Sydney?' she asked.

'Until tomorrow, then I fly to Melbourne,' he said. 'My time in Australia depends on how negotiations go with a start-up I want to buy.' She understood he would be tight-lipped about the details of his business. It must be highly competitive.

'I hope this lovely weather holds for the rest of your stay.'

The waiter came with their bill. In spite of the agreement that she would pay for the coffee, as he wouldn't let her pay for his dry cleaning, Josh went to pay for it. Eloise insisted she should pay. 'I invited you,' she said. 'Please.'

She didn't like it when men high-handedly insisted on paying, as it too often became a 'now you owe me' situation. Another way of them trying to assert control over her independence that she fiercely resisted. Not that she thought that would be the case with Josh. She suspected it was purely good manners on his part. Thankfully, he graciously conceded.

The waiter took their empty coffee cups away and an awkward silence fell between them that Eloise struggled to break. The sounds of the park—the clatter of cutlery in the café, Daisy's breathing—became something intrusive.

They spoke at the same time.

'I have to go—' she said.

'Would it be out of order to—?'

'To what?' She held her breath for his answer.

'Ask if you're free for dinner tonight?'

She didn't know who was more surprised, Josh or her at her rapid reply. 'Yes,' she said. 'I mean no, it wouldn't be at all out of order.'

CHAPTER THREE

JOSH COULDN'T BLAME the dog, or Eloise, or anyone else but himself for his spontaneous dinner invitation. At that moment, the need to see Eloise again while he was in town had overwhelmed good sense.

It had nothing to do with Tori or his self-appointed role of investigator. Fact was, he had enjoyed every second in Eloise's company and didn't want to say goodbye. There was something about her that fascinated him— and it wasn't just the resemblance to his friend. It had been a long time since he'd anticipated a date with such enthusiasm. And because he was a visitor in town only briefly, the encounter could be contained to just the one evening without there being any expectations of further dates. It could be awkward explaining to women that he didn't want the complication of commitment at this stage of his life.

But his obligation to Tori *was* a complication. Back in his hotel in Double Bay, not far from Eloise's atelier, he paced the room as he thought about what he would say to Tori. The time distance between Sydney and Boston meant late morning in Sydney was late evening back home. She would be anxiously waiting for his report on his sighting of her Australian lookalike, but he was curiously reluctant to speak to his friend. His reactions to the woman who must surely be Tori's long-lost twin were too new, too unexpected, too *private* for him to be interrogated or teased in best female friend style.

Josh wasn't a man to draw out decisions. He'd got where he was by being decisive, and acting swiftly on a mix of intuition and canny market knowledge. Yet he here was being indecisive as hell. Over a woman.

He knew that he could not lie to his friend about actually engaging with Eloise, sharing a coffee with her, arranging to see her again. Loyalty was important to him. In a world when even his own mother had ultimately proved disloyal, Tori and her family had been unfailingly loyal to him.

He picked up the phone. Tori reacted to his news with predictable excitement, demanding to know every detail twice over. The possible finding of a long-lost sister was a big deal and he knew it. He had lost a sibling, through unmitigated selfishness and greed on his brother's part, but it was a loss all the same and had left a brother-sized gap in his life. If Tori chose to make contact with Eloise she would find a kind person as besotted with dogs as she was. That could only be a blessing.

He recounted the incident with the dog and her ball and how it had brought him into accidental contact with Eloise. He told her they'd had coffee, how he was convinced the two women must be twins. And that even though they'd grown up separated from the age of two they had a lot in common and he was convinced Tori would like Eloise a lot. Fortunately, she didn't seem to pick up anything from his tone that revealed his unexpected and overwhelming attraction to Eloise.

Tori sniffed back tears. She thanked him effusively for tracking Eloise down for her. He told her he was seeing Eloise for dinner and she didn't object. Not that her objection would have stopped him. But he agreed again not to tell Eloise about Tori just yet.

As soon as he put down the phone he realised how difficult he had made things for himself. If at some stage the twins met each other, he would be the bad guy for not having told Eloise the truth straight away. Immediately he dismissed the thought. Surely Eloise would see he had done the right thing by staying silent about his real purpose for being in the park this morning. It was Tori's story to reveal, not his. He hoped she'd take action on it sooner rather than later.

He turned his mind to his work. From when he'd first started in his line of business he'd had dealings with people from all around the world and, while much of his business was conducted online, he liked to meet people face to face. His personal touch had won him business others had missed out on. He was tough in negotiations, but always fair. The ideal was that all parties to the transaction walked away from the negotiating table believing they'd got a good deal. That way led to ongoing, profitable business relationships. The end game was, after all, profit. Every new million he made was a kick in the teeth for the father and brother who had written him off as unworthy.

With recent world events, however, flights to Australia had been disrupted, so the point of this trip was to touch base with people he hadn't seen for far too long. But when an important client of his digital app marketplace called with a suggestion to meet for dinner that night he straight away declined the invitation. Then took a pause when he realised it was the first time he'd put a date with a woman ahead of a business deal.

Eloise had arranged for Josh Taylor to meet her at a favourite restaurant in nearby Potts Point. As her mother might say, it was wise to stay cautious about a man she had picked up in the park. No matter how genuine he seemed or how attractive she found him.

She'd quickly searched him online, of course—just enough to check if he was who he'd said he was—only to find he'd been remarkably self-effacing about his achievements. At twenty-nine, he was considered to be one of the world's leading tech moguls. He also appeared in several lists of 'most eligible bachelors' in the United States. Who knew? And she'd thought him just a friendly fellow dog lover. She could have read up on him all day but she'd had to rush into work.

But she made sure she and Daisy got back to her apartment in time for her to dress carefully for her date with Josh. Could she call it an actual date? He'd probably only suggested dinner because otherwise he'd be facing an evening alone in his hotel room and she was a friendly face. And that was okay because otherwise she would be curled up on the sofa, with Daisy at her feet, binge-watching TV.

But it didn't hurt to look her best. Despite its population of more than five million, Sydney was a small town—the eastern suburbs especially—and she never knew who she might see when she was out. Reputation was vital in her business and she couldn't be seen to be dressed anything less than stylishly. Not that it was a hardship. She adored dressing up and wearing make-up.

Tonight she was trialling one of her own designs, a heavy silk, full-skirted, calf-length nineteen-fifties-style dress in a flattering deep rose that she thought would be a hit for bridesmaids at a day-time wedding. She had a particular Bridezilla in mind, one who had told her she had directed her bridesmaids to lose weight so they'd all fit into the same size dresses.

This dress required a trim waist, so might work for those particular attendants. She'd had to use all her diplomatic skills not to retort that if she were a bridesmaid, she would immediately resign from bridesmaid's duties if any bride ever ordered her to lose weight, get a boob job, dye her hair to the wedding approved colour, or sign an agreement not to get pregnant before the bride's big day.

Eloise had heard them all. And every time was surprised at the women who went along with the crazy directives. Yet the perfect dress for the bride and for her attendants was a pivotal part of any wedding. It was her role to help every bride achieve her dream—the ideal gown for her fairy-tale wedding. What the bride and the bridesmaids did themselves wasn't Eloise's concern.

That wasn't a conversation she'd have with Josh over dinner though. Part of her success came from the fact that she always maintained strict confidentiality about her clients. Despite her design credentials, she would never have got the Roxee gig without her reputation for being scrupulous about her clients' privacy. She'd had no qualms about signing the strict non-disclosure agreements, and both before and after Roxee's wedding she had refused substantial sums to dish the dirt on what happened behind the scenes at celebrity weddings. In interviews she spoke about the thrill of working for the stars, snippets about her design process, but nothing that hadn't been cleared by her clients. Her business would soon dry up if she was indiscreet. And she fiercely protected her business. It was something that was all her own and that gave her a certain sense of security in a world that had been turned upside down when she was thirteen and had never quite spun on the same axis again.

Eloise was proud of what she had achieved. From making gorgeous original prom dresses for her friends at high school, to creating exclusive wedding dresses for clients including international superstars, her business brought her independence and fulfilment and she loved it.

The early days of her career, working in established fashion houses, had made her all the more determined to strike out with her own business, where she wouldn't be answerable to anyone. One well-known name had taken credit for her designs and then fired her when she'd asked for some acknowledgement—apparently all her work was his intellectual property and it said so in the contract she hadn't properly read. She'd resigned from another who used cheap materials but charged huge prices to the bride. With her own business she could work the way she wanted—and if it failed she could only blame herself. She'd worked hard to make Eloise Evans Atelier the success it was. She would do anything to protect it. How a man could expect her to give it up or let him take a hand in its management was beyond her. And that was what the most recent man in her life had expected her to do if she'd married him.

She should have seen the warning signs flashing around Craig sooner than she had. He'd been very good-looking and she'd fallen right back into that instant attraction trap. She'd been infatuated with him in the beginning and stupidly blinded to the reality of the man until finally her self-preservation mechanisms had kicked in. But not before he had inflicted serious damage to her self-esteem.

Craig had drip-fed criticisms of her—sometimes in the guise of barbed compliments or 'helpful' advice—until she had started doubting herself, censoring her answers to him so they wouldn't annoy him. He had pressed for an engagement but some deep instinct held her back. One day he had gone to kiss her and she hadn't wanted to kiss him back. Not then. Not ever. When she'd finally broken up with him, he had shown his true colours in a stream of invective that had shattered her. Then she found out he'd been cheating on her. No wonder she had soured on the idea of marriage. No wonder those old feelings of not being able to trust anyone close to her had resurfaced.

Fortunately, she'd then been plunged into the distracting workload of Roxee's wedding, which had involved several trips to LA, and there'd been no time for her to date.

Josh had arrived at the restaurant before Eloise. As she came in she saw him sitting at the table he'd booked, head down as he scrolled through his phone. She took the opportunity to admire him. The man was every bit as hot as she remembered. And as well dressed. Sophisticated in a lightweight charcoal sweater—cashmere, she was sure—with the sleeves pushed up to reveal that bank-balance-defying watch, and black linen trousers.

After the Craig fiasco more than a year ago, she hadn't dated at all. Casual dinners with trusted male friends only. She was surprised at how content she was being single. It meant she could live her life on her terms, could work all hours without being accused of not giving her man enough attention. Or having to worry what he might be up to while she had to work— a particular kind of worry she could well do without.

Of course, sometimes she got lonely for a man's company, a man's arms around her. Just that morning when she'd set off for her walk with Daisy she'd realised with a pang just how many couples there were in the park, from teenagers entwined around each other to silver-haired seniors holding hands. For a moment she'd felt suddenly alone in a world of couples. Until Daisy had sniffed out another single, quite probably the most attractive man in the park. And here he was now, waiting for her in her favourite restaurant. A casual, no-strings date with a handsome man might be just the lift her spirits needed.

He looked up, saw her, and smiled. Her eyes connected with his and for a long moment the noises surrounding them—the clatter of cutlery, the murmur of conversation—faded away. The shimmering thread of awareness drawing her to him seemed almost tangible until, flustered, she gave a shaky smile back and headed to the table. *What was happening here?*

The admiration in his eyes as he rose to greet her assured her that the pink dress had been a good choice.

She'd teamed it with a lacy knit vintage cardigan in a paler shade of pink embellished with silver beading and wore her favourite silver stilettos.

'You look lovely,' he said. 'One of your own creations?'

'But of course,' she said, preening just a little.

She took her seat opposite him, settling her full skirts around her. They ordered first drinks and then their meals. There wasn't any of the awkwardness of a first date. She marvelled at how she slipped into conversation with him as easily as she had at the park.

'Where's Daisy?' he asked, pretending to look around for a dog.

'Did you expect me to bring her?'

'It would have been nice to see her again,' he said with an obvious sincerity that pleased her. Craig had pretended to like dogs until he'd felt more certain of her. Then he'd let slip that he would never allow her to have a dog after they were married. *Allow* her! That might have been the moment her feelings for him had started to turn.

'She's safely asleep at my apartment, all tired out from her run in the park and then a visit to my workroom, where the staff all make a fuss of her.'

'You take your dog to work with you?'

'The advantage of being the boss. Of course, we have to keep her away from the expensive fabrics and laces we have in the workroom. Other foster dogs I've had haven't been as easy as this little one. She's happy to be crated if need be.'

'Do you usually work weekends?'

She leaned across the table towards him. 'I work any day I need to. Weekends suit some clients better. I like to do the final fitting for a bride whenever I can rather than leave it to one of my staff.'

'So I'm having drinks with a perfectionist?'

'Some say workaholic.' She laughed. 'I don't mind which label you use. There's a lot of hope and dreams invested in a wedding dress and I want that dress to look as perfect as it possibly can on my bride so she feels confident and comfortable.'

'There are a lot of dollars invested in your gowns too.'

'We use only the finest fabrics and trims; they don't come cheap.' She paused. 'How do you know how much my gowns cost?' She put up her hand in a halt sign. 'Wait. I get it. You looked me up online.'

'Of course.' He paused for a beat. 'Didn't you do a search on me?'

'Er...yes. Seems you own half the digital world. You were remarkably modest about your achievements.' She wouldn't say anything about the eligible bachelor lists that seemed to haunt his internet presence.

'So were you. *Bridal wear designer to the stars.* You don't get more famous than Roxee.'

'I know.' She grinned. 'I was positively star-struck when she got in touch. But she's a lovely, warm person and was wonderful to deal with. Her fabulous wedding and her commendations of my label have been brilliant for me. Business went ballistic. I've had to take on more staff and be prepared to fly more often to the US for personal fittings for her celebrity friends.'

Eloise waited for him to ask for inside gossip on the mega star—as so many people had since the wedding— and was relieved when he didn't. She would have thought less of him.

'It seems the designer became famous too.'

'Not really. It's second-hand fame, isn't it? I don't like being in the spotlight. I'm a backroom girl. I find interviews excruciating.'

'I don't care for the spotlight either, except when it serves my purposes,' he said shortly. 'My personal life is my own business.' She was glad she hadn't mentioned the eligible bachelor thing.

The waiter came with their starters—organic Sydney rock oysters for him and a salad of seared, cured trout for her.

'How did you get to be a wedding dress designer to the stars?' he asked when she had finished her salad.

'I'll ignore that label, if you don't mind,' she said, with a smile. 'I'm just as happy working with a girl from the suburbs who's saved up for one of my dresses, and gets to be a star for a day at her wedding.'

'Seriously,' he said, putting down his tiny oyster fork. 'When you were a little girl, did you say "I'm going to grow up and design wedding gowns for international superstars"?'

'Actually, I said I was going to grow up to be a mermaid.'

He laughed. 'Cute.'

'I don't know why, as I'm not a particularly keen swimmer. I think it was the idea of having a glorious tail, glistening with multicoloured scales. Which, when you think of it, is not so different from a bride's glorious long train trailing after her as she glides her way up the aisle, picking up the light from the beautiful beading and crystals stitched onto it.'

'You're obviously highly creative,' he said, a smile

twitching around the corner of his mouth. 'And imaginative.'

'Even as a little girl I loved colour and texture and fabrics. Most of all I loved clothes. My grandmother—my Australian grandmother, that is—was no fashionista but she taught me basic sewing and I stitched garments for my dolls as soon as I could use scissors and needles and thread. The same grandmother gave me a sewing machine for my eleventh birthday and I started making my own clothes. I was a puzzle to my mother. She's a scientist with, as she herself says, no real interest in fashion. She lets me choose her clothes for her now, which is fun.'

His eyes narrowed. 'So you don't take after your parents.'

She shrugged. 'I don't, and maybe I do. I'm the creative one in a family of intellectuals and scientists. But I'm adopted, so that's no great surprise.'

Every time she told people she was adopted she forced her voice to sound calm and even, as if it were no big deal. And maybe it wouldn't seem a big deal if she'd been told she was adopted from the get-go. But she would never forget the shock of discovering the hidden truth of her birth. The justification of that nagging feeling that she somehow didn't fit, the creative in the family of pragmatic academics. She had the same colouring as her father, so no one had ever doubted she was their birth child. But that shock, that feeling of betrayal and mistrust, was burned deep into her psyche.

'I don't know anything about my birth family except my birth mother worked in a department store, so maybe she was into fashion too,' she said.

Both she and her adoptive parents had tried to find out more, but with no luck. After a while, she'd asked them to stop the search. It seemed painful and pointless, especially when she had decided to forgive her parents for their deception and embrace the family who had chosen her rather than abandoned her.

Sometimes, when she sent one of her foster dogs off to their new home with a sense of satisfaction he or she would now get the good life they deserved, she wondered about the social worker who had placed her with the Evans family. Was that how it had felt for them, for the adoption agency, to place an unwanted little girl with a loving family who would care for her as if she were their own?

Always, she forced those thoughts to the back of her mind. To know she'd been unwanted was too hurtful. No one on either side of her birth parents' families had claimed her after her birth mother's death. Sometimes she rationalised that her adoptive maternal grandmother had made up for all those others who hadn't wanted her, but their rejection still stung deep down. No matter how exceptionally fortunate she had been with her adoptive parents.

'What about your birth father?'

'Father unknown,' she said making light of it by forming quote marks with her fingers. She wasn't telling him anything that she hadn't spoken about in interviews in the past.

'I'm sorry,' he said.

'Don't be. I couldn't imagine a better father than my real—that is, my adoptive—father was to me. Or my amazing mother, who did her very best to nurture and encourage the cuckoo she had brought into her nest.' Not that her mother had ever called her a cuckoo—that was Eloise's own term, devised to explain her role in the Evans family. 'She tells me it was an adventure to see how I would turn out. According to her, it was like seeing a flower bud unfurl, blossoming into possibilities that my pragmatic parents had never imagined.'

That was the truth. Except some of that had been recognised in retrospect. After she'd come to terms with the truth of her adoption, after she had struggled with her identity. After she had vowed to be the best daughter she could be to the people who had rescued her.

Josh raised his eyebrows. 'And you don't think your mother is creative? That's quite an analogy.'

'She's rather proud of her story, I think. But I never tire of hearing it. It's only as an adult that I truly appreciated how generous she was. She says I must have got my creativity from my first mother, the woman to whom she was so grateful. She couldn't have children of her own.'

One of the worst times in the six months of rebellion and trauma that had followed the discovery of the adoption document, had been when her mother had cried as she'd explained how much she loved her, what a gift she'd been to a mother who could not conceive a child of her own.

'Your parents sound great.' There was an edge to Josh's voice Eloise couldn't place.

She nodded. 'I was fortunate. I was cherished and loved and encouraged to follow my own interests in art and design. I won a dress-designing competition in a teen magazine when my dad was still alive. He said he couldn't have been more proud of me than if I'd been awarded a doctorate.'

'Sounds like the perfect childhood,' he said. 'If such a thing exists.'

She toyed with her linen napkin. 'Do I sound ungrateful if I say it was *nearly* perfect? There was always something missing.' She acknowledged her adoption to wonderful parents, but this was something she didn't often talk about. It had nothing to do with her adoption, and everything to do with her personal wishes. But there was no harm in it. His calm, accepting manner made it easy to open up.

'What was that?' he said.

'A sister. I longed for a sister. Not a brother, although I liked boys. I used to beg my mother to give me a sister. I was so sure of the sister I wanted, I drew a picture of her when I was about seven. My mother laughed when I handed her my sketch; she said I'd drawn an image of myself. She's still got it.'

Josh made a strangled sound that might have been a cough, suppressed laughter, or some kind of choking attack. Silently, she passed his water glass towards him. 'That's amusing,' he said finally, after he'd drunk some water. 'That you'd drawn a self-portrait, I mean.' She got the feeling he didn't find it amusing at all, but she couldn't imagine why.

The waiter brought their main courses. Eloise welcomed the interruption. She felt she'd talked far too much about herself without finding out anything much about him. He was dangerously easy to confide in.

Once she had tasted her favourite dish at the restaurant, a pan-fried chicken breast finished with truffle oil, and asked Josh how his steak was, she put down her knife and fork. Time to redress the balance.

'Do you have a sister or brother?' she asked. 'Or both?'

He paused for a beat too long before he spoke. 'How deeply did you burrow into the search engine when you looked me up?'

'I only had a quick look because I had to get to work. I figured if you really were a tech entrepreneur as you said, there would be something there on you beyond the usual social media. I didn't expect to find thousands of pages.'

'Did you read about the so-called scandal?'

'Not that I recall.'

She would certainly have remembered something *scandalous*. She shifted in her seat. Was Josh what he appeared to be? Her instincts were finely honed when it came to her business. Not so reliable when it came to men. Somehow she wanted to believe the best of Josh, but was that just because she found him so attractive? No, Daisy had trusted him too. Another day a good-looking man had come close to them in the park and Daisy had whimpered her fear then flattened her ears and bared her teeth at him. Eloise had walked briskly away—the complete opposite of what had happened with Josh.

'If I don't tell you you'll look it up as soon as you get home, won't you?' he said wryly.

'I might do just that,' she said lightly. 'You can't throw out the word *scandal* and not expect people to bite.'

'Fair enough,' he said. 'I guess I'll have to follow through.'

She groaned. 'Please stop dangling the bait. You've really got me intrigued now.'

Josh took a sip of his wine and settled back into his chair. His tension betrayed itself by his tight grip on the glass. What was the scandal he was about to reveal? Would it send her running from the restaurant?

'Like you, I had what might seem to be an idyllic childhood. I was born into one of the best families in Boston. A mansion on Beacon Hill. An illustrious heritage stretching back generations. A predetermined place in society. A big brother six years older than me who I looked up to. A father, distant but caring in his own way in that I lacked for nothing. A loving mother. However, also like you, I sometimes felt like the cuckoo in the nest. My brother seemed to excel in everything expected of him to take the path into the family's long-established legal firm. But I was a constant disappointment to my father. I'd rather have been on the sports field than in the library, although maths and computing came easily. I questioned rather than accepted the way things "had always been done".'

'Surely there's room for a rebel in every family?'

Again that wry smile. 'Rebel, perhaps. Interloper, definitely not.'

She frowned. 'What do you mean by interloper?'

'At the age of sixteen, a routine blood test proved I could not be my father's son.' Eloise gasped. 'All hell exploded at home. My mother confessed to an affair. Both she and I were expelled from the family.'

Eloise stared at him. 'I… I don't know what to say. Except that it sounds more a tragedy than a scandal.'

'You and I might say that; others didn't, I can assure you.'

Aching with sympathy, she leaned closer over the table. She longed to put her hand over his but didn't think it would be appropriate or welcome. 'It must have been terrible for you.' Just as traumatic as finding out she'd been adopted.

'You could say that,' he said with the understatement she was beginning to realise was part of him. 'My father—the only father I had ever known and who I loved—wanted nothing to do with me. I was forbidden to use the family name, banned from the family home and disinherited. He never paid another cent of support.' His words were underscored with bitterness.

Eloise's meal sat abandoned. She could only concentrate on the man sitting opposite her. The downward pull of his mouth, his set jaw, betrayed he was still struggling to come to terms with an old hurt. 'That seems unbelievably cruel.'

'I'd always known he was a hard man. But not that hard. He was furious he'd been fooled into bringing up another man's son. It appeared his relationship with me was collateral damage.'

'I can see he would have been angry. After all, his wife had lied to him in a major way. But to take it out on an innocent kid seems appalling. Who was your biological father?'

Since she'd discovered she was adopted, this kind of terminology came easily to her.

'My mother's tennis coach. She says she was in love, but that it was just a fling to him. He moved on. She wasn't sure I was his until after I was born. Luckily for my mother, I looked like her and no one questioned my legitimacy. But she could see her lover in me. When she tried to contact him, it was to find he'd died in a mountaineering accident. His family never knew about me. My mother never revealed my birth father's name—it was scandal enough that my father had disowned me. Even though she wasn't happy with my father, she stayed.'

'For your sake?'

'And for my brother's, she says. But she also liked the good life my father provided. She didn't come from a wealthy family.'

Eloise frowned. 'That sounds harsh.'

'Even she admits it was true. Although she told me she felt so guilty about deceiving him, she strove to be the perfect wife to a difficult man she didn't love to make up for her deception.'

'No one else knew the facts of your birth?'

'She hugged her secret to herself for sixteen years.'

'Your mother must have been on tenterhooks the entire time that she'd be caught out.' Had her parents even considered the possibility she would find out the truth about her adoption before they chose to tell her?

'With good cause. Her husband's reaction was swift and brutal. He's had no further contact with me since the day he booted me out.'

She noticed she didn't call his mother's husband his father. The hurt must run deep and bitter. He wouldn't trust easily either. 'What about your brother? Surely he stood up for you? Not that you'd done anything wrong.'

Josh pulled down his mouth in a grimace. 'He sided with my father. Why not when one day he'll get the entirety rather than half of a massive inheritance? He had a personal grudge too. When the scandal erupted he reckoned it ruined his chances of going into politics.'

'He blamed you? A teenager?'

'I was an easy target.'

'It all sounds terribly unfair.'

'I got through it all right,' he said, tight-lipped.

'You certainly have,' she said.

In terms of wealth and success anyway. In terms of personal damage, who knew how it had affected him? She remembered how vulnerable she had been at sixteen, determined to be an adult, to take risks, but buoyed by the security and guidance of her mother there for her. And, before he died, her father's loving support. 'Thank you for sharing that with me.'

He shrugged. 'I haven't told you anything that's not public knowledge—it's still often brought up in stories about my success. I thought I should clear the air in case you'd read about it.'

But she knew there must be so much more to it. 'I can understand, in a way, how you felt when you discovered the truth.'

'Really?' She could tell by the narrowing of his eyes he didn't believe anyone could ever understand what he'd been through.

'I didn't discover I was adopted until I was thirteen. And then it was only by accident.'

He frowned. 'Your parents hadn't told you?'

She shook her head. 'They said they nearly did on so many occasions but didn't know how to. They're highly intelligent people, so I don't quite get that, but there it is. I imagine you might have gone through some of the same struggles with identity as I did.' Only she had had parents who genuinely loved her to help her through it.

'You could say that, yes,' he said. 'I was sixteen, a kid, but savvy enough to realise what had happened. Why I hadn't fitted the family mould suddenly became clear.'

'For me too. Although I was lucky and my family embraced my differences.'

'Two different situations. Your parents chose you. My father felt I was foisted on him. He hated me for it.'

'Hate. That's a harsh word.'

'I was a kid of sixteen. A boy that age shouldn't have to learn to hate back. But I did.' His face was set in grim lines but she could see traces of the bewilderment he must have felt as a teenager.

'I'm sorry,' she said.

He shrugged again. 'In one way it was the making of me. I forged a new life in a different part of town, where no one cared where I'd fallen from. Forced into earning my own living to help my mother, I grew up quickly. Almost immediately I started refurbishing unwanted mobile phones and selling them on at a profit, all while I was still in high school.'

'You had to prove him wrong about you,' she said softly, gaining a glimmering of understanding of what it had been like for him.

'Correct,' he said.

She wondered why they were talking in such depth like this, as if it was a first date and there would be others. That wasn't going to happen.

He'd mentioned earlier that he would be flying down to Melbourne the next day, then flying back to Boston from there. There was an undeniable attraction between them—she could almost see the sparks. But it could go nowhere. She felt sad about that; it wasn't often she felt as comfortable with a man.

But she lived in Sydney and he in Boston. When she was nineteen, she'd snagged an internship in Paris working with a couture bridal house. She'd fallen crazily in love with a French guy and he with her. It had been real, not just a fling. After she'd gone back to Sydney, they'd tried to keep up the relationship long distance, but it had proved too difficult. It would be too difficult now. She reined in her thoughts. This was just one date. No one was considering romance, let alone a long-distance relationship.

'I'm glad I heard about the scandal from you rather than through an internet search,' she said. 'But I still say it's a tragedy.'

The waiter appeared at the table to ask if she and Josh had finished their meals. They looked at each other and laughed. 'We've been talking too much.'

'And I've enjoyed every minute of it,' Josh said, his voice deep and husky.

So had she. She didn't want the evening to end. And she hadn't felt like that for a long, long time.

Josh walked Eloise to her car. Purposely he took slow steps to extend his time with her for as long as possible. He didn't hold her hand, put his arm around her, or brush his shoulder against hers, although he wanted to. He gritted his teeth against the urge to pull her into his arms. She was gloriously sexy in that glamorous dress, although this rush of attraction was about so much more than that.

The way she tilted her head at a slight angle as she listened to him—really listened to him—and understood. Her wholehearted laugh. How that laughter reflected in those remarkable eyes, cornflower-blue fringed with thick black lashes that must be fake or enhanced with make-up, because he hadn't noticed them in the park. The lushness of her mouth slicked with deep red lipstick with a boldness that was almost theatrical. The sparkle of her creativity—she'd had him halfway to wishing he had a merman's tail. *Him*. Josh Taylor, who had no time for fanciful flights of imagination unless it led to something marketable and profitable. And yet the professionalism in the way she spoke about the business she was so passionate about had also struck a chord. In that drive to succeed, they were like-minded.

She and Tori might look alike but Eloise was entirely her own person. The whole evening he hadn't given Tori a thought. Except when Eloise had mentioned the way she'd sketched herself as an indication of her ideal sister and he'd nearly choked on his surprise. Apart from that, he hadn't remarked to himself on their similarities or their differences. Because Eloise was Eloise.

And he liked her, really liked her. But he had made a promise to Tori not to tell Eloise about their connection. If he took his interest in Eloise any further he would find himself tangled in a net of deception. That was not something he felt comfortable with. Not something Eloise would appreciate either, he was sure, even with his limited knowledge of her.

If he was wise, he would forget any further contact

with Eloise until the day Tori could explain how he had acted as an advance scout in her search for her twin—and, short of DNA testing, he was convinced they *were* twins—and they could have a good laugh about the way Daisy had engineered their meeting.

Apart from that, he wasn't in the market for a serious relationship. Not now. Maybe not ever. And Eloise had commitment and permanence written all over her beautiful self. How could he possibly fool around with Tori's sister? Tori might have been adopted into an Italian family but those Italian expectations of family loyalty she held were real and ran very deep in her. If he dated her sister, she would expect nothing short of a proposal. No. He would be wise to keep a very, very wide berth from this gorgeous woman.

They reached Eloise's car, a vintage Scandinavian sports car circa 1962, a collector's item in immaculate condition. A woman with a cool car. His admiration for her rocketed even higher. Eloise turned to face him, car keys dangling from her hand.

'Thank you. Dinner was an unexpected surprise and I enjoyed it very much.'

'I hope we can keep in touch,' he said. They had swapped numbers that morning in the park.

'I'd like that,' she said. Her voice was cool and contained and gave him no hint as to whether she really wanted to see him again or was being polite. It was just one date and they both knew it.

He would urge Tori to get in touch with Eloise soon, and give her the sister she'd sketched all those years ago. And let Eloise give Tori her imaginary friend for real.

'Next time you come to the States for one of your

celebrity clients, perhaps you can swing by Boston,' he said.

'It's a thought,' she said, again polite and non-committal.

She stood half in shadow but as she looked up at him the movement took her into the warm glow of a street light. Her eyes shone incredibly blue and the rich red lipstick gleamed on her luscious mouth. 'Goodbye, then,' she said.

'Goodbye,' he echoed.

But he couldn't break the irresistible pull of her gaze. He had felt it in the restaurant when he had first no-ticed she had arrived, an attraction so powerful it had transcended the space between them. Now she stood so close he was aware of her warmth, her tantalising scent. There were no further words to be said. The silence that hung between them could only be broken in one way.

He lowered his head to kiss her as she stepped closer to accept his kiss. He realised he had wanted this since the moment she'd laughed up at him in the park, had wanted to push his fingers through her thick hair. He did that now and she gave a little murmur of pleasure. Then he kissed her on her mouth. After an initial start of surprise, she kissed him back wholeheartedly. What started as a sweet and tender goodnight kiss flamed into something urgent and passionate that overtook him with its intensity. For minutes, or it could have been hours, all he was aware of was Eloise—her taste, her warmth, the excitement of having her in his arms.

But then, with a little sigh of regret, she broke away from the kiss, stepped back from him, her face flushed, her lips swollen, her hair in delicious disarray. 'That…

that shouldn't have happened.' Her voice wasn't steady as she tried to control her erratic breathing.

His voice was hoarse. 'I'm glad it did.' He put his hand on her shoulder, suddenly unable to bear the loss of her touch.

She gave a shaky smile. 'I don't do one-night stands—'

'I didn't expect—'

She put a finger across his lips to silence him. 'We both know what we'll want if we keep on kissing like that. We both know what would happen if I invited you into my car and back to my flat.' She paused to drag in air, and her breasts rose in a way he found almost unbearably alluring. 'Not a good idea,' she said.

She was so beautiful.

'No,' he choked out, while his body screamed *yes*. She wriggled out of his reach. Reluctantly, he let her go.

'Thank you, Josh, for a wonderful evening—I enjoyed every minute.' She flashed him a mischievous smile. 'Especially the last few minutes.'

He laughed and any awkwardness evaporated. 'Goodbye, Eloise.'

She swung her long, shapely legs into her car. It suited her, its era, her style. With just one backward glance and a fleeting smile, she drove away with a throaty roar of the engine. He watched the sleek, small white car until it turned a corner, raising his hand in a final, farewell wave he knew she couldn't see.

CHAPTER FOUR

DESPITE HIS RESOLVE, Josh could not get Eloise out of his mind. When had he ever met a more enchanting woman? Her lovely face, her warm laugh, their sensational kiss all haunted his thoughts. Why did it have to be so damn complicated?

Boy meets girl. Girl is most likely boy's friend's long-lost twin, but boy is honour-bound not to reveal his connection. Girl lives on the other side of the world. Boy does not want to be distracted by girl while he still has goals he has to fulfil. But boy is distracted no matter how he tries not to think about girl.

Man, was he distracted.

Josh particularly found his thoughts turning to Eloise while at the most important of his Melbourne meetings—with Courtney and Shawn, the people behind the phenomenally successful digital graphic design platform he had invested heavily in as a start-up. It had been one of his best decisions, as it had also brought him two good friends.

They were a couple, deeply in love and planning their wedding. He recommended Eloise Evans Atelier, only to be told by the delighted bride that she was already on the waiting list and his wedding invitation was in the mail. 'Plus one, of course.'

'Just keep it at me,' he said. 'No plus-one.'

Despite her not so subtle questioning, Josh did not enlighten her to the state of his love life. Nor did he allow Courtney—or Tori for that matter—to set him up with any of her single friends. His love life—or lack of it—was his own business.

His ex-father—what else could he call him?—and his ex-brother—ditto—had written him off as a future asset to the family firm from an early age. He had not fitted the mould. All the men in the family went to Harvard and Josh had had no desire to be a lawyer. His interests had lain in the digital world and a degree in computing. Then the truth of his parentage had come out and suddenly there had been no college fund, no support. He had been so shocked when the issue of his birth identity had erupted. 'But Dad—' he'd protested.

His father hadn't let him finish. 'Don't ever call me that again. I'm not your *dad*. You are nothing to do with me. You're the result of a sordid liaison between a deadbeat and a woman of dubious morals. I wipe my hands of you completely.'

His mother had gasped at that. But she hadn't tried to defend herself. Or him.

Even his high school girlfriend had dumped him when he'd been booted from the big house on Beacon Hill to live with his mother in his widowed aunt's apartment in the North End. He'd thought she'd been as in love with him as he'd been in love with her. Seemed it was the wealth and lifestyle he'd lost that had been the attraction.

That was when he'd started to grow the cynical shield around his heart that had now hardened into a barrier he liked to consider impenetrable. And he'd found truth in that old saying, *He who travels fastest, travels alone.*

'Perhaps you just haven't met the right woman yet,' Tori had been known to say.

But it wasn't that. His energy had to be put into proving to his ex-father and half-brother that, in terms of the material success their world judged people by, he not just matched but also exceeded them. He didn't want long-term relationships—and the emotional fallout that came with them—to get in the way.

Despite the cramped quarters at Aunt Lil's apartment, the enforced move had been a revelation. Boston's Little Italy neighbourhood, with its crowded old buildings dating back to the very early days of the city, was lively and convivial. He'd met Tori and her brothers, Ty and Tate, at his new high school and found both a warm welcome and income-producing gigs as a waiter at the Italian restaurant Tori's parents ran.

He still considered their trattoria to be a home from home. It had been a welcome escape from his mother's misery and depression. Looking back, he realised how much it must have hurt her to lose her home and contact with her older son. Back then, Josh had thought she'd blamed him—or the accident of his birth—for it all. He'd been at the trattoria more than he'd been at home.

Today, Tuesday lunchtime, he was eating with his Melbourne friends at a small, family-run Thai restaurant in one of Melbourne's famous laneways. It had the same kind of casual warmth and excellent food as the trattoria—as well as off-the-beaten-track privacy. As far as Josh was concerned, the good thing about being successful in the digital world, as opposed to something more 'glamorous', was that he tended to fly under the radar when it came to media attention.

Lately, however, his rocketing wealth and single status had been getting him unwanted attention—and he didn't like it. He'd complained to the publications about his inclusion in puerile 'eligible bachelor' lists—which had only excited them into asking for interviews. What did his relationship status—or lack of it—have to do with anything?

But here, he could enjoy his anonymity with his friends. While the food was good and the company excellent, he couldn't help but aware of the conspicuously empty chair at the four-person table. How would it be if Eloise sat there next to him? He'd never before met a woman he'd want to introduce to his friends.

Four successful young entrepreneurs would have a lot to chat about. He could imagine the spirited conversation, the laughter, the strong opinions tossed back and forth. The thought conjured up an image of her sitting there, smiling at him, holding his hand under the table. It almost seemed real. But the empty chair glared back at him.

The long lunch over, he farewelled his friends with promises of seeing them again at their wedding. Then he headed back to his luxurious suite in one of Melbourne's most stylish Southbank hotels. For several hours, he attended to the necessary phone and video-call catch-ups that being in a different time zone entailed. He had no more appointments for the day after those were complete though and now he was on his own.

Usually he valued time to himself. But this afternoon he only felt restless. And, unusually for him, lonely. Perhaps seeing Courtney and Shawn so happy together was affecting him. Making him think thoughts he usually pushed far to the back of his mind, to keep company with other repressed thoughts of love and family and the security of shared lives. *Not for him,* he reminded himself. Not now. He was only twenty-nine. Perhaps later. Much later.

He found himself looking out of the floor-to-ceiling windows over the winding Yarra River and the staggered skyline of a city that wasn't home. He flew back to Boston tomorrow. But he would be flying back to loneliness too, packing it in his bag and transporting it with him to his empty apartment. Being alone was the price he had willingly paid for the freedom to build his staggering wealth that disproved, dollar by dollar, that he hadn't been worthy of the family he'd been born into.

Boy could not forget girl.

Eloise intrigued him. He wanted to see her face again, hear her magical laugh. Just a friendly meeting. Not a date. No physical contact like kissing, which only complicated things. It made sense, didn't it, to act on that impulse when he was in the same country as her rather than half a world away?

Thoughts of her flashed through his mind: her uninhibited joy in her scruffy little foster dog; the sensual sway when she walked in high-heeled shoes; the understanding in her eyes when he'd told her some of his past.

He started to text:

I find I have to be back in Sydney on Thursday. Would lunch be out of the question? Josh T

He pressed *send* and stared at the screen. She'd be busy in her workshop. Perhaps fitting a client. Maybe even dreaming up a spectacular dress for Courtney. But within seconds, the phone pinged a reply.

Nice to hear from you. Thursday is a busy day for me, but I'd like to catch up. A quick lunch would be great. Suggest a café near my atelier.

She texted the address of the café and a suggested time, to which Josh agreed.

He put down the phone and realised, to his surprise, that his hand wasn't quite steady and his heart was thudding.

But he had no time to think about what that meant. He had to reroute his flight home via Sydney. If he had to, he would hire a private jet.

CHAPTER FIVE

ELOISE COULDN'T HELP checking her watch every few minutes. Josh should be here very soon. She'd got to the café early, a favourite lunch spot for her just diagonally over the road from work. Her usual waitress, a lovely girl named Mara, had shown her to a table outside under the shade of an umbrella—it was another perfect, sunny autumn day.

She was excited at the prospect of seeing Josh again, while also filled with a healthy dose of trepidation. That unexpected kiss had aroused long dormant appetites and emotions. It was true what she'd told him—she wasn't a one-night stand kind of girl. Yet once her car had turned the corner and he'd fallen out of sight, she'd had to fight the urge to turn it around with a screech of tyres, speed back and tell him to jump in the car. Her place or his hotel—it wouldn't have mattered once they'd got hot and naked.

She had to fan her face with her hand at the very thought. Obviously she'd been too long without a man to be having fantasies like that about someone she hardly knew. Yet Josh had not been far from her thoughts since she'd driven away from him. She found him hotter than hot—especially after that kiss—but she had also really enjoyed his company.

There was a straightforwardness to him she found refreshing. And she'd liked his kindness to Daisy, which she was convinced was genuine. Dogs didn't lie and Daisy had approved of him. She had been surprised and pleased when he'd texted on Tuesday. But he still lived in a country that was, at best, a twenty-one-hour flight away. Hardly conducive to dating.

However, dating and all the drama that went with it wasn't at the front of her mind right now. Since she'd had that text from Josh her world had imploded.

She really should have cancelled the lunch and concentrated on trying to put the social media fires out. But she wanted to see him, and who knew when lunch with Josh would happen again, if ever? For that reason, she decided not to share the story of the disaster that had erupted yesterday. Rather she would push it down under a cheerful façade to be the trouble-free woman he had dined with just a few days ago. She was used to solving her own problems. Although this particular nightmare might not be easily solved—and the impact on her business could be considerable.

She looked up, saw him striding towards her table and caught her breath. Josh in a dark charcoal, perfectly tailored business suit rocketed his degree of hotness to blow the top off the thermometer. She used to think tech people, no matter how wealthy, hung out in hoodies and sneakers. Josh was the sartorially splendid exception. She couldn't remember when she'd last found a man so attractive.

He got to the table and she rose to greet him on legs

that felt suddenly shaky. She looked up at him, his lean, strikingly good-looking face seeming already familiar. His nose, slightly crooked, saved him from being pretty-boy handsome, and his dark brown hair cut short seemed to resent being tamed, going off in rebellious spikes. And his mouth, his sensual mouth, his top lip slightly narrower than the bottom… A shiver of desire ran through her at the remembered pleasure of his kiss.

But she didn't trust that kind of instant attraction. Handsome Craig had hidden so well what kind of man he really was. She'd been like an insect, lured by the sweetness of honey, only to find herself sinking in a heavy, suffocating mass. Thank heaven she'd found the strength to struggle to the top and then fly away. When she next got into a relationship it would only be after a long getting-to-know-him process. She needed to embrace her feelings of mistrust towards men, not fight them. Only time could build trust.

But that kiss had happened and it seemed to make a handshake in greeting redundant. She looked up at Josh for a long moment, not sure what to do. He had no such hesitation. He claimed her mouth for a quick, warm kiss of greeting. 'Glad you were free for lunch,' he said.

She had to fight the temptation to raise her fingers to her lips, tingling with the pleasure of his touch. Even a simple kiss sent a shiver of awareness reverberating through her.

Then Mara the waitress was there again. She looked from Josh to Eloise and back again. 'Good to see you here again, sir,' she said to Josh with a big smile. 'So it was *her* you were waiting for.'

Eloise wasn't sure what Mara meant. Had Josh got here before her then gone again? It was possible.

Josh was quick to explain. 'I'm staying near by at the same hotel I stayed at last week. I came here for coffee then. When I got here, I was surprised to find it was the same café.'

'I see,' she said, not sure it was a full explanation but shrugging it off as nothing to worry about. She had enough real issues to worry about without angsting over imagined ones.

She sat down and he sat down opposite her. It was a table for two, so that wasn't far between them. She had to purposely angle her legs not to come into contact with his legs. When they accidentally brushed together, jolts of awareness reminded her of how she had felt when he had kissed her in the street outside the restaurant.

'How was your flight up from Melbourne?' she said.

'On time and comfortable. I can't ask for more.'

'It…it's nice to see you again,' she said. 'I'm sorry Daisy can't be here. She'll be upset she missed you, her favourite male human, or…or she would be if she were human and she knew about it, but of course she's not.' Well, that was a great start, mumbling inanely about her dog.

'I'm upset I missed her,' he said gallantly. 'Where is she today?'

'I like this café but they don't welcome dogs, so I left her at work.' She waved her hand to indicate her shop front, diagonally across the road. 'We're over there.'

'I walked past your building on my way here from the hotel. It's very smart and with great street presence.'

'Yes, we get passing trade as well as clients who

know us by reputation,' she said, knowing her voice sounded stilted. Where was that easy flow of conversation from their dinner last Saturday?

Trouble was, she couldn't stop worrying about what might be going on there over the road and it was strangling her thoughts. She should be there, not having lunch with someone. But she was here, and she wanted to enjoy the rare treat of being with a man as attractive as Josh.

'We should order,' she said. 'The food is excellent here.'

She handed Josh a menu. In doing so she knocked over the open bottle of sparkling mineral water Mara had brought to the table. Water spilled, fizzing, all over the table. She swore under her breath, the same word several times, as she tried to mop up the water with the paper napkins from the table. 'I'm sorry, so sorry. First my dog muddies your trousers and now I've spilled water all over you.' She was conscious of her voice rising. She took a deep breath to bring it back down.

'No need to apologise. There's no water on me.'

'Really?'

He grabbed some napkins and mopped up the water that had formed a puddle on his side of the table. 'There, all gone.'

'I'm sorry, I really am,' she said, feeling wretched.

'You've already said sorry twice, no need for a third. You've got nothing to apologise for.'

'So long as you're not drenched.'

'I'm perfectly dry,' he said.

'You're sure?'

'I'm absolutely sure.' His smile was kind and reassuring. It made her want to sob. *Pull yourself together, Eloise.*

'Good,' she said. 'I'll order another bottle of water when we order our meal.'

'Problem solved.'

She attempted a smile. 'Shall I try again?' Very carefully, she passed him the menu, which he took from her with exaggerated care and made her laugh.

'What do you recommend?' he asked.

'Anything I've tried on the menu is very good. It's simple café food but very well prepared. I… I'm not very hungry so I'll order a quinoa and hummus salad.'

'I'll try the salmon,' he said.

'Good choice,' she said.

He leaned towards her. 'Before we order I want to make it clear lunch is my treat.'

'Oh, but—'

'No buts. I invited you, I pay.'

She knew she would sound ungracious if she argued. 'Thank you.'

Mara came to take their orders, bringing with her a pile of new napkins. Josh asked her to bring more water, Eloise for her favourite white wine.

Josh waited for the waitress to be out of earshot. 'Are you okay? You don't seem yourself. Or at least not the you I know from our last two meetings.'

'Absolutely fine,' she said but to her horror her voice wobbled and she had to sniff back a sudden, threatening tear.

'Are you sure? You seem a little stressed.' His voice was calm and soothing.

'*Stressed?* Yes. I am a little stressed.' She paused.

'Something horrible has happened and I wasn't going to tell you and now I guess I should or you'll wonder why I'm all over the place.'

'I'm listening,' he said.

Eloise realised what a relief it would be to share the awfulness of the threat she was under. Her staff were too invested in the business to give an impartial opinion, although she was pleased at how they had banded around her with wholehearted support. Josh was a tech mogul. Maybe he would have some advice on how to shut her problem down.

The wine had arrived. Josh poured two glasses. As he reached across the table to hand it to her she became intensely aware of the fresh male scent of him. Whatever aftershave or cologne he wore, it made her want to swoon. When she got to know him better—if that ever happened—she'd ask him what brand it was.

She took a good slug of wine and put her glass back on the table, leaned across to him and lowered her voice. 'I've run foul of one of the local social media fashion influencers—an eastern suburbs woman who goes by the handle @lindytheblonde. She has more than two million followers and has threatened to ruin me. Soon, she told me, no bride will want to wear an Eloise Evans Atelier gown at her wedding.'

Josh frowned. 'That doesn't sound good.'

'It's not good. I know this woman. I've dressed her as a bridesmaid three times. She wasn't easy to deal with then. Now she's finally a bride, she's morphed into a fully-fledged Bridezilla.' She was aware her voice rose on the last words and forced herself to lower it.

'How did the threat come about?'

'The first conflict came when I wouldn't let her jump the waiting list. I got the "Do you know who I am?" thing then. I knew perfectly well who she was and, to be honest, wished she'd go somewhere else for her gown. After some huffing and puffing she had to wait for her name to come to the top like everyone else.'

'Your waiting list is a clever strategy. I suspect it makes people value your product.'

She smiled a shaky smile. 'It's quite deliberate. Exclusivity is our selling point.'

'And people are prepared to pay for it.'

'Yes,' she said. 'But not *@lindytheblonde*.'

Eloise looked around the café, just in case, but it was still early for lunch and the tables nearest to them were empty. Only a few people walked by on the street. She lowered her voice to practically a murmur. She and Josh had to have their heads almost touching for him to hear her.

'She came for her first consultation yesterday afternoon. She wanted a very extravagant, very expensive gown and was furious I wouldn't give it to her gratis in return for a social media tag. She expects everything for free and I don't give freebies. They devalue my brand. I have a marketing strategy that includes paid advertising and placements. I'm grateful to bloggers and social media—brides sharing their wedding dresses on their pages helped grow my business immensely in the early days—but I keep advertising and editorial separate. I didn't get the chance to tell her I would consider advertising in her space as she has such big numbers.'

'She wasn't happy?'

'She was outraged. She flounced out of my workroom telling me in no uncertain terms where I could stick my wedding dresses.'

'Not a nice lady.'

'Indeed not.'

'Good riddance to bad rubbish, I would say.'

'That's what I thought. Until she started a smear campaign against me. It's all over social media. She must have gone straight home and started posting—and you know how quickly gossip spreads on the internet.'

'What dirt could she find to smear you with?'

'Dirt? I hope I haven't got any dirt to find. But she's outing me as the wedding dress designer who never wants a wedding of her own. "Would you trust your dream dress with a woman who scorns your dreams? How can a designer who has sworn off marriage possibly understand the needs of a bride?" That kind of thing.' She shuddered. 'She's given me some horrible hashtags.'

Josh's eyebrows rose. 'Is that true? That you don't ever want to get married?'

'She's twisted my words somewhat but it's mostly true.' She shrugged. 'I've made no secret of it. Now I wish I'd kept my mouth shut about my views.'

'Why such a strong opinion?'

'To close down well-meaning people, basically. I broke off a long-term relationship more than a year ago. I nearly got engaged, but realised in time that he was totally and utterly Mr Wrong for me. I do *not* want to rush into another serious relationship.' She'd lost herself in trying to be what Craig had wanted her to be.

'I get that,' Josh said. She thought about the 'most eligible bachelor' lists he'd appeared on and thought he might have his own story to tell about relationships gone wrong.

'But the thing with brides is that they're in their own little bubble of couple love and they want you to be floating up there alongside them. Nearly every consultation, every fitting, sooner or later out it comes: "When will you be making your own dream dress, Eloise?" I found the easiest reply was to tell them I hadn't found the right man yet. That soon proved to be totally the wrong reply.'

'Why?'

'Because it inspired them with zeal to find me the right man. Their lonely brother/cousin/friend/bitter divorced uncle or even gay guy friend they were convinced hadn't met the right woman.' She made pretend tearing-out-her-hair motions. 'Aaargh! I didn't want to meet them, and they most likely didn't want to meet me. It became so much easier to say I didn't ever want to get married. I didn't think it would backfire on me like this.'

'You really meant it? About not wanting to get married?'

'Never say never. But it's true for me right now. I can't see a wedding on the horizon for me for a long time.'

'I get that,' he said.

'Working in the wedding dress business, I deal with some deliriously happy couples. Their glow can't help but wear off on you, like glitter. I sometimes envy them. But you can really get to see the underbelly of romance too. I'd never name names, but it's got so I can predict which of my brides' weddings won't last a year. It's made me realise too many people get married for the wrong reasons.'

He frowned. 'What are the right reasons?'

'Being darn sure you're compatible for one thing. I value my independence and I don't want to give over any part of my life for someone else to control. So yes, @*lindytheblonde* is partly right about me but she's very wrong that I'm not the right person to help another woman's wedding dreams come true. I think I've proved that and I can't bear that her vindictiveness might affect my business.'

'Has it affected your business?'

'Sadly, yes. Three names came off the waiting list within minutes of her first posting. Heaven knows what carnage is to come.'

'What do you intend to do? Take legal action?'

'I can see Mara heading our way with food. How about we talk about my options over lunch?' Eloise suggested. She felt so much better for having unburdened herself.

Today Eloise looked vintage sexy in a tight, red and white polka-dotted pencil skirt, a wide belt and a white knit top that looked fabulous with her wavy black hair and bold red lipstick. So very, very different from anything Tori would ever wear. The top was finished with a wide, loose bow that drew attention to the subtle cleavage on display. However, he doubted she wore it to purposely tease and entice. Those were the clothes she wore to work, she'd come straight from her premises across the road to this café. She was a fashion designer, she had a 'look' and it suited her natural sensuality superbly. Josh couldn't keep his eyes off her.

He was more and more intrigued by Eloise. He didn't

think he'd ever met a beautiful young woman with an anti-marriage stance. Guys, yes. Including himself. He wasn't a huge fan of weddings either.

There weren't enough good marriages in his family to make him aspire to the matrimonial state. His brother was a bully and on to his second wife. His mother, so she'd explained to him, had been lonely and unhappy in her marriage to his ex-father, hence the affair with her tennis coach. And yet, when Josh was eighteen years old, graduated from high school and already earning his own living, she had informed him she was going back to the man who had kicked them out. More for the affluent lifestyle she'd been used to and had sorely missed than anything to do with love, she had admitted. She hated living in the North End.

But there was a proviso—Josh himself wasn't to darken the door. His mother had to meet him off the premises. The unexpected betrayal had been a painful blow—he had still needed her. How could she accept separation from him in return for financial comfort?

Thankfully his aunt had stepped up to assure him he would always have a home in the North End. The security of Aunt Lil's love had done much to soothe the sting of his mother's betrayal. Now he was able to ensure his aunt was secure financially for the rest of her days.

Yet, to his mother's credit, she had worked to keep up her relationship with him, just as she had with her older son when he'd been forbidden to her. In recent years, he had tentatively rebuilt his relationship with his mother. Not to what it had been when it had been him and her against his father and his world, but something both of them were moderately happy with. However, he had never trusted her enough to confide in her about his vendetta against his ex-father. She was too beholden to him to be trusted.

Control. Eloise was right in her thinking. In that marriage his mother had ceded all independence to her husband's control. But surely men of his generation didn't behave like that with their wives? Even with his insistence that all dating was casual, he'd been stung by women impressed by his wealth, who saw him as a potential meal ticket. But to him a relationship had to be one of equals—his mother had been trapped in an unhappy marriage, as she'd given up her career to support her husband's and been financially unable to support her sons.

The waitress winked at him when she put his plate in front of him, not so Eloise could see. He couldn't tell Eloise but during his first days in Sydney he had spent quite some time in this café, watching her atelier in the hope of seeing her going in or coming out. This waitress had asked him if he was waiting for his fiancée to have a fitting at the exclusive bridal store over the road. He'd made a noncommittal answer she had obviously misinterpreted. Did she think Eloise was his fiancée? From the knowing way she looked from him to Eloise he believed so—and that she approved of their 'romance'. He swallowed a curse. How would he ever explain that to Eloise if the girl said anything about his prior visit to her café?

He was glad for the diversion of eating their meals. He didn't want to talk about weddings or anything related to them. But suddenly he didn't feel very hungry.

'Are you going to finish your salmon?' Eloise asked.

He noticed she'd barely touched her salad. 'No. If you'd like—'

She smiled. 'Not for me. But Daisy is very fond of salmon. If you don't want it, I could take a doggy bag back to her.'

'She'd be very welcome.'

'My mother will be picking her up soon to take her home with her. I asked her to mind Daisy for me, as I've been invited to a big pull-out-all-the-stops wedding out in the country this weekend.'

'It's convenient your mother could look after her for you.'

'Yes. Only it might be for nothing. I'm not sure I can bear to go to the wedding. Horrid *@lindytheblonde* is going to be there and I don't think I can face her.'

'That doesn't sound like you.' He corrected himself. 'The you that I've got to know, that is. Wouldn't she see it as a victory if you didn't go?'

'Probably. And Becca, the bride, might be disappointed if I cry off. We've become good friends. I dressed her for her first wedding and this is her second.'

'Do you often get repeat business?'

'Quite often. In this case she's got it right the second time. Husband number two, Simon, is a fabulous guy. I'd like to be there to celebrate with her. There's also the fact that among all those guests might be potential clients. But I really don't think I can face *@lindytheblonde*.' Her voice hitched. 'My presence will only point out the truth of what she's saying about me because I don't have a plus-one to take to the wedding.'

'I can be your plus-one.' The words slipped out as if of their own volition.

Her eyes widened. 'You could? But you're going back to Boston.'

'I don't have to. I'm my own boss.'

'Really? You'd really do that for me?'

'It would hardly be a hardship,' he said drily.

'It's out near Bowral, south west of Sydney, very posh. The wedding is to be held in a grand country house owned by the groom's family. I've been invited to stay the night. We made the bride's gown and the attendants'. It will be a beautiful wedding. But it does mean a nearly two-hour drive out there and then back the next day. If you're sure you can spare the time...?'

'I can do that,' he said. He didn't like seeing her being ill-treated by the woman.

'Thank you! I accept your offer.' She clapped her hands together in delight, her cheeks flushed. She leaned over and kissed him on the mouth. 'Have you got a tux with you?'

'No, I didn't see the need.'

'No matter. We can tailor one for you. We sometimes do that for special grooms. Actually, there are some brides who like a white tux as well. We have an excellent tailor on the staff. You'd just have to come in for a fitting. Now. After lunch. I'll take your measurements myself. Then another fitting tomorrow.'

Josh gulped at the prospect of Eloise taking his inside leg measurement. 'Great,' he choked out. What the hell was he letting himself in for?

CHAPTER SIX

THERE WASN'T TIME to waste. As soon as they finished lunch, Eloise ushered Josh over the road and through the door to Eloise Evans Atelier. She gave him a quick tour around the ground-floor salon. As she did, she immediately felt her tension ratchet down a notch. Her business was everything to her. She would defend it in any legal way she could. Josh had offered her a lifeline as her plus-one for the weekend wedding. With him by her side, she could hold her head up high against any barbs from that malicious influencer.

The spacious room proudly celebrated femininity. One of her clients had called it a shrine to brides and maybe that wasn't far off. The space was decorated in shades of white and cream, with plush carpets underfoot and silver vases filled with magnificent fresh flower arrangements strategically placed. Bolts of the finest fabrics sourced from all around the world spilled out of a large, open armoire she'd imported from France and shimmered under the light of a lavish antique crystal chandelier.

'We pride ourselves on luxury and exclusivity,' she explained. 'The salon is set up to see one bridal party at a time—the bride, her attendants, her mother, whoever she chooses to bring with her. Appointments are timed so that brides are unlikely to bump into other brides.'

'And the price reflects the level of service,' he said. She liked the way he took her 'girly' business so seriously and seemed to have an innate understanding of how she operated.

'And comfort,' she said. Upholstered chairs were strategically placed around the space. Champagne was chilling in a silver ice bucket, canapés would be offered. And tissues for the tears of those brides overcome by the beauty of their gowns and their mothers overcome by the beauty of their daughters.

All that was missing was a bride trying on a gown from the rack filled with garments in various shades of pale to see which shapes best suited her and twirling in front of the large mirrors with ornate gilt frames. A girl from a very wealthy northern suburbs family should have been doing just that right now. Only she'd cancelled at the last minute, citing 'philosophical differences with the designer' as her reason. Even the thought of it made Eloise grit her teeth.

Josh's expression was vaguely hunted, his eyes glazed as he looked around. 'Impressive,' he said.

'I wanted to recreate the kind of elegant salon that impressed me when I worked in Paris. Getting fitted for a wedding dress should be a memorable, happy experience and a real treat.'

'I'm sure it is,' he said. 'But—'

'There's a *but*?'

He shuddered. 'I feel totally out of place here. I'm too tall, too big, too *male*.'

He was all that without a doubt. *Oh, yes.* And so very handsome. She couldn't be happier that he had offered to escort her to Becca's wedding. He was perfect. And if @*lindytheblonde* got wind that he was a billionaire, that would be even better.

She laughed. 'Men aren't usually part of the wedding dress decision. Remember, it's thought to be bad luck for a groom to see the bride's dress before their wedding. Old traditions die hard. I think you'll be more comfortable in the workroom upstairs.'

'Perhaps I could go out and buy a tuxedo rather than you make—'

She shook her head. 'Not happening. The least I can do for you in return for accompanying me to the wedding is to provide a bespoke tuxedo. You're used to having your clothes made bespoke, I can tell.'

'I go to the best tailor in Boston.'

'Besides, I couldn't possibly have my plus-one accompany me in anything that wasn't classy and impeccably tailored.'

He looked at her, bemused. 'I'm uncertain if you're joking or not.'

'Mostly not joking. I'm judged by the quality of my clothes. I guess I'll be judged by the quality of your suit if @*lindytheblonde* really has the daggers out for me at the wedding. I don't want you caught up in it.'

Eloise led Josh up the stairs, and through another set of doors to the workroom.

'This is the heart of my business,' she said proudly. 'Where a bride's dreams of the perfect dress become reality.'

This large room was a constant hub of activity. Her

team of seamstresses sat at industrial sewing machines or hand-stitching garments, mostly white, some the myriad colours of bridesmaids' dresses. They all wore gloves to protect the very expensive fabrics.

Trolleys were hung with clipped-together bunches of brown paper pattern pieces. Dressmaker's dummies were draped with pinned and half-finished gowns. Various samples of lace and trims and ribbons dangled from metal racks. A mood board for a large upcoming wedding where they were dressing not just the bride and her attendants but also all the female members of their extended families dominated one corner.

Eloise breathed in the scent of freshly cut fabrics, of paper and sewing machines. She loved it all. Most nights it was a wrench to go home. She couldn't bear it being under threat.

She stood at the front of the room and addressed her team. 'I'd like to introduce you all to Josh Taylor. He's accompanying me to the Sanderson wedding and we need to get him into a tux, pronto. We'll need to pull out all the stops.'

She was surprised at the wave of giggles that rippled through the room. Her close friend and second in command, Vinh Tran, came over to her, unable to suppress an enormous smile. 'Hi, Josh; we were wondering when Eloise was going to introduce you to us,' she said, for the room's benefit.

'What?' The word exploded from Eloise.

She looked anxiously up at Josh. Surely he wouldn't think she'd boasted to her friends and colleagues about their date, blown it up to something so much more than it was? He shifted from one foot to the other, looking as uncomfortable as she was feeling.

She'd told Vinh she was going on her first date in for ever with a visiting American when they'd been working on the pink tea dress she'd worn that night, but that was as far as it had gone.

'You mean you haven't seen it?' said Vinh.

'Seen what? I don't know what you're talking about.'

Vinh brought over her tablet and, without a word, enlarged the images on screen to show her.

Eloise's hand shot to her mouth to stifle her gasp. There she was in close-up, in her red spotted skirt, leaning across the table in the nearby café and kissing Josh. It had only been a brief kiss, but the camera gave it so much more significance. There was another of them talking, their heads so close they were almost touching, smiling into each other's eyes. The images were close, intimate, and she was glowing. *They looked so good together.*

'Where did these come from?'

'They were posted on one of the local gossip sites.' Vinh read out the caption. '"*New man for celebrity frock queen?*" I must say you look gorgeous. And…er…so do you, Josh.'

Vinh, a petite Vietnamese Australian, had been friends with Eloise since the first days of their fashion design degree. Eloise had dropped out soon after her internship in Paris ended, as she figured she'd learned enough about the nuts and bolts of design and pattern-making and had keenly observed how the French bridal couture house had operated. Vinh had completed her degree and, while she was an excellent designer, she was also interested in the business side of running a label. But Vinh hadn't wanted to start her own. Each of the friends had not had good experiences working for established fashion companies.

Eloise had set up by herself on a small scale, working from an industrial site in Alexandria. Some of those girls for whom she'd made prom dresses had asked if she could work her magic on their wedding dresses. Word-of-mouth recommendations and exposure on social media had given her the bookings and the confidence to expand into Double Bay, or Double Pay as it was colloquially known. Two years ago she'd asked Vinh to join her in the business. It had proved to be an excellent decision.

Now Vinh was obviously taken with Josh and kept giving Eloise meaningful sideways glances of approval. Dear heaven, please don't let Josh notice, Eloise prayed.

Eloise frowned. 'But who—?'

'The waitress?' Josh said.

'Mara? Maybe.'

'A lot of people walk past there—it could have been anyone with a camera phone who recognised you,' said Vinh.

Josh turned to Eloise. 'Isn't this good publicity for you? It takes the sting out of the attack from the influencer.' He paused. 'And I agree, you look beautiful.'

A soft, collective sigh sounded through the room. Eloise felt the sudden sting of tears and blinked down hard on them. She was as susceptible to romance as anyone else—more so perhaps, given her profession— it was just she fought so hard against it for herself. She couldn't let herself get to like Josh too much. He'd soon be winging his way back home. There would be no chance to see if the attraction between them could lead to anything deeper.

'In fact, it's very romantic,' said Vinh. 'And if you're going to that big wedding together on the weekend, that's all the better.'

Vinh and the rest of the team were aware of her anguish over the influencer's damaging posts. And the fact if the business slid downhill their jobs could be at risk.

Eloise looked at the photo again. She'd like a copy for herself but didn't dare admit it. Later, she'd take a screen shot. 'You're both right,' she said.

'Let's hope it goes viral, then,' said Vinh. She turned to Eloise. 'Before I forget, your mum popped in to pick up Daisy. She said she was double parked and couldn't wait for you.'

'Thanks,' said Eloise, disappointed she wouldn't see her little foster dog until after the weekend. People sometimes asked her how she liked living alone. She would reply she was never alone, as she had a series of canine companions. When it came to love, dogs were so much more reliable than humans.

Josh seemed genuinely disappointed too. 'I'm sorry I won't see Daisy.'

Vinh then turned to Josh. 'We need to take your measurements for that rush order tux.'

Eloise caught Josh's eye. For a moment she was tempted to take the tailor's tape measure and do it herself, as she'd suggested at the café. But she couldn't bring herself to do it. There was a lot of body measuring involved for a bespoke suit so it would fit and drape

perfectly. She just couldn't. It would be somehow too…
intimate. She was too aware of him, of the feelings
aroused by that kiss, to trust herself.

'Yes,' she said to Vinh. 'Can you please handle him…
er… I mean, handle that? You know what I mean.' Her
friend laughed. Josh looked discomfited in a way she
found very appealing.

'I think the Italian wool and silk fabric in midnight-
blue,' she said. 'What do you think, Josh?'

He shrugged. 'I'll put myself in your expert hands.'
Eloise blushed high on her cheekbones and hoped he
didn't notice. *She'd like that very much.*

During the process of being measured for his tux, Josh
became aware of how liked and admired Eloise was by
her staff. How hard she worked. What a fair manager
she was. How very unfair it was that the spiteful actions
of a disgruntled Bridezilla should threaten the business
she loved so passionately.

If he were Eloise, he would be immediately seeking a way to ruin that influencer. He was vengeful and
didn't mind admitting it. Long after his opponent had
forgotten about his attack on Josh or one of his enterprises—or thought they'd got away with it—he would
strike. *The smiling assassin*, one of his business asso-
ciates had labelled him. And they hadn't meant it as a
compliment.

He hadn't always been that hard, vengeful person.
As a kid, he'd been sunny, good-natured, secure in his
family and status. All that had changed the day he'd
been evicted from his home and the life he'd thought
was his by birth. Then he'd had to use his smarts and

any weapon available to him to forge ahead. He treated people with honesty, and if he didn't get it in return then they would get their comeuppance. He knew he would never get the revenge he wanted against the man who had raised him—his ex-father's fortune was too blue-chip, too established—but he could certainly chip away at the edges of it. And, oh, how he would gloat to see him up before the bankruptcy court.

He was glad he was able to help Eloise by accompanying her to the wedding as her plus-one. How wise an action that was for him, he hadn't paused to think. Or how he would explain it to Tori. Eloise needed help, and on impulse he'd come to the rescue. Now he realised there was yet another way he could help her get revenge on her opponent.

He waited until he'd been measured, every bit as skilfully and thoroughly as by his gentleman's tailor in Boston, and been asked to return later in the afternoon for his first fitting. There would be two more the next morning.

Eloise escorted him downstairs. She paused at the entrance to the citadel of girliness. 'We'll see you in two hours. I've got half the team working on your tux.' She looked up at him, her blue eyes warm and sincere, fringed with those outrageously fake black lashes that were fun and glamorous on her but he'd think over-the-top on anyone else. 'Thank you again, Josh. The paparazzi actually played right into our hands. Hopefully there'll be some buzz ahead of us by the time we go to the wedding together on Saturday.'

He lowered his voice to be heard only by her. 'I've

thought of a way to get even more buzz and to knock the wind right out of your detractor's sails.'

Her brow pleated into a frown. 'And that would be?'

'What if I pretended to be your fiancé for the weekend?'

Her eyes widened. 'You…you'd be my fake fiancé?'

'In terms of business strategy, it's an excellent idea. If you turn up to the wedding with a fiancé on your arm, it negates everything the influencer says about your attitude to marriage.'

'That's true.' She paused. 'It's drastic though, isn't it? I'd have to give the idea some thought.'

He had a sudden inspiration. 'It would help me out too. Lately I've been put on a number of ludicrous "most eligible bachelors" lists and that really bugs me. Gossip of an engagement will put those lists immediately out of date.'

'So it could work for both of us,' she said slowly.

'It could,' he said.

She looked up at him. 'Okay. Let's do it.' Although her words were bold, the accompanying smile was a tad shaky.

'Then, after the wedding, you can take your real revenge.'

'What do you mean?' she said.

'This is how I would handle it if she were my opponent. You will already have weakened her by showing she was wrong about you not wanting to marry. Next, I would get my business analysts to go through her site looking for any inconsistencies and weaknesses in her enterprises. Presumably, she gets her income from advertisers who pay her for her endorsements of their products. I would look for even the slightest instance where she might have crossed the line that I could use against her. Then I would use my muscle to ensure the advertisers did not see her as being the best spokesperson or brand for their products any longer. Ultimately I would bring her down. As she intended to bring you down.'

Her eyes widened. 'That's really ruthless. And not very ethical.'

He shrugged. 'That's how the world works.' He'd learned from the best when it came to stone-hearted ruthlessness: his ex-father.

Eloise stayed silent for a long moment and he could see by the expressions flashing across her face that she was reassessing her opinion of him. And it was definitely downward. For the best, perhaps. He didn't want her building any expectations of him.

Finally she spoke. 'I don't know that I would want to go that far, regardless of what you might do in the same situation. However, the fake fiancé idea is a good one, if we can carry it off.'

'You'll have to guide me there. I know nothing about being engaged.'

'I would have to have a doting fiancé on my arm. What I mean is, we'll have to make it look believable. You know, that we…er…were actually in love with each other.'

'That's a point,' he said. 'We might get our first chance now. Don't turn around, but your friend Vinh is peeking around the door upstairs.'

Eloise smiled. 'Is she, now? Let's start how we mean to continue. Give her something to take back to the workroom, and get the gossip started, shall we?' She wound her arms around his neck and kissed him, her mouth sweet and warm under his.

Almost immediately Josh forgot that the kiss was staged as he pulled her close and kissed her back.

CHAPTER SEVEN

BY EARLY FRIDAY afternoon Josh's tuxedo was fitted and finished, the trouser hems breaking perfectly on the new dress shoes he'd bought the day before at a Double Bay boutique. The jacket had a whimsical blue-and-white-spotted silk lining, which had been a surprise to him.

'If I'd known you a little better I could have fitted the design to your interests, even had the lining custom-printed if there'd been time,' Eloise murmured so no one else could hear. 'After all, tuxedos can be a tad on the stuffy side for a young guy.'

He stood in his new tux at the front of the workroom for a final check. Eloise and her delightful friend Vinh then circled him, while he stood there captive in his new suit. The two women snipped loose threads, tucked, pulled, and prodded the fabric into place, laughing as they did so until it dawned on him they were making a game of it. Finally, laughing himself, he told them to cease and desist. Eloise's touch, no matter how light and playful, was altogether too distracting. Again he wondered what he might have unwittingly got himself into.

She looked sexy as hell in citrus-yellow hip-hugging retro-style cut-off trousers and a short swing top that gave a tantalising hint of the creamy skin of her waist when she turned. High heels gave her a delightful wiggle when she walked. She wore her clothes like a theatrical costume, he realised. Did she hide her real self behind the drama of vintage style? Or was the dressing up just part of her creative nature? It was no matter. It was fun. *She was fun.* He couldn't remember when he'd last felt more relaxed.

Again he thought how much Tori would like Eloise. He wished Tori would contact her twin soon. The longer Tori left it, the deeper Josh got into this friendship with Eloise—which was more than a friendship but less than a relationship or even an affair—the more difficult it would be to explain his role in their reunion when it ultimately all came out.

In the interests of transparency, he had called Tori that morning, Sydney time, to tell her his business dealings had taken him back to Sydney. It was stretching the truth somewhat, as, while he had actually made business appointments, the primary purpose had been that inexplicable and compelling urge to see Eloise again.

He'd told Tori about the lunch. Then casually mentioned he was acting as plus-one for a wedding on the upcoming weekend.

Immediately Tori had pounced. 'Are you sure you're not getting in a little too deep, Josh? I asked you to get a close look at her. Not to get close *to* her.' She'd paused. 'You're not developing a thing for her, are you?'

'Of course not,' he'd denied, knowing he was blustering, knowing he was not quite telling the entire truth.

Whatever Tori defined as a *thing*, he wasn't feeling it for Eloise. He found her undeniably hot, beautiful, smart. He liked her. She made him laugh, loosened him up, made him relax. Inspired him to do crazy things like pretend to be her fiancé to help her vanquish a business threat. But it wasn't a *thing*. He wasn't falling for her, definitely not. Tori needed to be absolutely clear about that.

So did he.

Now Eloise pulled him aside so they could speak without being overhead. 'Are you free for practice after work tonight?'

'Practice?'

'Fiancé practice.'

His thoughts ran in one rather exciting direction but he suspected she didn't mean that. 'Run that by me again?'

'We're meant to be an engaged couple and we have to be convincing at the wedding. That influencer woman will pick a phony couple a mile off. We have to seem genuine. That means we have to get our stories straight—you know, how we met, how long we've been together, that kind of stuff.'

'I didn't realise it would involve all that.'

'I didn't either until I started to think about it. I've never been a fake fiancée before. Or any kind of fiancée actually. Do you want to back out? You can at any time, you know. I won't hold you to it.'

'No, not at all. I gave my word.' He frowned. 'But I didn't realise it would involve so much lying.'

'Might be wise not to think of it as lying. Rather…' She thought about it for a moment 'Not a lie as such, but rather a targeted business strategy of purposeful evasion.'

He laughed. 'Where did you get that from?'

'I did a business course when I knew I'd be setting up on my own,' she said. 'I can talk the talk when I need to.'

'Well, I guess that's something I should know about you. There must be more.'

'Exactly. That's why we need to practise our stories.'

'Okay. Count me in.'

'Why don't I pop round to your hotel after I finish work? It's only around the corner. We could maybe get a pizza or something.' She put up her hand. 'No. Wait. As my fiancé, you would be expected to be familiar with my apartment. Do you mind coming round to mine? I'll give you the address.'

'Sure.'

'In the meantime, you think of a few questions to ask me, and I'll think of a few questions to ask you. I'll pick up some Thai take-out on my way home.'

Eloise was only too aware that Josh, charming as he might appear, was a tough, driven businessman. No one got to be a billionaire before the age of thirty without a finely honed edge of ruthlessness. His comments on her business revealed a shrewd eye for potential profit. That was verified in the many news and finance pages she'd delved into online to find out more about him.

Yet his revenge strategy for @lindytheblonde had shocked her. His eyes had narrowed and his face set hard as he'd outlined his plan. His fluency made her think he had exacted such a revenge before against someone who had crossed him. Perhaps more than one opponent. She realised she would have to keep her wits about her in any dealings with him. Who knew how ruthless he might be towards people in his personal life?

And yet she'd seen a different side to billionaire Josh. A man kind to a scruffy little dog. A man with a sense of humour who had completely won over her fiercely protective best friend, Vinh—not to mention everyone else in the atelier. Then there was the man who'd offered that whacky solution to her problem with *@lindythe-blonde.* She considered herself to be a creative thinker but a fake engagement wouldn't have crossed her mind in a million years.

Accepting his off-the-wall offer had kicked her relationship with Josh up to a different level that taking him as a plus-one to the wedding would not have. He was no longer a stranger, yet not quite a friend—she was way too attracted to him to put him in the friend category. She didn't have lustful thoughts as she did for Josh with her male friends. Yet their situations meant he couldn't be a potential boyfriend either.

They were co-conspirators in a fake engagement and that would involve a disconcerting level of fake intimacy. But it really was a good idea. If only she—they—could carry it off. Because if they didn't, if she and Josh were revealed as frauds, she'd be a laughing stock. And what that meant for her business could only be bad.

Now she sat opposite Josh, the coffee table between them, each on one of the two squashy cream sofas that formed the focal point of her living room. A half-empty bottle of white wine and their two glasses sat on the coffee table.

She'd inherited this spacious nineteen-thirties apartment from her grandmother—the same one who had taught her to sew—and it was her haven. That grandmother had loved her unconditionally, and had helped her understand the reasons her mother had kept her adoption from her. Still, she'd never been quite able to shake off the knowledge that her grandmother had known and been part of the conspiracy. Even someone as close and doting as her grandmother had lied to her.

She knew how fortunate she was; the price of real estate in this suburb was astronomical. In fact, Double Bay was the wealthiest area in the state with this adjoining area coming in second. The bow-fronted windows looked out over Rushcutters Bay Park and beyond to the waters of the harbour. She could actually see the spot where Daisy had so fortuitously redirected her ball to Josh.

Josh had changed into black jeans and a black cashmere sweater. He looked comfortable, relaxed and super-hot. Not only was he handsome, but he also exuded a male virility that she could not help but respond to with thoughts bordering on the sinful. She wouldn't have any trouble pretending to be attracted to him as his fake fiancée. Keeping her hands off him might be the problem.

They'd chatted generalities as they'd polished off the Thai dinner but, the meal cleared, it was time to get down to the business of prepping themselves to be a believable couple.

'Okay, let's start our preparation for operation fake engagement,' she said. 'Have you ever done any acting? Theatre? Drama studies at school?'

'No.' His expression told her he found the very idea disdainful.

'Me neither,' she said. 'I freeze with nerves the second anyone so much points me in the direction of a stage.'

'I find that hard to believe,' he said. 'You seem so confident.'

'On a one-to-one level maybe,' she said. 'But that does nothing for me when stage fright hits. So when it comes to playing our roles as an engaged couple, we're going to have to wing it.'

'Improvisation is what they call it,' he said.

She nodded. 'We have to think about what a real engaged couple would do and then improvise accordingly. Heaven knows I see enough of them around me.'

'My friends are starting to succumb to the lure of matrimony, so I know a few,' he said. He said *succumb* as if they were being felled by some noxious disease. With her own opinions on marriage being blasted all over the internet, she could hardly be critical of his.

'They're super-sweet to each other,' she said. 'Most have cutesie pet names.'

Josh shuddered. 'Can we please not go there?'

'I agree. I don't think I could do the pet names with a straight face. But some of my close friends call me Ellie. I won't mind if you drop the occasional "Ellie" in the interests of authenticity.'

'"Ellie". I like that. It suits you. But please, don't even think of calling me "Joshy".' The pained expression on his face made her laugh.

'Okay, no calling you J— No, I can't even say it in jest.'

She paused, not sure how to bring up the next subject. 'Engaged couples are usually very affectionate towards each other. Physically affectionate, I mean. Dropping little kisses on their beloved, lots of snuggling and smooching. You know.'

He looked at her for a long moment, and again she had that heady sense of connection. She realised she was leaning towards him, as if straining to be in his arms, and he was leaning towards her. He cleared his throat. 'I don't think we'll have any trouble doing that,' he said.

She sat back on her sofa. 'Me neither. In fact I... I... well, I think we—that is to say I—might have the opposite problem. Being too enthusiastic perhaps.'

'Yes,' he said slowly.

'So only public displays of affection. We need to turn down the dial in private. It's not that I don't trust myself... Well, it is, actually. But we've agreed that neither of us is ready for a relationship and I don't want—'

'I know,' he said hoarsely.

'So that's agreed?'

He nodded. 'Hands off in private.'

Eloise tucked her feet up under her on the sofa. She'd changed into skinny, cuffed nineteen-fifties-style jeans and a red-and-white-checked shirt. 'I'm thinking of the questions people might ask us at the wedding.'

'You go first,' he said.

'Where did we meet?'

He indicated the front window with a wave. 'The dog park out there.'

'Correct. And that would mean we were presenting as an engaged couple just a week after we really did meet. Not very believable in my opinion.'

'You're right. This takes a bit of getting used to,' he

said. 'Let me think. How about we first met in the US, say a few months ago?'

'Did you happen to be in Los Angeles at the time of Roxee's wedding?'

'So happens I did.'

'I was there too. Perhaps we met in LA. At a party. There were a number of parties leading up to the wedding.'

'To which, sadly, I was not invited,' he said with a mock-mournful expression.

'Shame. There was a party at a waterfront venue in Santa Monica. I went outside for a breath of fresh air. You were outside—'

'Taking a break from a particularly boring business dinner.' He paused. 'And I saw this dark-haired girl leaning against a palm tree. I was struck by her beauty.'

Eloise giggled. 'I like that. So what happened?

'I opened a conversation with a witty remark.'

'I responded with something equally witty.'

'We struck up a conversation. You hung on to my every word.'

'Huh! How about I made you laugh?'

'You do that in real life, so that could work. Then you said you had to get back to the party.'

'No! I'm sure I would have wanted to stay with you.'

'Would you?' he said.

'Yes.' Her gaze connected again with his in that surprisingly intimate way.

'Really?' he said, his voice husky.

'Really,' she said. Just as she had found an excuse to have coffee with him at the park. Deny it to herself all she liked, she'd been attracted to him from the start.

She snapped her eyes away. *This was just a game.* A game the success of which was important to her business, but a game just the same. She mustn't get carried away.

'So that's sorted.' She injected a no-nonsense briskness into her voice. 'What did you do next?'

'I got your number. And I called you straight away to check I'd got it right.'

'So when did you call me?'

'I asked you to call me when the party was finished. You did and we met up. Then I took you back to your hotel room.'

'And…?'

'We talked all night until the sun came up,' he said, a smile dancing around the corners of his sexy mouth. 'I was a gentleman.'

'And I was wishing you weren't.' She slapped her hand over her mouth. 'Scratch that!'

He laughed. 'But I wasn't such a gentleman the next night.'

'Really?' she said, trying to sound prim instead of turned on.

It took a real effort not to focus on imagining the exciting details of his fictional ungentlemanly behaviour and her fictional response. Since that first kiss she had spent too much time fantasising over the prospect of making love with Josh. Now he sat so near to her in the privacy of her home, it was impossible not to acknowledge that intense physical pull. 'And we spent as much time as we could together before you had to go back to Boston.'

'We did. In fact, we hardly left your hotel bedroom.'

His tone was so exaggerated in its lasciviousness it made her laugh.

'If you say so,' she said.

'I wished so,' he said with a grin.

She was glad she had decided not to sit next to him on the sofa. It would be only too easy to let this game get out of hand and practise for real.

'Let's be serious,' she said. 'After the big celebrity wedding was over, I had to go to New York City to meet with one of Roxee's friends who'd just got engaged and wanted me to design her wedding gown. That part of the story is true.'

'So I flew to New York and we took up where we left off.'

'Don't say it, we hardly left the bedroom again and I saw nothing of New York.'

'Actually, this time you said it,' he said, laughter still warming his voice.

'Yes, I did,' she admitted. What a slip.

'You pick up the story now,' he said. 'What happened next?'

'I stayed in New York for as long as I could, but I had to get back to my work in Sydney. We said a sad goodbye.'

'We kept in touch via video chat.'

'And had lots of phone sex.' Again she clapped her hand to her mouth. 'I'm sorry—I don't know how that slipped out. Too much of that white wine you brought to go with the Thai food.' Was it wishful thinking that was causing her to blunder like this?

'I'm sure it would be the case if...if our story were true.' Was he humouring her? Or did he feel it too?

'We realised it was more than a fling,' she said.

'Then I flew over to Sydney last week to surprise you and propose.'

'And of course I was delighted.' She sat back in the sofa. 'That works for me. I think we've come up with a reasonable story. We just have to remember the details and stick with them.'

And not feel inexplicably sad because it sounded like a really romantic story and for a minute there she'd found herself wishing she were in it. On that beachfront at Santa Monica and falling in love with a stranger. Only the man in the story wasn't a stranger. It was Josh, real-life Josh, who was playing along with the game. And who looked so hot in those black jeans.

She untangled her legs, took a sip from her wine glass. 'Next question. Have you thought of anything you want to ask?'

He shook his head. 'I think you might know more about the subject of engagements than I do.'

'I know one question we're sure to be asked: *When is the wedding?* The second anyone gets engaged people start asking that.'

He frowned. 'That's got me stymied. To be honest, it's not something that has ever crossed my mind. What do you suggest?'

'We can't go wrong by saying spring. That gives us time to organise the hypothetical wedding. Say November, which is spring Down Under. That's actually a lovely time to get married.'

'November it is,' he said. 'And the wedding is in Sydney not Boston?'

'Of course, as it's the bride's home town.' She had

to say *the bride*. She simply couldn't bring herself to say *my*.

'Might they ask if you are intending to move to Boston after the wedding?' he said.

'Or if you intend to move to Sydney?'

They both fell silent. 'It's a tricky one,' she said finally. 'Why don't we say we're still fine-tuning the details?'

'Because actually Boston is your home town too,' he said slowly.

The silence that fell between them was more uncomfortable than the mock-marriage plans warranted. Finally Eloise broke it. 'So, moving on. The other question we're sure to be asked is *Can I see the engagement ring*?'

'I didn't think of that.' He swore under his breath. 'Will I have time to buy one in the morning before we leave for the wedding?'

'Thank you for the thought, but there's no need. I have a ring we can use. I inherited it from my grandmother. It's a gorgeous ruby and diamond ring. She called it a cocktail ring but it will suit our purpose. I've had the ring resized to fit me but never had a chance to wear it. Let me go and get it.'

Eloise got up from the sofa and went into the bedroom, glad of the excuse to escape from Josh for a moment and get back her equilibrium. She was shaking. This game was a dangerous one. She'd too easily become engrossed in the fiction of falling in love with Josh, a man who, the second the hypothetical scenario of their wedding came up, immediately assumed she'd be moving to Boston. It was only an off-the-cuff remark, meaningless in its context. But it underscored the reasons why no matter how much she enjoyed his company, no matter how much she fancied him, she could never allow herself to even think about falling for Josh in real life. He didn't appear to be controlling, but he certainly had a ruthless side to him. Who knew what he was really like?

With a bright smile pasted on her face, she came back into the living room to find Josh flicking through the glossy decorating magazine that had published a feature on her renovation of this apartment. He got up on her approach.

'Impressive what you've done here,' he said. 'The article says you could make your living in interior design if you changed your mind about wedding gowns.'

'Flattering, isn't it? But fashion is my first love, and I don't ever want to do anything else. Eloise Evans Atelier is more than just my work—it's my life. I enjoyed doing this place up but I wouldn't want to do it for a business. The apartment was my grandmother's and I wanted to honour all the lovely times I had with her here while at the same time updating her old-lady décor.'

'You've done a great job,' he said, looking around. 'It's very elegant.' She realised he must have seen the photos of her bedroom in the magazine and resisted the urge to show it to him.

She held up a small, rust-spotted box. 'But this ring I've left just as she had it because I value it that way. It's a large stone and I believe the setting was quite avant-garde for its time.'

'May I see it?' he said.

She flipped open the box and handed it to him. 'I don't know when it was last worn.'

One thing was for sure, her grandmother would not have approved of her intended subterfuge. And her mother would be horrified when she heard about it. But protecting her business was her priority—and she intended to do everything she could to make *@lindytheblonde*'s attack on it fail.

Josh looked at the ring nestled in the very old velvet. 'I don't know anything about engagement rings but aren't they meant to be diamond? Will this be believable? I don't want to look cheap.' He was really entering into the spirit of the charade.

'I believe an engagement ring can be anything you want it to be. Anyone who knows anything about me knows I like vintage. I think this will pass muster. And it's actually very valuable.'

He held the little box awkwardly. 'Do…do I have to put it on your finger?'

She couldn't meet his eye. 'I… I think that would actually be a bit weird.' She took the ring from him and slipped it onto the third finger of her left hand. She held out her hand to display it, fingers splayed. 'This is how I'll show it off to anyone who asks. We don't need to give any details about where we got it or anything else.'

'It suits you,' he said. 'The ring suits you, your car suits you, so does the way you dress. You're your own woman. If people ask I'll say that's one of the reasons that attracted me to you.'

'Thank you,' she said, not sure what else to say, not sure if it was a compliment or not.

'It makes me wonder, do you actually need anyone else in your life?'

'I have friends, my mother—'

'I mean a life partner. Or are you like me, a lone wolf at heart?'

She looked up at him. 'I'm happy on my own but I… I don't think I'm a lone wolf. I've often felt there's something missing in my life, something intangible. Perhaps that's from being an only child. But as far as relationships go, I won't compromise and I've had bad luck with the wrong kind of man.'

A lazy smile hovered around the corners of his mouth. 'So, in fact, you haven't met "the right man" yet?'

She forced a laugh. 'Back to the old cliché. Perhaps in our role play at the wedding I can tell them I finally did meet him.'

She paused and the silence again became awkward. She had no experience to call upon to help her manage this situation. *A fake engagement.*

'I can't think of anything else we have to rehearse, can you?' she said.

She didn't give him a chance to reply. She really couldn't endure any more, alone here together in her apartment with all this make-believe talk of falling in love and phone sex and that undeniable, sizzling current of attraction between them.

'We'll have two hours in the car tomorrow to cover anything we've missed,' she said. 'The wedding starts at four. I need to be there around two as Becca, the bride, wants me to be there for a final check on her gown. I'd rather leave earlier than later. How about I pick you up from your hotel after breakfast?'

'Sounds like a plan to me,' he said.

She led him to the door. For a long moment they stood silently, facing each other. With her heels kicked off he seemed taller and she had to look a long way up. Finally, he put his hand to her face and traced a line to her cheek. Such a simple caress, yet it set her nerve ends tingling. 'I want to kiss you goodnight.'

She caught her breath. 'I want to kiss you goodnight too.'

'But you've set the rules. No kissing in private.'

She had to clear her throat to speak. 'I want to say we don't need to enforce the rules yet, but I can't. I like kissing you, Josh. A lot. But I meant what I said the first night. We know where that kind of kissing will lead us and I don't want to go there.'

She couldn't deal with a no-strings fling with Josh. Not when he'd be going home soon. Not when she was starting to like him too much as a friend. To be honest, as more than a friend. Not when she realised if she didn't keep him at arm's length she could end up getting hurt.

'So we start as we mean to continue,' he said. 'No kissing in private.'

'That's right,' she said, unable to take her eyes from his sexy, sexy mouth, trembling inside from the need to press her mouth against his lips, to wind her arms around his neck and pull him close.

He dropped his hand. 'Then I'll just say goodnight.'

'Goodnight, Josh,' she said. 'I'll see you in the morning.'

She closed the door before she could change her mind. For a long moment she stood staring blindly at the door. Something told her that Josh was still on the other side and she had to fight the urge to call him back and tell him she'd changed her mind. She held her breath until she heard his footsteps moving slowly away and then let it out on a sigh of what she didn't know was relief or regret.

CHAPTER EIGHT

Josh was thoroughly enjoying his ride in Eloise's vintage sports car. For a car that was almost sixty years old it had a lot of power. Back home, he had driven a new model luxury European car ever since he could afford one. It was an outward flag of status to wave under the nose of the Boston family who had rejected him.

Yet this smart little white car garnered more attention from passers-by than any of his exceedingly expensive vehicles.

'A friend of my grandmother's put it up for sale when I'd barely got my driver's licence,' Eloise said. 'My grandmother knew how much I wanted it and lent me the money to get it. I paid her back every cent, of course.'

She'd been young to have been so sure of what she wanted. Yet he had known what he wanted when he'd been booted out of home at the age of sixteen: to show his former family they'd been wrong about him. He continued to pursue that aim with fierce determination.

'It's probably worth much more than you paid for it now,' he said.

'This car has been an excellent investment. New cars

depreciate; this one continues to go up in value. Not that I'd ever sell it. I get stopped in the street by admirers all the time, with offers to buy it, offers to hire it.'

Jealousy, unexpected and shocking, hit him. Were the 'admirers' interested in the car or its beautiful driver? Even in the relatively subdued outfit she wore today, narrow-legged trousers in a mottled purple colour with a matching short jacket, she turned heads. Josh realised his fists were clenched tightly on his lap. He forced the feeling to go away. He had no claim on her whatsoever. 'Have you ever loaned the car out?'

'Just the once. To a movie production company. I knew someone there who begged me to borrow it and paid me a good fee. They returned it with a scratch on it and denied they'd put it there. My beloved car. Never again. I'm not known for my generosity in giving second chances.'

She said that last sentence in a light-hearted, almost throw-away manner. But he had no doubt she meant every word. Eloise was charming and fun, but you didn't get to run a successful business like hers with clients all around the world without a certain degree of toughness.

'I have, however, made a promise I intend to keep,' she continued. 'When Vinh decides to get married, I'll lend her my car for her wedding. Friendship trumps all.'

'Of course,' he said, thinking what a contradiction she was and how interesting it made her.

The wedding destination was on the outskirts of the town of Bowral in the southern highlands, south west of Sydney.

'I promise once we clear the city motorways the

scenery will get interesting,' she said. 'Bowral is known as Double Bay in the country, as it's always been a rural retreat for wealthy Sydneysiders. The place is dotted with mansions on magnificent estates. Silver Trees, where the wedding is to be held, is one of them. It's been in the groom's family for ever…prize-winning gardens, an ornamental lake, expansive grounds, tennis court, swimming pavilion, stables, you name it—all designed by a renowned architect in the nineteen-twenties.'

'I look forward to seeing it. I've never been outside of Sydney or Melbourne.'

'You didn't want to go up north to tropical Queensland for a holiday once you'd flown all the way here? An escape from the Boston winter perhaps?'

'I don't take holidays these days,' he said, more tersely than probably required.

'Fair enough,' she said. She drove in silence for a few minutes. 'Tell me, you asked me if I had childhood dreams of making wedding dresses for celebrities. I know your parents pretty much forced your hand to earn your own living. But was it your childhood ambition to be a billionaire tech mogul?'

He nearly choked from the shock of her blunt question. 'No one has ever asked me that before,' he said once he'd regained his voice.

She looked straight ahead as she spoke. 'Maybe because you seem quite formidable.'

'Formidable?'

'Your achievements are incredible. If I'd known who you were, I probably wouldn't have dared chat to you in the park.'

'I'm glad you did,' he said. Not for Tori's sake but for his own.

'Thanks to Daisy,' Eloise said lightly. 'But seriously, is that what you set out to be?'

'Does anyone actually set out to become that? I knew I wanted to work in the digital world, and planned on a degree in computer science, but that wasn't to be.'

'Because of what happened when you were sixteen?'

'It started even before then.' He paused. 'Do you really need to know all this?'

'If we were really engaged I'd already know it, wouldn't I?'

'I guess so,' he said grudgingly.

His past was his own private hell, not readily shared. But Eloise had a point: she would be expected to know more about him than she did if she was to be his future wife. *Wife.* He reeled at the thought, even in a hypothetical context.

He honestly didn't know why he had made that spontaneous offer of pretending to be her fiancé. It was all mixed up with his attraction to her, his loyalty to Tori, the fact that his time in Sydney was beginning to seem almost surreal. The meeting with the dog in the park. The paparazzi shot. The hilarity of being fitted for his tux in Eloise's studio. *These kinds of things did not happen to him.*

Then there had been the fantasy first meeting at Santa Monica they'd devised over a Thai take-out and a good Australian white wine. Against all logic, he'd found himself wishing that meeting had really happened. That he'd met Eloise somehow, somewhere, in a context that had nothing to do with Tori. And that he'd been a man open to love rather than one with a protective shield encasing his heart.

'Come on, spill,' she said. 'It can't be any more embarrassing than aspiring to be a mermaid.'

He couldn't help but smile at that. 'If you insist.'

'I do insist.'

'As I told you, even before I turned out to be genetically the wrong fit, I didn't fit the family mould. I showed no aptitude for the law or banking, the acceptable professions according to my ex-father.'

'You call him your *ex*-father?'

'What else fits? Technically my stepfather, I suppose, but that doesn't really apply, as he had no say in the matter. My mother tricked him into believing I was his own. I look at it as if he divorced me.'

I'm not your dad. You are nothing to do with me.

'I guess that's a valid way of putting it. By the way, he sounds utterly vile. How could you bring a boy up from a baby and then just turf him out? Weren't you his son in every way but by blood?'

'I don't think he particularly cared for me from the start, but he did his duty by me for sixteen years.'

'As he darn well should have, especially as he thought you were his own child,' she said indignantly.

He shrugged. 'Truth was, we never really clicked. I was a disappointment. Not academic. Certainly not a son to boast about at his club. When it came to career advice, he suggested I learn a trade, become an electrician or plumber. He'd say it with a sneer. Not that I thought there was anything wrong at all with learning a trade. I would have willingly done so. But he knew so little of who I was, he had no idea I was already supplementing my allowance by creating apps and trading gaming codes.'

'Your interests lay elsewhere.'

'In the burgeoning digital marketplace my conservative family barely acknowledged existed. Forget studying law at Harvard, I was destined to study at the Massachusetts Institute of Technology.' He paused. 'Until I wasn't. I was cut off with nothing, certainly no college fund.'

'The media calls you a self-made billionaire.'

'I don't deny the label. There was no one to give me a leg up. I got where I am under my own steam. I took risks, I had setbacks, but I pushed through. And I'm proud of it.'

'You've given your ex-father something to boast about now.'

He spoke through gritted teeth. 'I make very sure he knows what I've achieved. My ex-brother too. But neither of them would be boasting about me.'

A year ago, he'd seen his ex-father in the distance at the exclusive yacht club to which they both belonged. Josh was sure he'd seen him too but he'd turned away without acknowledging him. Not as his son, but not as his equal in the rich man's club. It had still hurt. And further fuelled his anger.

Eloise might think less of him if he admitted to the business deals he'd diverted from his brother, the wealthy clients he'd deflected from his father's law firm. She'd called him ruthless. She would be shocked if she knew just how ruthless. The power of having a lot of money had facilitated his actions. His fantasy wasn't of a happy-ever-after family reunion but of his father

admitting he was wrong about him. As a teenager he'd
been hurt and heartbroken at what his father and brother
had done to him. As an adult, no love or respect remained, and he despised them for how they'd treated a
kid who'd thought he belonged with them.

The car was stopped at traffic lights and Eloise
turned to face him. Her expression was troubled. 'So
when it boils down to it, your success has been fuelled
by bitterness and revenge?'

'You could say that,' he said. 'Although it was sheer
survival at first.'

'How good is that for you?'

'Satisfying in the extreme.'

'I mean for your health, your spiritual health if you
like.' The lights changed and she faced the road again.

'I've never felt healthier,' he said, knowing that
wasn't what she meant.

'For how long does it continue?' she said. 'I don't
want to say the wrong thing here but surely your…your
ex-father must see by now how wrong he was about you,
how you might not have been born to his grand family
but you were certainly worthy of it.'

The drive to prove himself had been his focus for
so long, Josh didn't know how to think any other way.
But when would enough be enough? 'I sometimes feel
nothing I do would be enough to make him admit he
was wrong.'

'He sounds a horrible man, not worthy of someone
as brilliant as you. Why do you continue to seek his
approval?'

'That's not what I'm doing,' he said tersely.

But underneath it all, was Eloise right? Was he still

making a futile effort to seek the approval of that cold, unfeeling man who had kicked the boyish love he'd given so unstintingly as a child back in his teeth?

'That kind of negative emotion isn't good for a person. I know we don't know each other very well, but it makes me worry for you, Josh,' Eloise said. 'It cuts you off from the kinder side of life.'

A cold shiver ran up his spine at her words, the echo of Tori's. *I worry about you, Josh. You're cutting yourself off from life.*

'I can look after myself,' he said gruffly. 'I've been doing so for a long time.'

'I'm sure you can,' she said, with the resignation of someone who knew she was fighting a losing battle.

'Chalk that up to being another thing you now know about me,' he said.

'It's actually not something I'd be introducing into the conversation,' she said. 'That's your personal business.' An air of disapproval lingered for a long time in the car.

With the outskirts of Sydney left behind, the road took them through vast tracts of bushland, the green fields of dairy farms and horse studs, vineyards and turn-offs to historic villages with names like Berrima and Yerrinbool. 'The names are from the language of the people indigenous to this area,' Eloise explained.

'It's beautiful countryside,' he said.

'People drive out here for the day to visit antique shops, art galleries and wineries, inspect beautiful gardens, go horse riding or just to get out to the country. There are hotels and bed and breakfasts for longer stays. And there are some very popular wedding venues. It's lovely but I wouldn't want to live here. I'm a city girl myself.'

'I prefer the city too,' he said.

'Wait, I haven't asked where you live. I should know that.'

'My apartment is in the Seaport District, a penthouse with awesome views across the harbour. It's a relatively new area, redeveloped waterfront in South Boston. There are excellent restaurants and facilities and it's incredibly convenient for the business district and the airport, which makes it great for me.'

'What's your apartment like?'

'Very contemporary, all glass and stainless steel.' Lonely and empty might be the words he would also use to describe it. But he didn't want her to feel sorry for him. His life was exactly the way he wanted it to be. 'I don't know that you'd like it. It's nothing like your elegant apartment. I had an interior designer do it for me and I sometimes wonder if she took the "bachelor billionaire" brief too seriously.'

'I'm sure it's lovely.'

'It's actually quite sterile,' he said, surprising himself. 'I don't know why I live there actually, though it's already doubled in value. I keep gravitating back to the North End. You may remember it's a very old part of town.'

'I haven't been to Boston since my father died, but I think I remember going there to a restaurant with my grandparents.'

'When my mother and I were evicted from the big house on Beacon Hill we went to live there with her sister, my Aunt Lily, in her apartment in Little Italy. The apartment was cramped and I had to go to a new high school, but I loved it.'

Eloise nodded thoughtfully. 'That's good information. If anyone asks I can maybe say we're thinking of moving to a house there instead of living in your bachelor apartment.'

'You'd like the area, I'm sure.'

All the best parts of his life were there. His Aunt Lily, who had given him a home. Tori's family trattoria and his close friendship with her family. Tori's bakery too; her spectacular cakes were to Boston's brides what Eloise's gowns were to Sydney's brides.

He could be himself there and judged for who he was and not by the size of his bank balance. So very different from the Boston where he had lived the first sixteen years of his life with his judgemental father whom nobody could please, not even his half-brother, who turned himself inside out in the process of trying. Warm, vibrant Eloise would fit right in in the North End. That she had actually been born in Boston would give her a head start. But she was a Sydney person too, with a thriving business she loved. A move there couldn't possibly work.

Josh shook his head to clear it of the invidious invasion of his thoughts. This fake fiancé game was messing with his head. He wasn't marrying Eloise, he wasn't dating Eloise, and when she found out he'd been hiding the truth about his visit to Sydney and his knowledge of her long-lost twin he wouldn't be talking to Eloise.

'Before we get there, I have a final question for you,' he said.

'Fire away,' she said.

'There's something I haven't asked you that I should probably know. Why is a beautiful woman like you without a date for this wedding? Without a real-life fiancé of her own to accompany her? What went wrong with your last guy?'

'He lied to me about who he really was,' she said flatly. 'And that's unforgivable.'

'I see,' he said. He didn't need to know the details. It just reinforced his earlier thoughts.

They were soon entering the salubrious small town of Bowral, with shops and businesses lining the main road and those intersecting it. 'We've made good time,' Eloise said. 'Do you want to stretch your legs? Take a walk, grab a coffee in Bowral, even a bite of lunch, before we head to Silver Trees, which is on the other side of town?'

'Coffee sounds great,' he said. 'And now that you mention it, so does lunch.'

Eloise parked the car on the high street, so she could keep an eye on it, she said. Before she made to get out of the car she turned to him, her expression very serious. 'The fake engagement starts here. There are likely to be people I know in town for the wedding. Last chance for you to back out.'

'I'm in,' he said.

Even though she was the driver—no one, but *no one*, got to drive her precious vintage car—Josh insisted on getting out of the car first to come around to her side and open the door for her.

'I intend to start as I mean to continue as your fiancé,' he said.

She tensed. Thank heaven he hadn't said 'fake fiancé'. These streets could have ears. She would have to force herself to relax and trust him to play his part.

'Thank you,' she said.

It seemed the most natural thing in the world for him to take her hand as she walked with him towards her favourite Bowral café, which served great coffee and the most delicious pastries baked on the premises. Enfolding hers, his hand felt warm and large and somehow comforting. He was on her side, even for only a very limited time.

She was looking up at him and smiling at something he'd said when she heard her name called out. Eloise turned to see a woman she'd dressed for her wedding two years ago. All must be going well, as she was proudly sporting an advanced baby bump.

'Eloise, I thought it was you. Are you in town for Becca's wedding?' She didn't pause for an answer. 'Of course Becca would be wearing one of your gowns. For the second time, that is.'

'Anna, how lovely to see you.' They air kissed. 'And I can see congratulations are in order.'

The other woman smiled. 'Do you design christening gowns by any chance?'

'Only for my most special clients,' she said. 'Call me and we can chat.'

Eloise kept a special linen bag of offcuts from each wedding. They came in remarkably handy for creating baby outfits, both traditionally styled and contemporary, for christenings and naming ceremonies, made with the fabric from the mother's wedding dress. She didn't advertise the service, as there wasn't much profit in it, but it was an added extra for clients and unique, as far as she knew, to her company.

People boasted about starting their own christening gown family heirlooms. But you had to have bought a wedding gown from Eloise Evans Atelier first.

Anna was not doing a very good job of disguising her interest in the tall, handsome man standing by Eloise's side.

'Oh, Anna, this is my fiancé, Josh.'

The words tripped so easily off Eloise's tongue, thanks to a dint of practising in front of the mirror the previous night after Josh had gone home.

'Josh, this is Anna, one of my clients who had the most beautiful wedding two years ago.'

'Fiancé?' Anna said, sculpted eyebrows raised. 'But I heard…' She collected herself. 'Congratulations. How exciting.' Her gaze went straight to the ruby engagement ring glinting on Eloise's left hand. She seemed puzzled by it.

No doubt Anna had seen the horrible hashtags on @lindytheblonde's social media. And believed every word. Yet here was wedding-hating Eloise Evans engaged to be married. You could almost see the cogs working in the woman's mind.

'It's only very recently that Ellie has done me the honour of agreeing to become my wife,' Josh said smoothly. He embellished his words by dropping a swift kiss on her cheek.

'Well, this is wonderful news,' said Anna.

'We certainly think so,' said Josh.

'Well played,' Eloise whispered, as Anna walked

away. 'I dare say by the time we arrive at the wedding the word will have started to spread.'

'Piece of cake,' he said.

He reached for her hand again.

'And so it begins,' Eloise said, as if she were murmuring an endearment in her fiancé's ear.

CHAPTER NINE

As Eloise swung her little white sports car up the gravel driveway to her friend's soon-to-be husband's family estate, Silver Trees, Josh wondered what the hell he was doing there, ready to embark in full force on the fake fiancé scam. It went against the grain for him to out-and-out lie the way he had to that woman on the main street of Bowral.

And yet when Anna had given Eloise that look of sly surprise when told she was engaged, he'd felt a fierce surge of protectiveness. Obviously the woman was aware of the gossip being fomented by the heinous influencer who was trying to ruin Eloise out of meanness and spite. Perhaps Anna had even been guilty of spreading it. Eloise needed help. If that meant Josh acting the loving fiancé, then so be it. If she needed his help later to exact the kind of deeper revenge he'd outlined—and believed she should—he'd be on call to guide her.

One thing was for sure—Eloise had better restrain him if he found himself anywhere near that @lindytheblonde, as heaven knew what words he might unleash on her.

Eloise did not deserve such meanness. They'd had a rapid getting-to-know-you process over the last few days. He had noted how thoughtful and caring she was towards others. That had led him to wonder who cared for her? It seemed she went home to that stylish apartment by herself every night to lavish love on Daisy, the little stray dog who had been instrumental in his meeting Eloise. But who lavished love on Eloise? He couldn't offer love, but he could offer his help in stopping this unfair attack on her livelihood. He vowed to do his utmost to be an impeccable fake fiancé.

Eloise pulled over in the designated parking area for the select group of guests who had been invited to stay at the house. She turned off the engine, put the stick shift into gear, and pulled on the quaint, old-fashioned handbrake. It was one cool car. She turned to Josh.

'About the accommodation,' she said. He got the impression she had been building up to saying this and now had to let it out.

'Yes?' he said.

'When I told Becca I would, after all, be bringing a plus-one, and my plus-one was actually my fiancé, she was delighted for me and assumed you'd be staying in my room. The thing is, the room I've stayed in here a few times before is very small.'

Josh had wondered at the sleeping arrangements but hadn't felt he could ask for details. She'd just mentioned they would be staying at the house where the wedding would be taking place. 'I could always book into a hotel in town. I'm sure it's not too late to get a room somewhere.'

She frowned. 'That wouldn't send the right message, would it? Not for a newly engaged couple supposedly madly in love.'

'No, it wouldn't. And we need to appear genuine.'

'I'm glad you think so too. But sharing this room might not be so bad. It must have been originally a child's room, I think. There's a single bed and a sofa. I'm happy to sleep on the sofa and give you the bed. Even then it might be a bit of a squash for a man but it's comfortable enough and—'

Josh put up his hand. 'I insist on taking the sofa. No further argument.'

It was a relief, in a way, that there was only a single bed. He wouldn't be taunted by the fact he couldn't share the bed with her.

'You're the one doing me a favour. I insist on you having the bed.'

The interior of the car was thick with unspoken words and denials and a simmering undercurrent of sexual tension centring around the word *bed*. The mere thought of the enforced intimacy of sharing a bedroom with her was arousing. Eloise in her nightwear, Eloise naked under the shower, Eloise there with him all night long. But he could not think like that.

To keep his equilibrium, he had to act as if they were platonic friends bunking down together to save costs in a backpackers' hostel. He'd certainly done that back before he started to make serious money. But not with a woman he found so intensely desirable. Not with a woman who was forbidden to him in so many ways. He felt sure she felt the same undeniable physical attraction, and had her own reasons for fighting it.

'A gentleman would take the sofa,' he said through gritted teeth.

He hadn't meant to use the word *gentleman* in that

context, as he had in the fiction they had devised to explain their first meeting. And their play on his gentlemanly—or, rather more importantly, his ungentlemanly behaviour. There'd been a distinct flirtatious undercurrent to that conversation—on both sides. But that was only talk. This situation was real and forced them into an uncomfortably intimate proximity.

'If we can't agree, why don't we toss a coin for who gets the bed when we get to the room?' she said.

'We'll see about that,' he said. No way would he allow her to sleep on a sofa. He could sleep on the floor if he had to.

'I didn't realise how stubborn you could be,' she said, obviously bemused.

He grinned. 'You've got that right. Although I'd say determined rather than stubborn.'

As it turned out, she needn't have worried about who was or wasn't going to get the bed versus the sofa. The Silver Trees housekeeper led them into the lift and onto the first floor. The woman opened the door to a luxurious room with an enormous king-size bed and an ensuite bathroom. French doors opened out to a balcony and a view of the garden.

Eloise stared at the housekeeper in ill-disguised dismay. 'But this isn't my usual room.'

Josh followed her gaze to the enormous bed that dominated the room. There was no sofa, just a big vintage cane chair that looked exceedingly uncomfortable. But they couldn't display misgivings. As far as their hosts were concerned, he and his fiancée should be delighted to have that big bed.

He put his arm around Eloise and squeezed her

shoulder, hoping she'd get the message she was giving the game away by her show of reluctance.

'I was told to swap you to this larger guest room, as your fiancé was with you,' the housekeeper said, obviously confused by the lack of enthusiasm.

'It's a marvellous room, isn't it, honey?' Josh said.

Eloise's eyes widened at his use of the endearment. But he was taking the role of fake fiancé and running with it.

She caught on. 'Yes. It's a beautiful room,' she gushed.

'And so good of you to organise it for us at such short notice,' Josh said.

The housekeeper looked gratified.

When he was growing up their housekeeper had been a very nice woman. She'd even cried when he and his mother had left. But she'd been too scared of losing her job to come and see them at his new home.

'We're thrilled,' Eloise said, right into the act now. 'Thank you. And thank you to Mr and Mrs Sanderson for giving us such a beautiful room. We'll be very comfortable here.'

Comfortable? He had to fight the images of him and Eloise making very good use of that bed. There wouldn't be a lot of sleeping going on, that was for sure. He wanted her. Badly. But the reasons for it not being a good idea for him to make love with her were still there, clamouring at him to keep his gaze away from the bed and the tantalising possibilities it evoked.

'Do you need help with your luggage?' asked the housekeeper.

'No, thank you, we can get it ourselves,' said Eloise very quickly.

Josh watched with Eloise until the housekeeper disappeared into the lift and they saw no one else was in earshot.

She turned to him. 'Only one bed. Not even a sofa. What the heck are we going to do?'

'I'll sleep on the chair. Or the floor.'

'No, you won't. I can't let you do that. Either way would be hideously uncomfortable and totally unfair to you when you're doing me a favour. The bed is huge; we'll just have to both sleep in it, trying…trying not to be aware the other person is there.'

'Are you serious? Do you honestly think I could sleep in a bed with you and not be aware you were there?' An image of her flashed into his mind, of her lying back against the rumpled sheets, her dark hair spilled across the pillows, her shoulders bare, her breasts… Her warm, sexy presence would be the only thing on his mind. 'That won't be easy.'

She looked up at him, her blue eyes huge, her cheeks flushed. 'It won't be easy for me either, Josh. Please be aware of that.'

Did she realise that knowing she wanted him as much as he wanted her did nothing to make it easier for him? She looked so woebegone he couldn't stop himself from opening his arms. 'Come here,' he said. She went towards him and he enfolded her in a comforting hug. It wasn't breaking her rule. They weren't behind closed doors. To anyone seeing them, they were an engaged couple embracing.

'This is going to be more difficult than I thought,'

she said, her voice muffled against his shoulder. 'Look how I missed that cue from you back then. The house-keeper must have thought I was very odd not to exclaim in delight at the beautiful room in this amazing mansion. I told you I wasn't a good actor.'

He pulled back from the hug so that, while she still stood within the circle of his arms, he could look down into her lovely face. 'You're doing fine,' he said. 'It will be worth it. Just think of the damage that influencer woman is doing to your business.'

'More cancellations this morning. Vinh texted me before I picked you up.'

'Put them right back on the bottom of your waiting list when they call wanting to be reinstated, which they will do once they realise they've been suckered.'

'I wouldn't do that.'

His voice hardened. 'I would. I told you, I'm venge-ful. Loyalty should be rewarded. Not betrayal. How stupid of them to be influenced by that—'

'That *influencer*.'

'That's the word.'

She laughed and he felt her relax.

'Let's try and have fun with this,' he said. 'From what you say, it's going to be a great party. Let's enjoy it, at the same time knowing we're sticking it to an enemy of your business. Nothing can be more satisfy-ing than that.'

Despite Eloise's protests, Josh insisted on carrying her overnight bag as well as his own while she carried her long dress in a special Eloise Evans Atelier garment bag to their room. He didn't have to pretend to be a gentleman, she thought, it was obviously innate to him. But she couldn't help her thoughts from straying to what he would be like when he was being ungentlemanly. In this very room.

She did her best to ignore the contentious bed while she hung her dress alongside Josh's tuxedo in a matching bag in the wardrobe. She walked over to stand beside him where he stood looking out of the French doors. They opened out to a wide balcony edged with lavishly planted containers and across the garden to the green fields studded with grazing horses.

'It's an awesome view,' he said.

'The other side of the house, where the family have their rooms, overlooks the lake and the stand of silver birch trees that gives the house its name. This house is incredible, yet it's a family home. I grew up in a comfortable house in Sydney's inner west, near Sydney University, where my father taught. I can't imagine what it must have been like for Simon to grow up with something like this.' She faltered to a halt. 'I'm sorry, Josh, you must have lived in a wonderful house before you had to move.'

'Home was a grand townhouse with a view to Boston Common. My grandparents—ex-grandparents—had a place something like this in Northborough, about an hour out of Boston, that we used to visit. But there are few happy memories. And now I can buy any house I choose to.'

'Which is a triumph in itself,' she said, not certain what else to say.

'I guess it is,' he said.

Not for the first time, Eloise thanked her lucky stars

for the stability of the childhood her happily married parents had given her. She'd long stopped wondering what her life with her birth mother might have been like. However, she sometimes wondered if her parents' romance had given her unrealistic expectations of relationships. She'd had her heart crushed a few times by seeing in a man what she wanted him to be, not who he actually was. Craig had played her by pretending to be someone he wasn't. He'd outright lied and, at the beginning, she'd been so besotted she hadn't seen the signs. No wonder she was wary of taking a man at face value.

'Will you be okay here by yourself?' she asked Josh. 'I have to go and check everything is perfect with Becca's dress and the bridesmaids' dresses. There are only two bridesmaids and a flower girl. Believe it or not, this is a relatively low-key wedding compared to some, as it's her second. But it's Simon's first and he wanted a big celebration. As you said, it looks to be quite a party.'

'I'm perfectly fine by myself. I'll see you when you get back.'

'I won't be long,' she said.

There was an awkward moment when she wanted to lean up and kiss him on the cheek but decided against it. *No kissing in private.*

CHAPTER TEN

FROM THE MOMENT Josh had first laid eyes on Eloise in the park with Daisy he had thought her to be an exceptionally beautiful woman. But nothing had prepared him for the sight of Eloise dressed for the wedding.

Already in his new tux, he'd gone out on the balcony and turned his back while she got ready. It had seemed way too intimate to be in the same room as her while she got dressed. Not that she used the bedroom for changing—the bathroom was there for that. No, it was the private female rituals that only a woman's lover would usually witness that he found too disconcerting, the primping and preening and perfecting.

What had made him decide to leave the room was when she, dressed modestly in a satin robe patterned with oriental dragons, had leaned in close to the mirror to fasten her outsize earrings. The hairdresser and make-up artist employed by the bride had done her hair and make-up, and Eloise's thick dark hair had been swept up into a glamorous style. As she'd peered into the mirror her robe had slipped off her shoulders to reveal the nape of her neck, slender and pale. She'd seemed somehow vulnerable and exposed, yet deeply

sensual at the same time. He'd been swept by the desire not just to protect her but also to make her his, and
he'd had to fight the impulse to press a tender kiss to
the base of her delicate nape and slide the robe all the
way down off her shoulders.

Instead he'd muttered an excuse that he needed to
get some fresh air and headed out onto the balcony. It
had been left to his imagination to guess what else she
was doing in there—was she wearing anything under
that robe?—and his imagination tantalised him. But
not once had he looked back to catch a glimpse of her
getting dressed. He respected her privacy and dignity
too much for that.

Then she was at the French windows. 'I'm ready
when you are,' she said.

He turned. And could do nothing but stare. His heart
started to thud into overdrive and his mouth went dry.
She stood in a strapless dress that cupped her breasts,
then hugged the curves of her body to her hips before it
floated down in a series of layers—he wasn't sure what
you'd call them…flounces maybe?—to the floor. The
dress was an iridescent deep blue that picked up the
light and shimmered through subtle tones of purple and
violet. The colour contrasted with the creaminess of her
skin and complemented the cornflower blue of her eyes.

Her black hair was twisted and turned up on her head
and, with her deep red lips and highlighted eyes, she
looked like some Hollywood movie star of a time long
before she was born. Glittering clear stones hung from
her ears but she wore no other jewellery save the ruby
ring that shone brighter in contrast to the blue dress.
He had never seen a more beautiful woman.

He stared at her for so long, she shifted from high-heeled shoe to high-heeled shoe. 'Do I look all right?' How could she imagine for even a second that she would ever look anything but much more than 'all right'?

'You look absolutely beautiful,' he said hoarsely. 'You just need long gloves and a jewelled cigarette holder to look like you stepped out of a vintage movie.'

She smiled, pleased. 'But if I wore the long gloves it would cover my ring, and what would be the point of that? And of course I don't smoke.'

'You look...breathtaking. Are you sure you won't outshine the bride?'

Eloise laughed. 'No one could outshine the bride! Her gown is exquisite and she's glowing with happiness.'

She picked up a filmy blue wrap and a small beaded purse from the bed. 'We don't want to be late.'

'It's an honour to escort you, Eloise. Truly.'

'I'm glad you're here. I wouldn't have worn such a glamorous dress if I'd come on my own,' she said. 'And may I say how handsome you look in your tux?'

'That's really thanks to you and your team,' he said.

'I don't know about that,' she said. 'I think the very good-looking man wearing the tux is what makes it look so good. They say clothes maketh the man, but in your case I'd say the man maketh the tux.'

He laughed. 'If you say so.' He liked her quirky outlook. Honestly, he'd never met a woman like her. Tori was her lookalike, of course, but they were so very different in personality. Eloise was incomparable.

Josh offered her his arm. 'Let's go and give that troublemaker influencer something to think about.'

'Like how to backpedal out of the lies she's spread about me.'

She tucked her hand into his arm and looked up at him. Again he caught his breath at how lovely she looked, how alluring with the subtle curves of her breasts, the shadow of her cleavage revealed by the strapless gown. 'It would be a different scenario all together if you weren't with me, Josh. Thank you again for being here.'

He couldn't think of anywhere else he would rather be.

Eloise had never felt more confident entering a room of people than with Josh by her side. Together they walked into the ballroom of the mansion, which had been set up for the marriage service with rows of white chairs forming an aisle and facing the front of the room. While the overwhelming focus of the wedding guests' interest was on the bride, Eloise soon became aware that her appearance with Josh was causing a secondary ripple of interest. She knew they were noticed as a couple and comments made, and she'd detected several glances towards her left hand. By the time she and Josh made their way to their seats for the ceremony, she felt satisfied the news of her 'engagement' was spreading.

Because she knew several of the bride's friends, and had dressed others as either brides or bridesmaids, Eloise knew quite a number of the other guests. She didn't look out for @lindytheblonde but she knew she must be there.

If she didn't have to see the woman ever again she would be grateful. She just wanted her nemesis to know that the basis of her attack had now been proved to be erroneous. Eloise was here with an incredibly handsome 'fiancé' and looking her best in a killer dress from her own label. The bride and her attendants were dressed in the most exquisite, money-no-object dresses from Eloise Evans Atelier. That should be enough. If not... well, Josh had presented her with a next-step option she would shudder to take.

She settled in to enjoy the wedding, Josh by her side. No matter her opinion about a wedding for herself, there was something about other people's weddings that always grabbed at her emotions. The favourite part of any ceremony for Eloise was to see the bride come down the aisle and then watch for the moment when her groom first caught sight of her. In this case Simon didn't disappoint with a look of wonder and love when he saw Becca walking up the aisle towards him, the joy shining from her.

It brought the sting of tears to Eloise's eyes. But beyond her usual sentimentality and happiness for her friends, she felt a deep and heartfelt yearning of her own. *Would it ever be her?* Not so much the dress and the flowers and all the fuss, but would a man ever look at her like that? And would she ever be able to trust a man enough to look at him with such unreserved love? For a deeply disconcerting moment she imagined that man was Josh and had to shake the image from her mind.

She clasped his hand tightly. 'I told you I always cry at weddings,' she whispered.

Eloise sniffled her way through the rest of the ceremony. Becca's first marriage had been short and miserable and her friend had vowed never to let a man into her life again. Then she'd met Simon, and risked her heart a second time. How had she found the strength to do that?

The ceremony over, the bride and groom walked triumphantly back down the aisle as husband and wife. Eloise realised she had been holding on tight to Josh's hand the entire time. He pulled a handkerchief—a crisp, white, old-fashioned handkerchief—from his pocket.

'You might need this,' he said quietly.

Her hands flew to her face. 'Panda eyes?'

He nodded. She scrubbed under her eyes with the handkerchief where she thought the smeared mascara must be.

'Let me,' he said, taking it back. She tilted her face upwards. Gently he wiped beneath one eye then another. She sat perfectly still, hardly daring to breathe. Loving his touch, even masked by a handkerchief. He sat back to look critically at his work. 'Better,' he said. 'Although you look beautiful even with panda eyes.'

'Thank you,' she said.

She smiled, he smiled too, and their eyes met for a long moment. Was he acting? Without thinking, she leaned across and kissed him on the mouth, a sweet, tender kiss of thanks, of gratitude, of sheer appreciation of how thoughtful he was. It wasn't staged. She meant it and she was smiling as she pulled away. He was smiling too and there was something warm and questioning she hadn't seen before in his eyes that sent a tremor of awareness through her. Josh took her hand again and she squeezed it tightly as they rose from their seats. The truth hit her with painful clarity—the truth she had been refusing to acknowledge.

She could so easily fall in love with this man.

But Eloise did not want to fall in love with a man she scarcely knew. She had to slam down hard on that inner voice that cajoled, *You've known him long enough.* She'd listened to that voice before with disastrous consequences. Right now, however, she wasn't going to fight it, just ignore it. Josh had suggested they relax, have fun and enjoy the party, and that was exactly what she intended to do.

The guests flocked around the bride and groom. Eloise and Josh waited their turn. Congratulations were said. Introductions were made. And Josh played the doting fiancé to perfection. 'You deserve someone like Josh,' murmured Becca. 'Well done for opening your heart again to love.'

Only of course she hadn't and her heart was still shut down to love. Everything about her and Josh being together was a sham. She was pretending to be in love to save her bridal business. How hypocritical of her was that? And he… She wasn't really sure why he had offered to help her. Could it be simply because he enjoyed exacting revenge for revenge's sake? Even when it was someone else's revenge? In spite of the ruthlessness he'd demonstrated, she couldn't bring herself to believe that of Josh. Not the Josh who was so sweet to Daisy and had been so kind to her. She had to tell herself it was because of a gentlemanly instinct. And she was just so glad he was here with her.

The bride and groom disappeared for more photos. The guests were directed into the large conservatory where first cocktails and then a sit-down dinner were to be served. Eloise was greeted by some women she knew quite well, and some she didn't know so well. Congratulations on her engagement flowed and Josh was given appraising and approving looks. She was gratified by people's happiness for her and dreaded how uncomfortable it would be to say, a few months down the track, that her long-distance engagement had, as it happened, not worked out.

But right now, she and Josh had their answers ready.

'Yes, a November wedding, we think,' she said.

'Boston is home for me, but then, it used to be home for Ellie too, so we're keeping our options open.'

'I have no intention of closing my business—never, ever. Oh, you're on my waiting list? Don't worry, I won't be too distracted by my own wedding to design you a fabulous wedding gown.'

'Yes, I knew she was "the one" straight away. How? I…uh…just knew.'

'You know I dressed Roxee and her wedding party? Josh and I first met when I was in Los Angeles for the wedding.'

'Yes, we have kept it quiet,' Josh said. 'We wanted to be sure.'

'Thank you. You're very kind to say we look like we're made for each other.'

'No, I don't have a brother just like me back home in Boston.'

'Oh, yes, Josh is a keeper.'

'Ellie is a keeper for sure.'

She found it emotionally draining to keep up the act and not slip and was glad when they were asked to head to their assigned tables for the speeches and dinner.

They were nearly at their table, when Eloise clutched Josh's arm. 'Don't look now but she's over there... *@lindytheblonde.*'

'Is she watching us?'

'If looks could kill...'

Josh pulled her close to him and looked deeply into her eyes, smoothing a wisp of hair that had tugged free from her updo as only a lover would do. 'Do I look suitably smitten?' he said in a voice only she could hear.

'I thought you said you were a terrible actor?' she murmured. 'Because you're being very convincing.'

He came closer, so close she felt giddy from his scent, weak at the knees from the contact. 'Maybe it's because I'm not acting,' he said, in a voice so low she wasn't sure she heard him correctly.

She didn't have a chance to ask him to repeat it because suddenly the influencer was at her elbow. 'I hear congratulations are in order,' she said with an insincere smile from her trout mouth's inflated lips that didn't reach her eyes.

'Yes,' Eloise said simply. She introduced her to Josh and the woman's eyes narrowed at the same time she mouthed platitudes. Josh acted the proud, loving fiancé as if he'd been born to it.

When Eloise had first read the influencer's mean social media posts, calculated to ruin her business, she had lain awake planning exactly what she'd say to this woman if she got the chance. Now she kept her mouth shut. Josh had, instead, offered her a way to defuse her

accusations. Then @*lindytheblonde* introduced her and
Josh to her fiancé.

Immediately, Eloise recognised his name. One of her
clients had cancelled her wedding when she'd discovered both his cheating and his over-active interest in
her wealthy father's bank balance. A schoolfriend had
also dated him and could only say he was bad news.
Perhaps it was karma, perhaps the influencer and her
fiancé had met their match. But Eloise decided she'd
be the better person and graciously accepted her congratulations while giving congratulations of her own.

'What was that about?' Josh said in an undertone
when the influencer had gone. 'I was looking forward
to watching you stick the knife into that awful, super-
cilious woman and twist it.'

'Because, darling Josh, sometimes karma takes hold
of the knife and twists it for you. I'd rather have one
night of being your pretend fiancée than a lifetime of
being a wife to that guy. I almost feel sorry for her.
Almost.'

'You'll have to explain that one to me later,' he said.
'It doesn't sound enough like revenge to me.' He looked
so puzzled she had to kiss him again.

'Thank you, thank you…' she murmured against his
mouth.

All the while she couldn't stop wondering if she had
correctly heard Josh. Had he really said he wasn't acting? And if so, what could he have meant by it?

CHAPTER ELEVEN

JOSH USUALLY WENT out of his way to avoid weddings. A generous cheque and an apology for his inability to attend was his stock response to an invitation. But to his surprise he found himself enjoying this wedding. The other guests on the table were pleasant company. The meal was superb. The speeches, usually interminable, were short, warm and witty. Just the kind of speeches he would like to have at his own wedding. He pulled up his thoughts. When had he started thinking there might actually be a wedding for him one day in the distant future, instead of never?

The answer was sitting next to him. *Eloise*. Enchanting, funny, gorgeous Eloise. He was getting in deeper every minute he spent in her company. Maybe he'd imbibed one too many toasts to the bride and groom with the plentiful French vintage champagne. Or the excellent Australian red wine with dinner before that. But the more he pretended to be in love with Eloise, the more he started to wonder what was stopping him from considering the actual possibility. Not of a real-life engagement. Of course not. But of somehow seeing more of her. Long-distance dating, even. Because he was thoroughly enjoying every minute of her company. And he dreaded having to say goodbye. A life without Eloise in it seemed somehow unacceptable.

She excused herself to go to the powder room in the company of one of the other women at the table. Immediately after she left her chair, he felt bereft. He watched that delightful sway of her hips as she walked away, the way she leaned down to smile at something her companion was saying. He could not keep his eyes off her.

Hurry back to me, Ellie.

Again he had that surreal feeling that, since he'd been in Australia, the foundations of his life were shifting on ground that had suddenly become unstable. His rules against a serious relationship were self-imposed. But then, he'd always been perfectly satisfied without a committed, meaningful connection with a woman.

Eloise had commented that his life was motivated by bitterness and revenge. He had proudly owned the truth of it. But spending time with Eloise was making him question that truth. Had the time passed for focusing his entire life on the relentless pursuit of extreme wealth to prove he was worthy of the old life of his childhood? Was he letting the cruelty of his father cut him off from what Eloise called 'the kinder side of life'?

His rules had been forged when he was sixteen, bewildered and hurting from the out-of-the-blue total rejection of his father. Now, four months away from the age of thirty, a new thought was percolating through: the best revenge against that cold-hearted man might be a life well lived. Personal fulfilment could be a fine shield against cruelty and rejection. What was stopping him?

Only his own old fears.

Perhaps it was time to flick the switch, to think forward to how he might treat his own son or daughter one day rather than back on how his father had treated him. *Kids?* He was thinking *kids?* He shook his head. That took reconsidering his life too far. There'd been some funny, teasing speeches about babies directed at the newlyweds. That must be where the thought had come from. He shoved it right back.

Eloise slid back into her chair beside him just as the band struck up. She held on to his shoulder as she settled into her chair. He reached up to hold her hand and she squeezed it. She was just playing her part as fake fiancée. He knew that. Yet with it came a thrill of possession as she left her hand in his.

The bride and groom danced their first dance together as husband and wife. Gradually the ballroom—cleared now of chairs—filled up with couples dancing. Josh turned to Eloise and saw that she was swaying in time to the music. He asked her to dance and they joined the other couples on the floor.

'You can waltz,' she said.

'So can you.'

'My grandmother said it was a desirable skill for a young lady. She taught me. It felt very strange when I first waltzed with a boy instead of an old lady.'

He laughed. How often had he laughed since he'd met her? More than in the previous six months, he felt sure. Laughter was meant to release feel-good endorphins. Maybe that was what was making him start to re-evaluate his life strategy. It couldn't be that other word starting with *L*. 'Your grandmother sounds like an interesting woman.'

'She was; we were very close—she and my mother too.' Eloise's glance went to the ruby ring. 'Where did you learn to dance?'

'At my old private school. Very unwillingly, I might add.'

She laughed and he whirled her around the dance floor. Perhaps because of his avoidance of weddings, where old-fashioned dancing still seemed to hold sway, he had forgotten how intimate a waltz could be. As intimate and exciting as an embrace.

He was intensely aware of where his body connected with Eloise's, of her warmth and curves. His arm around her waist held her close, her hand rested on his shoulder, her cheek felt smooth and cool against his cheek. Her scent was already familiar, rich and sweet and intoxicating. Other couples danced around them but he was scarcely aware of their presence—he was too lost in the rhythm of his private dance with Eloise.

It was part of wedding protocol that the bride and groom made their way around the dance floor to dance in turn with each of their guests. Josh smiled when they broke in on his dance with Eloise but in truth he felt like growling. He didn't want to let her go.

Eloise waltzed away with Simon, and Josh took his turn to dance with Becca. He held her at a polite distance. Even for a duty dance he did not want another woman in his arms, even a bride so obviously crazy about her new husband. 'A great wedding,' he said. 'The best I've ever been to, in fact.'

'Thank you,' Becca said. 'We're so glad you were

able to come with lovely Eloise. What a gem of a woman she is, in every way.'

'Yes,' he said. 'She is that.'

Becca laughed. 'You don't have to try to chat.'

'What do you mean?'

'You haven't taken your eyes off her since you relinquished her to Simon. You've got it bad, haven't you?'

It? He remembered his role as fake fiancé. 'Yes, I have. I…uh…had a crush on her the moment I met her.' And just maybe that wasn't a fib. But a crush was just a crush.

Becca smiled. 'You can't hide how you feel about her. I can see it in your eyes. Love is hard to find and to be cherished. Simon and I wish you both the kind of happiness we've found.'

Josh was too stupefied to find an answer for her. Thankfully he didn't have to, as Simon waltzed Eloise back to him. 'I'm returning your beautiful fiancée into your care,' he said.

Josh gladly took her back into his arms but he was too shaken by what Becca had said to think straight. He just held Eloise close and kept on waltzing.

Dancing with Josh was utter bliss. From the waltz, to the classic rock, to the crazy group dances that only half the guests knew the steps of, Josh had rhythm. He had rhythm, he had energy, he had the moves. And they moved well together. Not only was he hot, but also he was fun. There were times Eloise forgot their engagement was fake, and that the relationship was staged, his mock affection seemed so real. And that was dangerous.

Although she suspected he felt the same physical attraction she felt for him. That was more difficult to fake.

Early on in the evening, she'd gone past being on edge, worrying he or she might trip up on an answer about their engagement or wedding plans. However, people asked basically the same questions and the answers almost came by rote. They didn't trip up once.

She'd only sipped at a flute of champagne for the toasts—just in case there was another encounter with the influencer she wanted to keep a clear head. But @lindytheblonde had steered clear of her. So she couldn't blame champagne for the recklessness of her rising desire for Josh. She knew their time together was limited and she wanted him. Perhaps she wanted him so badly *because* their time was limited.

The band were playing the final set of slow dances. The bride had changed into her going-away dress—designed by Eloise Evans Atelier, of course—and she and her new husband were saying their final farewells to a group of their elderly relatives. Soon the wedding would be over.

'We haven't talked about what happens after tonight,' Eloise said in a low murmur.

'Again we stick to something close to the truth. It's a long-distance engagement. We just keep quiet about it until—'

'Until it becomes too hard, as long-distance relationships tend to do.'

'It quietly fizzles out.'

'Although we tried so hard to make it work.'

'All that,' he said.

They both dwindled away to silence. 'This is too

gloomy for words,' she said. 'Can we forget about to-morrow when we've still got today to enjoy?'

And tonight ahead of us, she thought, thinking of that big bed with a shiver of anticipation. How would she be able to resist the temptation of having him so close?

She laid her head on his shoulder and they swayed together to the medley of classic love songs, thigh to thigh, hip to hip as she dreamed silly daydreams about what might be if things were different with Josh. Then the music stopped and they gathered with the other guests to farewell the bride and groom. There was an awkward moment when Becca and Simon had gone and people started to leave as the band announced the final number. Lights were lowered for the last dance.

'Do you know how many women here have asked if my dress is for sale?' she said. 'Not this exact one, of course, but one of the same design. Or they've asked if I make it in white as a wedding dress. I haven't been actively looking for business, but it's come my way. I'm thinking maybe I should branch out with a party dress diffusion line or maybe…' There was something intent in his eyes that made her falter to a halt.

'It's a superb dress,' he said. He lowered his head to hers so only she could hear. 'It looks sexy as hell on you. But I can't stop wondering how it would look off you.'

'Oh,' she said, a tingle of want tightening her nipples and running down her spine.

'I've offended you,' he said. 'Taken the game too far.'

'No. Not at all,' she said breathlessly. 'You didn't offend me.'

'But I've overstepped the mark. I'll sleep out on the balcony with the plants tonight.'

'It'll be too cold. It's several degrees colder here than it is in Sydney.'

'Then I'll sleep in the car.'

'You won't fit,' she said. She wound her arms around his neck and pressed close to him as they swayed to the slow, romantic music in the darkened room. 'I'm afraid it will have to be the bed for you tonight.' She pressed her lips to his. Then she couldn't wait for the band to finish and for the lights to come on, to have to make farewells to the people she knew.

With a low murmur of invitation, she took his hand and led him from the ballroom.

CHAPTER TWELVE

ELOISE THREW HER inhibitions away as soon as the ballroom was behind her. Forget her 'no kissing in private' rule. Whatever had made her impose that dictate? Kissing Josh was a delicious pastime to be enjoyed whenever she found the opportunity. She wanted Josh and she could see no real reason why she shouldn't have him. If only just for the night.

They kissed and laughed and stumbled as they tried to walk at the same time as kiss, all the way back to their room, only stopping when there was another couple waiting for the small lift. Josh made a grand gesture to usher them—Becca's cousin and his girlfriend—into the lift ahead of them. Who cared if her lipstick was smeared from passionate kissing and she was hanging on to Josh as if she never wanted to let him go? To all intents and purposes *they were engaged* and acting entirely appropriately.

Once they reached their room, Josh slammed the door shut behind them. He pushed her against the wall and held her hands above her head with one of his big hands as he kissed her—hard, hungry, urgent. She kissed him back with equal urgency, meeting his tongue with hers, straining her body against his. He ran his other hand down her bare arms, the sides of her breasts, and she trembled at the pleasure of it. She wanted him so much it was a physical ache.

He kissed down the side of her neck to the hollow of her throat and she murmured her pleasure. Her breasts swelled above the top of the bodice of her dress. She ached for him to touch her. Forget caution, forget worry about how this might end, her world shrank to just him and her and how he made her feel, her need for more. *Josh.*

She attempted to hook one leg around his in an effort to get closer but her dress, tightly fitted to her hips, got in the way.

He released her arms. 'This dress needs to come off,' he said, his voice husky.

'Yes,' she said.

'Do you want that?'

'Yes, yes and yes again,' she said impatiently.

Desire had been relentlessly building since that first dance. The way he moved, the way he held her so close, so possessively. It might not be anything more than this night but she would regret it if she didn't take full advantage of his willingness, of that big, inviting bed.

'You're sure?'

'I told you what kissing like that would lead to. And I want— Oh!'

He deftly turned her around and kissed the nape of her neck, the backs of her ears. How did he know that was one of her secret turn-on spots?

Then he slowly pulled down the back zip of her dress. The dress was lined with fine silk and it was like an extra caress on her highly sensitised skin as it fell from her body to pool on the floor.

She stepped out of her gown and moved it aside so she stood in just her deep blue lace thong, a strapless bra and her glittering high-heeled stilettos. From behind, Josh caressed her back and started to unhook her bra, but she twisted in his arms to face him.

'My turn now,' she said, her breath coming unevenly, scarcely able to get the words out.

She planted small kisses over his face as, with impatient fingers that weren't quite steady, she undid the buttons of his jacket and slid it off his shoulders.

'It was fun to fit you for this jacket, but it's even more fun to take it off you,' she murmured as she placed it on the chair near the bed. Even giddy with desire and want, she couldn't throw that beautiful piece of tailoring on the floor. With impatient fingers she unfastened the studs and buttons of his dress shirt and slid it off his broad shoulders as he freed his arms from the sleeves.

She stilled as she took in the delicious sight of him, wearing only his trousers, broad-shouldered, well-built, skin smooth and lightly tanned.

'Do I pass inspection?' he said.

'Oh, yes,' she sighed, placing her hands flat on his muscular chest to slide them down his flat, washboard stomach. 'Are you really and truly a tech nerd? Because you look more like an athlete to me.'

'Both,' he said shortly, his breath coming faster as her hands went lower.

'And here I was thinking you couldn't get any better looking.' Her voice broke. 'You're perfect.'

'I don't know about that,' he said, scarcely able to

get the words out as she slipped her fingers under the waistline of his trousers, then went to undo his belt. 'Are you teasing me? Keep doing that and I—'

'Won't be responsible for what happens next?' Eloise looked up flirtatiously at him, not hiding the need from her voice. 'I'm looking forward to that.' She started to unbuckle his belt.

'Two can play at this game,' he said hoarsely as he unhooked her bra and tossed it onto the bed. He gazed at her in wonder, standing there in just her thong and her glittering stilettos. 'You're the one with the perfect body, *Ellie*,' he groaned.

She didn't let many people call her *Ellie* but she had given him permission and she liked how her name sounded when he said it in his deep voice.

He stroked her breasts, rolling her nipples between his fingers until they were hard and aching. As he slid his hands down her waist, her muscles contracted with pleasure and anticipation. He slipped his fingers under the scrap of lace that was her thong and she gasped. He would find her ready for him. What else had that slow, sensuous dancing been but a subtle and exquisite form of foreplay?

She unfastened his trousers and started to push them down over his hips. 'Getting these trousers off is easier said than done when you're standing up,' she murmured.

'Might be easier if we took this to the bed,' he said. The bed that had caused so much angst and yet was just right for the two of them.

She ran her fingers up his chest. 'I'd be happy to take you up against the wall,' she murmured huskily. 'Floor, chair—wherever we might happen to end up. But the bed might be more comfortable. I just want you, Josh.'

'I want you too, Ellie,' he groaned. 'I think you know that.'

She brushed her fingers lightly across the front of his trousers. 'Oh, yes, I can tell.'

He cupped her face in his hands and looked down into her eyes. 'But before we go any further—'

'To the point of no return?'

'There's something I have to tell you; it's important and I—'

'No. We've done more than enough talking.' She silenced him with a kiss. The kiss deepened and became more urgent. *She wanted more than kissing.* All she could think of was making love with Josh. If what he wanted to say was that important he could tell her later.

Josh effortlessly swept her up into his arms and carried her to the bed. He kicked off his shoes and she helped rid him of his trousers and boxers. As she did so, she made admiring comments about what she found beneath them. She had to touch and explore, which made him groan with want and heightened desire for both of them.

In turn, he kissed his way down her stomach, giving her almost unbearable tremors of pleasure and anticipation. He took her lacy thong in his teeth and tugged it over her hips and down her legs, managing a lot of highly arousing kissing of very sensitive places on the way.

She took him by the shoulders. 'Josh. No more. I want you inside me. Now. Please.'

He reached for protection from his wallet and obliged.

'Yes,' she moaned as he pushed inside her body. *Josh.*

He felt so hard, so powerful, so *right*. Almost immediately, she shattered into a climax and then another followed when he came.

'Oh, my gosh, what happened there?' she said, flushed and satisfied, with post-orgasmic tremors still rippling deliciously through her. *The best sex of her life.* 'I couldn't wait.'

He pushed her hair away from her face where it was falling out of its pins. 'There's a time for fast and furious and now there's the time for a slow exploration,' he said.

She shimmied her body under him. 'That sounds very good to me. Shall I start by exploring you?'

'Let's explore each other,' he said. 'There's still more to learn about pleasing you.'

He was a fast learner.

Afterwards, she fell asleep in his arms. Some time later they both woke, very early—near dawn, judging from the light in the room—and wordlessly they made love again, as she let her body say what she couldn't say in words.

Josh woke to the morning sun streaming through the French doors. He and Eloise had had more important activities to occupy themselves with the previous night than to draw the curtains. Naked, she lay close to him, one hand resting on his shoulder, a long, slender leg resting across his. The sheets were rumpled across her hips, leaving her beautiful breasts bared. Her hair glinted blue-black in a shaft of sunlight that fell across her face, the same shaft he suspected had woken him.

She looked…different. Then he realised her face was free of cosmetics. He vaguely remembered her getting up at some stage to go and wash her face, saying she never slept in her make-up.

Her skin was ivory pale and smooth with a smattering of light freckles on her cheekbones, her natural lashes dark and luxuriant, her mouth an unadorned pink. Her fingernails painted red were the only artifice, short and neatly shaped. He imagined it wouldn't be so easy to negotiate a sewing machine with long nails. She'd taken off the ruby ring. This Eloise, without her props of attention-getting vintage-style clothes and careful make-up was lovely, a natural beauty. But he liked both looks. He liked Eloise, period.

Aware, perhaps, of his gaze on her, she stirred and opened her lovely blue eyes. She blinked. 'Josh?' Then smiled. '*Josh*,' she said, this time with warmth. She stretched with unconscious grace then rested on her elbow to face him. 'Last night. We broke every rule. And wasn't it wonderful?' A slow, sensual smile spread across her face.

Her hair had tumbled down from its style of the night before, and he pushed it back from her face. 'It was indeed wonderful. *You* were wonderful.' He dropped a kiss on her bare shoulder. He had kissed practically everywhere else on her body last night.

'Thank you. It goes without saying so were you.' She paused. 'It…it wasn't just sex for me.'

'No. Not for me either.'

'I wish—'

'I want—'

They spoke at the same time.

'You say what you were going to say,' she said.

'No, you go first.'

'I was going to say, I wish you didn't live in Boston.'

'And I was going to say, I want to find a way we could continue to see each other after I go back.' He'd been thinking of nothing else since they'd first made love. That, and how he could explain why he hadn't told her about Tori, and that their meeting hadn't been accidental. Fact was, the more he'd got to know her, the harder it had been to tell her because the more there was at risk in terms of him and her.

'You mean long-distance dating? I'm not sure that—'

'We can try and make it work. If we want it enough. And I do, Ellie—'

'I like it when you call me Ellie.'

'I'm glad,' he said. 'But don't change the subject. I want to try to keep something going between us. At least try and see how it pans out.'

She traced a finger down his nose and over his mouth. He caught it with his teeth. 'I like that,' she murmured as she took it away. 'It's not just the long distance. I... I'm frightened of liking you too much.'

'Why is that?'

'The more I like you, the more I open myself to hurt.'

'I wouldn't hurt you.'

'Not intentionally, perhaps.'

'Certainly not intentionally. Have you been hurt before?' He felt a rush of anger at the thought of anyone hurting her.

'Hasn't everyone?' she said.

'That's not what I asked,' he said. He had to know what he was up against.

'I've been hurt. Of course, I've hurt people too. Men I never should have dated.'

He didn't give a flying fig about the men she had hurt. Although maybe he should. She could have the power to hurt him too—there were definite fissures in that shield around his heart, chiselled by each kiss from this wonderful woman. 'I don't care about them. It's you who interests me.'

She sighed. 'I started off a romantic, totally believing in happy-ever-after. My parents had a wonderful marriage—classic love at first sight, totally devoted to each other. I honestly thought it would be as easy as that for me too. Meet Mr Right in a shower of moonbeams, fall in love, glide up that aisle. The realities of teenage dating soon beat that delusion out of me. Me, all starry-eyed; him willing to gabble *I love you* as many times as it took to get what he wanted.'

'That guy was a jerk. Not all boys were like that. Boys get their hearts broken too.'

'Did you?'

'Yes. Probably part of the reason I'm propelled by bitterness and revenge.'

She bit her bottom lip. 'I'm sorry I said that. It was harsh.'

'But true. You were right. Meeting you has made me think about how I'm living my life, that maybe it's not, as you say, so healthy. I need to look forward, not trip myself up by looking backwards for my motivation. But that doesn't explain why you're frightened of liking me too much.'

'When my father died, my mother fell to pieces. An intelligent, capable person like her was utterly lost without him. It took her years to get back on her feet, though she's never remarried. I saw that and it scared me—the power of love, the pain when you lose it for whatever reason.'

'So you anticipate the end before you risk the beginning? I'm sorry. But that was your parents. What about you?'

'The first time I really fell in love was with a guy in Paris. He loved me too. But we couldn't keep it going long-distance. I was heartbroken. Couldn't look at anyone else for a long time.'

Jealousy, irrational but powerful, seared through him. He couldn't bear the thought of her with any other man. It shocked him. He'd only known her a week.

'How old were you?'

'Nineteen.'

'You probably couldn't have afforded to keep it going. That wouldn't be an issue with us.'

'True. But you know it isn't your wealth that interests me?'

'If I thought that for even a second, I wouldn't be here.' He dropped a kiss on her mouth.

'I value my independence and I'm frightened of giving over even part of my life for someone else to control. That last guy...the one I told you about who lied to me about who he really was? He made me distrust my own judgement.'

'Why does it have to be like that? My father had to have everyone under his control. Your parents were of a different generation. So were mine. When I turned eighteen, when she thought I didn't need her any more, my mother went back to my father. Of course, *I* still wasn't welcome at the house.'

'Oh, Josh, no wonder you're bitter.'

'I haven't got a great track record with relationships. As I told you, I've been a lone wolf. "He who travels fastest, travels alone." That kind of thing. But meeting you…meeting you is making me look at things differently. Making me think it could be worth taking a risk.'

'I seem to attract men who want to take charge of me. The last guy was like that too.'

'What foolish men they must be,' he said, smiling. 'If I've ever seen anyone who is her own woman, it's you. It's one of the things I like about you.'

'But would you want to change me?'

'I don't think so. I like you exactly as you are. But how would we know that, if we didn't get to know each other better? It's only been days, though it seems I've known you longer. I haven't had much practice in making compromises, and maybe you've made too many. We won't know unless we try.'

'All I ask is honesty,' she said. 'I can't forgive lies. Oh, I know we've fibbed our hearts out about the engagement, but that's different; that's—'

'A targeted business strategy of purposeful evasion,' he said.

'You remembered?'

'How could I forget?'

'You're laughing at me.'

'I'm not. I think it's brilliant. But there is something I have to tell you. There's someone back in Boston.'

'A girl?'

'Yes, but it's not what you think. She's a very good friend and—'

'I don't think I want to hear about it.'

'You should because—'

The phone in the room rang. He looked at Eloise and she looked back. 'I suppose we'd better answer it.'

She got out of bed and walked over to the desk where the handset was. She was completely unselfconsciously naked, and utterly enticing. He lay back against the pillow and admired the shapely lines of her beautiful body. That feeling of being on shifting ground returned. He felt as if he was on the edge of something new and important and life-changing. *Because of her.*

She picked up the phone and listened. 'Thank you,' she said and hung up. She turned to him. 'Breakfast for the house guests is being served in the conservatory for another hour. Do you—?'

'I'd rather skip breakfast and have you back here in bed with me.' Could he ever have enough of her?

'Other appetites, huh?' she said. 'I couldn't agree with you more.'

She slid back under the covers. 'Thank heaven they gave us this great big bed.'

'Oh, I don't know,' he said, pulling her close to him. 'I think we could happily have found our way around any size bed.'

CHAPTER THIRTEEN

By the time he and Eloise had left Silver Trees, stopped for lunch in Bowral and driven the two hours back to Sydney, it was mid-afternoon when she dropped Josh back to his hotel. He'd arranged to spend a few hours there and then go around to her apartment to take her out to dinner. They planned to talk seriously about how they might be the couple who could actually make long-distance work.

But before he did that, he had to call Tori. He hadn't been honest with her about how he felt about Eloise. But then, he hadn't been honest with himself—fighting the fact he was falling for her. Right from that first meeting in the park.

Tori was pleased to hear from him. He realised how difficult it must be for her not to know what was happening on the other side of the world. But why the hell hadn't she connected with Eloise as soon as he'd told her he was certain they were twins? It would have made it so much more straightforward for him. Now it was complicated. Too complicated.

'How did the wedding go?' Tori asked.

'So you remembered that was yesterday?'

'That you were my twin sister's plus-one at some big society wedding? Well, yeah. That wasn't something I'd easily forget.'

He'd known Tori since he was sixteen, but he wasn't sure how to voice this. 'It was good. Very good. But I haven't been completely honest with you.'

He could sense her frown through the phone. 'What do you mean?'

'About Eloise. And me. Remember you told me not to develop a thing for her? It was already too late. It's more than a thing. I'm in love with her.'

There was an indrawn hiss from Tori. 'Josh. That wasn't meant to happen.'

'I know. But it did.'

'You've fallen in love with a woman who looks just like me? Don't you think that's a little weird?'

'Not weird at all. She's actually nothing like you. I mean that in a good way. You complement each other. You'd see that if you met her. What I'm saying, Tori, is that you have to get in touch with her. I can't keep lying—to her or to you.'

'Are you serious, Josh?'

'Serious about Eloise?' He paused. 'Yeah. I am.'

'I've never heard you say that before. Finally he meets the right woman. And it has to be the twin sister I've never met. In Australia. You should have told me earlier.'

'I wasn't sure. But I've told you now. Call her. Please.'

It was corny, he knew, but Josh arrived at Eloise's apartment building that evening bearing flowers. It wasn't something he remembered ever having done since he'd bought a corsage for his prom date back in high school. The florist in the lobby of the hotel was open and on impulse he bought a huge bunch of voluptuous deep pink roses that he thought she might like. A gesture, perhaps, of how different he intended his life to be now. All part of him embracing 'the kinder side of life'. A life with Eloise in it.

He still firmly believed that her connection with Eloise was Tori's secret to tell, and the truth of their sisterhood should only be revealed twin to twin. And yet there had to be total honesty between him and Eloise for their fledgling—so new the feathers were still damp and crumpled—relationship to have a chance. Tori had had a few hours to call Eloise. He hoped like hell she had. Because he couldn't move forward with Eloise until she knew about Tori. And about the part he'd played in the discovery of the twins. How he'd seen that magazine article and pointed it out to Tori; how he'd offered to help by looking up Eloise while he was in Sydney—and why he'd had to evade the truth.

As he waited for Eloise to buzz him through the security door to the block, he tried to put a name to the way he was feeling. Finally he settled on elation. Elation at the prospect of seeing her again. Of being able to explain what had happened. Elation at the prospect of her becoming someone significant in his life. He hadn't felt like this about a woman for a long time. In fact, he'd never felt like this about a woman because he'd never met a woman like Eloise.

However, the second she opened the door of her apartment to him he knew something was amiss. Her face seemed drained of her usual vivacity, her mouth set in a grim line. She seemed, in a way, diminished. When he lowered his head to kiss her, he really knew something was wrong.

She averted her face, shrugged him away. 'Don't touch me,' she said coldly. She looked at the flowers with an expression he could only describe as scorn.

'What's wrong?' he asked, perplexed. How fleeting had been that feeling of elation. It had come crashing down to smother him.

Eloise stomped away from him into the living room, as if she couldn't bear to even breathe the same air as him, then whirled back to face him. 'I've just spent the last hour on a video chat with Tori. My twin sister Tori. The sister I had no idea I had, but of course you did.' Her cheeks were flushed.

Good. Tori had delivered. But her call didn't seem to have had the effect he'd hoped for.

'She called you.' He put the flowers down on a side table.

'She did. Can you imagine what it was like for me? First to find out I had a twin sister. And second to discover you're a friend of hers and have known about this all the time. That you've completely misrepresented yourself. And let me…let me get to like you. You played games with Tori too, with our fake engagement. I had to sort her out about that.'

'But how—?' What had Tori said?

'Funnily enough, Tori follows *@lindytheblonde*. I told you, millions do. So what does she see but a post mentioning our engagement? With a photo of us dancing very close and looking as though we wanted to tear each other's clothes off on the dance floor.'

'Which we probably did.'

'That's beside the point. For me, *you* are now beside the point.'

Her words felt like a kick to the gut. There were no words of his own he could summon up in reply.

'You'd know better than I do why she hadn't contacted me earlier, but apparently seeing us "engaged" put a bomb up her. I suspect she wasn't at all happy about it.'

'No,' he said. He had omitted to tell Tori about the fake engagement. He should have. She didn't know it was fake. It hadn't seemed important. Not as important as Tori contacting Eloise and telling her the truth. But it must have been a shock. And to see him looking so intimate with Eloise when she'd only just found out they were together.

Tori would be furious he hadn't told her he was engaged. Even though he actually wasn't. And that was on top of him not telling her about his feelings for Eloise until today. But his attraction to Eloise had been a force of its own. What had happened with Eloise had developed completely independently of Tori. It had been too private, too personal to share with anyone. It had overridden even his loyalty to his friend. Quite frankly, his intimate time with Eloise was none of Tori's business. Being lovers, a couple, meant sharing their own private, special world with no one else but each other. He'd found that magical world with Eloise, and now he could see it slipping away.

'Tori contacted me over social media, outlining the story of the twins adopted separately when they were two years old, telling me she believed I was her sister.'

He took a step towards her, wanting to comfort her. 'That must have been a shock.'

She took a step back, pointedly rejecting him. 'You could say that. It brought back in its entirety the shock of finding I'd been adopted. Tori had only just discovered that Baby One—me—had been adopted to a Boston couple, Dr Debra Evans and Dr Adam Evans—my parents, of course. Tori was Baby Two, adopted to Marissa Preston and Tom Preston, also of Boston.'

'She'd been waiting for that information as confirmation.' Josh felt as if he was pushing his way through thick sand, caught in a quagmire of deception that hadn't been entirely of his own making.

'And you knew that. *You knew.*' She spat the accusation.

'Yes,' was all he could manage to choke out, his mind racing to see how—if—he could salvage something from this.

'She sent me a photo of her. It was like looking at me with short hair. A…a different version of me. I nearly hyperventilated. You see stories in the media about this kind of thing. You don't expect in a million years that you could find yourself in the story.'

'I'm sorry.' He'd made a few abortive attempts to tell her something of the story, but had still not been sure how much had been his to tell.

He could have prepared her for this. Or could he have? Not without revealing she might have a twin sister. He was stymied whichever path he took. But at least Eloise was telling him what had happened and hadn't booted him straight out of the door. Although that might be because he was the only other person she knew who also knew Tori and she needed to talk about her.

Eloise raked her fingers through her hair. 'Tori asked could we video chat? Before I considered that option, I called my mother. She was as shocked as I was—she'd had no idea there were two babies; neither apparently did Tori's adoptive mother. I suspect both the mothers would have had a moment, even for a split second, of wondering what it would have been like if they'd been given the other baby.'

'Why didn't you call me?'

'I had no idea there was a connection to you at that stage. It was something so intensely personal I had to do it for myself. *A sister.* Then tell you about it afterwards.'

'So what happened on the call?'

Tori was obviously so cranky with him about leaving her out of the engagement news, she hadn't presented him in a favourable light. He wished he'd known that before he'd come over here with his goofy bunch of roses. Because he knew where this was heading. Had known when Eloise had so pointedly averted her face from his kiss. But he wouldn't give up without a fight. He was in love with her.

'I couldn't believe it,' she said, the wonder and shock still in her voice. 'At first we just stared at each other for what seemed a long time without saying a word. I saw *myself* on the screen. I wanted to put out my hand to touch her. To see if she was real. It was seriously like looking in the mirror. We're the same, yet I think we're very different people. She dresses in a rock chick kind of style. But then, you know that, don't you? You've been friends since high school. Only friends, she reassured me. Strictly platonic.'

'I think of her like a sister; her family were good to me,' he said. 'Remember I told you how my mother and I went to live with my aunt in the North End? I met Tori at my new school. She took the new kid under her wing.'

'Yeah. She said that.' Her tone was frigid. As if his role in this was irrelevant. As if he was no longer relevant to her.

'She has two brothers. Great guys. Did she tell you that?'

'She did. Our lives growing up were very different. But it seems we both had good adoptive parents.'

'So did you like each other? I was sure you would.'

Her face softened. But for Tori, not for him.

'Immediately we clicked. Certain things fell into place. We were together until we were two years old, so must have buried memories of each other. We both felt something was missing in our lives. Turned out I was her imaginary friend. She was the picture I drew for my mother as the sister I wanted. There were other weird things. We both broke our left arms when we were ten. Had our appendix out at the same time. Both creative and into art and design. Both work with rescue dogs. And seriously weird that we each have wedding-related businesses. Dresses for me, cakes for her.'

'Not weird but a twin thing, I guess.' Maybe a bit weird considering the sisters hadn't seen each other for twenty-six years. 'I'm so happy for you both—it's an amazing thing to have found a sister.' He didn't want to point out that he was the one who had actually found her. It would not be appreciated, he was certain of that.

'It got very emotional; we were both crying by the end. Of course we'll get DNA tested. Did you know identical twins share almost one hundred per cent the same DNA? But we don't need a test to know we're sisters. And there was another thing. I talked to her on my laptop in my bedroom. She noticed on the shelf behind me a small, pink stuffed rabbit. I've had it ever since I can remember. Tori left the camera for a minute and came back with an identical one in her hand. A bit more battered than mine, as she grew up with two brothers, but she'd been told it was from her birth mother. I guess mine was from my birth mother too. But of course I'd never been told that. Maybe my parents didn't know its significance.'

Josh ached to take her into his arms and comfort her. Finding out about Tori was obviously a positive thing for her, but a deeply emotional one. One she would need quite some getting used to. He wanted to hug her and tell her everything he knew about Tori and what a wonderful person her newly found sister was. But she'd folded her arms across her chest and the emanations coming from her were distinctly hostile.

'I won't offer you a drink or a snack or even a seat,' she said. 'Because you won't be staying. I can't believe I was fooled by you when I so wanted to believe in you.'

'But you can still believe in me, Ellie.'

Her bottom lip stuck out, just like Tori's did when she was angry. They were sisters all right. 'Don't call me Ellie.'

Another kick to the gut.

'How can you honestly think I could believe anything you say? Tori told me everything. How you discovered a picture of me in a magazine and pointed out the resemblance. How you volunteered to look me up when you were here to report back to Tori in Boston.'

'I had no doubt, that first day in the park, that you were twins.'

'And you kept that to yourself. Even…even when we became lovers. How could you have done that?'

'Out of loyalty to Tori. It was her right to tell you. Wouldn't you do the same for a friend? Wouldn't you want to help if it was, say, Vinh? If you had a friend, a good friend who had taken you into her family when your own family had dumped you. A friend who had always felt something—someone—was missing in her life. Wouldn't you help her find her look-alike who just might be her identical twin?'

'I wouldn't completely misrepresent myself like you did.'

'Tori made me promise not to say anything to you. I respected that. It was her secret, her story. Your story and your sister's story. It wasn't mine to tell.'

'But you let things get so far between us.'

'That's where Tori doesn't know the full story. I said I'd try to find you and get a close look at you to check you really were her double as you appeared to be. Photos can lie. But I didn't count on being attracted to you. On not being able to stop thinking about you. That's why I flew back up from Melbourne—just so I could see you again.'

'But you said—'

'I know. I made new business appointments in Sydney to justify the trip, unable at that stage to admit to myself it was really all about you. That was real. What happened last night was real. Those…those feelings were real.'

Slowly she shook her head. 'It doesn't change anything, Josh. I could never trust another word you said. Everything you said to me last night and this morning, I wanted to believe it. And you know what? It makes me distrust Tori too.'

'You can trust her. Tori had no idea about our fake engagement or what happened between us at Silver Trees.'

'Don't talk about what happened between us. Don't remind me that I trusted you, believed in you. Now I… I never want to see you again, Josh.'

'Please, Eloise, don't say that. I'm sorry about how I handled this. Above all, I didn't want to hurt you. Ever.' He wasn't one to beg and plead, but he also didn't want to let go what he'd found with her without a fight.

'Hurt? Why would I be hurt? It was, after all, only one night. I… I hadn't had time to get attached.'

One night had been enough for him to change his entire way of thinking. 'We talked about making it more than one night.'

'That was before I discovered how you'd lied to me.'

She was hurting, even if she was denying it. He knew her well enough to know that. And that pain had been inflicted by him. He'd tried to do the right thing by Tori and by Eloise too. Reuniting these two sisters could be a wonderful thing for them. The imaginary friend and the girl in the drawing. Now they were both angry with him. A united force.

'Can't we try and start again, Eloise? Now that you know the truth about Tori.'

'No,' she said flatly.

'Perhaps we could meet tomorrow and talk this through?'

'There is absolutely no point. Unless you have further business in Sydney, I suggest you fly back home to Boston.'

'Did last night mean anything to you?' he challenged. It sure as hell had meant something to him.

She raised her chin. 'It was great sex,' she said.

'It was that,' he agreed. Their lovemaking had been so awesome because emotions had been at play that neither of them had been prepared to admit to. Until they'd let down their guards in the morning. *This morning.* It seemed an age ago now. Her barriers were right back up again.

'But that's all,' she said, making absolutely sure he got the message.

It had been so much more than sex for him. But he had no right to argue the point. He had to disengage from her. This aftermath of relationships gone wrong was one of the main reasons he had avoided them for so long.

'The only thing I ask, is if we can keep up the pretence of the engagement for a while longer,' she said. 'If it gets out now that we're frauds, it will do more harm than good and I'll be a laughing stock.'

'Sure,' he said. 'We'll stick to the timeline. Give it a few months to peter out. You can tell people we're in touch. Fabricate a few phone calls. Whatever you need to do. I'll be in Boston, right out of your way. If someone should happen to ask, I'll give them the same story. Just text me when you decide it's gone on long enough, so we keep our stories straight about ending it. I have no intention of returning to Sydney.' He'd been planning to buy a house here to make it easy to see her.

He was hurt. But he'd had plenty of experience of hiding his hurts. That old shield around his heart would still do its work, and the cracks would eventually mend. He'd stay clear of the Tori-Eloise reunion. He'd done his best to bring them together. Time to bow right out.

'Let me know if you change your mind about meeting,' he said.

Her silence told him she wasn't going to change her mind.

'I'll fly out tomorrow.'

'Good,' she said.

There was nothing good about it, not as far as he was concerned anyway.

'Don't take what happened between us out on Tori,' he said. 'You'll like having her as a sister.'

Wordlessly, she nodded.

'Goodbye, Eloise.'

He turned on his heel and walked out, not looking behind him.

Eloise was left staring after Josh. She had to hold on to the back of a chair for support, take deep breaths to steady herself. How had this wonderful new phase of her life suddenly gone so horribly, horribly wrong?

She'd gained a sister. A twin. *A miracle.* But she'd lost a man she'd thought she could fall in love with. A man she'd started to spin dreams around.

She breathed in the lingering scent of him, mingling with the rich sweetness of those magnificent roses. How did he know they were her favourites?

The same way he knew how to please her in bed, how to make her laugh, how to make her think she was with the most wonderful man on earth. And she'd believed in him. Only to have that belief thrown back at her by the discovery of his deceit.

She'd had a lucky escape. More time spent with him and she would have been back in that sticky, sweet trap of infatuation. She'd made the same old mistakes, thrown away all her hard-won caution. All for a few exciting kisses, a thrilling time in bed.

Deep down, she knew it had been more than that. There had been an undeniable connection between her and Josh, something so compelling it had overridden caution and common sense. That was what had made it so agonising to find out the truth about him. That he was there in the park that day had been no accident. He'd been there specifically to watch out for her. Mara, the waitress, had recognised him because he'd been sitting at her café hoping to catch sight of her to report back to Tori. What else didn't she know about him? She'd thought she knew enough to trust him.

Eloise knew she couldn't stay here by herself. She'd go crazy with regrets and self-recriminations and a chorus of *what ifs* hammering into her brain. Home. She'd go home to her mother, who'd said for her the discovery of her twin was almost like finding another daughter. She would want to talk about Tori. She'd pick up Daisy, the little dog whose instincts she'd trusted over her own. Which was a kind of crazy all by itself.

CHAPTER FOURTEEN

Three weeks later

THE LAST TIME Eloise had flown into Boston's Logan Airport she'd been fifteen years old and accompanied by her mother and father, arriving from Sydney for their annual trip to her father's hometown. Her grandparents—her father's parents—had been waiting for them when they'd come out of Security. Family. That was what it had been all about then. Her memories were bittersweet: her father had died not long after and she hadn't seen her grandparents since. She was tempted to contact them while she was here—maybe they'd mellowed—but wasn't sure she could handle their rejection.

Today she'd flown in from New York and she was also being greeted by family. Her twin sister, Tori. Her blood family. Since the first day they'd connected online they'd chatted most days, even if only for minutes at a time. The need to see each other face to face had become overwhelming. And the opportunity to meet came sooner rather than later. She could hardly wait to hug the sister she hadn't seen since she was two years old.

She'd be meeting Tori's parents and brothers too,

which was exciting. As for Josh... Tori knew to keep his name right off the reception committee. During their online chats, Eloise had specifically asked her new-found sister not to talk about Josh. How could she forget him any other way?

Eloise had spent the last week in New York City. Roxee's actress friend's wedding had turned into a mega celebration with twelve bridesmaids and three changes of gown for the bride. It was a job that had required Eloise's hands-on presence. The American side of the business was burgeoning and getting more and more time-consuming. Not just for the actual design and production of the garments but also the tariffs and taxes on importing Australian-made products into the United States and the consequent paperwork. Then there were the celebrities impatient at being put on an ever-growing waiting list.

It was getting to the stage that the balance was starting to tip between her Australian clients and her clients in the USA. She had to be careful not to overstretch herself—that could be the death of creativity, and she'd seen it too many times when designer friends had started their own labels and ended up bankrupt.

She might have to establish an atelier in New York, perhaps put Vinh in charge. But the fact was it was her name on the label. And it was Eloise Evans those demanding new clients wanted to see, certainly in the first instance.

She should be deliriously happy about her business's rapid expansion. Trouble was, she couldn't take much joy in it.

'You've had too many emotional ups and downs,' her

mother had said soothingly. Her mum knew about Josh, as Eloise had sobbed out her distress on her shoulder.

'There are plenty of other fish in the sea,' her mother's advice had been. That was always her relationship advice. She didn't think any of Eloise's boyfriends had been worthy of her daughter. This time, Eloise suspected she was secretly glad things hadn't worked out with Josh. She didn't want to lose her only child to Boston.

Her mother had joined in some of the video chats with Tori. 'We've found each other, but we've also each found a new family,' Tori had said several times in delight.

So the deeply hidden gap in Eloise's life caused by her long-lost sister had been filled. Sadly there was now another painful gap: Josh. True to their agreement, they hadn't contacted each other. For her own well-being, she needed to forget he'd ever been in her life. So why did she miss him so much? She couldn't go to her favourite café in the park, the restaurant where they'd had their first date, even Mara's café near her work. So many memories for such a short time together. And that was apart from the dreams that haunted her sleep and had her waking to tears when she realised he wasn't there. Poor Daisy had had her fur wetted with tears, but the little dog had only given her comfort. Eloise didn't know how she would bear to give this dog away. She might have to admit to being a foster fail and keep her.

She cleared Security and watched out for…well, someone who looked like herself. And there she was: black hair like hers but chopped short and spiky, wearing urban chic black jeans and boots. And a huge smile.

Her sister. *The sister Josh had found for her.* She hadn't appreciated just what he'd done and the conflicting loyalties he'd had to struggle with, the integrity with which he had treated both her and Tori. Only now, meeting her twin and realising the incredible odds against having found her, did she realise just how grateful she should have been to Josh. Instead she had pushed him away. And wounded herself in the process. But she couldn't think about that now. She was in Boston. She would have to swallow her pride and seek him out. Grovel a little—okay, grovel a lot. And hope he would give her the second chance she'd refused to give him. Even if only to be friends as they had Tori in common.

She and Tori hugged, then drew back to look at each other and exclaim at their resemblance and then hugged again. Tears flowed too, happy and emotional.

'I didn't think we'd look quite so alike,' Tori said. 'It's uncanny. Even the video chat didn't give the complete story. Our height, the way we move, our expressions.'

'The full dimension. If we'd grown up together, can you imagine the fun we would have had swapping places and tricking people?' Eloise said.

'Oh, yes!' said Tori, laughing. Her laugh was like an echo of Eloise's own. 'We would have been menaces.'

'We were cheated of that childhood,' Eloise said slowly. 'I wonder why?'

'I couldn't find out why the adoption agency split us up.'

'I guess they had their reasons. But it turned out well for both of us, didn't it?' Eloise said. She couldn't stop smiling.

'We were both so blessed with our adoptive families,' said Tori.

'We were indeed. And now we've found each other.'

'With no intention of ever losing one another again.'

Arms around each other, they walked towards the area where Tori must have parked her car. A few people did a double take when they saw them together and Eloise and her sister laughed. 'There might be possibilities for us to be menaces still,' Eloise said. They both giggled. In harmony.

When they'd stopped laughing, Tori spoke. 'There's someone I want you to meet. A friend of mine.'

'A bride in need of a dress?'

'No, a guy friend.'

Eloise stopped her with a hand on her arm. 'Please, Tori, that's sweet of you, but I really don't want to be set up with anyone. Seriously. I'm happy on my own. I don't have time to date or the inclination.' Or the heart. No one could compare to Josh.

'This guy's a really good friend and…'

And then Eloise saw him. Her heart jolted. *Josh.*

He saw her at the same time and he stared, momentarily transfixed. Then he strode towards them. 'Tori, what the hell—?'

All Eloise's denials of her feelings for him, all the anger she'd tried to build up for him deceiving her, were lost in a rush of sheer joy. *Josh.* Josh, even more handsome than she remembered him in a dark, charcoal business suit.

Frowning, he looked to her then to Tori and back to her. He'd been set up. He obviously had no idea why he was here. A well-meaning yet clumsy attempt by her sister to force them together? She wanted to cringe with the humiliation of it. Then she looked at Josh, really looked at him. And saw the same emotions she was trying to control herself reflected in his hazel eyes. And, strangely, he didn't look as if he wanted to be anywhere but here.

'This is my friend Josh Taylor,' said Tori, as if Eloise had never met the man before. Or made love with him, or laughed with him, or teased him as she'd pinned him into a tuxedo.

Tori continued. 'Josh is an excellent friend. The absolute best. He actually found you for me, my long-lost twin. He saw you in a magazine and realised we must be related. Although I think there's actually more to it than that. Josh saw something in that Australian fashion designer that absolutely fascinated him. What he didn't expect was that when he actually met her—at my request—he'd be so madly attracted to her he'd go right off plan in his pursuit of her. Until it wasn't as much about Josh finding my twin for me but about Josh finding the ideal woman for him.'

Eloise swallowed hard against a sudden lump in her throat. She looked up at Josh. 'Is that what happened?' she asked him.

The busy airport around her faded away. Even Tori disappeared. It was just him and her and that connection that had been there from the get go, which she'd done her best to sever with her own insecurities and fears.

'Sounds accurate,' he said, his gaze on her face as if he'd been starved of the sight of her for too long. Something that had been shrivelled and frozen deep inside her since she'd watched him walk out of her apartment started to warm and thaw. *Her heart.*

'Then Josh somehow lost his ideal woman and I don't really know why.' Tori turned to Josh. 'But I think he could tell you that better than I could.' She looked at her watch in an exaggerated manner. 'Heck, I've got to go and see a lady about a cake. Josh, could you get Eloise to the trattoria for me? No rush. In your own time. You okay with that, Eloise? We can catch up later.'

Eloise nodded. Bemused, she watched her sister stride away. 'Is she always like that?'

'She's her own woman. Like you. And she's got it into her head it's her fault that I lost you. Whereas I did a perfectly good job of doing that on my own.'

'You didn't lose me, Josh. I misjudged you. Behaved stupidly. And didn't trust in what we had together.'

'I didn't fully recognise what we'd found. Because I'd never felt it before. Too used to being fuelled by bitterness and revenge I guess.'

She smiled at that. 'I've done pretty well on the bitterness front myself,' she said. 'There I was, lecturing you about the kind side of life, and I was so mean to you.'

Over and over again she'd gone over that final confrontation in her living room, scented with his beautiful roses. 'I cannot believe I told you that you were "beside the point".' She shuddered. 'I'm surprised you're even talking to me.'

'It wounded me, I won't deny it. But you were in shock. I've thought about it a lot. That day. A call from a sister you didn't know existed. Your world knocked off its axis. I wouldn't—I don't—blame you for anything you said. I should have handled it better. Stuck around in Sydney, for one thing. So I'd be there if you needed me. To talk you through things. Helped you understand what had happened.'

'But I pushed you away.'

'I shouldn't have gone. I've been miserable without you.'

She looked up at him. 'I've been miserable without you too. Utterly miserable. Every minute of every day. I think the word might be heartbroken. And I'm so grateful to Tori for engineering this meeting.'

'She didn't need to trick me into seeing you. I've got a ticket to fly out to Sydney tomorrow.'

'But you said you'd never visit Sydney again.'

'I said a lot of things I didn't mean. And left unsaid too many others.'

'Like what, Josh?' She had a few words left unsaid of her own. She held her breath for his answer.

He cupped her face in his hands and looked deeply into her eyes. 'That I love you, Ellie.'

She let out her breath on a sigh of happiness. 'Funnily enough, those are the exact same words I left unsaid. I love you too, Josh. So much. I feared I was falling in love with you at Silver Trees, but I realise I was already head over heels.'

'You've got nothing to fear now, darling Ellie.'

At last he took her in his arms and his kiss was long and tender, at the same time hinting at the passion she knew could ignite so quickly. But, while they were in a busy arrivals hall, where no one would look askance at a couple kissing, she'd rather take the kiss further, which meant going somewhere more appropriate. Like his apartment. She would suggest they detour there on the way to Tori's family trattoria, where a welcome lunch was planned for her.

'Another thing, Josh.'

'Yes?'

'Did you enjoy being my fake fiancé?'

'Very much so. I've never enjoyed myself as much as at the wedding at Silver Trees.'

She took a deep breath. 'Would you consider being my fiancé for real?'

He didn't look the slightest bit perturbed by her proposal. 'On one condition,' he said. 'Two, in fact.'

'What would they be?'

'One that we get our own engagement ring. A ring that's significant just to us that we choose together. You can wear your grandma's ruby on your other hand if you like.'

'Yes. I'd like that. And the other condition?'

'That you be my real-life wife as soon as we can possibly get married. I don't want to wait.'

Joy bubbled through her. 'Yes to that too. I can't think of anything I'd like better. If anyone can organise a wedding in a hurry, it's me. I've got all the contacts.'

'We've wasted enough time apart. Let's get on with our lives together, starting from now.' And he kissed her again.

CHAPTER FIFTEEN

Another three weeks later

ELOISE'S WEDDING DAY. Her twin sister, Tori, and her best friend, Vinh, as her bridesmaids. Josh waiting for her at the altar of the beautiful old sandstone church near Bowral with Tori's two brothers, Ty and Tate, beside him. Eloise thought it couldn't be more perfect. Except her father wasn't there. But her mother was here in the vestibule of the church with her, ready to walk her down the aisle, and she was so grateful for that.

Vinh fussed around her, smoothing and tucking her gown into place. Vinh had helped her design it. Made in heavy white silk, with a full skirt, a stand-up neckline and long, heavy lace sleeves, it gave a nod to her beloved nineteen-fifties vintage style, but was very much a contemporary masterpiece from Eloise Evans Atelier. There was, of course, a detachable train, glistening with crystals, harking back to her mermaid days.

'I've never seen a more beautiful wedding dress,' Tori said wistfully. 'If I ever meet a guy I want to marry, can you make me one just like it, please?'

'I'll make you whatever dress you'd like,' Eloise said.

She and Tori had further bonded through tales of their lacklustre love lives. Pre-Josh, of course, for her. Tori had a huge crush on one of the customers of her bakery, a wealthy architect, but had never done anything about it.

'As alike this one as you can make it, please,' Tori said. 'It's my dream dress.'

'Mine too,' said Eloise, giving her sister a quick at-arm's-length hug so as not to disturb her dress and veil.

The organ started to play the wedding march. Her mother took her arm. 'Time to walk up that aisle, sweetie,' she said. 'There's a good man waiting for you at the altar.' Josh had won her mother over completely and reassured her she would always be welcome to visit, and that they would be in Sydney often.

'I know,' Eloise said simply.

Tori walked first, then Vinh, and finally Eloise started her journey up the aisle of the church full of family and friends towards the man she adored. She realised it was happening just as she'd hoped it would all those years ago before she'd let herself get cynical. Love at first sight. Moonbeams and roses. And a walk up the aisle to where Mr Perfect was waiting for her. All set for the happy-ever-after that awaited them.

So many times at so many weddings, she'd watched for the groom to catch his first sight of his bride. Now she was waiting to see when Josh first saw her. He did not disappoint. Love and wonder and awe shone from his eyes. Her heart turned over and she hoped he saw love and trust and joy in hers as she held his gaze. Her husband-to-be.

* * *

Josh placed the platinum wedding band on the third finger of Eloise's left hand above her exquisite diamond ring as he promised to love, honour and cherish her for as long as they both did live. *His wife.* Then he smiled at her as she placed the matching wide band on his ring finger. In fact, he couldn't stop smiling. 'I love you,' she whispered. When the priest pronounced them man and wife, he thought his heart would burst with pride and love.

This was what a kinder life was about. Love. Friendship. Family. Not that he would stop making millions. It was in his nature to strive and succeed, be ruthless when he needed to be. But everything he did would be for Eloise and the children they hoped to have. Not for an ill-placed, unhealthy revenge.

When the priest said he could kiss the bride, he didn't want to stop.

Eloise had followed the newer custom of changing into another less formal white gown for the reception, which was being held at Silver Trees, thanks to the generosity of Becca and Simon. It was easy for her to have two dresses—after all, she owned two branches of her atelier. Or she would soon when Eloise Evans Atelier, Boston, opened in the exclusive shopping area on Newbury Street.

The timing had been perfect. She'd taken Vinh into partnership with her for the Double Bay branch, while she would work between Sydney and Boston. She and Josh would live in his Seaport apartment while they looked for a house near the North End. She'd be near her twin too.

There was another reason she had chosen to wear a second dress. Her bridal gown was now carefully wrapped in acid-free tissue paper and boxed for Tori to take home with her to Boston. She sought her out, to tell her it was waiting for her in her room.

'It's a good luck wedding dress, I just know it,' Eloise said. 'We're the same size. Take it home with you. I had to learn to trust and open my heart to love. Go after your dream man, the architect. What's his name again?'

'Clay Ramos. But Ellie, I'm not sure—'

'Who knows what might happen? And the dress will be ready for you if it does.'

She hugged her twin, already so loved. She might not see her again until she got back to Boston when she and Josh returned from their honeymoon on a luxury tropical island in far north Queensland.

Josh was over near the table where their magnificent wedding cake—whipped up by Tori—was displayed. He'd been talking to his Melbourne friends and fellow billionaires, Courtney and Shawn. Now he was chatting with his mother, who had defied her husband to travel to Australia to attend her younger son's wedding. His Aunt Lily was here somewhere too.

'You know, I was just telling Mom that the only person—well, not a person—we love who's missing from our wedding celebration is Daisy the dog.'

'Funny you should say that,' Eloise said. 'My mother has darling Daisy in her room, with Becca's permission, of course. I thought I'd surprise you by having her at the church but she's still too nervous around a crowd.'

Her move to Boston had made it problematic to adopt Daisy. But her mother had fallen in love with the little dog and decided to adopt her instead, which was nearly as good.

'So Daisy is the dog who introduced you?' Josh's mother asked. Eloise had liked her immediately and looked forward to having her at their home in Boston.

'In a manner of speaking, yes. She will still be part of our lives when we spend time in Sydney. And we can say goodbye to her before we leave.' Tori had already lined her up as a foster carer for a dog rescue organisation in Boston.

'Sounds like the perfect wedding all round,' said Josh. 'Here, where it all started for us.'

'It's the start of our perfect life together as husband and wife,' she said, lifting her face for his kiss.

* * * * *

A NEW FOUNDATION

ROCHELLE ALERS

Thy wife shall be as a fruitful vine
by the sides of thine house: thy children
like olive plants round about thy table.

—Psalms 128:3

Chapter One

"Momma was really full of surprises today. I still can't believe she waited until today to tell us that she bought a condo in a gated community, listed the house with a Realtor, and now she plans to take a two-hundred-forty-five-day around-the-world cruise. But what really threw me for a loop was willing us a dilapidated property and expecting us to restore it."

Taylor Williamson met his sister's eyes for a millisecond before he shifted his gaze back to the road and the bumper-to-bumper traffic heading for the tunnel leading into New York. "Firstly, Mom is a widow and an empty nester, and that means she doesn't need a house with six bedrooms. And she'd always talked about taking an around-the-world cruise when Dad was alive, but she knew he would never go with her because his parents were killed during a boating accident."

"I'm aware of that, Taylor, but why didn't we know that Daddy had inherited a mansion he'd planned to restore once he retired?"

"That's something I can't answer, Viola."

"And when Momma asked if you would supervise the restoration of his ancestral home I couldn't believe you said yes."

Elise Williamson had waited until her children were all together at the same time to reveal the details of her late husband's will. Conrad Bainbridge Williamson had left her and their sons and daughter a mansion in northern New Jersey.

"I agreed because it's something both Mom and Dad wanted. And, don't forget I wasn't the only one to agree. Tariq said he was willing to get involved once he finished his postgraduate program, and then later fulfill his obligation at the horse farm. Even Joaquin is willing to become involved as the landscape architect. Only you and Patrick are the holdouts."

"But that means you have to quit your position at the engineering firm where you've just been promoted to an assistant project supervisor."

A hint of a smile tugged at the corners of Taylor's mouth. "I know, but if I assume the responsibility of overseeing the restoration, then not only will I supervise my own team, I'll be working for the family." His mother had given him two steamer trunks filled with blueprints, floor plans, correspondence and documents linked to Bainbridge House. Conrad had stored the trunks in the attic of the farmhouse with the intent to review them once he retired.

"Right now, you're the only one in the family that has actually committed. There's no guarantee that Joaquin and Tariq won't change their minds a year or two from now."

Taylor wanted to ask Viola why she insisted on being a Negative Nelly. He really did not want to argue with his sister, not when he'd grown tired of her complaining that she wanted to run her own restaurant kitchen. As a professionally trained chef she had secured a position at an Upper East Side Michelin-starred restaurant. And if she did agree to come on board once the hundred-room mansion was restored to its original magnificence she would have the autonomy she'd craved since graduating culinary school. She would supervise her own staff at the family-owned business Taylor had planned to convert into a hotel and venue for weddings and private parties that could accommodate up to three hundred guests. It would take some time before the property would be fully restored, and while Taylor didn't want a firm commitment from Viola he did want her to consider it.

"I know a lot can happen in that time, but right now I have to believe they're willing to get involved."

There was more than a hint of confidence in his pre-
diction.

His brothers Joaquin and Tariq seemed genuinely
interested in becoming involved in the restoration of
Bainbridge House, and Patrick had offered to oversee the financial component. He had worked for their
father as a CPA after graduating college. Then he'd
become involved with a woman whose father and
uncles were winemakers. Patrick subsequently divided his time between working in their father's office and at a Long Island vineyard, and after a few
years decided growing grapes and turning them into
wine was his passion.

"We'll see," Viola replied, her voice skeptical.
"What I don't understand is why did Momma wait
until now to tell us about the abandoned property?"

Taylor knew he had to be truthful with his sister because it would eventually come out that he'd
known what Elise Williamson was prepared to reveal once all of her children were together for the
first time since the passing of her husband of forty-
nine years. That had been the second week in Janu-
ary, and now it was late March and Easter Sunday.

It was a Williamson family tradition for everyone
to get together at Easter. Conrad's death was unexpected because at seventy-four he hadn't exhibited
any health issues. Elise said he'd complained of feeling tired and had gone to bed earlier than usual, and
sometime during the night he'd died from what the
medical examiner documented as natural causes.

From that time until now, Taylor had established a routine of sharing dinner with his mother the first Sunday of the month.

"Mom kind of hinted to me that she had some news that involved all five of us, and if we were amenable it would change our lives," Taylor admitted.

"Did she tell you that Daddy had inherited a huge old house sitting on over three hundred acres in North Jersey?"

Taylor stretched his right arm over the back of Viola's headrest when traffic came to a complete standstill. He'd wanted to leave earlier to get back to Connecticut before ten, but first he had to drop his sister off in Greenwich Village, and with the buildup of holiday traffic he estimated he'd probably make it home sometime around midnight.

"She did tell me a couple of months ago that Dad had left us some property, and he'd talked about restoring it once he retired. He'd gone so far as to file for permits and approval for variances to convert the property from residential to commercial. But we all know that golfing took precedence over everything."

After their father sold his private equity/venture capitalist company he'd hired a golf pro to teach him the game. The only time he wasn't on the green was when it rained or snowed.

"Since Daddy's gone and a developer wanted to buy the property, why wouldn't Mom sell it?"

Again Taylor met Viola's large hazel eyes, and he noticed the dark circles under the brilliant orbs.

He didn't know whether she wasn't getting enough sleep or she was putting in too many hours at the restaurant. "She told me when Dad updated his will he'd wanted her to keep the property in the family."

Viola bit her lip. "I don't want to sound callous, but there's nothing keeping her from not honoring a dead man's wishes."

Taylor removed his arm and ran a hand over cropped coarse hair. "Maybe when you've been married to a man for almost fifty years you might feel an obligation to honor his last wishes."

As soon as the words left his lips he saw a flush suffuse Viola's light brown complexion. Although they were brother and sister, they did not share DNA. In fact, none of the Williamson brothers and sister were biological siblings.

"You're right," she said, apologizing after a pause. "Maybe because you're closer to Momma than any of us, you know her better."

"I'm not any closer than you. I just get to see her more often."

"That's not what Patrick says. He claims you're Momma's favorite."

"I don't know why Patrick would say that when she has treated all of us the same. And if she did have a favorite it would be you because she always said she wanted a daughter."

Viola laughed. "Being the only girl with four brothers definitely has its advantages."

A special bond had developed between Conrad

and Elise Williamson's five foster children, and it had grown even stronger when they all stood together in the courtroom to make their adoption legal. That day was imprinted indelibly in Taylor's memory.

At six, he had been the couple's first foster child. A year later two-year-old Joaquin joined the family. He was nine when fourteen-month-old Viola became his foster sister and the darling of the family. The year he celebrated his tenth birthday eight-year-old Patrick and five-year-old Tariq became his third foster brothers. Elise had joked they would not get another sibling because the farmhouse in Belleville, New Jersey, had six bedrooms and seven baths, and she wanted everyone to have their own bedroom.

For Taylor, not having to share a bedroom or a bed with another child was something that had taken him a while to get used to. That, and having enough food to eat. There were times when he slept and woke that he feared the social worker would knock on the door and take him to another foster home, and when he verbalized this to his foster mother Elise had insisted he call her Mom promised he could live with her as long as he wanted.

Not knowing who his biological father was and losing his mother before he'd celebrated his third birthday and then going to live with his mother's sister, who took him in because it meant more money in her social services check, had emotionally scarred him as a child. As a preschooler he'd grown used to seeing his aunt's belly growing bigger whenever she'd become pregnant with another child, and her drunken binges where she would pass out while he and his cousins had to find whatever they could in the refrigerator to keep from starving.

Taylor's deprivation ended when his first-grade teacher contacted the school's social worker because she suspected he was being neglected. He'd worn the same clothes for a week and appeared undernourished. Child Protective Services became involved and he was placed in foster care. Unlike some children that were shuffled from one foster home to another he was lucky because he had been assigned to the home of Conrad and Elise Williamson. Unable to have children of their own they had decided to become foster parents. He didn't attend regular classes like most kids his age because as a former teacher Elise had decided to homeschool him. In the sprawling farmhouse, she'd turned a space in her library into a classroom, and by the time he was eight he was reading at a seventh-grade level.

"If you're serious about overseeing the restoration, then I know someone that may be able help you," Viola said.

"Who?"

"I have a friend who's an architectural historian, and when I saw the furnishings in the mansion I immediately thought of her. She's currently working at a Madison Avenue art gallery, and she has an uncanny gift for recognizing and authenticating antiques. In other words, she's an expert and a genius in her field."

Taylor knew Viola was right about the antiques in the French-inspired château known as the Bainbridge House. Many were stored on shelves in the mansion's cellar, while others were in ballrooms and bedroom suites. The property was set back off a private road, surrounded by ten-foot stone walls with a massive iron gate. An on-site caretaker had taken up residence in one of the half dozen guesthouses.

"I know I'm going to have everything appraised for insurance purposes," Taylor said.

"And I'm certain Sonja will be able to ascertain what is authentic and what is a reproduction." Reaching into the tote on the floor between her feet, Viola took out her cell phone. "I'm going to call her to ask if she's willing to help you out."

"I don't want to impose on her if she has a job."

"I don't believe it would be an imposition because she works part-time."

Taylor glanced at Viola as she tapped the number and then activated the speaker feature. The phone rang twice before being answered.

"Happy Easter."

"Thank you. Happy Easter to you, too, and your family. I hope I'm not calling at a bad time."

"No, not at all. What's up, Vi?"

"I'm calling because I want to know if you would be willing to appraise some items in a house that has been in my father's family since the 1880s."

"Where is it?"

"It's in north Jersey. I have you on speaker because I'm in the car with my brother who will be responsible for the restoration."

"How many pieces are you talking about?"

"A lot, Sonja. The house sits on three hundred acres and has more than a hundred rooms."

There was a noticeable silence until Sonja's voice filled the interior of the SUV again. "That sounds like quite a project."

Viola shared a smile with Taylor. "It is. Maybe you and Taylor can meet, and then he'll be able explain everything to you."

There came another pause. "Okay. I have to go into the gallery all this week because we're having an exhibition Friday night, but I'm free Saturday and Sunday."

"What if I make a reservation at the restaurant in Taylor's name for you to meet him Saturday night." Taylor nodded when Viola's eyebrows lifted questioningly.

"That sounds good. It isn't often that I get to eat at The Cellar."

Viola smiled. "I guess that settles it. How does seven work for you?"

"It works."

"Good. I'll give my brother your number so if something comes up he'll be able to contact you."

"Saturday at seven," Sonja confirmed.

"Thanks, Sonja."

"No, thank you, Viola. You know how excited I get whenever I'm approached about a new assignment."

"Even though I'll be in the kitchen, I'll make certain to come out and see you." Viola rang off and then turned to smile at Taylor. "That's one thing you can cross off your to-do list."

"I really appreciate that." And he did.

Viola took Taylor's phone off the console and programmed Sonja's number. "I think you're going to like Sonja. And don't get your nose out of joint, because I'm not trying to hook you up with her—she's currently not into dating," Viola said quickly.

Taylor stared straight ahead as traffic began moving again. He'd lost count of the number of times Viola had attempted to set him up with a few of her friends. The year before, he'd read her the riot act, and she finally took the hint that he'd never had a problem asking a woman out. But he hadn't been in a relationship for a while—not since he'd dated an attorney exclusively until she decided to reconcile with her ex-husband.

"She sounds like someone I could get along with."

"You two are like bookends."

"Why would you say that?" Taylor asked Viola.

"Both of you are laser focused on your careers."

Taylor wanted to tell Viola that he'd had to make up for the five years when he'd dropped out of college before deciding to return to complete the courses he needed for his degree. He accelerated as he entered the tunnel and twenty minutes later he maneuvered up to the curb in front of the four-story apartment building along a tree-lined street in the West Village. Viola lived in a two-bedroom apartment in a renovated building with a doorman and rented the extra bedroom to a nurse that worked the night shift at a local hospital.

Viola unbuckled her seat belt, leaned over and kissed Taylor's cheek. "Thanks for the ride."

He patted her short curly hair. "Anytime, kid."

"I'll try and see you when you come in Saturday."

"Don't stress yourself if you can't get out of the kitchen." Taylor had taken the train down from Connecticut and into Manhattan a week after Viola had been hired at the restaurant. He'd wanted to discover why the establishment had earned the prestigious Michelin star and was more than impressed with what he'd ordered. The Cellar opened for dinner Tuesday through Saturday, and reserving a table was highly recommended.

"Just send me a text when you arrive, and whenever I get a break I'll come out to see you."

Taylor knew it was useless to argue with Viola, because once she set her mind to something, she was like a dog with a bone. "Okay." Viola grasped the handles of her tote and opened the passenger-side door. He waited until she walked into the lobby of the building and then programmed the navigation app for the best route to Stamford, Connecticut.

During the drive he thought about how his supervisor would react to his resigning within weeks of getting a promotion. Not only would he leave the firm, but also he had to make plans to relocate from Connecticut to New Jersey. The decision wouldn't be an easy one because he liked his job, but when he had to weigh it against not leaving or undertaking a family project the latter won out. He owed everything that he'd become to Conrad and Elise Williamson and for Taylor it was family above all. He tapped the screen on the dashboard and activated the Bluetooth for his mother's number. She picked up after the first ring.

"I just got a text from Viola that you dropped her off."

Elise was overly protective when it came to Viola. Initially, she'd been apprehensive about her daughter living alone New York City, fearing she would become a crime statistic. "Mom, you're going to have to stop pressuring Viola to check in with you. She's not a child—she's a twenty-eight-year-old woman living and working in the city that is now her home."

"I know, Taylor, but I can't help it. You don't know how many times I've blamed myself for homeschooling all of you. Perhaps if I'd enrolled my children in traditional schools where they were able to interact with other kids or signed you up for sleepaway camp and had other kids for sleepovers, then I wouldn't be so overprotective."

Taylor did not remind his mother that he and his siblings did not have sleepovers because they had one another. "Don't beat up on yourself, Mom. You did a fantastic job raising us. Just try and ease up on Viola. I know you're selling the house, and I'd like you to ask your Realtor to find a rental for me within a ten-mile radius of Bainbridge House." Taylor estimated it would take at least two years for the main house suites and guesthouses to be completely refurbished, and he intended to make one of the guesthouses his permanent residence.

"You don't need a rental because you can live in my condo for as long as you want. I've already furnished it. I plan to live here until closing."

"Do you think you'll be able to sell the house before you leave for your cruise?"

"Hopefully, yes. I have another four months and the Realtor reassures me he will be able find a buyer by that time. If not, then I'll close it up, take the cruise and deal with selling it once I return."

The 5000-square-foot farmhouse built on four acres with an in-ground pool and tennis and basketball courts would be perfect for a large or extended family. It was where Taylor had learned to swim, shoot hoops and play tennis. He and his brothers and sister had not needed a day or sleepaway camp during the summer months when they cooked and played outdoors from sunrise to sunset. The Williamson kids agreed they'd had the best childhood possible. They had also grown up with pets ranging from dogs, cats, birds and fish, plus a family of rabbits that kept multiplying until Elise decided to give them to pet shops.

"Thanks for offering your condo. I recently got a notice for a lease renewal, so the timing is perfect." Before he vacated the apartment he would have to pack up the furnishings and ship them to a New Jersey storage facility.

"You don't have to thank me, Taylor. You know there isn't anything I wouldn't do for my children. When I see you next month I'll give you a set of keys and the remote device for the gate. I'll also put your name on the management list in case you're approached by security. Better yet, the next time you come down I'll take you to see my new home."

Although Elise had dropped hints about Bainbridge House, she had been completely mum when it came to her purchasing the two-bedroom unit in a gated community with amenities that included indoor and outdoor pools, tennis courts, an on-site concierge for laundry, dry cleaning, recreation center, supermarket and coffeeshop. Conrad's death had left Elise a very wealthy widow. He had also established a trust to restore Bainbridge House with the proceeds from the sale of his investment company totaling more than a half billion dollars.

"Okay. I'll talk to you later."

"I love you, Taylor."

"Love you, too, Mom." It didn't matter that she hadn't given birth to him—he couldn't have loved her more even if she had. She was soft-spoken, patient, affectionate and fiercely protective of her children. Elise, aware of the traumas her sons and daughter had experienced before being placed in foster care, made certain all had been in therapy, individually and as a family group. The sessions had allowed them to work through their unresolved issues while at the same time forming and tightening the bond as a family unit. This is not to say Taylor and his siblings didn't have their squabbles, but as they grew older they learned to settle their differences without spewing hateful words with the intent to hurt one another.

Taylor groaned under his breath when he saw the traffic signs indicating delays on the New York State Thruway. Slumping lower in the seat, he turned on the satellite radio, tuning it to a station featuring cool jazz. The melodious sound of a tenor sax filled the interior of the SUV as he recalled the events of the day. He had reunited with Joaquin and Patrick, who'd flown in together from California, and Tariq, who had driven up from Alabama earlier in the week.

Tariq was on spring break from Tuskegee University where he was enrolled in postgraduate courses in veterinary medicine and had planned to spend the time with their mother. Patrick and Joaquin would fly out from Newark International at the end of the week. Patrick had delayed his return to go over the trust their father had set up for the restoration project in which Conrad had named his accountant son the executor.

Elise was ecstatic once Taylor agreed to assume responsibility to restore her late husband's ancestral home to its original magnificence. He planned to focus on the exterior before the interiors. It wasn't only the château that needed work but also the guest cottages, vineyard, orchards, stables, formal gardens, a bridle path, and a nine-hole golf course all of which were in poor condition.

Taylor had been forthcoming with Viola when he told her Elise had dropped hints about inheriting property from her husband she'd wanted to share with her children. She'd finally revealed that not only was Bainbridge House listed in the National Register of Historic Places, but a trust had been established more than seventy years ago to cover property taxes and salaries for future generations of resident caretakers.

Taylor estimated it would take at least two years to completely renovate the house, barns and outbuildings, and hopefully by that time it would be ready to become a successful family enterprise.

Chapter Two

"Do you still want me to pick you up at nine?"

"Yes," Sonja told her cousin, estimating her dinner meeting with Taylor Williamson shouldn't go beyond two hours.

Sonja alighted from the car and made her way down the staircase to the below-the-street dining establishment that had operated once as a speakeasy during Prohibition. This would be her second time eating at The Cellar. The first had been two years ago when Viola was hired as an apprentice chef. The restaurant had just earned a Michelin star, and if it hadn't been for her friend setting up a reservation for her she would've had to wait three weeks for a table. The food, ambiance and professional waitstaff were exceptional.

If Viola hadn't asked her to meet her brother, Sonja knew she would've spent the day sleeping late and watching her favorite movie channel, because she'd just had the week from hell. It had taken more than a month for the gallery owners to decide what they wanted to exhibit after they'd purchased the contents of a home in the Hudson Valley during an estate sale. Their constant bickering had worn on Sonja's fragile nerves, and she'd found herself leaving the gallery several times a day to walk around the block. The indecisiveness ended when Sonja became the mediator and there was consensus to exhibit a limited collection of crystal and silver pieces. They had belonged to the descendants of a Dutch shipping merchant who had amassed a sizeable fortune when New York was still a British colony. His subsequent descendants continued the family passion for purchasing crystal and silver for generations.

The restaurant's solid oaken doors with stained glass insets opened, and she exchanged a smile with the maître d'. The slightly built man wearing all black inclined his head. "Good evening. Welcome to The Cellar."

"Thank you. I have a reservation for seven."

"Your name, miss."

"Martin. However, the reservation is under Taylor Williamson."

The maître d' beckoned to one of the hostesses at the podium. "Please show Ms. Martin to Mr. Williamson's table."

She followed the young woman into the dining room with round tables covered in white tablecloths, with seating for two, four or six. Lit votives, bud vases with fresh flowers, Tiffany-inspired sconces and gaslighted fireplaces created an ambience that was inviting and intimate. She savored the mouth-watering aroma of grilled meats from a tray carried by waiter balanced on one shoulder as he passed her.

The hostess stopped at a table at the same time a tall man rose to his feet. Sonja felt as if someone had caught her by the throat, cutting off her breath, when she recognized the man staring down at her. She had never met any of Viola's brothers so there was no way she would have been able to connect Taylor Williamson with T.E. Wills.

Recovering quickly, Sonja extended her hand and her voice. "Hello, T. E.—Sonja Rios-Martin," she said, introducing herself. He took her hand, cradling it gently in his much larger one.

"It's just Taylor now."

Taylor pulled out a chair, seating her. He lingered over her head and she inhaled the subtle scent of his cologne. Sonja curbed the urge to give him an eye roll when he retook his chair opposite her. T.E. Wills was to men's fashion what Tyson Beckford was to Ralph Lauren's Polo brand. His image had graced the covers of countless magazines while he'd also be-come a celebrity spokesperson for a men's cologne and a popular luxury automobile. Despite his public persona, very little was known about his private life.

It is was if the mystique had enhanced his popularity and marketability.

She met the large dark eyes with her own curious stare. His complexion reminded her of the color of autumn leaves that had turned a shade of brown much like black coffee with a splash of rich cream. To say her friend's brother was a beautiful man was truly an understatement. It was as if Michelangelo had carved David from onyx rather than marble and had been branded the Nubian Prince. Taylor's royal blue suit appeared to have been expressly tailored for his tall, slender physique. He looked and smelled delicious, and she wondered if he was wearing the cologne he'd been paid to endorse.

"Does it bother you if folks call you T.E. Wills?"

Taylor lowered his eyes. "No, because that is my past and that's something I can't erase."

A slight smile parted her lips. Modeling may have been his past, but Taylor still had the ability to elicit gawking. "Viola told me you're a structural engineer."

He gave her a direct stare again as the corners of his mouth lifted in what passed for a half smile. "I am. And she told me you're an architectural historian."

Sonja nodded, smiling. "That I am," she said proudly. "You design and build structures, while I write about the history of architecture, and help to restore and preserve historical buildings."

"What made you decide to become a historian?"

She was preempted from answering as a waiter approached the table. He handed Taylor a binder. "Would you like to order a cocktail before I take your dining selections?"

Taylor accepted the binder containing a listing of wines and liquors. He was glad for the man's interruption because it gave him time to concentrate on something other than his sister's friend. Everything about her screamed sophistication—the shoulder-length dark brown wavy hair framing her round face, barely there makeup highlighting her best features and the pearl studs in her ears that matched the single strand around her long, graceful neck. He'd noticed men staring at her when she'd passed their tables and he was no exception. He didn't know if it was the sensual sway of her hips as she walked, the way the vermilion sheath dress under a matching peplum jacket that hugged her curvy, petite body, or her full lips outlined in the same red shade. But it was her sexy mouth that had garnered his rapt attention. He knew staring at her was impolite, but it had taken all his self-control to lower his eyes.

Taylor glanced at the beverage selection before handing Sonja the binder. "Would you like me to order something for you from the bar?"

A beat passed. "Yes. I'd like a glass of Riesling."

He signaled for the waiter standing a comfortable distance away from the table. He ordered Sonja's Riesling and a merlot for himself. Taylor shifted his attention to Sonja, and he watched her as she studied the menu. He'd arrived at the restaurant earlier than his appointed time because he knew if he couldn't find a parking spot close to The Cellar he would be forced to park in an indoor garage nearly a half mile away.

Taylor always looked forward to coming into Manhattan, and whenever he spent time in the city he chided himself for giving up the apartment in a Brooklyn brownstone to move to Stamford once he'd secured a position with the Connecticut-based engineering and architectural firm. The alternative had been taking the subway to Grand Central Station and then the Metro North to Stamford, and in the end he decided moving would offset having to spend close to ninety minutes, barring delays, each way commuting to and from work.

He'd grown up in Belleville, New Jersey, and it wasn't until he was twelve that his father would occasionally take him into his Manhattan office. He would spend the time reading or staring out the skyscraper's windows at the New York City skyline. Then he'd been too intimidated by the number of yellow taxis and pedestrians crowding streets and sidewalks to leave the office unaccompanied.

After he'd been accepted as an incoming freshman at New York University, he had fallen in love with the city that exposed him to people and neighborhoods he'd seen on television or read about in books and magazines. He hadn't realized how cloistered his life had been up until that time.

"Do you come here often?" he asked Sonja as she studied her menu.

Her head popped up. "No. Whenever I eat out it's usually in my neighborhood."

"And where's that?"

"Inwood."

Taylor smiled. "Have you ever eaten at La Casa Del Mofongo?"

Sonja's smile matched his, bringing his gaze to linger on her straight, white teeth. He'd warned his sister not to attempt to hook him up with any of her gal friends; however, Sonja definitely could have been the exception. Everything about her demeanor radiated poise—an attribute he looked for in a woman he found interesting.

"More times than I can count. My aunt and uncle eat there several times a month." She paused. "So, how are you familiar with La Casa Del Mofongo?"

"I attended college with guys from different New York City neighborhoods, and on weekends we would take the subway uptown and occasionally into Brooklyn and Queens to eat at different restaurants. La Casa Del Mofongo became one of our favorites."

"I try to go on weekdays because it's always very crowded on weekends."

Taylor angled his head. "How long have you lived in Inwood?" Culturally diverse in Upper Manhattan,

Inwood was one of the most affordable neighborhoods in New York City's most expensive boroughs. The few times he'd eaten at the restaurant he'd thoroughly enjoyed the delicious Caribbean-inspired dishes and live Latin music.

"Not long."

When she did not indicate a timeline, Taylor decided to switch the conversation from personal to professional. "How was the showing at your gallery?"

Sonja's expression brightened. "It was incredibly successful. We managed to sell everything on display."

"What did you exhibit?"

"Silver and crystal pieces dating from 1625 to 1710."

"Is it difficult for you to identify pieces of different styles and periods?" Taylor asked.

Sonja gave him a steady stare. "Not really. For example Derby porcelain was mostly unmarked until circa 1780. After that time to present day there are nearly thirty marks. However, some early pieces were marked only by a model number."

Taylor angled his head, his eyes meeting Sonja's. "My family owns a late-nineteenth-century mansion that was abandoned in the 1960s when the last Bainbridge died at the age of ninety-four. My father was the last surviving direct descendant of the original owner. He inherited the property and had planned to restore it once he retired, but never got around to it."

"Vi sent me a text telling me your father had died, but I was in Europe and couldn't get a flight back to the States in time to attend the memorial service."

"Everything was done very quickly," Taylor explained. "My father had instructed my mother that he wanted to be cremated if he died before she did. He used to tease Mom that he would come back and haunt her if she had a wake where folks came and stared at him in a casket. However, she felt it was only right to host a memorial service for his friends and former employees shortly after following his passing."

A slight smile played at the corners of Sonja's mouth. "My dad is the complete opposite of yours. He already has a plot at Arlington National Cemetery with instructions that he wants to be buried with full military honors."

"Your father is in the military?"

"Was," Sonja corrected, smiling. "He's retired, and he and my mom live in a lakefront house in the Adirondack Mountains, where he spends most of his time boating and fishing. After thirty years of moving from base to base he claims it feels good to be in one place for more than a couple of years."

"Did you grow up a military brat?"

She nodded. "Yes. In fact, I was born in a hospital near Fort Campbell. At first I really didn't like moving so much when I'd just made friends with other kids on the base, but as I got older and we were transferred abroad a different world opened for me. My mother, who taught romance languages, would take my brother and me on holiday to Spain, Portugal, France and Italy, where we toured museums and medieval cities and soaked up the local culture. Keith, who is ten years older than me, hated it. He claimed he didn't see the sense in staring at statues and old paintings, and eventually stayed on the base with my father. Whenever we toured a medieval church, art gallery or museum I felt as if I'd been transported back in time. I was sixteen when I told my parents I wanted to study art history." Sonja held up a hand when Taylor opened his mouth. "And before you ask about my brother. He's followed in my father's footsteps and plans to become a lifer. We never know where he is because he's Special Forces and comes and goes like a specter. My sister-in-law says she's in a state of constant anxiety until he walks through the door after being away for weeks and sometimes months."

"It takes a special spouse to be married to an active duty soldier."

Sonja's eyebrows lifted slightly when Taylor said spouse rather than wife. Unknowingly, he had gone up exponentially on her approval scale. She'd married a man who had assigned specific gender roles for men and women, and it wasn't until she'd had enough years of being her husband's *little wife* that she finally filed for divorce.

"I agree. But now that she's the mother of twin boys, she has a welcome distraction."

A wide grin spread across Taylor's face. "So, you're an auntie."

"I prefer Titi Sonja to auntie."

"Should I assume you speak Spanish?"

She nodded again. "You assume right. I speak Spanish, Portuguese and Italian, and understand French, although I'm a little rusty when it comes to speaking it."

Taylor stared at something over her head. "I'm somewhat deficient when it comes to foreign languages." His gaze swung back to her. "My mother, who is fluent in French, taught all her children the language, but for me it did not come as easily as math and science. I managed to learn enough to read a French-language newspaper, but having a conversation was and still is definitely out of the question."

"If you don't speak it, then you'll lose the facility to have a conversation. Maybe languages came easy for me because my mother is Puerto Rican and my *abuela* insisted on speaking only Spanish in the home to her son and daughter. Mami said her mother always tuned the radio and television to Spanish-language stations."

Taylor gave Sonja a steady stare. "How did she learn English?"

"She grew up in West Harlem, but when she entered school for the first time she was fully bilingual. Years later she married her neighbor's brother."

"So, that's why you're Rios-Martin?"

Sonja laughed softly. "Yes. Mami is an avid

feminist and claimed she didn't want to give up her maiden name when she married, so she opted to hyphenate it."

"What would happen if you married?" Taylor asked. "Would you be Rios-Martin while adding your husband's last name?"

"I still would be Rios-Martin." Her refusal to change her name had become a source of contention between Sonja and her ex-husband. She may have given in to a lot of his demands, but she had remained adamant about not changing her name.

"Good for you. There's no reason you should give up your identity because of marriage. I know several career women who have opted to keep their maiden name."

Sonja noticed he'd said career women. Would he feel the same if she did not have a career? On the other hand, that was not her concern. Her association with Taylor, if she did help with the restoration, would be strictly business. She was now thirty-four and no longer the wide-eyed impressionable graduate student that had fallen under the mesmerizing spell of her worldly professor. Her mantra had become *once burned, twice shy*. And at this time in her life, her focus was on her career and not a relationship with a man.

"There were times when I felt jealous of Vi," Sonja said, hoping to divert the conversation away from the subject of marriage.

"Why?" Taylor asked.

"It was when she told me she grew up with four brothers. Mine was so much older than me. By the time I'd entered the first grade he was already a teenager, so I always felt like an only child."

"That's because we spoiled her. Every once in a while we let her win when we played board games. However, she was a natural when it came to swimming. Even though I was older and stronger than Viola, I rarely ever beat her swimming laps."

"It sounds as if you had a lot of fun growing up."

"I know I speak for my brothers and sister in saying we had the best childhood any kid could ask for. Did she tell you we were homeschooled?"

"Yes," Sonja confirmed. "I've tried imagining what it would be like to be homeschooled and having my mother as my teacher. She probably would've been harder on me than those in a traditional school setting. My teachers told her I could've been an exceptional student if I'd applied myself. For me it wasn't about making the honor roll but passing my courses. However, I did excel in languages, art and history."

"Even if you hadn't lived abroad, do you think you would've become an architectural historian?" Taylor asked.

"I would've studied art even if we'd stayed in the States."

"Do you think you would ever live abroad?" Taylor asked yet another question.

The seconds ticked while Sonja thought about

Taylor's question. There was a time when she'd wanted to leave the country of her birth and live in Italy to complete her graduate studies. Her personal life had been in shambles and she was experiencing an emotional crisis. She'd moved into her parents' retirement home, living there while her father awaited approval for his honorable discharge as a lieutenant colonel. It was her mother who had urged her to stay in the States and deal with her dilemma, because running away would not resolve her problem. Maria Rios-Martin had become her staunchest ally and protector as she went through a contentious divorce and was finally able to exorcise the man that sought to control her life.

"There was a time when I'd considered it," she said truthfully. "Why do you ask?"

Taylor gave her a long, penetrating stare. "I only ask because if you decide to become involved in the restoration project, then I'd like a commitment of at least a year, with an option renewal for an additional year."

"You sound very confident that I will accept the commission."

"I did say *if*. I would never assume anything, Sonja. Especially since you do have a job."

Although Sonja felt properly chastised, she tried to conceal it behind an impassive expression. "I won't be able to commit to anything until I see what I'll be responsible for."

"That's understandable," he countered quickly.

"Viola mentioned the house has more than one hundred rooms."

Taylor nodded. "Bainbridge House was built in 1883 and is listed on the National Register of Historic Places. The main house is designed like a French château with turreted towers and steep-pitched roofs. The outbuildings are tiled-roof cottages."

"Does it really sit on three hundred acres?"

"Yes. It's closer to three hundred fifty acres with overgrown gardens, neglected orchards, a vineyard, a nine-hole golf course and a bridle path. I have copies of blueprints for the house and the grounds. *If* you accept the commission, then I'll make copies for you."

Sonja's smile was dazzling. "You got me when you said French château. When can I see it?"

"Are you free tomorrow?"

"Yes."

"While you two were making plans to get together I decided to bring you your wine. I waylaid your waiter and decided to surprise you."

Sonja's head popped up at the same time as Taylor's. Viola stood over the table holding a tray with their beverage selections and a shot glass filled with an amber liquid. She was wearing chef's white, and her curly hair was concealed under a white bandanna.

Taylor was so entranced with his dining partner that he hadn't detected his sister's presence. Pushing back his chair, he stood and kissed her forehead. "Are you doing double duty as chef and server?" he teased.

Viola placed the wineglasses on the table and then picked up the shot glass. "No. I told Joseph to let me know when you were here and that gave me the excuse to leave the kitchen for a few minutes."

It wasn't often Taylor got to see Viola in what she called her *zone*: the restaurant. As a young girl she'd been drawn to cooking and the kitchen had become her favorite room in the farmhouse. "You've got a full house tonight."

"We're always busy on weekends. I probably won't get out of here until well after midnight. We seat our last customers at ten. I just wanted to say hello." She raised her glass, waiting for Taylor and Sonja to follow suit. Viola touched each wineglass with her own. "Here's to friends and family."

"Friends and family," Sonja and Taylor said in unison.

Viola tossed back her drink while her brother and her friend sipped their wine. She set the glass on the tray. "Sonja, we'll talk later."

Taylor waited until Viola had left before returning his attention to Sonja. "How long have you and Viola been friends?"

"We met a couple of summers ago at a Washington Square street fair. I'd overheard her haggling with a vendor selling pen-and-ink sketches. He cursed at me when I accused him of inflating his prices and that I knew an artist selling similar sketches that weren't overpriced. I told Sonja about a friend who owned a little art store near the South Street Seaport, and said if she was serious about pen-and-ink drawings then I would put in a good word for her. She asked me if I would go with her because she needed artwork to decorate her apartment's entryway. We went to the store and I helped her select what she liked. Afterward, we went to eat and wound up talking for hours. It was the beginning of what has become a wonderful friendship."

Taylor recalled the collage of framed pen-and-ink drawings lining the walls in his sister's apartment and had complimented her on her choice of artwork. "I'm glad you could help her out. By the way, there's an extensive collection of paintings at Bainbridge House. I have no idea what they are worth."

"That's why people hire experts. I'm really looking forward to seeing everything."

He heard confidence and not bravado in Sonja's pronouncement. "I don't think I'd have the patience to go through duplicate sets of china, silver, crystal, paintings and other knickknacks wealthy folks felt they needed to fill up every inch of space in a house. I wasn't aware my father owned the house until a week ago. My mother kept dropping hints after the reading of his will that he'd left her some property he wanted her to give to their kids, but it wasn't until I was able to see what she'd been talking about that I was completely overwhelmed with the enormity of it. Talk about sensory overload."

"That's because during the Gilded Age those with a higher concentration of wealth became more conspicuous. Art is divided into periods and the Bainbridge House falls between the Gilded Age and the Progressive Era in the 1890s." She paused. "What do you plan to do with it once it's fully restored?"

"I want to operate it as a hotel and wedding venue."

Sonja flashed a bright smile. "Long Island has the Oheka Castle, North Carolina the Biltmore House, and now New Jersey's Bainbridge House will once again become a premier estate in America."

Taylor's smile matched hers. "I like the sound of that. I'd like to pick you up around ten tomorrow morning. If that's not too early."

"It's not too early."

"I recommend you wear boots because it rained earlier this morning and the ground may still be a little muddy." When Sonja nodded, he continued, "Where should I pick you up?"

"I'll be in front of La Casa Del Mofongo."

All conversation about the Bainbridge House ended with the waiter's approach to request their dining selections. Sonja ordered a mixed-green salad with lardoons and vinaigrette, and an entrée of ricotta gnocchi with white truffle oil, while Taylor selected salad lyonnaise, veal Milanese and marinated asparagus spears.

The seconds ticked while Sonja took another sip

of wine, peering at him over the rim of the glass. "I like Vi's toast to friends and family."

Taylor nodded. "I like it, too." Not only did he want them to become friends, he also wanted to hire her as the architectural historian for the restoration project.

"I'd like you to answer one question for me."

He sobered. "What's that?"

"How much do you know about your father's ancestors?"

"Not much," he answered truthfully. "Dad was raised by an unmarried aunt after his parents were killed in a boating accident. He was twelve at the time, and he claimed his aunt resented having to take care of him because she never wanted children. He left home to attend college and never moved back. His parents had set up a trust fund for him, which he was able to control when he'd turned twenty-one."

"Once I research the history of Bainbridge House, I will let you know what I uncover on your family."

It was obvious Sonja was unaware that he and Viola had been adopted; otherwise, she would not have assumed that they'd claimed Bainbridge blood. Years ago, following their legal adoption, the Williamson siblings had pledged not to advertise that they did not share DNA and consciously neglected to reveal they were adopted. It did not matter they were a mixed-race family. They were brothers and sister, and their parents were Conrad and Elise Williamson.

Taylor had had no knowledge of Bainbridge House or of the family for which it had been named until

Easter Sunday, when Elise revealed that the property willed her by her late husband now belonged to her children for them to share equally. Bainbridge House and the land on which it sat made them instant multimillionaires. Taylor and the others agreed it wasn't about money but carrying out the wishes of the man who had provided them with love, protection and selfless support in helping them realize their dreams. Conrad was a businessman, but he had taken on the role of father seriously. Although he'd put in long hours at his office, he always made certain to spend weekends with his family.

"Do you have a timeline to complete the restoration?" Sonja asked.

"I'm projecting at least two years. I have a brother who is an architectural landscaper. He currently has commissions to design the grounds of several A-list actors' properties, but once he fulfills his obligations he'll be able to focus on the gardens at Bainbridge House."

Sonja's lips parted in a smile. "Are you saying it's going to be a family affair?"

"Yes." It was going to become a family affair. "Patrick promised his fiancée he would join her family's winemaking business once they are married. He's a CPA and will financially monitor every phase of the restoration remotely."

Dinner became a leisurely affair as Taylor listened to Sonja talk about the cities and countries she'd lived in and visited during her childhood. He was enchanted with her exuberance when she recalled the first time she saw the Mona Lisa and art masterpieces from the Renaissance. She admitted she'd been so enthralled with the Eternal City that more than once she'd considered moving to Rome to live. Their time together ended all too soon for Taylor when Sonja declined coffee and dessert saying she had to leave because someone was picking her up. He settled the bill, leaving a generous tip, and escorted her up to the street level.

"I see my ride across the street," Sonja said. "I'll see you tomorrow at ten."

"Okay. Get home safely."

He watched her walk across the street and get into the passenger seat of a late-model sedan. Viola said she wasn't into dating, but that did not mean the man sitting behind the wheel was someone his sister did not know about. Although he'd found himself attracted to Sonja, Taylor knew nothing would come of it. It was to be business and nothing but business between them. Waiting until the car with Sonja pulled away from the curb, he turned on his heel and walked the three blocks to where he'd parked his SUV.

What he did not want to admit to himself was that he'd spent a most pleasurable couple of hours with a woman who had unknowingly bewitched him with her beauty, poise and intelligence, and he looked forward to spending countless more hours with her if and when she signed on to the restoration project.

Chapter Three

Sonja walked into the kitchen in her aunt and uncle's apartment to brew a cup of coffee and was surprised to find both sitting at the table. They usually attended early-morning church service followed by brunch at one of their favorite neighborhood restaurants before returning home to watch either a sporting event or movie. In a month, her uncle would join a group of retired police and firefighters for Sunday afternoon baseball games in Central Park.

The table was littered with travel brochures, and her aunt was busy scrolling through travel sites on her laptop. Her uncle was a recent NYPD retired sergeant, while her aunt had retired the year before as an underwriter for a major insurance company.

"Have you guys finally decided where you want to go to celebrate your twenty-fifth wedding anniversary?" she asked as she removed a coffee pod from the carousel and popped it into the single-serve coffeemaker.

Her mother's brother shifted slightly on his chair, peering at her over a pair of reading glasses. "I still want to go to Alaska, while your *titi* keeps going on about Hawaii."

Opening the refrigerator, Sonja took out a container of creamer. "Why don't you compromise? You're going to be on the West Coast. You can spend a couple of weeks in Hawaii, and once you return to the mainland you can take a cruise up to Alaska. That way it's a win-win for you both."

Nelson Rios blew his niece an air kiss, then reached for his wife's hand. "What do you say, Mama? First Hawaii and then Alaska?"

Yolanda glared at Nelson. "Now, why didn't we think of that?"

Sonja winked at her aunt. She'd just turned sixty yet appeared at least ten years younger. There was just a sprinkling of gray in the neatly braided twists styled in a ponytail, while her nut-brown face was wrinkle-free which she attributed to good genes.

Sonja always felt Yolanda Clark was the perfect partner for her uncle after he lost his first wife during a hit-and-run, leaving him a grief-stricken widower and single father of an eight-year-old son. Nelson and Yolanda had dated off and on for more than a year before he'd asked her to move in with him. She refused, reminding him it would send the wrong signal to his son. Nelson had confessed to Sonja that marrying Yolanda was one of the best decisions he'd ever made.

She'd filled the void and had become a wonderful mother for Jaime.

Her mother and uncle were born with red hair, a recessive hair color they'd inherited from their great-grandmother. Maria and Nelson were referred to respectively as Red and Rusty by neighborhood kids, and the nickname had followed Nelson through adulthood. Many of his colleagues on the police force still called him Rusty although the red strands had faded to a shimmering silver.

It was Yolanda who had urged Sonja to move into their spare bedroom six years ago after Jaime married his high school sweetheart. Her offer had come at the right time: she'd left her husband, enrolled at the Pratt Institute to concentrate on completing her degree, while commuting between New York and Boston to file and eventually finalize her divorce. Although she'd volunteered a few times to pay them rent for living in the apartment with panoramic views of the Hudson River and the New Jersey Palisades, her aunt and uncle rejected her offer with the recommendation she save her money to eventually purchase a house or condo.

Their suggestion had made her aware that she'd gone from living with her parents to sharing a dorm

room with another college student and then with the
man who would become her husband. After she left
Hugh, Sonja had moved into her parents' retirement
home, wallowing in a morass of self-pity until she
shook off her lethargy with the intent of completing
her education. She'd applied and was accepted into
the Pratt Institute with the promise she would live in
Manhattan with her aunt and uncle until she graduated and secured employment.

She'd earned her degree and been hired to work
in the Madison Avenue art gallery, yet still did not
live alone. Sonja told Viola that she envied her because she'd grown up with four brothers, but what
she didn't say to her friend that she was jealous of
her independence. Viola had left her parents' home
to attend culinary school, and rather than return to
New Jersey she'd rented an apartment in the West
Village. Viola's tenure had been short-lived when
working for a few hotels, and then she found her
niche at The Cellar. Sonja's best friend, six years her
junior, had unknowingly become her role model for
what it meant to be an independent woman.

She cradled the mug with both hands. The weekend was her time to sleep in. It was only on a rare
occasion she got out of bed before noon. And when
she did it was to brush her teeth and take a leisurely
bath. Sweats were her favored attire, and after preparing something to eat or heating up leftovers, Sonja
left the apartment to visit the local nail salon for her
weekly mani-pedi. She always called the owner mid-

week to set up the appointment in order not to sit and wait for her favorite technician.

"I have to meet someone for a possible commission."

Yolanda powered down the laptop. "What kind of commission?"

"Cataloguing the contents of a New Jersey mansion."

"Where in New Jersey?" Nelson questioned.

"Somewhere in the northern part of the state. I'll let you know where once I get back."

"Are you going to accept it?" Yolanda asked.

"I don't know."

And Sonja *didn't* know. It was not as if she wasn't employed. The gallery owners paid her well, covered her health insurance and gave her a percentage of the final sale showings. If she did agree to assist Taylor Williamson with his restoration of Bainbridge House, it would have to be financially beneficial for her to leave the gallery.

"If you do accept it, you know you'll have to quit your position at the gallery," Nelson said.

"Before I make any decision I'll have to weigh my options."

Her options would include travel time, salary and benefits. Taylor had also mentioned he needed a one- and maybe even a two-year commitment from her. Yes, she thought. She had to weigh and examine all her options, because if she did assist in restoring Bainbridge House to its original magnificence, then she could add it to her résumé to secure similar commissions.

Sonja had to constantly remind herself that she wasn't married, didn't have children, and therefore she was free to come and go by her leave. She would celebrate her thirty-fifth birthday in November and decided it was time for her to map out what she wanted for the next decade. Living independently topped the list.

She finished her coffee, rinsed the mug and placed it on the top rack in the dishwasher. "I'm going to head out now because I have to meet someone at ten." Sonja estimated it would take her less than fifteen minutes to walk to 207th Street.

She had taken Taylor's recommendation to select footwear other than her favored ballet flats, which she wore to work, or running shoes when strolling around Inwood or Washington Heights. What she truly loved about living in Inwood was she could visit The Cloisters, a medieval-style museum devoted to medieval art and culture. She'd spend hours there viewing paintings and tapestries without having to travel to Europe.

Sonja pushed her sock-covered feet into a pair of well-worn leather boots, tied them and then slipped into a waist-length down-filled jacket. In keeping with the unpredictable fluctuating New York City weather, the unseasonably warm early spring temperatures had been replaced by a chill hovering just

above freezing. After picking up her cross-body bag
and camera case, she walked out of the apartment.

Taylor double-parked in front of the restaurant,
drumming impatient fingers on the steering wheel
while taking furtive glances in the rearview mirror
for a passing police cruiser. Sonja had asked him to
pick her up outside La Casa Del Mofongo when it
probably would've been easier to park near her apartment building.

*I'm not trying to hook you up with her—she's
currently not into dating.* Viola's pronouncement
came rushing back in vivid clarity. Had she meant
Sonja wasn't dating anyone because she was already
in a relationship? And was the man that had picked
her up outside The Cellar her boyfriend? Had she
wanted to avoid having to explain that she'd shared
dinner with another man?

Although he'd found Sonja attractive he knew
nothing would come from it even if she was unencumbered. She was his sister's friend as well as a
possible future employee, and Taylor did not believe
in mixing business with pleasure. He'd witnessed
firsthand how office romances imploded after a vol-
atile breakup.

After he'd told his family that he would oversee
the restoration project, it had taken Taylor five days
to compose his letter of resignation. Viola was right
when she'd reminded him that he'd recently been
promoted—something he'd wanted for more than

two years. Based on the recommendations of several of his college professors, he had been hired by a major Connecticut-based engineering and architectural company, and it had taken a number of large projects and five years before he was rewarded with a promotion and more responsibility.

He'd planned to stay on until the end of the month, and then reversed his decision. He sent a memo to the director of HR that he was leaving his position at the end of the workday and was utilizing more than three weeks of accrued vacation time to offset the mandated two-week resignation rule.

Taylor was now free to concentrate solely on his family's property.

Patrick had emailed him, requesting estimates for restoring and updating the main house and outbuildings, stables, barn, gardens and orchards, bridle path, golf course, and vineyard. Taylor had emptied one trunk, and it had taken an hour of sorting through personal correspondence, bills of lading and other paperwork before locating revised blueprints and surveys. It was then he discovered that Charles Garland Bainbridge had spent ten million dollars in 1883 to build the castle, and once the property was fully restored it would be worth more than one hundred and fifty million. Taylor had replied to Patrick's email with a promise to give him tentative numbers before the end of the month.

Patrick's email was a reminder that he had to interview and hire employees to begin work on the main house. Time was not of the essence to restore the stables because Tariq had another two years to complete his graduate studies and fulfill his obligation as one of the vets at a Kentucky horse farm. Joaquin also had professional obligations that would not free him up for more than a year. Taylor had decided not to put any pressure on Viola to leave The Cellar to become executive chef for Bainbridge House, or for Patrick to oversee Bainbridge Cellars. If they decided not to come around, then he would hire an experienced chef and vintner.

It was 9:50 a.m. when Taylor spied Sonja, wearing sunglasses. Jeans, pullover sweater, boots and jacket had replaced the body-hugging ensemble and sexy heels she'd worn the night before. And with her approach he noticed her bare face and hair styled in a ponytail. Yesterday she was the sophisticate, and today she could pass for a college coed. He exited the vehicle and opened the passenger-side door.

"Good morning."

Sonja smiled up at Taylor, who was towering over her. Without her four-inch heels, his height put her at disadvantage. She stood five-four in bare feet, and she estimated he was at least a foot taller.

"Good morning. Have you been waiting long?"

"Not too long. I give myself extra time when driving down, anticipating traffic delays on the Thruway."

Sonja did not have time to react when Taylor's

hands circled her waist, lifting her effortlessly and settling her on the leather seat of the late-model Infiniti QX80. She peered over her shoulder at the three rows of seating before fastening her seat belt. "Your car is gorgeous." She pretended interest in the SUV rather than Taylor Williamson. Fortunately for her, he wasn't able to see her lustful stare behind the lenses of the dark glasses. He was wearing the same cologne, but had exchanged the tailored suit for black jeans, an off-white cotton pullover and well-worn work boots. Dressed up or down, he had the ability to turn heads.

Taylor smiled as he slipped behind the wheel. "Thank you."

"It smells new."

"I bought it as a birthday gift to myself."

"When was your birthday?"

"November first."

Sonja went completely still. "You're kidding?"

Taylor checked his mirrors and then pulled out into traffic. "No. Why?"

"Because my birthday is November second."

Throwing back his head, Taylor laughed loudly. "What are the odds that we would almost share a birthday?"

She stared out the windshield. "What would be even more weird was if we were born during the same year."

"I'll be thirty-six in November."

"You have me by a year," Sonja admitted. "I'll be thirty-five."

"So, I'm a day and a year older than you." Taylor paused. "I'm curious to know if we like the same things."

"If you believe in astrology then we probably do."

"There's only one way to find out," he said cryptically.

Sonja turned to look at Taylor as he stopped for a red light and met his eyes. "How?"

"There's a pad and pen in the glove box. I'm going to mention certain categories, and you write down your favorite. Then you can give me your choices, and I'll let you know if I agree or disagree."

If Taylor was curious about her likes and dislikes, then she was equally curious about his. She'd told her aunt and uncle that she had to think about whether she was willing to leave the gallery, but during the walk from the apartment building to the restaurant to meet Taylor she had made her decision to accept his offer. After earning her MFA, she'd worked temporary jobs as a museum docent and a substitute art history teacher for an Upper West Side prep school. And when her tenure ended, she was left looking for future employment. She had discovered her current position when she saw a help-wanted sign in the window. She contacted the owners of the gallery and was hired on the spot when she was able to correctly identify every item on display. Now, after nearly two years, it was time for a change.

She retrieved the pad and pen. "I'm ready, Taylor."

"What genre of music do you like?"

Sonja jotted down her choice. The list grew with each interest. "Let's see if we're alike or polar opposites. We'll begin with music. I picked hip-hop and R & B."

"Cool jazz."

She put an *X* next to her choice. "Sports."

"Baseball."

"That's our first match," Sonja said, smiling. "How about books?"

"Legal thrillers."

"Romance or art," she countered. "But I have read John Grisham."

"Then, that should be a half match," Taylor argued quietly.

"Have you ever read a romance novel?"

"Yes. Viola is addicted to them, and one day I read one to see what the allure is. I must admit I enjoyed the book because the writer didn't treat the hero like a jerk. In fact, I really liked him, while I was pissed off that the heroine made him jump through hoops before she admitted she wanted to marry him."

"That's the genre, Taylor. It's boy meets girl, boy loses girl, and then boy finds girl and they live happily ever after."

"But all of the novels are the same."

"That's where you're wrong," Sonja countered. "The theme is the same because it's a genre, but the plots vary and the protagonists are different."

Taylor tapped the navigation screen displaying the programmed route. "Like the movies on the Hallmark Channel?"

She gave him an incredulous look. "For someone who is into legal thrillers, you know an awful lot about romance novels and the Hallmark Channel."

"That's because I'm the only one Viola could convince to sit and watch them with her. My brothers always found something to do whenever she asked them to join her."

"So, you're the good brother," she drawled.

Taylor smiled. "No. Currently, I'm the one living closest to her. Two of my brothers live in California and the other one is in Kentucky. Whenever I drive down to see my mother, I try and stop by Viola's apartment to hang out with her for a few hours, and her television is always tuned to the Hallmark Channel. What I don't understand is why they show Christmas-themed movies during the summer."

Sonja had no intention of getting into an exchange with Taylor about the channel that had become one of her favorites. "They feature them because viewers love Christmas anytime of the year," she said with a hint of finality.

"I'd like you to answer one question for me before we go to the next category."

"What's that?"

"Why do you read romance novels?"

The seconds ticked. "Well, for me it's the predictability. I know it's going to end happily for the hero and heroine."

"But it's fantasy, Sonja."

"It's not fantasy, Taylor, but escapism. For a few hours I'm able to escape into a place where two people will overcome the obstacles and conflicts threatening their happiness."

"So, it's not that you're living vicariously through the characters?"

"Not at all," she protested. "Even though I'm not married or in a relationship, that in no way translates into my identifying with fictional characters." She didn't see the smile tilting the corners of Taylor's mouth at the same time she glanced at the notations on the pad. "The next one on the list is color."

"I'm partial to blues and grays."

"That doesn't get a check because I prefer earth tones. What about art?" she asked.

"African masks. I have a collection of masks and paintings with masks."

A gasp of shock slipped past Sonja's lips. "That gets a double check. I've just begun collecting them. When I was in Venice earlier this year I bought one from an African street vendor to add to those worn at carnival. Where did you get your masks?"

"One of my former coworkers has a brother in Nigeria who is a sculptor, and I have bought a number of his pieces."

"I'd love to see your collection."

"Right now they're packed away, but perhaps one

of these days you'll get to see them. What's next?" Taylor asked.

"Favorite foods. I like Caribbean and Southern."

Taylor chuckled. "Again a double check."

"Favorite time of the year."

"Fall and winter."

Sonja angled her head. "That gets a half check because I like the change of seasons."

"Okay. I'll accept that. What's next?"

"Photography."

"Black and white," Taylor said.

"That's another check," Sonja confirmed.

"Favorite time of the day?"

"Late night."

"Bingo," Sonja drawled. She counted the number of checks. "It looks as if we are more compatible than not."

"That's good to know."

"And I agree, if we're going to be working together."

Taylor's fingers tightened on the steering wheel. He didn't know what had transpired in Sonja's life in less than twenty-four hours for her to hint about becoming a part of the restoration team he'd hoped to establish over the coming months. He'd also wanted to pump his fist in triumph when she'd revealed she wasn't married or in a relationship. He did not want to have to deal with a jealous or controlling husband or boyfriend.

"There's also something else we have in common."

"What's that?" Sonja asked.

"I noticed you brought a camera, and I also have one in the cargo area. There's so much to see that I know I won't be able to recall it all."

Sonja pressed her head against the headrest. "I've thought about what you've told me about Bainbridge House and I'm willing to accept your offer based on salary, benefits and perks."

Taylor had informed Patrick that he would assume the responsibility to establishing salaries based on an applicant's education, licensing and certification. The total restoration budget would support Taylor hiring the best tradespeople in the region.

"We'll discuss salary and bennies later. Do you have a valid driver's license?"

"Yes. Why?"

"I am willing to provide you with a leased car and put you up in a nearby hotel to cut down on the time you'd have to commute from Inwood to an area north of the Delaware Water Gap."

With wide eyes, Sonja gave him a lengthy look. "It's that far?"

"Yes. Bainbridge House was built close to the Dryden Kuser Natural Area known as the highest point in New Jersey."

"It sounds as if it's in the boonies."

"Not quite. There are a lot of small Jersey towns

in the area, and New York's Port Jervis is a short drive away."

"How long will take it us to drive from Inwood to Bainbridge House?"

"At least ninety minutes, barring traffic delays."

Sonja shook her head. "There's no way I want to spend three hours a day driving to and from work." She paused. "What about you, Taylor? Do you plan to commute from Connecticut?"

"No. I've already made plans to live in my mother's Sparta condo. It's about an hour's drive so that's manageable for me."

"What about your place in Stamford?"

"I'm not renewing my lease. I've arranged for a moving company to pack up everything and take it to a New Jersey storage facility."

"It appears you have all of your ducks in a row."

"I have to because I don't like surprises or chaos."

"Are you warning me that you're going to be a harsh taskmaster?"

A silence filled the vehicle for several seconds. "No. I don't yell or threaten, Sonja, and on a project, any foreman who does that will be terminated on the spot. As a new hire with my former employer I had a supervisor who was verbally abusive to everyone, and I swore once I was promoted to a supervisory position I'd never treat adults like recalcitrant children. The overall morale was so low and the construction site so toxic we'd talked about walking out en masse and quitting. It ended when word got back to a VP and the supervisor was fired. I was promoted as an assistant construction site supervisor. Unfortunately, my promotion came only a few months before my mother revealed she wanted us to restore the property, and it didn't go over well with some of my coworkers."

"They know you, Taylor, and are probably apprehensive as to who they would eventually get to replace you."

"You're probably right, but I can't dwell on it because it's my past."

Like your modeling career, Sonja mused. She marveled that it was so easy for him to dismiss his past while she was still struggling to deal with the events in her failed marriage. They were traumatic enough for her to reject any man who expressed an interest in her—and that included dating.

"Your position will be vastly different from the other workers."

She blinked slowly. "Why would you say that?"

"Because you'll be autonomous. You will be responsible for appraising every item in the mansion while deciding which architectural features should be repaired or replaced."

"I hope you're patient, because that means I'll have to go through every room in the house and give you a report."

"That's not going to pose a problem, Sonja. I've projected up to two years to restore the interior and exterior of the main house. I'd like to start work on the exterior before it gets too cold."

For the first time since she'd answered Viola's call, Sonja experienced an excitement that made her look forward to beginning a new artistic venture. Taylor unknowingly would assist her in becoming more independent once she moved to a hotel as he'd promised. She didn't have a problem sharing the apartment with her aunt and uncle, but at her age she should've been living alone. She'd dreamed of decorating her place and occasionally hosting little get-togethers for her friends, coworkers and family members. Hopefully, after she completed her commission to restore Bainbridge House, she would be able to concentrate on moving into a condo or co-operative.

She settled back against the leather seat and watched the passing landscape as Taylor followed the road signs leading to the Governor Mario Cuomo Bridge. It would be her first time crossing the new twin cable-stayed bridge spanning the Hudson River between Tarrytown and Nyack.

Living temporarily in a hotel and having a car at her disposal was a pleasantly unexpected perk.

"Cool jazz or R&B?"

Sonja knew Taylor was asking what she wanted to listen to. "Cool jazz."

He winked at her when she gave him a wide grin. "We'll listen to R&B on the return ride."

"Thank you, Taylor."

He shook his head. "I should be the one thanking you. You're going to make my job easier because I don't have to search for an appraiser. We have a tentative estimate that once the property is fully restored it will be worth one hundred-fifty million. But that doesn't consider the contents. You will be responsible for authenticating the value of silver, crystal, china, paintings and furnishings."

"It's going to take time to go through everything, but I promise to do my best to make Bainbridge House a showplace for the twenty-first century and beyond."

Chapter Four

Sonja hadn't realized she was holding her breath until she felt constriction in her chest forcing her to exhale. She was a sightseer, staring out the passenger-side window at the passing towns named McAfee, Sussex and Quarryville. She'd become more alert once Taylor maneuvered off the main road and onto a private one. A fading sign indicating the number of feet to Bainbridge House came into view as Taylor slowed and maneuvered into the hidden driveway. Age-old trees lining a cobblestone roadway were just beginning to display their spring yield, and she tried to imagine what they would look like during the height of summer.

Within minutes of hanging up after Viola's phone

call, Sonja had wondered about how the Williamsons were connected to the historical property. Were Viola's ancestors free people of color who had made a fortune before or following the Civil War and had purchased three hundred acres on which to build their mansion? She did not want to think of another possible scenario where a wealthy white man had fathered a child of color and had left him the property in his will. Sonja knew the questions would plague her until she was able to begin an intensive search on the Bainbridge family.

Taylor drove through a massive open iron gate and Sonja felt as she'd been transported back to a time in Europe where châteaus were country retreats for royals and nobility. A gasp escaped her when she got her first glimpse of Bainbridge House. The château was built on a hilltop overlooking a broad expanse of recently mowed green fields; soot and fading stones did little to lessen her enthusiasm to view the interiors. The authenticity of the design made her wonder if the château had been disassembled in Europe, transported to the States, and then rebuilt brick by brick.

Taylor stopped and cut off the engine in the circular driveway. "What do you think?"

Sonja removed her sunglasses, setting them on the console between the front seats, and then undid her seat belt. "I can see why you said you were overwhelmed. Bainbridge House is magnificent. It reminds of the castles in the Loire Valley. By the way, I noticed the grass has been cut."

"The caretaker keeps the grass from being overgrown." Taylor also unsnapped his belt. "Are you ready to see what's waiting for you?"

He had asked her if she was ready, but Sonja wasn't certain she actually was ready to take on what she assumed was a monumental project. She'd viewed and toured more châteaus, monasteries, castles, museums and churches than she could count both as a child and an adult, and being a student of art, she never ceased to be awed by the exteriors, interiors and their contents. However, this was different. This was to be the first time she would be responsible for cataloguing and managing artistic and cultural collections. She did not have the postgraduate degree to become a curator at a national museum; however, she did have knowledge of restoration and art history.

She gave him a bright smile. "Yes."

Reaching for her camera, Sonja waited for Taylor to get out and come around to help her down. He'd rested his hand at the small of her back and then dropped it. "I called Dominic Shaw to let him know we were coming today to leave the gate open and air out several rooms on each floor of the house."

"He lives here year-round?"

"Yes. Mom says he calls her whenever he's going on vacation, and that means the property is left unattended. I informed him yesterday that I'd scheduled a security company to wire the house and the grounds because once the renovations begin work people will be coming and going at different times and days."

"I'm surprised it wasn't done before."

"So was I," Taylor admitted. "I'm guessing that because the house is off the beaten track and surrounded by high walls and a fence it hasn't become a target for vandals and trespassers. I'm certain folks in the area being aware that the property isn't abandoned also acts as a deterrent."

Sonja wanted to tell Taylor that walls, gates and resident caretakers were no match for those intent on burglarizing the house and taking off with valuable items that were irreplaceable. And if Charles Bainbridge had spent ten million dollars to build his home, she was certain he had spared no expense decorating it.

They mounted the half dozen steps to the front door, flanked by window boxes with overgrown ferns. Taylor opened the door, and Sonja followed him into an entrance hall with rooms branching to the right. Grit on the marble flooring made a crunching sound as she glanced up at curving twin staircases leading to the second story. A massive chandelier, covered with cobwebs, sat on a drop cloth in the middle of the expansive space.

She shivered slightly from the cool air filtering through open windows and decided not to take off her jacket. "This place is going to need a good cleaning, Taylor."

He nodded. "I'm waiting for a callback from a maintenance company to schedule a time for them to come in and clean the entire house. I don't want to bring them in until cameras are installed. And I really didn't want to bring you here until it was thoroughly cleaned. But I needed to know if you were willing to join the project because my brother Patrick is doing double duty as the restoration's CFO and working for his fiancée's uncle's Napa vineyard. He divides his time between California and Long Island. He's been sending me emails every day asking for figures so he can draw up a tentative payroll."

"Have you hired your team?"

"Not yet. I plan to hire an architect as project manager, while I'll continue to supervise the overall restoration. I've given also given Patrick the figures for the prevailing pay scale for architects, carpenters, plumbers, electricians and painters."

"Do you know how many workers you'll need?"

"No. I gave him an approximate number that can always be adjusted either up or down. Now I'm going take you upstairs to see several bedroom suites, and then we'll go downstairs to the cellar, where the collection of paintings, china, silver and crystal are stored."

There were many more questions Sonja wanted to ask Taylor but decided to wait. She wanted to know if he'd projected a date when he wanted to begin work because it would take time for him to interview and hire his team.

She climbed the staircase, noticing the worn carpeting on the stairs and on the second story hallway. There were several rooms stenciled with Water Closet on the doors. She stopped, opened the door and saw a narrow space with a commode and shower stall. Sonja entered the first bedroom suite on her right at the top of the staircase. Massive mahogany pieces made the space appear smaller than it actually was. The queen-size bed with a decoratively carved headboard and two bedside tables, an enormous armoire, overstuffed armchairs, a round table with four pull-up chairs, a woven rice container under a console, storage chest at the foot of the bed and a cushioned rocker under tall, narrow windows would have made her feel claustrophobic if she had been assigned to this bedroom.

"What do you think?" Taylor asked as he stood behind her.

"The mahogany pieces are exquisite, but less would be better." Raising her camera, Sonja took several shots of the furnishings.

He moved closer, his moist breath feathering over her ear. "Can you imagine getting up in the middle of the night without turning on the light while attempting to find your way to the door through this maze?"

Sonja couldn't help laughing. "No." She sobered. "What I like is the Caribbean influence in the mahogany carvings on the headboard and armoire. The console, which is in the French Regency style, has an intricate Martinique-style carving."

"Are you saying it's an antique?"

"I won't know for certain until I examine it closely."

"I have two steamer trunks filled with correspondence, bills, canceled checks and documents linked to this house. I haven't had the chance to go through everything except to pull out blueprints and floor plans."

"Would you mind if I take a look at them? Maybe I can find receipts to ascertain where a particular item was purchased."

"Are you sure that's what you want to do?"

Sonja turned to look at Taylor. "Yes, I'm sure. Some of these pieces could have been ordered from Europe or won at auction."

"I'll wait until you move into the hotel before I bring them over."

"I noticed we passed several motels during the drive here."

Taylor shook his head. "A few are not much better than flophouses. I much prefer one belonging to a chain. I'll set up an account for you once you check into an apartment suite where you will have the option of ordering room service or cooking for yourself. I'll give you a salary commensurate with your education and experience, and you can set your own hours. Once the property is secured, you will be given an electronic key card that will allow you access to come and go whenever you like."

"That sounds like an offer I can't refuse," she teased.

"I don't want you to refuse it. You're not going to become my employee, but a contract worker. Right now I don't have time to look for another architectural historian. It's going to be a lot easier finding painters, carpenters, and masons than someone with your expertise. I told you before that I don't yell or threaten, but I am no-nonsense when overseeing a project. I have a timeline as to when I want the exterior and interiors completed, and that's before my brothers leave their jobs to become involved with the business."

"What about Viola?"

Taylor's eyebrows lifted slightly. "I'm hoping she will eventually come around. But, if she doesn't then I'll contact culinary schools to recommend their best graduates."

"You really have everything figured out, don't you?"

"I have to. I owe it to my dad to fulfill his last wish to my mother."

Sonja noticed Taylor's voice had changed when he'd mentioned his father. There was no doubt the two had been very close. She wanted to tell him that she would do whatever she needed to help him fulfill his father's final request to his mother. "And I promise to assist you in making Bainbridge House a pretty girl again because she's been neglected far too long. She may have a little dinge, but it's nothing we can't get rid of."

He gave her skeptical look. "Are you saying Bainbridge House is a girl?"

"Of course she's a girl. Are you familiar with the French term *belle époque*? It means *beautiful epoch*."

"I've read about it. But that was a long time ago."

"It is a period in French history dating between 1880 and World War I, and because Bainbridge House is designed as a French château built in 1883 and falls within this architectural era, I think of her as a girl. But after she has been restored both inside and out she will once again become a stunning woman flaunting her beauty for those stopping long enough to marvel at her."

Taylor crossed his arms over his chest. "I don't want you to take offense because this may sound sexist. Once the exterior of the house is power washed it will appear pink, and traditionally that's a color usually attributed to girls."

"I'm not offended, Taylor. I happen to like the color, and if I ever have a girl I'll definitely would dress her in pink."

"You want children?"

Sonja went still, meeting his eyes. There was something in Taylor's query that annoyed her. Did he believe she was so career focused that she eschewed motherhood? Even before she'd agreed to marry Hugh Davies, they'd talked about starting a family after she'd earned her degree. She had become

Hugh's second wife, and although he was nearly twenty years her senior he claimed he was looking forward to becoming a father for the first time.

However, Sonja had known before they'd celebrated their second wedding anniversary that she had no intention of bringing a child into a hostile environment where his or her parents spent more time arguing than making love. Now, as a single woman, her plan was to have a career and children. Rather than give birth, she would foster and eventually adopt an older child or children.

"Yes. I plan to adopt."

"Good for you."

She was taken aback by his response. "Good for me?"

Taylor unfolded his arms and rested both hands on her shoulders. "Yes. There are too many children languishing in foster care that need a forever home."

With wide eyes, Sonja stared at Taylor like a deer caught in the bright beam of headlights. She couldn't help comparing him to her ex-husband. On a scale of one to ten Hugh came in at a low-two while Taylor was a ten. She'd found him to be open-minded and nonjudgmental. And, more importantly, he wasn't a sexist.

"You would rather adopt than have your own biological children?" she asked.

Sonja's question gave Taylor pause when he recalled his own upbringing. Elise was unable to have children, yet that hadn't stopped her from becoming a mother of five. "There's no reason why I couldn't have both, Sonja. A lot of couples have blended families with biological kids and adoptees of different races." He didn't tell her that he was talking about his own upbringing and family.

During a heart-to-heart discussion with Elise during one of their first Sunday meetings, she'd asked him if he ever intended to marry or if he wanted to father children. Taylor had been forthcoming when he told her yes to both. He wanted to fall in love, marry and start a family. And it didn't matter whether he fathered or adopted them. Elise had become emotional when he told her he knew he would become a good father because she and Conrad were the best role models for him to nurture the children he'd hoped to have.

"Do you realize you're an anomaly."

"Why would you say that?"

"I've met a lot of men that claim they prefer fathering their kids to adopting someone else's."

"I don't see a problem with that, Sonja. What I take exception to is their not taking care of their kids. Sometimes it is impossible for couples to live together, but that doesn't excuse a man from not having a relationship with his kids. Too often it becomes out of sight, out of mind."

Taylor didn't want to go on a rant and talk about men he'd known who were serial fathers and had felt the need to impregnate every woman with whom they'd had a relationship. And then there were those who were missing in action once a woman revealed she was carrying his child. It had had happened to his biological mother, who'd lived with her boyfriend, and once she discovered she was pregnant and told him, he disappeared. Aware of the circumstances surrounding his birth, Taylor had made it a practice to develop a relationship and always use protection whenever he slept with a woman.

He released Sonja's shoulders and took a step back. He'd enjoyed touching her, inhaling her sensual perfume and staring into the large dark eyes brimming with confidence. In fact, he'd enjoyed it much too much for him to remain emotionally disconnected.

"Now that we've established that Bainbridge House is a girl, I'd like to ask how you would decorate this bedroom to make it appear less crowded."

Sonja pressed her palms together. "The round table and chairs will have to go, and the armoire should be moved, facing the bed. Shelves in the armoire have to be removed if you want to install a flat screen. The console table, doubling as a desk, could be positioned under the window to take advantage of daylight. I suppose the bedside tables can stay where they are."

Taylor knew Sonja's suggestions would make the room less crowded and more inviting. He walked over and opened the door to a walk-in closet. "There's plenty of space for clothes and storage." He opened another door to the en suite bathroom. "Come, Sonja, and check out the bathroom."

Sonja stood next to him and snapped a picture of a sculptural sink on a ribbed column with brass fittings and a deep soaking claw-foot bathtub also with brass fittings. Then she took photos of the commode and bidet. "There's a fireplace!"

"The original plans included fireplaces in every bathroom suite on the first and second floors."

"Why only those two floors, Taylor?"

"Anyone that was a Bainbridge occupied the first two floors. The upper ones were reserved for guests."

Sonja laughed softly. "Were they trying to send a message that they didn't want their guests to wear out their welcome? Taking a bath in an unheated bathroom in the dead of a northeast winter had to be torture."

"I agree. Revised plans dated 1912 included running water and the installation of central heating." Taylor knew the house's electrical system had to be upgraded and Wi-Fi capability added, and the plumbing had to pass code before Bainbridge House could be licensed as a hotel.

"What are you going to do with the water closets?" Sonja asked.

"Convert them into spaces to keep linens and cleaning supplies for the housekeeping staff, and stockrooms to store personal products for the restrooms. The house has two elevators, but I won't know if they're operable until they have been inspected. We'll probably need two more elevators, but I'll have to confer with the architect to determine where they will be located."

"When you open Bainbridge House as a hotel and wedding venue, what will be the capacity?"

Taylor pinched the bridge of his nose as he attempted to recall the original floor plans for several rooms. "I believe the larger ballroom can hold three hundred and the smaller one somewhere around a hundred. I'm considering making modifications to the bedrooms. I'd like to remove walls to convert them into connecting suites. Right now, there are one hundred bedrooms and I doubt whether we'll be able to book that many rooms at any given time."

"How many connecting suites are you talking about?"

"Probably seventy-five. Bainbridge House has gone through a number of architectural and structurally modifications since 1889 and must undergo even more to make it viable as a business."

Sonja nodded. "Most of these mansions have servant quarters. Do the plans include one?"

"Yes. In fact, it is quite large, which may indicate the Bainbridges needed a full staff to keep the house operational. Once you go through the documents, you'll have to let me know how many were in their employ."

"I recall you saying something about cottages."

Taylor realized Sonja had remembered a lot of what he'd told her. Then he realized she must have an incredible memory if only to be able to identify thousands of years of relics and works of art. "The caretaker lives in one, which leaves five unoccupied."

"Does he live there with his family?"

"No. He's not married."

"What do you intend to do with the other five?" Sonja had asked yet another question.

Taylor's plans for the cottages included turning them into family residences. "Unlike the Bainbridges who occupied the first two floors in the main house, I plan to live in one of the cottages."

"What about the rest of your family?"

"We'll see when that time comes. The floor plans show one large bedroom and two smaller ones. There's also a kitchen, bathroom and an area for a living and dining room."

Taylor talking about the cottages had Sonja wondering what they had been used for when there was more than enough space in the main house to accommodate friends, guests and family members. If they weren't occupied by tenant farmers, then the only alternative could have been for guests who had insisted on complete privacy, or men of wealth and privilege who'd sequestered their mistresses on the property away from the prying eyes of their wives and her friends.

"Maybe the next time I come I'd like to see inside one," she told Taylor.

"I'll make certain they're cleaned and aired out.

Do you want to see a bedroom on the third or fourth floors?"

"No. I'd rather to go up to the turrets and look out over the property."

Taylor reached for her hand, and Sonja felt a slight shiver sweep up her arm. Whether Taylor was assisting her in or out of his SUV, resting his hand at the small of her back or touching her hand, it had become a struggle not to pretend she was a heroine in a romance novel and he the hero, and they would live happily ever after. Everything about him made her feel safe and protected. However, she had to remind herself she wasn't a character in a novel, but a real flesh-and-blood woman with deep-rooted trust issues when it came to men.

When she'd first walked into Professor Hugh Davies's classroom Sonja had been awestruck by the middle-aged man with the handsomeness of leading men in 1940s and 1950s movies. And when she'd glanced at the other female students, she realized their reaction was like hers: they were mesmerized. Professor Davies was the total package: tall, slender, perpetually tanned, and he'd been blessed with a velvety baritone voice.

He periodically conducted a slideshow quiz, and students were required to name a painting and painter or piece of sculpture. Because she'd been able to identify each slide every time, she'd believed he had taken a special interest in her whenever he'd asked her to stay after class to discuss her grades.

Her fellow students were unaware she'd grown up visiting European medieval cities with museums and churches displaying priceless artifacts.

Her passion with art also extended to photography and she owned coffee table books depicting black-and-white photographs of the celebration of Black culture and the struggle for freedom dating from 1840. Many of the photographs were now a part of the Smithsonian.

As a twenty-year-old art major at Boston College, Sonja hadn't realized she was in over her head with Hugh until it was too late. She hadn't told her mother she was involved with one of her professors until after they were married. There was complete silence on the other end of the call, and then the sound of a dial tone. Her mother had hung up on her. Telling Maria that Sonja had become the second wife of a man old enough to be her father had shocked and disappointed her mother. Her father's reaction was different. He'd wished her well. It was what he'd said next that proved prophetic. He said because she was an adult and responsible for her own actions, she had to be willing to accept all and any consequences of her marriage.

Although she thought of Taylor Williamson as the total package, there was no way she would allow her heart to rule her head. She'd married once, and that was something she did not want to repeat. Been there, done that. And she didn't need a man in order to have a baby because she had the option of adopting.

She glanced up at Taylor when he tightened his hold on her fingers as they climbed the winding staircase to the turrets. She noticed he wasn't breathing as heavily as she was from the exertion, which indicated he was in excellent physical condition.

"Do you work out?" she asked him.

He smiled at her. "Yes. There's a sports club for the residents in the development where I live."

"You told me you're moving into your mother's house. Is there space there where you can work out?"

"Yes. She has a condo in a gated development with a lot of on-site amenities. She's still staying at the house where I grew up. It's now on the market, and she's waiting for someone to buy it."

"Mortgage rate are low, so right now it's a buyer's market."

"True. But it's not your traditional three or four-bedroom home. It's a five-thousand-square-foot farmhouse built on four acres with an in-ground pool and tennis and basketball courts. With six bedrooms and seven baths, it would be perfect for a large or extended family."

Taylor's revelations that he'd lived on what Sonja thought of as an estate now confirmed her suspicions once she and Viola had become friends. Her friend had grown up privileged. Viola had revealed she and her brothers did not have to apply for student loans to subsidize their college tuitions and that her father had paid her rent on her West Village apartment until she'd secured permanent employment. Viola had also hinted her father had inherited a small fortune after the death of his parents, while Taylor had admitted his grandparents had set up a trust for his father, which he was able to gain access to at twenty-one. Even if Taylor hadn't grown up with the proverbial silver spoon in his mouth, it was purported he'd earned a great deal of money as a top male model.

Viola would talk incessantly about her brothers in glowing terms that made Sonja slightly unhappy she didn't share the same closeness with her brother because of their ten-year age gap. Viola said one of her brothers had married, but the union did not last a year, and another had recently proposed to his long-time girlfriend, while Taylor and another brother were still single. And she was adamant that Taylor did not want to be introduced to any of her gal friends, and the one time she ignored his warning he'd read her the riot act. Sonja was quick to tell Viola that she echoed his sentiments. She didn't want or need a man at this time in her life because her career took precedence over any relationship.

Sonja felt the muscles in her calves straining from climbing the staircase. "Will you continue to live with your mother once she sells her house?"

Taylor stopped at the top of the staircase and opened a narrow door. He walked in, glanced around and beckoned her to follow. "Yes. My mother is scheduled to take an around-the-world cruise. She says if she doesn't sell the house before August, then she'll close it up. I promised her I would check on it at least once a week."

"How long is her cruise?"

"Two hundred forty-five days."

"Well, damn," Sonja whispered under her breath.

Taylor chuckled, the sound rumbling in his chest. "That's what I said when she first told me about it. She claims she's making up for all the times she asked Dad to go on cruise with her, hoping he would change his mind about his parents' boating accident. Now that Dad's gone, she's convinced her best friend to be her cabinmate. They met as college roommates, and their friendship has spanned fifty-plus years."

"It's not often people remain friends that long. Either they move to another city or state, or their lives change once they marry and have a family. Most times, it's like life gets in the way of maintaining a friendship of that duration."

"Life got in the way and that's why you want nothing to do with men?"

Her jaw dropped and her mouth opened, but no words came out. She wondered if Viola had disclosed to Taylor the details of her failed marriage. Viola Williamson was as close to a friend that she could count or rely on, yet when she'd poured out her heart to the chef about how she'd allowed her husband to turn her life upside down, she hadn't told her to keep the conversation between just the two of them.

"Who said I want nothing to do with men?" Sonja

knew she sounded defensive, but at that point she didn't care.

"You did in so many words, Sonja. You're not married, don't have a boyfriend, and you plan to become a single mother. To me, that translates into you being content to live your life alone."

She glared at him. Taylor had no right to attempt to psychoanalyze her when he knew very little about who she was. "You make it sound as if I'm a man-hater," she spit out between clenched teeth as she struggled not to lose her temper.

Sonja walked over to the narrow window to give herself time to calm down. She didn't want to say something that would ruin her chance to become the architectural historian for the restoration project. She concentrated on the landscape unfolding before her eyes, taking deep breaths to slow down her respiration. She saw a pond with ducks and swans. Her gaze shifted, and she spied the roof of one of the cottages. She went completely still when she felt the heat from Taylor's body seep through her jacket and into her when he pressed his chest against her back.

"I didn't say you were a man-hater, Sonja," he whispered in her ear. "And I'm not accusing you of being lonely. Being alone and lonely are not the same."

Sonja knew she didn't have to explain herself to Taylor, especially if he was to become her employer. And it wasn't because she was his sister's friend. It was her education and experience in the field of art history that made him want her to become a part of his restoration team.

She turned to face him. "What are you saying, Taylor, if not that?"

He stared down her at the same time the beginnings of a smile tilted the corners of his strong mouth. "I think you are an incredibly talented woman that any man with half a brain would respect."

Sonja felt hot tears pricking the back of her eyelids, but she refused to cry and embarrass herself. Hugh had driven her to tears so many times that he would provoke her just to see her cry. She was damned and determined not to let Taylor see her that way.

"I had a man tell me almost those exact words and, unfortunately, I fell hard, hook, line and sinker, into his trap. I gave him four years of my life, and then I knew I had to get out before I allowed him to destroy me. It took another two years to end the legal entanglement because he refused to let me go. That's when I swore I would never become involved with another controlling man as long as I was in my right mind."

"You are lucky because you were able to get on with your life. I know you don't want to hear it, but not all men are like your ex-husband."

Sonja closed her eyes for a few seconds. "It's been difficult for me, but that's something I've been trying to convince myself."

"I'm not saying I'll try to convince you one way or the other, but I'm available if you need a friend."

She managed a brittle smile. "You want to be my friend *and* my boss?"

One of Taylor's eyebrows lifted. "Boss aside, I'll always make myself available to you if you need to talk about something."

Sonja chided herself for misinterpreting his motives. Maybe it was because she was his sister's friend that he didn't want any romantic entanglement. Besides, he'd warned Viola about attempting to set him up with her friends, and for Sonja she thought of it as a win-win. Not only would she add the restoration project to her résumé, she would also interact with a man with whom she could have a no-pressure ongoing friendship.

She extended her right hand. "All right. Friends."

Taylor took her hand and dropped a kiss on her fingers. "Friends." He released her hand. "Now, friend, it's time we head down to the cellar so you can see what's waiting for you."

Chapter Five

Sonja clapped a hand over her mouth when she saw crates filled with china, paintings, crystal pieces, monogrammed silverware, a collection of snuff boxes, framed prints, porcelain figurines, vases and military swords and paraphernalia, and worn leather-bound books she suspected were first editions.

She found shelves lined with dusty wine bottles, Bainbridge Cellars labels indicating the year the grapes were harvested. The entire cellar contained a treasure trove of items that would take months, possibly a year, to go through.

"What do you think?"

She turned to find Taylor standing several feet away, arms crossed over his chest. "I feel like a kid walking into FAO Schwarz during the Christmas holiday season. I don't know where to begin."

"I told you it was overwhelming."

She sighed. "Yes, you did. I'm going tackle one crate at a time, but I can't work down here." The space was dimly illuminated with several overhead naked bulbs.

"Don't worry, Sonja. I'll set aside a room you can use as an office. And once you're set up, I'll bring the steamer trunks here instead of leaving them at your hotel. You'll have enough to do here, that once you get back to your hotel you shouldn't have to look at anything that remotely resembles work."

"Thank you." She paused. "I'm sure there's a library in the house, and that would be perfect place to set up my office."

Taylor lowered his arms. "Let's go upstairs and see."

They found the library on the east wing of the château. Sonja stared at the walls. "You'll have to hire faux bois specialists to restore the wall, and the plaster moldings in here and in the ballrooms," she told Taylor.

"After I take care of securing and cleaning the house, I'll need you to come back and go through the entire house and recommend the craftspeople needed to restore everything to its original state."

"That's not a problem. The interiors have held up well after not being occupied for sixty years. I've been inside homes that were practically falling around the owner's head because of neglect. Bainbridge House has what I call good bones."

"We'll find out once I inspect the foundation."

"When are you going to do that?" she asked.

"One day this week. A moving company is scheduled to take the contents of my apartment to a storage unit sometime next week. Once that's done I can move into my mother's condo. Living in Jersey…" His words trailed off. "Is that your stomach making those noises?"

Sonja bit her lip as she averted her gaze. "Yes. All I had was coffee, and it's probably reminding me that I need to eat."

"Why didn't you say something earlier? We could've stopped to eat before coming here." Reaching into the pocket of his jeans he removed his cell phone and tapped the screen. "I just sent Dom a message that we're leaving, and he should close the windows and the gate."

Sonja was relieved to leave the cavernous unheated house and feel the warmth of the sun on her face. She'd hoped by the time the office was set up for her to begin working she wouldn't have to wear a coat.

"Where are we going to eat?" she asked Taylor as she secured her seat belt.

"There's a restaurant in Yonkers I sometimes frequent. The food and service are excellent."

She shared a smile with him. "All right. Let's go."

Taylor winked at her. "Yes, ma'am."

* * *

"How's your omelet?"

Sonja's fork stopped in midair as she smiled across the table at Taylor. They'd arrived at the restaurant as brunch diners were leaving and were able to get a table in the enclosed patio with views of the Hudson River. "It's delicious." She'd ordered the farmer's omelet with a medley of finely diced peppers, onions, mushrooms, bacon, ham and sausage. "How did you find this place?" Taylor had had to drive down several narrow one-way streets before he was able to find parking.

"I told you my college buddies used to search out restaurants to visit, and one day we missed the turn-off for City Island. We decided to keep heading north and ended up here."

"I thought you said you took the subway uptown and to other boroughs."

Taylor gave her a direct stare. "Do you remember everything I say?"

"Just about," she admitted.

"Which means you could catch me in a lie."

"Do you lie?" she asked, deadpan.

"Hardly ever," Taylor countered. "I learned a long time ago that if you tell a lie, then you have to tell another to correct that one, and after a while you're busted."

Sonja popped a piece of fluffy egg into her mouth, chewed and then swallowed it. "Back to my question about how you ended up in Yonkers. Whose car did you use?"

"It was my rental."

"Renting a car under the age of twenty-five is pricey."

"Not for me, Sonja, because I'd just turned twenty-five."

"How did you get into modeling?"

"I sort of fell into it."

Propping her elbow on the table, she cupped her chin in the heel of her hand. "Tell me how you fell into it."

There had been a time in his life when he'd forgotten his career goals. He'd known at ten when his parents gave him a Christmas gift of Lego that he'd fancied himself a builder. Using the interlocking pieces, he spent hours creating entire cities with imaginary office buildings, hospitals, restaurants and even malls. Instead of his obsession waning as he grew older, it intensified. Whenever he went into Manhattan with his father he'd found himself transfixed with the towering buildings and wondering how they were able to stand without falling.

"Earth to Taylor."

He smiled. "I'm sorry about zoning out on you."

"Are you or aren't you going to tell me how you became a model?"

Now he knew why Sonja and Viola were friends. They were like dogs with bones when seeking information. "I'd just begun my sophomore year at NYU when a student asked if she could take some photos of me for a photography project because she said I had an interesting face. I told her I would think about it, but then she told me not to think too long because she had to complete her project and submit it in a couple of days. I said okay and she gave me a form to fill out with my name, address and phone number. There was also a section certifying that she owned the photographs.

"I met her the next day in one of the classrooms set up as art studios, and after about twenty minutes she was finished."

"Did you have to take off your clothes?"

Taylor wagged a finger. "Get your mind out of the gutter, Ms. Rios-Martin. I wasn't auditioning for a porno flick."

She narrowed her eyes. "But you did take off a few garments."

Taylor wondered if he was that transparent or she that perceptive. "She did ask me to remove my shirt and shoes."

"Even if she'd asked you to take off all of your clothes, as an artist she would've viewed your nude body as art."

"I'm not a prude, but I wouldn't have complied in case she wasn't going to use the photos for her school project."

"Did you know her?"

"Not personally, but I would see her around campus and always with a camera. I ran into her a month later, and she told me that her professor gave her an A. Her prof said I might do well if she sent the photos to a modeling agency. I told her to do it just to humor her. I'd returned to Jersey for the winter break when I got a call from a woman asking if she could rep me because a modeling agency was interested in booking me.

"I'd forgotten about the pictures until she mentioned the photographer's name. I was curious, so I agreed to meet her at a midtown restaurant. I listened to her spiel and told her I had to talk it over with my parents. Mom and Dad really didn't want me to drop out, but I promised then I would do it for two years, and then go back to school. Two years turned into five and even though I'd earned a lot of money I knew it wasn't what I wanted to do long term."

"So, you just walked away." Sonja's question was a statement.

"Yes. And I've never regretted it."

"How did you manage to remain an enigma when your face was so recognizable?"

Other women had questioned him about his career as a model and most times he was able to gloss over it without going into detail about a time in his life when he'd lost focus on his goal to become an engineer. However, Taylor felt differently when it came to Sonja. Not only was she his sister's friend, but they would also work together and he wanted her to trust him.

"I had a clause in my contract prohibiting the agency from disclosing anything about my personal life. Professionally I'd become T.E. Wills, while in private I could be Taylor Edward Williamson."

"What I don't understand, Taylor, is once you become a public figure it's virtually impossible for you to claim you want your privacy. Fame isn't arbitrary or negotiable."

"I know that. I insisted on privacy to protect my family more than myself. I knew how my life would change the instant my image appeared in a commercial or on the page of a slick magazine, but no one in my family wanted their lives disrupted or dissected because I'd chosen a career where I was earning money using my face and body."

"I was in my nail salon when I picked up *People*'s Most Beautiful issue—in which you were included."

Taylor rolled his eyes upward. "Please don't remind me of that. That was a couple of weeks before I was scheduled to retire, but my agent pleaded with me to go to the shoot. I really did it as a favor to her."

Sonja wanted to tell Taylor that his favor had extended to millions of women because he was the epitome of elegance as he leaned against a low-slung sports car in formal dress with a mischievous smile parting his lips. His expression was hypnotic and inviting.

"Going out on top means you'll never be labeled a has-been."

Throwing back his head, Taylor laughed. "A has-been at twenty-four is really a stretch."

"Don't laugh, Taylor. Think of all the child actors that weren't able to transition to adult roles."

He sobered. "You're right."

"What's going to happen when you open Bainbridge House as a hotel, and it's covered by the press? Then the whole world will know that Taylor Williamson is the legendary T.E. Wills."

"I doubt…" His words trailed off when Sonja's cell phone rang. "Aren't you going to answer that?"

Sonja recognized Viola's ringtone. Reaching into her cross-body, she tapped the screen. "Hello."

"Hey, girl. I'm calling to find out how it went with my brother last night."

"Can I call you later?"

"Are you with him now?"

"Yes."

"Don't forget to call me."

"I won't. Later." Sonja ended the call, set the phone on the table next to her plate and picked up her napkin, touching it to the corners of her mouth. "I don't think I can eat any more." The three-egg omelet was very filling.

Taylor raised his hand to signal for their waitress. "Do you want dessert to take home?"

"No, thank you. My aunt is watching my uncle's sugar intake, and I would be sabotaging him if I brought dessert home."

"Speaking of home, it's time we headed out, and beat the traffic."

* * *

"My building is at the end of the block," Sonja told Taylor as slowed along the tree-lined street and maneuvered into an empty space. She unbuckled her belt. "Thank you for everything."

Taylor also removed his belt. "I'll walk you in."

Sonja rested a hand on his arm. "It's okay. My building is pretty safe."

He met her eyes. "Are you sure?"

"Yes, Taylor." Leaning to her left, she kissed his cheek. "Later."

She knew she'd shocked him with the gesture, and got out unassisted and walked toward her building. After entering the vestibule, she unlocked the inner door and made her way to the elevator. She'd just gotten in the car when her phone's text tone vibrated. Sonja pushed the button for the tenth floor and then tapped the icon for messages.

Taylor had sent her a contract offering the average salary for museum director or curator. It was more than double what she earned working at the gallery. She hadn't broached the topic of salary with him because she had wanted him to make the first overture. Well, he had, and now she would be able to save enough to purchase a condo sooner rather than later.

Sonja exited the car when it stopped at her floor. Her step was light when she strolled down the hallway to the apartment. She unlocked the door, closed it and left the camera case on a chair in the entryway. She tossed her keys in a large candy dish and then sat on the chair to remove her boots, leaving them on the mat inside the door.

The flat screen was off in the living room, indicating she was alone in the apartment. Her uncle turned on the television as soon as he got up and didn't turn it off until he retired for bed. She went into her bedroom, changed out of her street clothes and into a pair of cotton drawstring pants and oversized tee. Settling into a cushioned rocker, Sonja retrieved her cell phone and sent him a grinning face emoji, and then tapped Viola's number.

"Tell me everything and don't you dare leave anything out."

"What happened to 'hello, Sonja'?"

"Hello, Sonja. Now please tell me everything."

"I've decided to work with Taylor on the restoration project."

"I knew that would happen. But, what about you and Taylor?"

"What about us, Vi?"

"Do you like him?"

"What's not to like? I must admit I was shocked to discover he is T.E. Wills."

There was a pause before Viola said, "I couldn't tell you because he really values his privacy. I know that sounds crazy when he is so recognizable. My family has more than its share of secrets. I never told any man I dated that my dad came from wealthy family, because I didn't want to be viewed as a dollar sign. You know a lot more about me than a lot of people because I trust you, Sonja."

"Yeah, right," she drawled. "You trusted me so much that you didn't tell me your gorgeous brother was a top male model."

Viola's sultry laugh came through the earpiece. "Sorry about that."

Sonja pushed out her lips even though Viola couldn't see her. "I got to see the château today."

"What do you think of it? It reminds me of Disney's Magic Kingdom."

"It's beautiful."

"You would say that because I know how much you love old buildings and castles."

"You don't like it, Vi?"

"It's not that I don't like it. What I am is ambivalent. Taylor wants me to take over the kitchen once the hotel is up and running, but I'm still not certain that's what I want to do."

"Why not? Is it that you don't believe you have enough experience to be the executive chef?"

"Maybe not now, but I'm certain I will be in a couple of years."

"Don't play yourself, Viola. You went to one of the top culinary schools in the country and graduated at the top of your class. And you're talented enough to have secured a position at a Michelin-starred restaurant. Women executive chefs are still as scarce as hen's teeth, while you're dragging your feet about whether you want to become involved in your family's business."

"I don't know if I have the personality to supervise a commercial kitchen. Besides, I need more experience. Right now, I'm waiting to be promoted from a line cook to sous-chef."

"Stop making excuses, Viola."

"I'm not making excuses, Sonja. Running a kitchen is a daunting task and at this time in my life I don't feel confident enough to become an executive chef."

"Do you realize how many times you've complained about your tyrannical boss who gets his jollies off browbeating his staff?"

A beat passed. "I suppose too many times," Viola admitted. "But I've learned to tune him out."

"You shouldn't have to tune him out, Vi, when you're not obligated to stay on once Bainbridge House opens for business. I'm looking forward to the grand opening when you and your brothers gather in front of the mansion for a ribbon-cutting ceremony—you in your chef's whites with Bainbridge House, Viola Williamson, Executive Chef embroidered on your coat."

"Why do you make it sound so over-the-top?"

Sonja smiled. "Because it would be. Food critics will be lining up to eat at Bainbridge House, and then writing about the food and service. And I'm willing to bet there will be articles in cooking magazines about you being an up-and-coming chef to watch."

Viola laughed. "Maybe I should hire you as my publicist."

"You don't need a publicist, Vi. Your dishes will speak for themselves."

"I'm not going to promise anything, but I'll tell you what I told Taylor. I'll think about it."

"Don't think too long, Vi. Time will go by faster than you think." Sonja wanted to tell her friend she'd short-circuited her own career when she opted to marry rather than complete her education. And while she hadn't been able to make up for the lost years Sonja had made herself a promise to maintain her emotional wellbeing at the same time making her career a priority.

"I know. I can't believe I'm having second thoughts even though I've always wanted to run my own kitchen. My real quandary is giving up my apartment and moving back to New Jersey. You know how much I love living in the Village."

Sonja did not want to debate with Viola that moving across the river paled in comparison to the possibility of making a name for herself in a male-dominated field. "I know, Vi, but you have to think of yourself as a role model for not only women, but particularly women of color who want a career in culinary arts."

"I've never thought of myself as a role model, but you always know what to say to bring me back to reality."

"I learned it from you, my friend. When we first

met, I was still healing emotionally. You listened to me go on and on about my ex and what he'd done to me. Then you told me that I had to stop blaming myself for someone else's negative behavior."

"I had a similar experience with a guy I'd believed was the love of my life. When I found out he was cheating on me I told him it was over. He pleaded and begged, said that it would never happen again. I forgave him over and over until I realized he would always be a serial cheater. The only way I could get over him was to go into therapy. It took more than six months for me to completely exorcise him not only from my life but also my head."

Sonja was slightly taken aback with her friend's revelation. Viola rarely talked about her past relationships. She'd mentioned occasionally dating yet never admitted to having had a serious relationship. "Fortunately, I didn't have to lay on a therapist's couch because I had you to give it to me straight, no chaser."

"I know there are times when I'm a little too candid for my own good, and that's when Taylor has accused me of not having a filter."

"I've concluded it is better to speak up rather than remain silent." Sonja knew she wasn't the same woman who'd fallen under the spell of a much older man and married him. She didn't hate men. She was just wary of their motives. However, it would be different with Taylor. They would be friends.

She chatted with Viola for few more minutes and then ended the call.

Last summer Taylor's sister had hosted a Sunday brunch buffet at her apartment and Sonja had been amazed with what she'd prepared. The gathering was small—less than a dozen people—and included Viola's waitstaff coworkers, her roommate's colleagues and her neighbors. One of her neighbors that had taken an interest in Sonja, and everywhere she turned he was only a few feet away. Then he'd asked if they could go somewhere later that evening for drinks. She had turned him down politely with the excuse that someone was coming to pick her up at six. Of course, he didn't believe her and offered to walk her down to the street. She was hard-pressed not to laugh at his crestfallen expression when she got into the car with Jaime. Her cousin had proved invaluable when it came to discouraging men attempting to come onto her.

She retrieved her camera, booted up her laptop and downloaded the photos she'd taken at Bainbridge House. Sonja had described the mansion as having a little dinge, which did not in any way diminish the graceful beauty of the architecture.

She had just enlarged the photos of moldings in the library and the smaller ballroom when her phone rang. Glancing at the screen she saw Taylor's name. She tapped the speaker feature. "I hope you're driving hands free."

His deep laugh caressed her ear. "I'm not driving. I'm home."

"How did you get there so quickly?"

"Stamford is only thirty miles from Inwood."

"That's all?"

"That's it. Should I interpret your emoji to mean that you've accepted my salary offer?"

Sonja bit on her lip to keep from laughing. "Yes."

"Good. Send me your email address, and I'll have Patrick send you a list of documents he'll need for your personnel file. I know he'll want a résumé and unofficial copies of your college transcripts. He'd wanted to ask for letters of recommendation, but I told him I'd vouch for you. He's setting up payroll for direct deposit so he will need your banking information. I'm projecting your start day will be the first week in May. Meanwhile, I'll search for hotels in the area and instruct Patrick to set up a corporate account for you. It will be the same with the leased car. I'll arrange for it to be delivered to you the day you check into the hotel. You're going to need a credit card for anything that's business related. Just make certain to save the receipts because my brother is—excuse the expression—a tight-ass CPA who will go ballistic if he can't account for every penny."

"Tight-ass or scrooge?"

"Both. I'm willing to go along with his edicts because Patrick is a genius when it comes to accounting and taxation."

* * *

"Will I get to meet him?" Sonja asked.

"I doubt it. Right now, he's living in Napa with his fiancée. She comes from a family of winemakers. A few years back Patrick worked for her uncle, who'd begun a startup vineyard on Long Island's North Shore. Next year will be the first time from the initial planting that they will get their first harvest. He told me the first vintage probably won't be bottled for another two years after that."

Sonja recalled dozens of dusty and cobweb-covered wine bottles in the château's cellar. "Does he plan to become the vintner for Bainbridge Cellars?"

Taylor's sigh reverberated through the speaker. "I'm hoping he will. But, if he doesn't, then I'm going to bring in a wine taster to judge the quality of the wine in the cellar. If he gives it a thumbs-up, then I'm willing to hire a vintner and workers to restore the vineyard and put in new plantings."

"I just had an idea, Taylor."

"Talk to me, sweetheart."

Sonja went completely still, wondering if Taylor had meant to call her 'sweetheart,' or if the endearment had slipped out unconsciously. "You'd talked about the gardens and orchard, but have you given any thought to putting in a farm?"

"What type of farm?"

"A vegetable farm. After all, New Jersey *is* touted as the Garden State."

"That it is, but who's going to maintain the farm?"

"Really, Taylor? You hire someone. You'll save a lot of money if you grow your own produce in greenhouses year-round and offer farm-to-table dining."

A beat passed. "Do you have any other suggestions?"

"I have a few more."

"Do you want to tell me about them?"

Sonja smiled when she registered laughter in Taylor's query. "I'll wait until I see you again."

"I'm always open to your suggestions as long as they are within the realm of possibility."

"Like raising chickens, ducks and sheep?"

"That's enough, Sonja. I have no intention of operating Old MacDonald's farm."

"Why not? You'll have stables for horses, so why not house the chickens, ducks and sheep in the barn? There's nothing better than fresh chicken and duck eggs."

"Where is all of this coming from?"

His accusatory tone was beginning to annoy Sonja. "Forget it, Taylor."

"No, Sonja, I'm not going to forget it."

"We don't have to talk about it now. The next time we get together I'll have put everything on paper."

"Okay."

"After I hang up I'll text you my email."

"Okay," Taylor repeated.

"I'll talk to you later." Sonja ended the call. If Taylor had been willing to listen without prejudice,

Sonja would have explained she'd toured the Loire Valley and had stopped to eat at a château offering farm-to-table meals. The owners raised their own chickens and ducks, and the difference between store-bought refrigerated eggs and ones gathered daily were remarkable. It was the same with the freshly picked vegetables and free-range poultry.

As promised, Sonja would write down her ideas, suggestions and recommendations, and present them to Taylor. It wouldn't bother her if he rejected them— just the fact that he would take the time to listen was enough. She texted Taylor her email address and then returned her attention to the photos she'd taken at Bainbridge House.

A knock on her bedroom door got her attention. She smiled. Her aunt had come home. "Hi, Titi Yolie." Sonja shifted on the bench seat in front of the table where she'd set her laptop and printer. "Come and see the pictures I took of the mansion."

Yolanda walked in, sat beside Sonja and slowly shook her head. "That's what I call wretched excess. I'll never understand why rich folks in this country felt the need to build these monstrosities."

"During the Gilded Age, America's nouveau riche flaunted their wealth to emulate European royalty," Sonja explained. "They had everything but the titles, while Europe's landed gentry needed money to run their estates and were willing to trade their titles for cash. It became a win-win when young American heiresses married English nobility to become a princess, duchess, viscountess or a marchioness. Winston Churchill's mother was an American socialite, Consuelo Vanderbilt married the Duke of Marlborough, and Princess Diana's American great-grandmother had been a baroness."

"That's so tacky. Selling yourself for a title."

"Word," Sonja said in agreement. "American heiresses that married into the British aristocracy were referred to as 'Dollar Princesses.' Marrying an aristocrat was seen as a way for them to raise their social status."

"That's crazy, Sonja. If they are millionairesses, shouldn't that be status enough?"

"Not for them. They were the daughters of self-made men who didn't have the social standing of longtime members of high society."

"Are you saying they were shunned?" Yolanda asked.

"Yes, because they were new and not old money, and they'd believed a title would enhance their position among America's social elite. Unfortunately for some of these titled princesses they did not have a happily-ever-after. Princess Diana's great-grandmother divorced her husband, while Consuelo Vanderbilt also divorced her husband."

Yolanda snorted delicately. "What did they expect when they sold themselves just to be accepted by those that looked down on them because they didn't have the proper pedigree."

"You are preaching to the choir, Auntie."

"Now that you've seen the mansion, are you going to accept the commission to help restore it?"

"Yes." Sonja knew she'd shocked her aunt when she revealed she would have to live in New Jersey. "I don't want to drive ninety minutes to work, put in six or seven hours, and then sit in a car for another ninety-plus minutes in rush hour traffic, to turn around and do it again the next day."

"When are you leaving?"

Sonja draped an arm around her aunt's shoulders. "Not until early May."

"I suppose that means you'll be leaving the gallery."

"Yes. I will let them know that I'll stay until that time." Sonja knew that once she become a part of the restoration team, her life and her future would not be the same. She was looking forward to her involvement in the restoration.

"What do you know about the family that built this mansion?"

"Not much," Sonja admitted truthfully. She would set aside as much time as necessary to research the Bainbridges and hopefully discover Taylor's father's connection to the wealthy family that had erected an exact replica of a French château in northern New Jersey.

Chapter Six

Taylor took one last look around the apartment and then left the keys, as instructed by the building manager, on the kitchen countertop. The movers had come earlier that morning and transported the boxes to their van to take them to a storage unit near his mother's condo. Meanwhile, he'd packed and stored his clothes, personal items and the steamer trunks in the cargo area of the SUV. He'd called Elise to let her know he planned to stop and see her in Belleville before they drove up to Sparta.

His week had begun with him going to Bainbridge House because the security company was scheduled to wire the house and install cameras around the property. Even with a team of eight technicians it had taken nearly a week to set up everything. The caretaker had admitted he felt more secure now that the property was electronically monitored.

Taylor found Elise sitting on the porch knitting, the familiar rhythmic clicking of the needles reminding him of a time when his mother spent her spare time knitting sweaters, gloves, scarfs and hats for his sister and brothers. If she wasn't knitting, she could be found reading. Although a woman came in three days a week to clean and do laundry, Elise had insisted on preparing meals for her family.

Walking up the porch steps, Taylor leaned over and pressed his lips to his mother's graying strawberry-blond hair. "Hello, beautiful."

A flush suffused Elise's face following his compliment. When the social worker had brought him to the home of Elise Williamson, Taylor had believed she was a princess. He'd been told the tall, slender woman with a pale complexion, wavy reddish hair and sapphire-blue eyes was to become his new mother. She had insisted he call her Mom even though, at six, he knew she couldn't be his mother because his cousins looked like his aunt, and all of the kids in his class looked like their mothers. His greatest fear was going to school and having this woman come and identify herself as his mother and having his classmates laugh or call him a liar. It was only when he realized he didn't have to leave the house to attend classes, and that his foster mother had planned to homeschool him, that Taylor's fears vanished and he was able to call her Mom.

"You should be sweet-talking a young woman around your age instead of your seventy-two-year-old momma."

"I don't have time to sweet-talk anyone, Mom."

She gave him a long, penetrating stare as he folded his body down on a rocker facing hers. "I hope you don't get so caught up in restoring your father's property that you forget to relax."

Stretching out long legs, Taylor crossed his booted feet at the ankles. "I'd wanted to ask you about Dad's property."

Elise's hands stilled. "What do you want to know?"

"When did Dad know he'd inherited Bainbridge House?" He had learned not to ask Conrad about his family because the older man would give him a look that told him that he was prying. It was Elise who had occasionally revealed a few incidents in her husband's life that he'd loathed talking about.

"It was after his aunt died. He'd talked about owning land in the northern part of the state, but whenever I asked him what he intended to do with it he claimed he didn't know. A couple of months after he sold his company he took me to see it. I was so shocked that I was at a loss for words. Before that, he'd had the property appraised with the intention of selling it, and because he didn't say anything I'd assumed he'd sold it."

"Did he ever live at Bainbridge House?"

"Yes. He said he lived there before his parents' boating accident. He said he loved riding the horses. And when the ewes had lambs, he would give them all names. He said the caretaker didn't have to cut grass in the area where the sheep grazed because they were four-footed lawn mowers."

Taylor bit back a smile. Sonja had talked about chickens, ducks and sheep. "Why didn't you tell us about this before Easter Sunday?"

Leaning to her right, Elise put her knitting into a quilted bag beside her chair on the floor. "Conrad added a codicil to his will, and it wasn't until the reading of the will that was I made aware that he'd left the estate to me and his children. Meanwhile, I wanted to wait until the entire family was together to give everyone the news."

Taylor pressed his head against the back of the rocker and stared at the glass-topped wicker table and matching chairs in a corner of the wraparound porch. "If you were shocked when you first saw Bainbridge House, I know I speak for the others when I say we were also stunned by it."

"I'm glad you decided to take the lead when you said you would supervise the restoration, because if you hadn't, then I don't think Joaquin and Tariq would've agreed to join you."

"You underestimate them, Mom. I believe given the option of working for someone or one's self, most would choose the latter."

"Maybe for you, Tariq and Joaquin, but not Viola and Patrick."

"Patrick is involved, Mom. Don't forget he's overseeing the project's fiscal component. And I'd rather have him signing checks than a stranger."

Minute lines fanned out around Elise's eyes when she smiled. "You're right about that. Patrick is more nitpicky than Conrad ever was when it comes to money."

Taylor had to agree with his mother. His father had a sixth sense when it came to investing his clients' money, but it was Patrick's gift of total recall that proved invaluable to the company's ongoing profitability.

"That's four out of five, Taylor. I need you to convince Viola to join the rest of the family."

"You know if you tell Viola to go left, then she'll go right. Although she's always talked about running her own kitchen, I feel she'll come around even before we open as a hotel and wedding venue."

"I hope you're right."

Taylor wanted to tell his mother he knew he was right. Within days of Viola graduating culinary school, her future plans included opening her own restaurant. Every once in a while she would bring up the topic, and whenever Conrad offered to give her the start-up capital, her comeback was always she needed to be more experienced.

There was a swollen silence before Taylor asked his mother a question that had been nagging at him for months. "Are you selling this house and taking an extended cruise so you won't be reminded of Dad?"

Elise closed her eyes, and when she opened them they were shimmering with unshed tears. "It doesn't matter where I go because I'll never be able to forget Conrad. I knew he was special the first time he bumped into me at Princeton and spilled coffee on the front of my sweater. I yelled at him for not looking where he was going. He calmly told me he was sorry and would buy me another sweater. I told him I didn't want another sweater, and there was no way I could go to class with brown stains on my white sweater and smelling like coffee."

"Did you skip class?"

"No. Conrad took off his sweater and gave it to me. He stood there in just an undershirt. He told me to take off my sweater and he would have it cleaned. I told him there was no way I was going strip in front of him. The impasse ended when I walked behind a tree and exchanged my sweater for his, because all I had on was a bra. I gave him my off-campus address, and a week later he showed up with a box from Bloomingdale's with a cashmere twinset in a beautiful shade of cobalt blue. When I told him I couldn't accept something that expensive because I didn't know him, he claimed if I allowed him to take me out to dinner, then we could get to know each other."

Taylor laughed softly. "It looks as if Dad knew what to do and say to get his woman."

Elise's laughter joined his. "That he did. We set up

a date for dinner, and when he picked me up in his dinged-up two-seater sports car I was wearing the twinset with a strand of my grandmother's pearls. To say I was impressed is an understatement. Not only was I, a sophomore, going out with a senior, but I was totally unaware that he'd been born into wealth."

"When did you find that out?"

"The day he proposed marriage. By that time, I was so much in love with him that I couldn't say no even if I'd felt I was too young to marry. My father, who was a judge, married us, and we had a small reception on the patio with relatives and a few of my sorority sisters in attendance. He'd invited his aunt, but she'd declined because she had come down with pneumonia and her doctor had recommended she remain at home. We delayed going on a honeymoon until she recovered, but unfortunately she never did. Conrad honored her wishes to have her cremated, and four months after our wedding we were finally able to take our delayed honeymoon to Hawaii. We were living with my parents because we were waiting for this house to be renovated. Conrad had bought it below market value because it been abandoned for years.

"Meanwhile, I'd gone back to school to get a graduate degree in education. I'd just begun teaching when I discovered I was pregnant. I knew something was wrong because I kept cramping. I left school early and called my doctor to let him know I was coming in. I'd just walked in when I began hemorrhaging. I don't remember anything after that, but hours later when I woke up in the hospital was told that I'd lost my baby, and because they couldn't stop the bleeding I'd undergone a hysterectomy."

Elise sucked in a breath, holding it until she finally let it out. "I went into a depression because I realized I would never give Conrad children. When I told him this, he said we could always adopt. It was when I spoke to my former college roommate who'd become a social worker that she convinced me to become a foster parent, because the adoption process was a lengthy one." She smiled. "That's when I got you."

Taylor's smile matched Elise's. "You got me, and then you couldn't stop until you filled every bedroom in this house."

"That's because you were the sweetest little boy any mother could wish for. Then I rolled the dice and requested another foster child. I'm not going to say it was easy raising children who had been neglected and had experienced a myriad of traumas, but I was willing to accept the challenge. And once I decided to homeschool you and saw you thrive, I knew that's what I wanted for the others. My mother accused me of setting up a safety net for my children where they wouldn't be able to survive outside the bubble I'd created."

Taylor hadn't had much interaction with Elise's parents, who'd relocated to Florida to take advantage of the warmer climate. "Thankfully, they did live long enough to see us survive."

"You're right. My mother finally had to admit that Conrad and I had done a good job raising their grandchildren."

Taylor would readily admit to anyone that he'd had the best upbringing any child could wish for. Although Conrad was a workaholic, putting in long hours at his office Monday through Friday, on the weekends he devoted himself totally to his wife and children. Once the family increased, he'd arranged for an in-ground pool and basketball and tennis courts. On Saturdays or Sundays, he could be seen shooting hoops with his sons and daughter or swimming laps with Viola.

"And I'm certain once Patrick marries and has children he will also become a good father."

Elise's mouth twisted into a sneer. "I shouldn't say this, but I really don't like my future daughter-in-law."

Taylor angled his head. "Why would you say that?"

"She's a bit too pushy and immature for my tastes. When Patrick doesn't do what she wants, she tends to pout like a little child."

Taylor wanted to tell Elise he agreed with her but didn't think it was his place to comment on his brother's choice as a potential wife. "It's apparent that it doesn't bother him."

"Well, I still don't like her," Elise mumbled under her breath.

He sat straight, wondering if his mother would approve of the woman he would choose as a wife. "I'm ready to move into your condo."

Elise stood, Taylor pushing off the rocker and rising with her. "I just have to get my keys."

Sonja had drawn up a list of things she had to do before she relocated to New Jersey. She'd handed in her resignation, giving the gallery owners two weeks' notice. In the interim she'd gone through her closet to select garments for spring and summer, and then went online to purchase a number of tees and khakis that she'd planned to make her work ensemble, along with boots and running shoes.

She and Taylor communicated with each other electronically, either texting or emailing her with updates and emojis. He sent her a thumbs-up after it'd taken the security company a week to set up their system, and a thumbs-down after the maintenance company used more than a dozen workers over the span of a month to clean the entire house from the turrets to the cellar.

When she wasn't working at the gallery, Sonja went online to research Bainbridge House and had gleaned more about the house than the family for which it had been named. However, she did discover an article written about Charles Garland Bainbridge that recorded he'd been prevented from building his summer cottage in Newport, Rhode Island, like millionaire owners of The Breakers, Marble House and Chateau-sur-Mer because there were rumors that his wife may have been a mulatto. Sonja was anxious to go through the contents of the trunks to uncover what secrets the Bainbridge family wanted to hide or deny.

Bainbridge House had survived while Newport's summer retreats of wealthy Gilded Age industrialists hadn't after World War II. The Victorian-era mansions had become impractical and out of style. Many were converted into schools or condos, and others were neglected, razed or abandoned until the Preservation Society of Newport County began buying up Gilded Age mansions and opening them to the public as museums.

She'd just finished packing a Pullman when her cell phone rang. Smiling, she picked it up. "What's up, boss?"

Sonja did not realize how much she'd missed Taylor until he called her. And not seeing him for weeks had exacerbated the longing she'd continually denied acknowledging. There was something about her best friend's brother that turned her into an emotional pretzel whenever she asked herself what she wanted from Taylor and the answer continued to evade her.

Taylor's laugh caressed her ear. "Not hardly," he teased. "I'm calling to let you know I've leased a furnished condo for you less than ten miles from Bainbridge House, because the only extended-stay hotel was too far away. Your car is parked in the attached garage. Whenever you're ready, I'll pick you up and drive you back here."

"I'm ready now, Taylor. I just finished packing."

"How many bags do you have?"

"I have a Pullman, a smaller one with wheels and a carry-on bag with my laptop."

"I'll come up to your apartment and help you with your bags."

"That's not necessary. My uncle will help me."

"Are you sure?"

"Yes, Taylor. I'm sure."

"I'm on my way. I'll call you once I reach the bridge."

"Okay." Sonja wheeled her bags out of her bedroom to the entryway. She'd alerted her aunt and uncle days before that she would be leaving before the weekend.

Nelson pushed to his feet. "I guess this is it."

Sonja nodded. "Yes. But I'm not going down until Taylor calls to let me know he's on the GW Bridge."

Yolanda came out of the kitchen wiping her hands on a dish towel. "Don't get so involved in your work that you forget to take time to relax."

Sonja laughed. "I don't plan to work weekends." Taylor told her she was responsible for her own hours, and for her that meant taking Saturdays and Sundays off.

Yolanda approached Sonja and hugged her. "Good for you."

She returned her aunt's hug and kissed her cheek.

"I have some time before Taylor will be here to pick me up—I'll help you in the kitchen." Since she'd retired, Yolanda spent most of her time in the kitchen scrolling through the internet and trying out new recipes.

"I'm making your uncle's favorite. Puerto Rican lasagna."

"It's called *pastelón*."

Yolanda waved her hand. "It should be called *delicioso*, because the first time I tasted your mother's I've always wanted to make it. And this time I won't get a recipe from a book or the internet because Maria sent me her recipe."

"You're kidding? Mami never gives out her recipes." Sonja's grandmother had earned a reputation as one of the best cooks in her neighborhood and had passed her culinary skills onto her daughter.

Yolanda flashed a Cheshire cat grin. "I told her Nelson missed her *pastelón*. I wanted to know if she would send me her recipe. At first she said if he wanted some then all he had to do was drive up and she'd make a pan for him. When I opened my email to find the recipe, I had to assume she changed her mind."

"Lucky you."

"If you want, I'll forward a copy to you."

"*Gracias*, Titi."

Sonja sliced overripe plantains on a cutting board, making certain she yielded four slices per plantain and set them aside to be fried. The mouthwatering aroma of sautéed garlic and sofrito filled the kitchen, and she recalled the times when she'd sat on a stool watching her mother concoct the most delicious Caribbean-inspired dishes, and when older she became Maria's sous-chef. Sonja had inherited her love of cooking from her mother and grandmother, and she was looking forward to moving into the condo, where she could cook for herself.

When she got the call from Taylor that he was on the George Washington Bridge, Nelson helped her with her luggage, riding the elevator with her to the street level. "Will you get time off for a vacation?"

Sonja stared at Nelson as if he'd taken leave of his senses. She was only moving two—not two hundred—hours away. "Of course. If I decide to come home on a weekend, I'll call you beforehand." She did not want to remind Nelson that he played baseball with his retired buddies on Sundays, and when he wasn't playing ball he spent hours in front of the television watching whatever professional sport was in season.

She spied a gleaming silver SUV with Connecticut plates. "That's Taylor's Infiniti."

Nelson's eyebrows lifted. "Nice ride."

Taylor slowed and maneuvered next to a parked car. He tapped a button and the hatch opened. Sonja and the man he assumed was her uncle were wheeling the luggage to the rear of the Infiniti at the same time he got out. He took the handle of the Pullman from Sonja, lifting and placing it in the cargo area with the smaller suitcase and carry-on.

Smiling, he extended his hand to the slender middle-aged man. "Taylor Williamson."

Nelson stared at the proffered hand, and then took it. "Nelson Rios. Sonja's uncle. Make certain you take good care of my niece, Taylor Williamson."

"Tío!"

Taylor noticed the rush of color darkening Sonja's face. Her uncle had obviously embarrassed her. "It's okay, Sonja. Your uncle is just trying to protect you."

"I don't need protection," she snapped angrily. "Not from *any* man." Turning on her heel, she walked over to the passenger side of the Infiniti, got in and slammed the door harder than necessary.

Nelson threw up both hands. "What the hell did I say?"

"It must have been the wrong thing, for her to go off on you like that."

Nelson shook his head. "Tell her I'm sorry."

"I think it would be better if I don't say anything to her for a while." Taylor hadn't seen this side of Sonja, and instinct told him this wasn't the time to try to defend her uncle. "And I do want you to know that I intend to take good care of her."

Nelson nodded. "Thanks, son."

Taylor closed the hatch, then rounded the SUV and took his seat behind the wheel. He gave Sonja a sidelong glance as he fastened his seat belt. She was so still she could've been carved from stone and it was obvious she was in a funk. There was something about her expression that reminded him of Patrick's fiancée. Sonja was pouting like Andrea.

Well, Taylor mused, he wasn't his brother and Sonja wasn't his fiancée. He didn't have to plea and cajole her to talk to him, and there was nothing for which he had to apologize.

There was just the sound of the radio for nearly a half hour before he detected a grunt.

"Did you say something?"

"I said I don't need you to protect me."

Taylor's hands tightened on the steering wheel. "I didn't say I would protect you. It was your uncle asking that I take care of you. Try and see his side, Sonja. He sees you moving out and going away with a man he's never met and knows nothing about. That's what I call being concerned."

"I told him I would call and let him know where I'm staying."

"Why did you tell him that, Sonja?"

"Because he'd know where to contact me in case of an emergency."

"Couldn't he do that if he has your cell number?"

"Yes, but—"

"But nothing," Taylor interrupted. "Even if he didn't know your address, he could always track your cell. It's obvious the man loves you, but you failed to see the pain on his face when you screamed at him."

"I didn't scream at him."

"Yes, you did."

"Are you saying I should apologize to him?"

"It would behoove me not to tell you what to do. After all, you're a strong, independent, professional woman in control of her life and her destiny."

"Now you're being facetious, Taylor."

"Am I? Aren't you all of those adjectives?"

A beat passed. "I am."

"If you are, then own it, sweetheart."

Sonja met his eyes. "Do you realize this is the second time you've called me sweetheart."

"Really?" Taylor hadn't realized the endearment had just slipped out. And he had to ask himself if he wanted Sonja to be his sweetheart and the answer was a resounding yes. She was everything he liked in a woman. Her beauty aside, he was drawn to her intelligence and confidence.

"Yes, really, Taylor. Do you call all your women sweetheart?"

"No, because I don't have any women. I'm sorry, it was just a slip of the tongue."

"Apology accepted."

He couldn't tell Sonja that his father had always called his mother sweetheart and she probably would've thought it creepy that he was doing the same thing to her. As a young boy Taylor had been confused because he'd thought her name Elise, and when he'd asked Conrad why he'd called her that he said it was because she was the sweetest woman he'd ever known and he'd given her his heart.

Taylor recalled the time when he'd first come to

live with Conrad and Elise Williamson and found
their behavior strange. He'd watched Conrad stare
at his wife with what he would interpret once he
entered adolescence as longing and lustful stares.
Conrad would rest a hand at the small of her back,
and when he suspected no one was looking, his hand
would slip lower to cradle her hips. Blushing, Elise
would whisper in his ear and he would remove his
hand. He'd known his parents loved each other unconditionally and that love was transferred to the
children they'd fostered and then legally adopted.
Elise had always professed she would fight like a
lioness protecting her cubs if anyone attempted to
harm her children, and it was apparent her attitude
was the same when she professed her displeasure
toward Patrick's fiancée.

"Tell me about your parents," Sonja said after a
comfortable silence.

Taylor wondered if Sonja could read his mind.
"They were insanely in love," he said quietly after
a moment. "I never heard my father raise his voice
to my mother even when he was angry. He would
walk away, leaving her talking to empty air. Then
they would be lovey-dovey, acting as if nothing happened."

"Is that why you don't yell?"

"Yes, Sonja. Yelling and screaming never solves
anything. What it does is make a bad situation worse
and can only lead to unwarranted hostility."

Sonja locked eyes with him when he came to a

stop at a red light. "Are you talking about me and my uncle?"

"Yes. I think you misinterpreted what he'd said to me. What if I were a psychopath masquerading as an engineer to lure young women to a place where I'd torture and kill them?"

Sonja laughed. "It's apparent you watch shows depicting kidnapping, murder and mayhem."

"Don't laugh, Sonja, because it happens every day in every large and small city around the world."

"The difference is you're not a psychopath, and if you were then my former NYPD uncle and my active duty Special Forces brother would bypass the legal system and take you out."

"You wouldn't know that if you were dead. And maybe it was because your uncle was a cop and had taken the pledge to protect and serve that he felt the need to say what he did to me."

Sonja wanted to tell Taylor that he was being an alarmist, that she had nothing to fear from him. But when she thought about what her uncle had said to Taylor, she realized it was the first time Nelson had seen her with a man since she'd moved in with him and his wife. She hadn't revealed the intimate details of her failed marriage to anyone except Viola. She had trusted her friend to be neutral, unlike her father and brother, who probably would've confronted Hugh and made a bad situation worse. She'd told her parents that her marriage wasn't working because she'd felt like more of a daughter than a wife to her much older husband, and decided to file for divorce.

"You're probably right about my uncle."

"I know I'm right."

"I suppose I should call him and apologize."

"I agree."

"There's no need for you to act so smug, Taylor," she countered. "I'll have to call him later because I put my cell phone in the carry-on bag."

Taylor tapped the navigation screen. "My number is synced to Bluetooth. You can call him from here."

She tapped in Nelson's number. It rang twice before he picked up. "What's the matter?"

Sonja registered fear in her uncle's strident query. "Nothing is the matter, *tío*. I'm using Taylor's cell because mine is in one of the bags. I'm calling to apologize for screaming at you. I'm sorry I overreacted."

"There's no need to apologize, *muñeca*. I've forgotten about it."

"Well, if you have, then it is the same with me. *Te quiero*."

"Yo también te quiero."

"What does *muñeca* mean?" Taylor asked after she'd ended the call.

"Doll. My uncle has always called me that."

"Would it bother you if I called you *muñeca*?"

"What happened to sweetheart?" she teased, smiling.

"What if I use them interchangeably?"

Sonja sobered because she felt they were about to

embark on something neither needed nor possibly wanted. Especially not her. She couldn't afford to become involved with someone she had to see and work with every day. Taylor Williamson was too potent a man for her to completely ignore. There were times when he looked at her and she felt as if he could see beyond the wall she'd erected to keep men out of her life; that her lips professed one thing while her celibate body screamed for her to sleep with a man, if only to assuage the frustration she'd denied for far too long. She'd filled her spare time with work, reading romance novels and watching television programming dedicated to love and romance. And she'd been successful until coming face-to-face with her best friend's brother.

Even if she was able to dismiss his gorgeous face and body, it was his soothing and calming voice, intelligence and down-to-earth personality that drew her in and refused to let her go. And his wealth never factored into the equation that he was a certified trifecta.

At that moment Sonja realized she was tired. Tired of pretending that she did not need a man, when she wanted a relationship where she was treated as an equal and not an ornament or trophy taken out and put on display whenever it suited her partner. Taylor had offered to be her friend, and not seeing him for many weeks made her aware that she wanted more than friendship. And she knew she had to be the first to thrown down the gauntlet to ascertain whether he would be receptive.

"It wouldn't bother me if you called me doll or sweetheart." She knew she'd shocked him when his foot suddenly hit the brake, the SUV coming to a complete stop in the middle of the street, followed by a cacophony of blaring horns. Her heart was pumping a runaway rhythm when she realized they could've been rear-ended by the car behind them. "Taylor, you're holding up traffic."

He eased off the brake and resumed driving. He took his right hand off the wheel and covered her left, resting on her thigh, brought it to his mouth and kissed the back of it. "I believe we're going to have a lot of fun working together."

Sonja had fought the dynamic vitality he'd exuded effortlessly and failed. "You think?"

Taylor winked at her. "I know."

He'd said the two words with such confidence that it buoyed hers. They had time, at least a year, to discover where their friendship would take them.

Chapter Seven

With wide eyes, Sonja stared at the gatehouse. "Isn't this where your mother lives?" she asked Taylor. He'd told her his mother owned a condo in a gated community.

"No. Her condo is in Sparta. It's about thirteen miles south of here."

Taylor decelerated and then came to a complete stop at the gatehouse. He lowered the driver's-side window and spoke to the man inside the enclosure. She couldn't hear what they were saying. The attendant leaned down and peered in at Sonja. Smiling, he waved to her, and she returned his wave with one of her own.

The gate rose smoothly, and Taylor drove through,

following a paved road to an enclave of two-story farmhouse structures with broad porches, second-floor balconies and attached garages. There were signposts along the road indicating the direction to shops, the recreation center, movie theater and restaurant.

"How did you find this place?" Sonja asked.

"I contacted a Realtor, who told me the developer was having a problem selling units, and rather than leave them vacant he'd opted to lease a few. From what I've seen of the development I think you'll enjoy living here."

"I like what I see. It appears I won't have to leave to shop for food or eat out." She paused. "Do you know why it has been difficult to sell all the units?"

"Personally, I believe even with the number of on-site amenities they're overpriced. Folks could buy a four- or five-bedroom home in the Poconos built on half an acre for a lot less than these two- and three-bedrooms."

"How much does a three-bedroom go for?"

"Why? Are you thinking of buying one?"

Sonja shook her head. "Not hardly. If I was going to purchase property, it wouldn't be in the middle of nowhere even with on-site amenities. However, if I were looking to downsize later in life, then maybe I would consider it."

"Are you saying you couldn't see yourself living at Bainbridge House?"

"I could if I was a docent."

Taylor pulled into the driveway to a house at the end of a street and shut off the engine. "Bainbridge House is not going to be a museum."

Shifting on her seat, Sonja turned and gave Taylor a long, penetrating stare. "It could be a hotel *and* a museum. I told you before that I have some ideas about the property, so if you want we can talk about it after I settle in."

Taylor unsnapped his belt. "Okay. Why don't you take a few days to get used to your surroundings before you begin working."

"What are you going to do?"

"I've scheduled interviews for several days this week."

She nodded. "I'd like to ask a favor."

"What's that?"

"I'd like to go through the trunks during my downtime."

"You want me to bring them here?"

"Yes."

"Are you sure, Sonja?"

"Yes, I am sure." She had carefully enunciated each word. "After spending hours attempting to identify the period and style of a particular plate, fork or candlestick, examining the contents of the trunks will be like a breath of fresh air." Sonja didn't tell Taylor that she was curious to uncover additional information about the original owners of the historic house. Old letters, journals, bills of sale were helpful when authenticating items.

"I'll bring them over later tonight."

She inclined her head. "Thank you, sir."

Taylor smiled. "You're welcome, ma'am. Let's go inside so you can check out your new digs.

Sonja stared, tongue-tied, as she surveyed the open floor plan of the house that was to become a place she could call home. White walls, with creamy upholstered furniture, heightened the illusion of openness in the living, dining, and family rooms, which made the space appear even larger. White cabinets, yellow and cornflower blue tiles, and cobalt blue countertops and colorful accessories created a cheerful mood in the contemporary kitchen. The classic combination of blue and white was timeless and was repeated in throw pillows, area rugs and the dining area chair seat cushions.

Looking over her shoulder, she smiled at Taylor. "It's perfect. Thank you." And for Sonja it *was* perfect. Move-in ready with a large wall-mounted television and audio components in the family room and under-cabinet radio in the kitchen.

He moved closer and put an arm around her waist. "I was hoping you would like it."

"Of course, I like it."

"It's one of two two-bedroom model units."

Moving into the condo would signal a significant change in Sonja's life. It would be the first time in twenty years she would live independently of others. First, she'd lived on base with her parents; then she'd shared an off-campus apartment with a roommate before marrying Hugh and moving into his house. During their separation she'd gone from her husband's house to her parents' retirement home in the Adirondack Mountains to heal and plan the next phase of what had been her tumultuous life. And once she decided to return to college, it wasn't in Boston, but in New York City, where she'd moved in with her aunt and uncle.

Taylor kissed her hair. "I'm going back to the car to bring your bags in."

"And I'm going upstairs to see the rest of the place."

Sonja felt as if she was walking on air as she climbed the staircase to the second story. The condo contained two bedrooms: one master and another smaller one she could use as an office. The master had a sitting area and an en suite bath. She thought of the bedroom as a romantic retreat with voluminous pale silk drapes covering floor-to-ceiling windows and sliding doors with built-in blinds that opened out to the balcony. She focused her attention on a king-size four-poster mahogany bed. The bed linens, with layers of pillows in differing patterns, repeated the first floor's blue-and-white palette. A creamy-white armchair with a matching footstool, close to a small round mahogany table in the seating area, was the perfect place for her to kick back and relax before retiring for bed.

Sonja left the master suite and walked into the bedroom across the hall, wondering if Taylor had chosen this unit because he'd believed she would like the colors and furnishings. Suddenly she recalled his preference for blues and grays while she preferred earth tones. Had he, she mused, selected this unit because of his affinity for blue? She recalled the exquisitely tailored royal blue suit he'd worn during their initial meeting at The Cellar.

The decorating style in the smaller bedroom was Swedish country with wood furniture painted in tones of white. The decorator differed from the classic approach by including French provincial and country influences. Duvets in a toile de Jouy pattern covered twin beds with off-white headboards, and white linens and a crocheted bed skirt beneath the duvets artfully corroborated the Swedish theme of elegant white. A table and chair next to a blue-and-white-checkered upholstered chair and ottoman would do double duty as her desk. Sonja had walked out of the bedroom when she spied Taylor coming up the staircase carrying her Pullman.

He had removed a sweatshirt to reveal a tee stamped with a college logo; it hugged his muscular upper body like second skin, and her mouth went dry when Sonja realized she was lusting after a man with whom she would have to work closely over the next year. And she didn't need anyone to tell her that she was being a hypocrite. Taylor was her boss and he'd offered friendship, but for Sonja that wasn't enough. She wanted more and the more translated into what had been missing in her life even before she'd considered ending her marriage: intimacy. The very notion of her wanting to sleep with Taylor shook her to the core.

"Where do you want me to put this?" Taylor asked her.

She blinked slowly as if coming out of a trance. "You can put it in the master. I'll go and get the other bags."

"Don't bother. I'll bring them up."

She wasn't about to argue with him. "I'm going downstairs to get my cell and bag from the carry-on. Then you can put it in the other bedroom." Sonja knew she had to put some space between them for a few minutes if only to regain control of her fragile emotions.

Smiling, Taylor executed a snappy salute. "Okay, boss lady."

"Yeah, right," she drawled, trying not to smile. Sonja discovered the two bags at the foot of the staircase and removed her cell phone and cross-body from the carry-on.

Taylor returned and hoisted the two bags, his biceps bulging from the exertion. "After I come down I'll give you a key card for the house, fob for your car and the corporate credit card. I'll hang onto the extra key card and fob in case you either lose or misplace them. There's a remote device under the visor that will allow you access at the gatehouse."

Sonja nodded. She wanted to tell Taylor she'd never lost or misplaced her keys, but if it made him feel more secure then she wasn't going to argue with him. Walking into the kitchen, she opened the French-door refrigerator. It was empty except for a box of baking soda. Sonja opened the cabinets, finding them empty, and then a door in a far corner of the kitchen and discovered a pantry and half bathroom. A stackable washer and dryer were set up behind café doors.

She detected movement behind her and turned to find Taylor standing only feet away. Her heartbeat kicked into a higher gear.

"You can't do that," she said in a breathless whisper.

"Do what?"

"Sneak up on me."

Crossing muscular arms over his chest, Taylor smiled at her. "Sorry about that. Next time I'll make some noise."

Sonja blew out a breath. "Thanks. I need to go food shopping to stock the fridge and the pantry, and also buy plates, cups, glasses and flatware."

Taylor held out his hand. "Come with me. I have to pull my car out the driveway before you can get yours out of the garage."

"What did you get me?"

He winked at her. "You'll see."

Sonja doubled over laughing hysterically when Taylor tapped the button on the automatic garage opener and she saw the vehicle he'd leased for her.

It was an Infiniti QX50—the smallest model of the QX SUVs.

"I can't believe you got the same style and color as yours."

"When you admired mine, I thought I'd get you the smaller version."

"Thank you." The two words sounded empty to Sonja once she realized Taylor was thinking about her when he had made the decision to lease the SUV. "I really appreciate the thought, Taylor."

He handed her the fob. "Anything to make the lives of my team easier. You're going to have your work cut out for you once you begin going through those crates. What you saw in the cellar wasn't even half of what has been stored there."

Sonja went still. "What are you talking about?"

"The maintenance people discovered a door to a storeroom hidden behind several armoires. The space is filled with as many crates as what you saw."

"Oh no!"

"Oh yes," Taylor said, smiling. "I didn't even bother to look at what was written on them—I just closed the door."

"Your ancestors probably were hoarders."

"Either hoarders, collectors or packrats."

Sonja was tempted to mention the museum again to Taylor but held her tongue. Bainbridge House was large enough to operate as a hotel, wedding venue *and* a museum. "Let me get my bag with my license so I can drive Silver Bullet to see if she purrs or roars."

Taylor ran a hand over his cropped hair. "Please don't tell me you just named your car."

"Of course. Doesn't yours have a name?"

"Yeah. QX80."

She made a sucking sound with her tongue and teeth. "That's the model number."

"Well, that's what it is."

"Well, my new baby is Silver Bullet."

Taylor shook his head. "Go get your bag, Sonja."

Sonja adjusted the seat to accommodate her shorter legs, tapped the start-engine button and slowly backed out of the garage. It was a while since she'd been behind the wheel, and this was her first time driving a sport utility vehicle.

"How does it feel?" Taylor asked. He sat in the passenger seat as she drove slowly in the direction of the business area.

"Nice, even though I'm not used to sitting up this high. I think I'm going to enjoy driving on the parkways." She came to a complete stop at a stop sign, then continued, not exceeding the posted fifteen miles per hour.

Sonja drove into the lot behind the strip mall, parking near the supermarket. The condos may have been overpriced, but for her the trade-off was convenience. She was certain to patronize the hair and nail salon, variety store, dry cleaner and restaurant.

"I'm going to the variety store to pick up some housewares." Not only did she need pots, pans and dishes, flatware and serving pieces, but also linens, kitchen and bath towels, and a laundry basket.

Taylor nodded. "I'll meet you in the supermarket. You said you need to stock the pantry, so I figured I'd pick up canned goods and nonperishables."

"Okay."

She peered into his cart near to overflowing with cans of beans and other vegetables, boxes of pasta, rice, sugar, flour, vinegar, cooking and olive oil, and a variety of cleaning supplies. "You did good."

"Thank you, sweetheart. What's for dinner?"

Sonja gave him a level look. "You want me to cook for you?"

"Yes. If you cook for me tomorrow night, then I'll return the favor and cook for you the following day."

"You cook?"

"Duh! Who do you think feeds me?"

Sonja felt as if she'd suddenly come down with a case of foot-in-mouth. She didn't know why she'd assumed Taylor was unable to prepare a meal for himself. "All right," she said, hoping to cover up her faux pas.

"What are you making?"

"I don't know. I'll think about it once we get home."

Once we get home.

Taylor repeated the four words to himself. Had

Sonja actually thought of the condo as theirs? When he was shown the two model units he'd purposely selected the one with the cheerful blue-and-white furnishings because he felt it complemented Sonja's romantic nature. She'd admitted she read romance novels and watched Hallmark movies.

Taylor knew he'd been lying to himself for weeks. He'd almost convinced himself that there could never be more between him and Sonja Rios-Martin than friendship. Even though he'd told himself that over and over, he knew it was a lie, and he'd purposely kept his distance, hoping his feelings for her would translate into out of sight, out of mind. But even that had proved unsuccessful.

There was something about his sister's friend that was so different from any other woman with whom he'd been involved. Sonja wasn't reticent when it came to speaking her mind, and that meant he did not have to guess what she was thinking or attempt to interpret something she'd said. She was intelligent, poised and confident, qualities he admired most in a woman. Then there was her sensual beauty. Just looking at her, inhaling the intoxicating scent of her perfume, touching her hand or a part of her body, and the husky quality of her voice he never tired of listening to. The only thing missing was how she tasted. Taylor longed to kiss her sexy mouth with a need bordering on obsession, and it had taken all his self-control not to act on his fantasy.

"You can ring up these two carts together," he told the register clerk.

He emptied his cart, bagging everything. And then he bagged the items in Sonja's cart. He handed the checker a credit card. Between him and Sonja they'd bought enough food to last her for several weeks. He took the receipt and returned the card to a case in the pocket of his jeans.

"Let's go, *muñeca*," he said, grinning and winking at Sonja.

"I'm ready whenever you are, *papi*."

His eyebrows shot up. He'd lost count of the number of times he'd heard Spanish-speaking girls call their boyfriends *papi*, and it was always said as a term of affection. Taylor pushed his cart and pulled Sonja's as he followed her to the SUV.

"So, I'm your *papi*?"

"Only if you want to be."

Taylor stopped and met her eyes. "I do." The two words were firm, final, and in that instant he knew he and Sonja had silently acknowledged both were open to see where their friendship would lead. "What on earth did you buy?" he asked, moving the bags behind the rear seats to make room for the contents of the shopping carts.

"Pots, pans, dishes, sheets, towels, small appliances and other knickknacks for the kitchen and bathrooms. I also bought a single-serve coffeemaker and an electric kettle, because I need my coffee in the morning and chamomile tea at night."

He gave her a sidelong glance as she handed him

bags from the carts. "Do you have a problem going to sleep?"

"Sometimes. But that's only when I'm overthinking something."

"I hope that doesn't happen when you begin working. I've told you I have a two-year timeline in which to fully restore the house and property. Even though you have a lot to appraise and catalogue I don't want you stressed out about it. You can set your own hours and at no time will you be obligated to check with me unless you have a question or problem. I'll have enough to do, working with the contractors and making certain I don't incur too many cost overruns. I don't want too many verbal rounds with my brother."

"Do you have a final budget for the entire project?"

"Not yet. Patrick has been adjusting the budget for the house as needed. He has one for the château, one for the outbuildings, including the cottages, stables and barn, and another for the gardens, golf course, reflecting pools and fountains. Why did you ask?"

"I haven't seen the entire property, but based on restoration projects I've observed in France and Italy I guesstimate it will cost you between ninety and one hundred million dollars."

"That sounds about right," Taylor said, neither confirming nor denying the dollar amount.

"Sounds about right, Taylor?"

Taylor knew it was impossible to deceive Sonja. "You're right. How did you know?"

"I know you're going to have to hire electricians, plumbers, roofers, carpenters, stonemasons, and landscape architects. Faux bois specialists are necessary to restore the walls in the library and the moldings in the ballrooms. A cleaning crew and exterminators also factor into the cost along with workers needed to haul away debris. Replacement doors and windows will have to be ordered from Italy, and if there's a need to replace roof tiles, I can give you the name of a Vermont quarry that can ship them to you."

Taylor wanted to ask Sonja how she knew the doors and windows had come from Italy. Did she only have to glance at an object to ascertain its origin? "You're going to prove invaluable and an essential member of the restoration team."

"I hope so."

"I know so, Sonja—otherwise I never would've hired you."

"I thought you hired me because Viola pressured you to."

He blinked slowly. "Is that really what you think?"

"I don't know, Taylor. You tell me. You didn't believe me when I told you I was an architectural historian?"

"I believed you because Viola, who rarely gives out compliments, said you're a genius when it comes to identifying antiques. When Patrick asked for letters of recommendation and I told him I would vouch for you, it had nothing to do with Viola singing your praises. I don't have time to look for another architectural historian so, regardless of what you think or believe, you're it, Sonja."

A mysterious smile parted her lips. "Are you saying we're a good combination?"

"Yeah. Like peanut butter and jelly," Taylor said teasingly.

"No, Taylor. Like shrimp and grits."

"Nice. But how about bacon and eggs?"

She scrunched up her nose as she handed him another bag. "I've got one better. Chicken and waffles."

"Hell, yeah! I've got a special recipe for chicken and waffles, and one of these days I'm going to make them for you."

"I usually have chicken and waffles along with mimosas for Sunday brunch."

Taylor closed the door to the hatch. "I suppose that means I'll have to come over one Sunday morning and put my money where my mouth is."

Sonja bit her lip, bringing his gaze to linger on her mouth. "We will see."

"Yes, we will. If you don't mind, I'd like to drive Silver Bullet back to the house," Taylor volunteered.

"I don't mind since you acknowledged her correctly."

Cupping Sonja's elbow, he steered her around to the passenger side, opened the door and assisted her up. Taylor stared up at her. "If you had to name my vehicle, what would it be?"

"Gray Wolf."

Taylor angled his head. "I like that. Gray Wolf it is. After I help you put everything away, I'm going up to the house to get the trunks and copies I made of the blueprints and floor plans. By the way, the papers are wrapped in oilskin, which has preserved them from moisture and rot, and the floor plans and blueprints have been stored in metal tubes."

"Bring them by tomorrow. I need to unpack and put everything away."

"I have morning meetings, so I probably won't be able to come over until late afternoon," Taylor said.

"That'll work. Don't forget I'm making dinner."

He wanted to tell Sonja there was no way he would forget. "Do you want me to bring anything?"

"No. I think I have everything I need."

Taylor drove back to the condo, and he and Sonja made quick work of unloading the bags and carrying them to the kitchen. "Do you need help putting things away?"

Sonja shook her head. "I don't think so."

"It looks as if you're really going to be busy, so why don't we put off sharing dinner for a couple of days."

"That's not necessary. I'm going to stay up tonight and finish everything."

"So, we're still on for tomorrow night?" he asked. "Yes."

Taking a step, Taylor lowered his head and brushed a light kiss over her parted lips. "I'll see you tomorrow." He knew he'd shocked her when he heard her hushed gasp.

Turning on his heel, he left the kitchen and walked out to where he'd parked his vehicle.

Chapter Eight

Taylor tapped a button on the steering wheel, increasing the radio's volume as he sang to Bruno Mars's "Uptown Funk." Knowing he was going to share dinner with Sonja put him in a party mood. It had been impulsive when he'd invited himself to her home and then asked if she would cook for him.

And if he were honest with himself he would have to admit he had been intrigued before Sonja introduced herself to him at The Cellar. When Viola called her from his car, putting their conversation on speaker he'd been mesmerized with the timbre of her voice. And the expression on her face when he opened the garage door to reveal the vehicle he'd leased for her was imprinted on his memory like a permanent tattoo. It was a combination of shock and then pure joy. It had been the same when she'd walked into the condo. She may have thought of them as perks, but he viewed them as necessities to make her life less stressful and had given her the option of setting her own hours. He did not relish the task of going through hundreds of crates, examining each item and cataloguing or authenticating it as an antique or a reproduction.

Taylor lowered the volume on the radio when a familiar name appeared on the navigation screen. "What's up, stranger?"

"That's what I should be asking you, Williamson."

"It's all good, Robbie. Right now I'm living the dream."

"I'm glad you are because I'm so sick and tired of Lansing, Allen and Payette's dog-and-pony show that I'm seriously thinking about walking into HR and quitting, but not before giving them the middle finger."

Taylor smothered a laugh even though what Robinson Harris had said was no laughing matter. After the company's merger several years back things began to change. It was gradual at first, but after a number of Payette's board members gained a monopoly, the entire culture of the company changed—and not positively. Layoffs escalated, salaries and promotions were frozen, and supervisors were told to lean heavily on their workers to complete construction projects before the designated date in order to maximize profits.

"I'm sorry I didn't get back to you sooner, but I just got the message. Kendall took my phone when we broke up. She only gave it back once she'd let me into her apartment to get my things. In the interim I was using a prepaid phone."

Taylor suspected the woman in Robinson Harris's life had tired of being his girlfriend when she'd hinted to Taylor that she wanted to become Mrs. Harris. "I'm sorry to hear that."

"It's okay. I'm over it."

Taylor wanted to ask him how he could be over a woman he'd dated for more than two years. He wasn't calling Robinson about his love life but about whether he wanted to work for him as his project manager. He was a brilliant architectural engineer who had been passed over for a promised promotion before the merger.

"Do you want to leave the dog-and-pony show?"

There was complete silence from the other end of the connection. "You know I do."

"I just might make that a reality if you agree to come and work for me."

"For you and not with you? What are you into, Williamson?"

Taylor chuckled softly. "Why do you make it sound as if I'm involved in some shady business?"

"Are you?"

"Hell, no! I'm working with my family, and we'll need a project manager for the next two years."

Taylor made certain to say *we* rather than *I*. Although he'd supervise the restoration of the house and outbuildings, his brothers and sister had their assigned tasks before Bainbridge House was approved to operate as a hotel and wedding venue.

"You want me to come and work with you?"

"That's why I called you, Robbie." Taylor told him about the project and how he had set aside several weeks in which to interview licensed general contractors. "If you're interested I'd like you to come up and see what I am talking about."

"When can you make time for me?" Robbie asked.

"Next week. I'll let you know when I can block out time to spend the entire day with you."

"Where is the property?" Robbie asked.

"North Jersey."

"I'm familiar with the area because my sister lives in Hackettstown."

"Good. I'll talk to you later."

"Taylor?"

Taylor was taken aback—Robbie had always called him by his surname. "Yes."

"Even if you don't hire me, I want to thank you for thinking of me."

"You misunderstood me, Robbie. I do want to hire you."

"If you want me, then I'm your man."

"I'll be in touch."

When he'd called Robbie and hadn't heard from him, Taylor didn't know what to make of it. It wasn't like his friend not to return his call, and now he knew why. If his former coworker was willing to accept the position as project manager, then he would have filled the two most important positions.

Sonja had mentioned hiring faux bois specialists to restore the walls and moldings, and he planned to give her the responsibility of finding them. Once Robbie came on board, together they would examine the château's foundation to make certain it was stable before any work began.

He also thought about what Sonja had said about ordering windows and doors from Italy and roof tiles from a Vermont quarry. The latter was more easily obtainable than the imported items. If he wasn't able to get the windows installed before the cold weather, then they would have to wait until the following spring.

Taylor had given himself a two-year window in which to refurbish the château, barn, stables, and cottages, to take undue pressure off himself and everyone else involved.

Within that time frame Joaquin would've fulfilled his contracts and could begin to redesign the gardens, and Tariq could purchase horses for the stables.

A sixth sense told him that Viola would eventually supervise the kitchen because she'd never been one to let her brothers exclude her from any of their joint plans. And he was okay with Patrick's role as

CFO of the foundation, because no one else would monitor the bottom line like his certified accountant brother.

Conrad had made Elise promise to carry out his wish to restore his ancestral home, and Taylor had promised his mother he would see it to fruition.

Sonja checked the dining area table for what seemed the umpteenth time before realizing old habits die hard. She'd set the table for two with cloth napkins, water goblets, wineglasses and a vase of daisies as the centerpiece. She had also lit jars of scented candles and set them on tables in the living and family rooms.

As Hugh's wife, she had presided over so many dinner parties that one blended into the next until she'd lost count of how many she'd hosted in the four years they'd lived together. Her then mother-in-law would come by and check on how she'd set the table, and then lecture her in a too-sweet soft voice that a spoon or fork wasn't in its proper place. After a while she'd come to resent the presence of the passive-aggressive woman who doted on her only son.

It was only after Sonja freed herself of the invisible shackles of her husband and mother-in-law that she had come to the realization that Hugh hated his controlling mother, but rather than confront her as a fortysomething-year-old adult, he'd transferred his resentment onto his wife. The day Sonja worked up the courage to put whatever she could carry in a bag and climb into the back seat of a taxi to take her to the nearest bus station was the moment she'd taken control of her life. She had boarded a bus from Boston to Burlington, Vermont, where she checked into a motel for the night. The next day she'd called her mother let her know she'd left her husband and asked her to take the ferry and pick her up. Within minutes of the ferry docking and her mother alighting from the car Sonja did something she rarely did. She cried. Somehow she'd worked up the nerve to free herself from a man who'd controlled every aspect of her life from morning to night. Her mother also cried when she saw her because Sonja was a former shadow of herself. She had lost weight she could ill afford to lose. It taken her nearly a month to plot her escape, and during that time she had been so stressed out that Hugh would uncover her plan that she found it hard to eat more than a few forkfuls of food at any given time. And if Hugh noticed her weight loss, he did not mention it because of his preference for waiflike models.

And that night, once she'd settled into the guest bedroom at her parents' lakefront home, Sonja cried inconsolably. While the tears were cathartic, it would be a long time before she'd completely rid herself of the man. In her naïveté she had replaced her father with Hugh. He'd initially been her protector, but whenever she sought to exercise a modicum of independence he'd quickly quash it. Sonja had overlooked it until it was apparent he did not want to be challenged but obeyed, without her questioning his motives. He'd referred to her as his "little wife," and that was what she'd become because it was easier to acquiesce than argue with him.

Sonja shook her head as if to rid it of her past. It was now time for her to concentrate on the present and her future. When she awoke earlier that morning she'd found herself completely disoriented, and it had taken a full minute before she realized where she was. She knew she wasn't in her regular bedroom because of the sunlight coming in through the windows. Her Inwood apartment had southern exposure, and the sun didn't fill the space until the afternoon. She'd lie in bed, staring up at the ceiling waiting for the butterflies in her stomach to go away, because at that moment she was a butterfly emerging from the cocoon and becoming free—freer than she'd ever been in her life.

Sonja hadn't realized it until now, but Taylor Williamson had become the hero in one of her romance novels. He unknowingly had offered her something she wasn't consciously aware that she needed—independence.

Once she knew Taylor had hired her, she'd called her mother to let her about her new position and that she would have to take up residence in a hotel to be closer to the work site. Maria congratulated her, while reminding Sonja that she was entitled to every good thing coming her way because she'd worked for it. Sonja knew her mother was talking about over-coming a toxic marriage to return to college to complete the courses needed to become an architectural historian.

She smiled. It had taken twenty-four hours for Sonja to fall in love with her new home. All of the units were connected; however, fenced-in backyards provided privacy from her nearest neighbors. The second-story balcony was the perfect spot for her to sit and enjoy her morning coffee, while offering unrestricted panoramic views of a forested area in the distance. She was looking forward to witnessing the change of seasons. The master bathroom had a soaking tub, oversize shower stall with twin shower-heads and a double vanity. This would be her personal retreat, where she could spend as much time as she wanted without someone knocking on the door to ask when she was coming out. Her uncle's two-bedroom apartment had only one bathroom.

The kitchen was a cook's dream—eye-level ovens with a warming drawer, microwave, double sinks, and a stovetop with six burners and a grill. The built-in refrigerator and freezer was large enough to store meat and perishables for months at a time.

The intercom buzzed, startling Sonja as she glanced at the clock on the microwave. It was minutes before six o'clock. Taylor had sent her a text indicating he would arrive at her house around six. Walking over to the wall, she tapped the button.

"Yes?"

"This is the gatehouse. There's a Mr. Williamson here to see you."

"Please let him in."

She didn't know why he'd asked to be announced when he had a remote device that would allow him access onto the property. Leaving the kitchen, she walked to the door and opened the inner one. Her pulse quickened when she saw Taylor get out of his vehicle and walk around to the rear. He removed a hand truck and loaded it with two steamer trunks. With wide eyes, she stared at the logo on the luxury beige and brown trunks. The monogram with quatrefoils, flowers and LV were recognizable as the Louis Vuitton brand. He balanced another carton on top of the trunks.

She opened the outer door and allowed Taylor to enter. The familiar fragrance of his cologne wafted to her nostrils as he moved past her. He'd exchanged his ubiquitous jeans, tees or sweatshirts, and boots for a pale blue linen shirt, navy slacks and black leather slip-ons. Her heart rate kicked into a higher gear when he smiled at her. It was the same apparent smirk he'd affected when modeling. It seemed to say I see you looking at me, and do you like what you see?

Hell, yeah, her inner voice said. Not only did she like what she saw, she also liked him. Sonja knew she had to stop denying that she liked and wanted Taylor for more than friendship. She'd had a few guy friends before and after her marriage, and now it was time for her to acknowledge that she wanted a relationship with someone willing to accept her and her imperfections, and for her it would be the same with him. Sonja wasn't looking or asking for declarations of love, but rather respect. She wanted and needed a man to respect her and for him to treat her as his equal.

"Do you still want me to take the trunks upstairs?" Taylor asked, hoping Sonja didn't notice the huskiness in his voice. He'd promised her they would remain friends, but now he wasn't certain he would be able to keep his promise.

Sonja nodded. "Yes. I can't believe someone would use luxury trunks rather than file cabinets to store paperwork. If I wanted to buy one of these today, the price tag would be more than forty thousand."

"That's crazy," Taylor spit out. "I'd rather donate forty thousand dollars to my favorite charities instead of a single piece of luggage."

"You're preaching to the choir, Taylor."

He gave her a narrow look. "How do you know the price tag?"

"I spent a month in Italy on holiday at the beginning of the year. Instead of going to museums, I spent most of my time eating in restaurants off the beaten track and browsing through countless shops. There is a Vuitton shop in Milan's Galleria Vittorio Emanuele II. That's where I saw the trunks. I was told if I live in the States and wanted to purchase one, then it would be a special order."

He slowly shook his head. "No, thank you."

Taylor tried not to stare at Sonja and failed miserably. He couldn't pull his gaze away from the wealth of curls framing her face and ending above her shoulders. When he'd met her at The Cellar he'd thought of her a seductress in red. If he had to give her a label, then it would be chameleon. She was able to smoothly transition from a seductress in red with a profusion of waves framing her face and makeup accentuating her best features to a fresh-faced ingenue while affecting a ponytail, jeans and running shoes. Tonight she'd changed again when she'd selected a tangerine-orange sheath dress, black ballet flats and a subtle hint of makeup. Smoky taupe shadow on her lids complemented her large brown eyes, and the orange lip color contrasted beautifully with the gold undertones in her complexion. And her curly hairstyle reminded him of a doll—the nickname with which her uncle had tagged her.

He set the carton of wine on the floor and sniffed the air, smiling. "Something smells delicious."

Sonja closed the door, locking it, and then flashed a mysterious smile. "I know how much you liked the dishes at La Casa Del Mofongo, so I decided to make *arroz blanco*, *frijoles rosados, pollo asado* and flan for dessert."

"I understood flan, and that's about it. And I'm

not ashamed to say that I could eat Spanish food every day."

"I'm serving white rice, pink beans and roast chicken. Instead of a salad, I've decided to prepare a cheese and fruit platter. By the way, have you ever eaten *pastelón*?"

He shook his head. I don't think so. What is it?"

"Puerto Rican lasagna. My mother gave my aunt the recipe and she in turn gave it to me. I'll make it for you one of these days."

"I suppose I'm going to have to up my game when cooking for you."

Sonja rested her hands at her waist. "Are you talking about a throwdown, Taylor?"

"Not quite. But I can't have you show me up."

"Who taught you to cook?"

"My mother. In fact, she taught all of her children because she claimed once we left home she wanted us to be totally independent, and for her that translated into the ability to put a meal on the table." He paused. "I'm going to take these trunks upstairs, then we can talk about cooking for each other."

Taylor pulled the stair-climbing hand truck up the staircase and down the hallway to the smaller bedroom Sonja had claimed as her office. He noticed she had already put her personal touch on the space. She'd placed a laptop and printer on the desk, and framed photos occupied every flat surface. He peered closely at one with Sonja, her brother and her parents when she'd graduated college. There were others of her uncle, brother and father in uniform. Then there was another one with Sonja holding a baby in a christening gown. Not only was she *titi*, she was also a godmother. He left the trunks on the floor next to the desk, returned to the first floor and joined Sonja in the kitchen.

"It looks as if you've done more shopping." Bottles of red, white and rosé were stored in a wine rack on the countertop.

Sonja turned and smiled at Taylor over her shoulder. "Yes, I did. Thank you for the wine. I didn't know whether you were bringing anything." Not only had she visited the wine shop, but also the florist and a craft shop where she'd purchased scented candles, bundles of potpourri and framed prints with pressed leaves and flowers for the bathrooms. She'd also stopped at the variety store to pick up an ample supply of paper clips, folders, notebooks, legal pads, rubber bands, sticky notes, a stapler, tape and a desk organizer caddy.

"I must admit your house now looks like a home."

Sonja met his eyes. "It's the little touches that make a house a home." The supermarket had a section with plants and live flowers, and she'd selected a combination of potted ferns and succulents.

"You've done well, Sonja."

She affected a graceful curtsy. "Thank you."

Taylor winked at her. "You're welcome. I'm going to put the case of wine in the pantry, then I'm going to wash my hands."

"I'd also bought a case. It looks as if we have enough to last for a while."

"Don't forget, you're going to live here for at least the next two years."

"You're right, Taylor."

Sonja wanted to ask Taylor if she would be obligated to stay if she completed her project before the lease expired. Would he allow her to continue to live in the condo, or would she be forced to find another residence? Thinking about where she would live in a couple of years meant she was projecting. She hadn't even begun working, and now she was planning her future once her tenure with the restoration ended.

Opening a drawer under the countertop, she took out a bibbed apron and slipped it over her dress. The rice was done and so were the beans, and she'd placed them in the warming drawer. Meanwhile the timer on the oven indicated the chicken needed another twenty-five minutes before she could remove it and allow it to rest before carving. She retrieved the platter with a variety of cheese and fruit from the lower shelf of the fridge and set it on the breakfast bar.

"Wow! It's like a work of art."

Sonja's head popped up as Taylor returned to the kitchen. "One can do wonders with cookie cutters." She'd cut strawberries, cantaloupe and honeydew into stars, balls and triangles, and cheese into balls and cubes, alternating each and placing them around a small cluster of white, red and black seed-less grapes.

Taylor moved closer to her. "They look too pretty to eat."

"Pretty or not, we have to eat them or they're going to spoil."

"Have you taken a picture of it?" Taylor asked.

She laughed softly. "No. I have no desire to be-come a food blogger."

"Well, you should start, because once I concoct my dishes I'm going to upload them to your phone."

Sonja gave him a sidelong glance. "I thought we weren't going to compete."

"It's not a real competition. I just want to keep track of the dishes because I don't repeat one too often."

"If it's not real, then it must be fake. Real or not, wannabe Wolfgang Puck, it's on. I just want to warn you that I come from a long line of incredible cooks, and when my dishes beat yours I don't want to see any tears."

Taylor cradled her face. "I never figured you for a trash talker."

Sonja felt his breath feather over her cheek, his mouth mere inches from hers. She'd been totally un-prepared the day before when he'd kissed her. It had happened so quickly that she did not have time to react. "What are you doing, Taylor?" Her query was a whisper.

"Something I shouldn't be doing."

"And what's that?" Her voice had dropped an octave.

A hint of a smile tilted the corners of his mouth. "Deciding whether I should kiss you. If I do, then that negates our promise to be friends."

"And if you don't?"

"Then I will spend the rest of my life wondering how you taste."

Sonja lips parted in a mysterious smile. "How long do you expect to live, Taylor Edward Williamson?"

His smile did not slip as his eyebrows lifted slightly. "Probably ninety-five or maybe even one hundred."

Going on tiptoe, she brushed her mouth over Taylor's. "I'm not going to let you wait—" Her words were cut off in midsentence when Taylor deepened the kiss, caressing her lips until they parted under his. "How do I taste?" Sonja whispered.

Taylor groaned deep in his throat. "Yummy."

"Just yummy?"

"Nah, sweetness. Delicious."

Resting her palms against Taylor's chest, Sonja eased back, breaking off the kiss. Taylor said if he kissed her, then their promise to remain friends would no longer be valid, but what he hadn't known was that she wanted more than friendship. Although she'd vowed, once her divorce was final, that she would never become involved with a man with whom she would work closely, Sonja was no longer a vulnerable starry-eyed coed who had succumbed to her erudite professor. She wasn't that twenty-year-old wooed by a much older man and married to him at twenty-one. What she hadn't known after their living together for four years was that she would have to plan her escape, and then wait another two years of court appearances with escalating legal fees for her to obtain her freedom.

That was then and this was now. She'd achieved her career goal and was now a part of a team responsible for restoring a historic house she predicted would be written about and photographed for architectural and travel magazines. Her becoming involved with Taylor would be very different from her involvement with Hugh, because she was ready for a mature relationship where they could relate to each other on equal footing. And she had no intention of marrying Taylor, because their relationship had an expiration date. Two years.

"You're going to have to let me go so I can check on the chicken." Although her voice was steady, normal, it wasn't the same with her heart rate. It was beating so hard and fast she could feel it against her ribs.

Taylor pressed a kiss to her forehead before releasing her face. Sonja exhaled an inaudible sigh as she walked to the oven and opened the door. The roaster had turned golden brown. She inserted a digital thermometer into the thigh to monitor the bird's internal temperature. To allow the skin to crisp, she had periodically basted the bird in its own juices during the roasting process until it was close to doneness. The thermometer registered 170 degrees. Sonja added another twenty minutes to the timer. The temperature needed to read 180.

She turned to find Taylor staring at her. "It's going to be a while before the chicken is done."

Taylor nodded. "That will give us time to eat what looks like a still-life prop."

Sonja agreed with him. She'd arranged the platter to resemble objects for still-life painters. She motioned to the stools at the breakfast bar. "Please sit. I'll get some plates and forks."

Chapter Nine

Taylor's forefinger traced the stem of his wineglass as he stared across the table at Sonja. Sharing dinner with her had exceeded his expectations.

He had always been very selective when it came to dating. He knew it stemmed from not knowing the identity of his biological father and feared he could possibly be dating his biological half sister. He was certain he and Sonja did not share DNA because of her father's military career. She'd said she was born in a hospital near an army installation on the Kentucky-Tennessee border, whereas the year before, his mother had given birth to him in a Newark, New Jersey, municipal hospital.

Taylor did not have what he thought of as a type

when it came to a woman. He didn't judge them by their appearance, but rather their intelligence and ability to hold his attention, and it was a plus if they shared the same interests.

Picking up the wineglass, he took a sip. "I think you missed your true calling," he said as he smiled over the rim at Sonja.

"And what is that?"

"You should've become a chef. Everything was delicious, beginning with the cheese and fruit, and the rice, beans, and chicken were comparable to what I've eaten at La Casa Del Mofongo."

Sonja shook her head. "I like to cook, but not enough to spend hours on my feet cooking for a lot of people. Been there, done that."

Taylor sat straight. "When?"

"Viola didn't tell you?"

"Tell me what?"

"That I'd been married."

He blinked slowly. Although Sonja had said she didn't have a husband or boyfriend, she hadn't mentioned an ex-husband. "My sister and I don't discuss you."

Sonja gave him a long stare. "I was married while still in college. He—"

"You don't have to tell me about it if you don't want," Taylor said, interrupting her.

"But I do, Taylor," Sonja said in a quiet voice. If she hoped to have a normal relationship with Taylor, then he needed to know some of what she'd gone through with her ex. "I was twenty when I enrolled in an advanced art history class and got involved with my much older instructor. When I agreed to marry him, I had no idea I would become the quintessential trophy wife. I dropped out eighteen credits shy of earning my degree in order to become the hostess for his friends and colleagues."

"How long were you married?"

"We lived together for four years. Once I felt I was being smothered I knew I had to get out, so I waited until he was scheduled to lecture at an exhibition in Denver and left."

"Where did you go?" Taylor asked.

"I stayed with my parents at their retirement home in the Adirondack Mountains and sued Hugh for divorce. He countersued me for abandonment, and I was forced to commute between New York and Boston for court hearings. More than half the time they were postponed when Hugh's attorney wouldn't show up or he would have his doctor claim he was unable to appear because of a medical emergency. This went on for two years until he met someone else and decided it was time to let me go. Meanwhile, I'd moved downstate to live with my aunt and uncle. I enrolled at Pratt and finally got my degrees. End of chapter."

Taylor pushed to his feet, rounded the table, pulled a chair close to Sonja's and draped an arm over her shoulders. "It's the end of that chapter and now a beginning of another, sweetheart."

Sonja rested her forehead against Taylor's. "I

should've said 'end of story' because that's a scenario in my past I don't intend to repeat."

"Are you talking about marriage, Sonja?"

"Yes." The single word was flat, emotionless.

Taylor kissed her curls. "Not all men are like your
ex."

"I know that, Taylor. I just don't want to marry
again."

"What do you want, *muñeca*?"

Sonja knew this was her opening to talk to Taylor about several ideas she'd thought of for Bainbridge House. "Do you remember when I talked to
you about establishing a farm on the property?"

He laughed softly. "How can I forget. You did
promise to put everything down on paper."

"I did before I decided to scrap it."

"Talk to me, sweetheart."

Sonja turned her head slightly so Taylor wouldn't
see her grin of supreme satisfaction. His fingers gently stroked the nape of her neck as if she were a purr-
ing cat, and the gentleness in his voice indicated
he could possibly be receptive to hearing her out.
"Have you ever eaten at a restaurant with farm-to-
table service?"

"No, I haven't."

"If you had, then you'd know what I'm proposing. I haven't looked at the blueprints of the property,
but with more than three hundred acres it wouldn't
take that much for you to erect greenhouses to pro-

duce fruits and vegetables year-round. The dining menu could change with the availability of whatever is in season. There's nothing tastier than freshly picked herbs and greens to accompany a meat, fish or chicken entrée. Sorrel in a salad adds an intense lemony tang. Once you eat a fresh jicama slaw with mango, cilantro and lime you'll want to order it over and over."

Taylor's fingers stilled. "What about chickens?"

This time Sonja did flash a smile for Taylor to see. "There is a distinct difference in eating an egg laid by a chicken earlier that morning and one in a supermarket refrigerated case."

"What happens to the chickens once they stop laying?"

"You kill and eat them, Taylor."

A beat passed. "When I asked my mother about Dad growing up at Bainbridge House, he'd told her they had sheep and ducks on the property."

Shifting slightly on her chair to face Taylor, Sonja met his eyes. "Didn't you say something disparaging about Old MacDonald's farm?"

"Did I really?"

"Yeah. And you know you did."

Wrapping both arms around her shoulders, Taylor pulled her closer. "I'm going to talk to my brother Tariq about your proposal. He's the vet, and he'll be responsible for taking care of any and all of the animals on the property."

"What about the vegetables?"

"After Joaquin restores the garden he'll have to confer with a farmer about where to set up the greenhouses. I can't promise you my brothers will go along with what you propose, but I will do my best to try and convince them."

"I suggest you also talk to Viola about creating a farm-to-table setup. It works so well when held outdoors under a white tent—of course, weather permitting—with long tables and benches, strings of overhead lights, lanterns with flickering votives and music. Depending on the number of guests in any group, you can offer them an alfresco luncheon or dining under the stars."

"That's really casual dining."

"Casual and very chic," Sonja confirmed. "I've toured Italy and France, where I was able to experience farm-to-table dining. During one of my visits to Brittany, I'd checked into a château where I witnessed a late afternoon formal outdoor wedding reception. The groom wore a black wedding morning coat, with a cobalt blue ascot and vest, dove-gray top hat and matching gloves, while the bride was an ethereal vision in Chantilly lace. It was a fairy-tale fantasy in living color."

"Did you take any pictures?"

"Of course I did. Whenever I go abroad I usually have at least three memory cards because I take so many photos."

"What do you do with them?" Taylor questioned.

"I print out the ones I like and then frame them.

Someday, when I buy a house, I plan to transform one of the rooms into an art gallery."

Grinning like a Cheshire cat, Taylor winked at her. "Do you intend to have an exhibition and sell your photos?"

"You got jokes, T.E. Wills?" she asked teasingly.

His grin vanished quickly. "No. And please don't call me that."

"Was your modeling career so traumatic that you want to erase it from your past?"

Taylor dropped his arms and eased back, putting some separation between them. "It wasn't traumatic. In fact, it was very exciting and extremely profitable. I'd rather not talk about that time in my life because it is a reminder of how narcissistic I'd become. For me it wasn't so much about the money as it was which product would give me the highest visibility. After a couple of years, if I had to describe myself, then it would be jaded. I hated going to photoshoots, fittings and fashion shows where I'd have to change in and out of up to ten outfits within minutes. I knew it was time for me to quit the business when someone touched me inappropriately and I went ballistic. Once I calmed down I apologized, but it was too late because behind the scenes I was labeled difficult to work with."

Sonja rested her hand atop his fisted one. "Did you ever think maybe you were experiencing burnout?"

"I knew I was, but I'd become so ego driven that

I feared stopping. I didn't want people to forget or brand me as a has-been. Then, there was my mother constantly asking when I intended to go back to college. I kept telling her one more year and after a while she stopped bringing up the topic. My parents couldn't use the threat of not paying my tuition if I didn't give in to their demands because I was earning enough in one month to cover a year's tuition including books and room and board."

"What did you do with your earnings?"

"I gave them to my father to invest. Dad headed an investment and private equity firm. He had a sixth sense when it came to investing, which made many of his clients extremely wealthy. Dad had instituted a tier system for his clients. The lowest tier was for blue-collar workers who wanted to play the market but didn't have a lot of money to invest. The middle tier was for middle-income professionals, and the top tier was for wealthier clients. He'd assign his clients to designated teams to concentrate on moving those in the lower tier to the middle and the middle to the top."

Sonja was intrigued by Taylor's late father's business model. "Did it work?"

"Yes, it did. His clients had dubbed him the miracle worker, though he was anything but. Dad always said he did not want to take someone's savings and squander it. When the news broke about Bernie Madoff's Ponzi scheme, I saw another side of my father when he talked about hiring a hit man to break every bone in Madoff's body. This pronouncement shocked everyone because we had never witnessed Conrad losing his temper or raising his voice even when he was angry."

Sonja had given Taylor a brief overview about her failed marriage, and now she wanted to know about him aside from his modeling career. "How was it growing up with three brothers?"

Taylor unclenched his fist. "It was a lot of fun, considering we spent so much time together. What's really surprising is we're not competitive with one another."

"Who's the oldest?"

"I am. Patrick is thirty-four, Joaquin thirty-three, Tariq is thirty, and Viola is twenty-eight."

Sonja gave him an incredulous stare. "Your mother had three children a year apart?"

Throwing back his head, Taylor laughed with abandon. "What can I say? When she and Dad bought the house, Mom said she wanted as many children as they had bedrooms. Once she had Viola she claimed her life was complete because she finally had a daughter. Viola upset the equation because it was no longer two against two whenever we formed teams, and we had to figure out a way to include her. To say she was spoiled is an understatement. Mom spoiled her. Dad overindulged her, and she looked to me to protect her against her other brothers whenever they played tricks on her."

Sonja smiled. "There must have been a lot of activity in your home."

"It was whenever we didn't have classes. Mom had transformed her library into a one-room schoolhouse and because we were so close in age, excluding Tariq and Viola, we were given the same instruction."

"Why did you choose to become an engineer?"

"By the time I was ten I knew I wanted to build things because I was obsessed with Lego. I had a table in the corner of my bedroom where I'd created an entire town, and then it was a city with bridges and tall skyscrapers."

"How did your brothers choose their careers?"

"Patrick is a math prodigy. He spent more time at our father's office than any of us. Once he passed the CPA exam he went to work for Dad. We all knew Tariq would become a vet because he took care of our pets. We had dogs, cats, birds, fish, and a family of rabbits that kept multiplying until Mom finally gave them to various pet shops. Joaquin was an enigma because he couldn't decide what he wanted to be until he'd enrolled in college. He'd applied for a part-time position at a local nursery, and that's where his love affair with plants and flowers began. He also fell in love with the nursery owner's daughter and married her."

"Are they still married?"

Taylor shook his head. "No. They were married less than two years and even when pressured Joaquin refuses to discuss the reason behind their breakup. As a landscape architect he has a number of celebrities as his clients."

"Will he also refurbish the golf course?"

The seconds ticked while Taylor appeared deep in thought. "I don't know. That's something I'll have to discuss with Patrick and Joaquin. We have to determine whether having a nine-hole course would be advantageous to guests looking to play several rounds of golf. Perhaps if it could be expanded to eighteen holes, then it could possibly be used as a golf club or for local tournaments."

"What services do you plan to offer your hotel guests?"

"Bainbridge House will become a full-service luxury hotel with restaurants, lounge facilities, meetings rooms, bell and room service."

"What about specialty shops, Taylor? And I'm not taking about the standard gift shop."

Taylor affected a mysterious smile. "What ideas are you hatching in that beautiful head of yours?"

Sonja blushed when Taylor called her beautiful. As the daughter of a black father and Puerto Rican mother she had always thought of herself as an attractive woman of color, but not what she would deem beautiful. "Most luxury hotels have upscale jewelry stores, spas and boutiques. And because Bainbridge House is listed on the National Register of Historic Places you could have an on-site museum shop."

"And what would we sell at the museum shop?"

Her eyebrows lifted. "Do you mean you, Taylor?"

"No, Sonja. I mean *we. If* we do open a museum shop, will you assume the responsibility of running it?"

Her pulse kicked into a higher gear when she thought of the possibility of managing what would become an art gallery. "Yes. If that's what you want?"

"You're the one making the suggestion."

Sonja chose her words carefully. "After I catalogue everything, I'd confer with you about what you'd want to exhibit for sale. Wealthy families during the Gilded Age always purchased duplicate sets of china, silver and crystal for their over-the-top banquets with hundreds of guests. You'll be able to use some of the sets for weddings and retirement dinners, although I recommend purchasing commercial dinnerware, preferably stamped with BH for the restaurants and lounges."

"I can't believe you've planned all of this out even before you begin going through the crates."

Sonja wanted to remind Taylor that she was an art historian and that she'd been involved in countless estate sales. "This is not my first rodeo, Taylor."

"That's obvious." He held up his hands in a gesture of surrender. "I give up, Ms. Rios-Martin. You are hereby responsible for every glass, dish, knife, fork, spoon, table, chair, lamp and rug on the property. And there's no need to confer with me about anything you believe you can resolve on your own."

"Does this mean you're going to consider opening a museum shop?"

"I can't commit to anything until I meet with an architectural engineer. We'll have to reconfigure the entire layout of the first story."

Sonja wanted to remind Taylor there were endless possibilities when renovating an 86,000-square-foot private residence into a hotel and catering venue. While he'd estimated it would take a minimum of two years to completely restore and renovate the mansion and the outbuildings, she had her own time-table for examining, cataloguing and authenticating thousands of items.

"How many hotels have you put up?"

Taylor lifted his shoulders. "I've been involved with a few."

Sonja stared at him as if he'd suddenly grown a pair of horns. "A few! I can't believe you let me go on and on about what goes into a hotel other than rooms—"

"Enough, sweetheart," Taylor said, cutting her off. "I didn't stop you because I wanted to know what you were thinking. I've warmed to your idea of a farm-to-table setup and opening a museum shop on the premises. How many guests can say that they've stayed in a historic hotel and had the option of purchasing an original item that once belonged to the owners."

"I suppose not too many."

"You suppose?"

"All right," Sonja conceded. "Hardly any."

She had visited enough museums and their shops to occasionally purchase a replica of a particular item she just had to have. She had duplicates of Michelangelo's *Pietà* and the *Head of David* in various sizes, and framed reproductions of countless Renaissance Dutch and Spanish painters. Sonja also had begun collecting the work of African American artists from colonial to modern times.

Purchasing her own home had become a priority for both her independence and the ability to display the pieces she'd begun collecting following her divorce. Whenever she purchased a painting, print or sculpture she would have it shipped to her parents' home for safekeeping, with a promise that one day she would come and take her treasure trove to her own home.

"Thank you, Taylor."

"For what?"

"For indulging me."

He gave her a direct stare. "It's not an indulgence, Sonja. I'm open to whatever you have to say."

"Thank you," she repeated.

Sonja did not want to compare Taylor to Hugh. Her ex rarely listened to anything she had to say. The exception was when it benefitted him. Otherwise, he tended to wave her away as if she were an annoying insect. Now that she looked back she wondered how she had surrendered her will to him, and she didn't need sessions with a therapist for the answer. She'd taken her marriage vows seriously while loving Hugh Davies unconditionally.

"Are you ready for coffee and dessert?"

Taylor pressed a kiss to her cheek. "Yes. I'll clear the table while you brew the coffee."

Sonja walked into the kitchen, grinning from ear to ear as a silent voice said Taylor Williamson was a keeper. He was who she needed to start over with—a man who respected her and treated her as his equal.

"I made enough for leftovers," she said over her shoulder. "Should I put away some for you?"

"Of course. What time is dinner tomorrow?"

Sonja went still and then slowly turned to face Taylor. "You want us to eat together every night?"

"That's up to you, Sonja. It can be every night or every other night. The choice is yours."

"Tomorrow is okay. At that time, we can come up with a schedule that works for both of us. If I'm going to make my own hours, then there may be times when I'll work through dinner."

Taylor set stacked plates on the countertop. "Don't…"

"Don't what?" she asked when his words trailed off.

"Just don't overtire yourself."

"I won't. How do you take your coffee?"

"Black."

"Okay. One black coffee coming up."

* * *

Sonja stood at the door watching Taylor as he backed out of the driveway. She waved to him and he returned her wave before she closed and locked the door. Sharing dinner with him was not only enjoyable but also enlightening. After coffee and dessert, he'd stayed behind to help put away leftovers and clean up the kitchen. He'd scraped and rinsed dishes and pots for her to load the dishwasher. How different it was when she'd been left to clean up everything following a dinner party for Hugh's friends and colleagues.

She knew she had to stop comparing Hugh and Taylor, yet the differences were so acute it would take her time—a lot of time—to erase the memories of what she'd had with her ex-husband. When she'd answered Viola's call on Easter Sunday asking whether she would meet her brother, Sonja had no way of knowing her decision would change her life. Turning on her heel, she headed for the staircase. Although curious to open the trunks to see what she would find, Sonja decided to wait until tomorrow.

Chapter Ten

Sonja woke early, showered, slipped into a pair of
sweats, and fortified herself with a breakfast of grits,
scrambled eggs, crispy bacon, wheat toast and coffee.
Then she sat on the floor of the office, opened one
trunk and found copies of the floor plans and blueprints Taylor had made for her. She set them aside
and began removing bundled letters, receipts, led-
gers, and bank and tax records. It was going to take
her an inordinate amount of time to put everything
in chronological order.

She picked up an envelope with the initials MS—
Happy Birthday written on the front in calligraphy.
She removed an invoice stamped Paid and a hand-
written date of September 4, 1906, for a diamond-

and-emerald necklace from Tiffany's. Sonja jotted the initials, date, item, vendor and the price of the gift on a legal pad. There were more invoices from various jewelry stores in New York, Boston, San Francisco and Philadelphia for MS with dates ranging from 1906 to 1914. The baubles included rings, earrings, multiple strands of cultured and South Seas pearls, totaling more than ninety thousand dollars, which would be the equivalent of more than two million today. Sonja was anxious to determine the identity of MS, who had paid for the jewels, and their connection.

She selected another envelope and spilled out its contents to find ticket stubs and newspaper clippings. Sonja quickly scanned the articles. They were about infamous 1920s gangsters: Bonnie and Clyde, John Dillinger, Charles Arthur "Pretty Boy" Floyd and George "Baby Face" Nelson, just to name a few. There were even more *about* the exploits of Al Capone.

Sonja found herself engrossed in articles about Harry Houdini's death in Detroit, women's official right to vote in the United States, Babe Ruth setting a new home run record, and Lindbergh's first solo flight across the Atlantic. She heard a buzzing and then realized she'd left her phone on vibrate. Scrambling off the floor, she picked the phone off the table. It was her mother.

"*Hola*, Mami."

"*Hola*. How are you?"

Sonja smiled. "I'm okay. No. I take that back. I'm very, very well."

"That's good. I got your text with your new address. I thought you were moving into a hotel."

She flopped down on the blue-and-white-checkered upholstered chair and rested bare feet on the ottoman. "That's what I thought, but my when boss couldn't find one close enough to the work site he rented the condo."

"He sounds like a very generous boss."

Sonja detected a hint of facetiousness in her mother's tone. "He's a very considerate boss, Mami. He needs my expertise, therefore, he's willing to do what has to be done for me to perform at my best."

"Is he married?"

"No."

"Is he engaged?"

Now Sonja was becoming annoyed with her mother's questioning. "I don't think so." She knew Taylor wasn't married, otherwise Olivia would've mentioned it to her. And it was the same with him being engaged. "Why are you asking these questions, Mami?"

"I'm asking because I don't want you to get in and over your head when it comes to him."

Sonja frowned. "Why would you say that?"

"Remember you went gaga over Hugh. When I asked about you spending so much time with him, I recall you saying that he was a helpful and very considerate professor."

Closing her eyes and biting her lip, Sonja struggled to control her temper. She didn't think her mother would bring that up when she'd promised they'd never discuss her ex again once the divorce was finalized.

"Taylor is nothing like Hugh."

"How did you meet him?"

"He's my friend's brother." She told Maria about the phone call between her and Viola, and her subsequently meeting Taylor. "Working at the gallery allowed me to save money, but I knew it really wasn't going to advance my career. But, becoming the architectural historian to restore a residence listed on the National Register of Historic Places was an offer I couldn't refuse."

"I'm not doubting your professional ability. It's just—"

"It's just that you doubt my ability not to mix business with pleasure," Sonja said, interrupting her mother.

Well, she wanted to tell Maria that it was too late. She was doing exactly that, yet there was a difference. She was no longer that twenty-year-old woman who had fallen victim to a much older man who had a habit of preying on his young female students. It wasn't until much later in their relationship that Sonja became aware of his reputation. And when she confronted him, he'd proposed marriage. Shocked and taken aback that he loved her enough to make her his wife, she rationalized the rumors were nothing more than lies and agreed to become Mrs. Hugh Davies.

"I'm not as naive or gullible as I used to be. And I have Hugh to thank for that."

"I'm not trying to run your life, baby. It's just that I don't ever want you to go through what you did with that monster."

"I know that. I told you before that if or when I get involved with someone I'm like a traffic light. Green means go, yellow is proceed with caution and red means stop and don't look back."

"I'm going to ask you one more thing about your boss, and then I promise to stay quiet."

"What's that?"

"Is he nice looking?"

Sonja covered her face with her free hand and inhaled deeply. "No, Mami. He's gorgeous."

Her mother's soft chuckle came through the earpiece. "I rest my case. I never thought when I used to drag you around with me to museums that you would become an architectural historian."

"I love history and I love art even more."

"What are you working on?"

Sonja told her mother about Bainbridge House. "I'm certain if you were to see it restored with the original furnishings you would love it."

"Are you saying they're going to modernize it?"

"No. The exception will be updating the plumbing and electricity. Once the restoration is complete it will look like a French nobleman's country estate.

I'll send you photos when some of the work has been completed."

There was a noticeable pause on the other end of the connection. "When are you coming up to see me?"

Sonja grimaced. She usually tried to visit her parents for a weekend every two to three months, but that was when she worked part-time. "I'm not sure now that I'm working full-time. I don't plan to work the Memorial Day weekend, so I'll probably drive up then."

"We're not going to be here that weekend. Your father and I are driving down to Savannah. He's meeting up with some of his army buddies who rented a boat to sail down to the Caribbean."

"How long will you be gone?"

"About ten days. They plan to use the boat as a hotel while they visit different islands."

"That sounds like fun."

"I'm really looking forward it. I told your father if he agrees to another golf outing that I was going to leave him."

Sonja wanted to tell her mother that she'd threatened to leave her husband so many times over minutiae that James Martin tended to ignore her. "I suppose the next holiday is the Fourth of July. Do you guys also have plans for that holiday weekend?"

"James was talking about surprising me with something because that's our anniversary week, so right now I can't commit to anything."

"I can't believe you're going to be married forty years."

"It doesn't feel like it's been that long," Maria admitted. "I also know you're fixated on your career but—"

"Please don't say it, Mami." Sonja had cut her mother off in midsentence. "I know you want me to find someone and settle down and give you more grandbabies. Of course, I'd like to fall in love and perhaps even marry, but that is not at the top of my wish list. If or when I decide I want to become a mother, I'll adopt."

"I just want you happy, Sonja."

"But I am happy, Mami. I have my health. Right now, I'm living in a beautiful condo where all my needs are met. And I'm working on the sort of project I've always wanted. The only analogy I can think of is an archaeological dig and discovering ancient artifacts."

"I don't want you to think I'm meddling in your life. It's just that I saw you so emotionally wounded that as your mother I, too, felt your pain."

"I've healed and I've never been happier."

"That's what I want to know, baby."

Sonja knew she had pacified her mother because she'd called her baby. "Yolanda told me you sent her your *pastelón* recipe and I got it from her."

"That's because every time I talk to her she nags me until I couldn't stand it anymore and I sent it to her."

"Well, now I have it. I know Abuela is smiling in heaven because her granddaughter will continue the tradition of making her incredibly delicious *pastelón*."

"When we hang up, I'm going to go through some of the recipes my mother left me and send them to you."

"Have you ever thought about writing a cookbook using Abuela's recipes? You could publish it in English and Spanish. You can call it memories of a Puerto Rican kitchen. Before each recipe you can include a little narrative about the events that made that dish so memorable. I remember you telling me how the entire family had to pitch in when making *pasteles* for Christmas." The first time Sonja tasted the tamales filled with pork, chickpeas, yucca, olives, capers and other spices they'd become her personal favorite for the holiday season and other family celebrations.

"Ay dios mío," Maria said, lapsing into Spanish. "Why didn't I think of that?"

"Yo no sé," Sonja answered. It wasn't often she got to speak Spanish, because her mother and uncle, like a lot of New York Puerto Ricans tended to combine the two languages when speaking.

"I'm going to get all of her notebooks and go through them. After I decide what to include, then I'll start writing the narratives. Thank you, baby, for giving me something to do other than sit on the porch and read or watch television."

"Let me know what you come up with."

"I will. I'm going to let you go because I know you have work to do. You can call me whenever you have some spare time."

"Will do, Mami. Love you."

"I love you, too."

Sonja ended the call, smiling. Placing the phone on the charger, she returned to the floor to examine the ticket stubs spanning decades. There had to be hundreds of them from operas, concerts, stage plays, state fairs, circuses, movie theaters, museums and auctions.

Sonja decided the clippings and stubs would take up too much time to catalogue at this time and put them back into the envelope. A collection of flyers garnered her rapt attention. Someone had crossed the Atlantic on a steamship to attend six world's fairs, had taken the train across the country to attend two in San Francisco, driven to Philadelphia and had chartered a yacht to Havana, Cuba. She put them in chronological order. The first was in 1881 to Paris, France, for the International Exposition of Electricity and the last in San Francisco in 1915 for the Panama-Pacific International Exposition's Palace of Fine Arts. She noticed three of the expositions were geared to electricity, and she wondered if the Bainbridges had an interest in Edison's electric lighting system and subsequently invested in General Electric. The trip in 1881 preceded the completion of the château by two years. Where, she wondered, had the

Bainbridges lived before that time? And where and how had they amassed a fortune of at least ten million to build their castle?

Taylor's head popped up when he realized he wasn't alone. The caretaker had entered the room he'd set up to conduct interviews. Earlier that morning he'd met with two licensed electricians and one plumber, and based on their prior experience he wouldn't hire any of them.

"I just closed the gate," the caretaker announced.

Taylor pointed to the chair on the opposite side of the table. "Thanks. Please sit down, Dom." When Elise had talked about a resident caretaker he'd imagined a middle-aged or elderly man living in one of the cottages, not the tall, slender man in his mid-thirties with a black, lightly streaked gray man bun and dark green eyes in a deeply tanned face.

Dominic Shaw sat, stretched out his legs and crossed his booted feet at the ankles. "How did it go?"

Taylor laced his fingers together atop the table. He liked Dom and had come to rely on him to be available when the applicants arrived for their scheduled interviews. He met them at the entrance to the property and escorted them to the main house.

"Although licensed, they are not what I need."

"Not enough experience, Taylor?"

"It's not that, Dom. One electrician admitted that he couldn't get along with his last two supervisors, and for me that is a red flag for someone with a problem accepting and following orders. The other one once had his license suspended. It was recently reinstated, but I didn't want to know why. To be truthful, I'm on the fence with the plumber. He's young, licensed and hasn't had much experience, but I may be able to hire him as an assistant."

"Do you intend to supervise them?"

"Not directly. I'm hoping to hire someone I've worked with in the past to assist me."

"How many general contractors do you need?"

Taylor angled his head. "Why? Do you have someone in mind?"

A hint of a smile parted the caretaker's lips. "Yes."

"Who?"

"Me."

"You?" Taylor repeated.

Dom's smile vanished. "Yes. I'm the fifth generation Shaw caretaker. I learned the ins and outs of repairs from my father and grandfather. They taught me everything about installing electrical wiring and plumbing. By the way, I happen to be a licensed plumber."

Taylor knew the estate's caretakers were paid from a trust set up by Charles Garland Bainbridge in 1898, and at least one Shaw male from each succeeding generation had accepted and maintained the position, including Dominic Shaw.

"Are you asking to work for me?" Taylor asked him.

"No. I won't work for but *with* you," Dom countered. "Conditions set out in trust prohibit me from working for anyone because my sole responsibility is taking care of the estate."

Suddenly Taylor was intrigued with the caretaker. This was the first time they'd had more than a cursory exchange with each other, and Dom's offer to help with the repairs was an unexpected and pleasant surprise. "*If* I agree to let you help with the restoration, what do you want to do?" His query appeared to shock Dom, and he sat up straight.

"I really like plumbing. I renovated my kitchen, put in a half bath, and updated the toilet and all the sinks in my cottage. Would you like to see it?"

Pushing back his chair, Taylor stood. "Sure."

He left the main house with Dom and walked to the six two-story cottages situated far enough from one another for privacy. Dom opened the door to one and stepped aside to let him enter. Taylor wiped his booted feet on the thick straw mat and walked in. The spacious foyer with a circular pedestal table afforded easy access to the living room furnishings from another era. Taylor took in the overstuffed sofas and chairs covered with busy prints, rough-hewn side tables and built-in shelves filled with books, model ships, bottles of spirits and fragile stemware. There were framed black-and-white photos of couples and groups of people from other centuries, and Taylor wondered if perhaps they were Dom's relatives. He smiled seeing the billiard table in an area off the living room.

Dom, noting the direction of his gaze, asked, "Do you play?"

Taylor's eyebrows lifted slightly. "Not in a long time." Conrad had set up a pool table in the game room and had taught all his children to play. There was a chalkboard with a tally, and although he was good Taylor could never beat Joaquin, who demonstrated incredible eye-hand coordination.

"I know you're busy, but you're always welcome to come and test your skills."

"Spoken like a true pool shark."

A flush darkened Dom's tanned face. "I've been known to make a few dollars to supplement my meager income."

"Well, if I'm going to play, then it's not going to be for money because I don't like being hustled."

Crossing his arms over his chest, Dom leaned back on the heels of his boots. "I wouldn't mind playing for a bottle of premium scotch to add to my illustrious collection."

Taylor pointed to the bottles lining the shelves. He'd noticed some were premium aged scotch. "You play for bottles?"

Dom nodded. "Not only am I connoisseur of scotch, but that's the only liquor I drink. I have a few bottles that are at least thirty years old."

"That must have cost the loser a pretty penny."

"It did," Dom said proudly. "But I always say if you can't pay, then don't play."

"I didn't say I can't pay," Taylor countered.

"When do you want to play?"

"Since you issued the challenge, you set the date and time, and I'll let you know if I'm available."

"Tonight?"

"It can't be tonight because I have a prior engagement." He had promised to cook for Sonja. "What about tomorrow night? Say, around eight?"

Dom nodded and extended his right hand. "Tomorrow it is. Shouldn't we establish the wager beforehand?"

Taylor shook the proffered hand. "I don't think that's necessary. You want a bottle of aged scotch and I want to clean your clock."

Dom's expression shifted from smug to one exhibiting uncertainty. "Are you some kind of clandestine pool hustler?"

Taylor couldn't help laughing. "No. I grew up with three brothers, and although we all managed to get along we also were very competitive. And it's the same with my sister. It has been a while since I've played the game, but I'm warning you that I'm not an easy target. Now, I want to see what you've done to your kitchen and bathroom because I have to leave and get home."

He'd scheduled the interviews for the morning because he needed time to shop for the ingredients for dinner. He'd sent Sonja a text earlier that morning asking if he could prepare dinner at her place. It would save him having to transport hot dishes from his mother's condo to hers, and she'd quickly replied in the affirmative.

Taylor had to admit the changes Dom had made to the kitchen and bathrooms were remarkable. The sage-green kitchen cabinets, recessed lights, natural plank flooring and a granite-topped table mahogany doubling as an island combined the elements of modern and rustic with the stainless steel refrigerator and dishwasher.

He opened the door under the sink, lay on his back and examined the plumbing hookup. Dom had installed a garbage disposal sink. Taylor checked the strainer basket and the rubber gasket preventing leakage between the strainer body and the sink. Dom had also installed a locknut for tightening the joint between the draining circuit and the end piece. He got up and closed the door. He'd seen enough. The pipes for the cold and hot water supply line, spray hose and the shutoff valve had been expertly installed.

Wiping his hands on the front of his jeans, he nodded. "Very nice."

"Do you want to see the bathrooms?"

Taylor shook his head. "That's not necessary. I'd like to know if I hire a supervisory plumber, are you willing to work with him?"

Dom smiled, exhibiting a mouth of straight white teeth. "I'm your man."

Taylor patted his shoulder. "That means I'll have two plumbers." He needed to interview one more with a license and extensive experience. "I'm telling you this in advance—once I have the entire restoration team, I will have an orientation session where everyone will be introduced to their supervisors. And if anyone has a problem, then the supervisor will handle it, and if they can't then either I or my assistant will step in. At no time will I tolerate bullying or intimidation. And anyone caught or reported will be immediately dismissed and escorted off the property."

"I suppose you mean we'll have to work well with one another."

"That's exactly what I'm talking about, Dom. I will not tolerate a hostile work environment because I'm projecting a two-year timeline."

A slight frown marred Dom's smooth forehead. "Isn't that a little long?"

Taylor shook his head. "No. Remember we're not putting up a building, but restoring a structure to look the way it did one hundred forty years ago. All of the guest rooms will be replicas of that period but with modern amenities like heat, running water, air-conditioning and Wi-Fi. It will be the same with the bar and lounges and meeting rooms. It is much easier to gut a structure and renovate it than restoring it to appear the way it did during a particular era."

"What about the cottages, Taylor?"

"The bedrooms, kitchens and bathrooms will still retain some of the charm of a late-nineteenth-century cottage but with updates that will include air-conditioning and Wi-Fi." Taylor still hadn't decided whether to keep or remove the wood-burning stoves that were used, along with fireplaces, to heat the structures.

"When do you expect to begin the restoration?"

Taylor mentally counted off the weeks. It was now the first week in May and he'd projected it would take him at least a month or maybe even six weeks to interview and hire his teams. "Hopefully before the end of June. I'd like to begin work on the exterior before the cold weather sets in." He recalled what Sonja had said about the windows and roof tiles. "But if I can't get the materials I need to replace the windows and roof tiles before the winter, then we'll concentrate on the interior work until next spring."

"That sounds like a plan."

"Thanks again for volunteering to help. I have to leave now, and I'll see you tomorrow night for our game." It would be another two days before he was scheduled to interview an electrician. And Taylor was still waiting for Robbie to return his call with a date and time for when they could get together.

"No problem, Taylor. You have the remote device for the gate, so just let yourself in."

Wiring the gate electronically was advantageous for Taylor and Dom. Before that he had to call the caretaker to ask him to manually open and close the gates. He walked back to where he'd parked his car. He pressed the remote attached to the visor, opening the massive iron gates, and drove over a metal plate that automatically closed them behind him.

Taylor was looking forward to seeing Sonja again. He knew it wasn't possible for them to spend time together every day, but when they did he wanted it to be special. He'd asked himself whether he wanted to sleep with her, and the answer was a resounding yes. Yet their sleeping together wasn't as much a priority as getting to know each other well enough to say whatever came to mind without insults or reprisals. He didn't want their relationship to become a power struggle as it had been with his former girlfriend. She was one of three female lawyers in a firm of more than twenty, and Taylor had had to remind her over and over they were lovers and not competitors.

Taylor headed for a shopping center several miles from Sonja's condo to buy what he needed to make for their dinner. He loved Italian food and had perfected a favorite recipe, hoping Sonja would enjoy it as much as he did.

Chapter Eleven

Sonja took one last look in the mirror before going downstairs to answer the doorbell. Taylor had called to let her know he would be at her place at four, and that had prompted her to jump in the shower and change out of the sweats and into a pair of stretchy black cropped pants and a black-and-white striped boatneck cotton pullover. She'd brushed her hair off her face and secured it in a bun on the top of her head. She'd just stepped off the last stair when the door opened. It was apparent Taylor had decided to let himself in. He gripped large canvas bags in both hands.

She quickly approached him and closed the door, struggling not to let him see her staring lustfully.

He had paired a white golf shirt with a popular logo with a pair of light gray slacks. Whether in casual or formal wear, his tall, perfectly proportioned physique garnered a second and even a third glance. And there were times when she believed he had caught her gawking as she silently admired his dark complexion and sculptured features.

"Let me help you with some of those."

"It's okay. I've got them."

"Okay, superman."

Sonja followed him into the kitchen. "What on earth did you buy?"

Taylor wiggled his eyebrows. "Stuff."

Bracing a hip against the countertop, she met his eyes. "What's for dinner?"

"Italian bread, Caesar salad, baked clams, penne with ground sausage, sangria and hazelnut gelato."

"You are singing my song. I love Italian food."

"I figured that because you've spent so much time in Italy."

"Do you need a sous-chef?" she asked as he set jars of dried spices, plastic bags of green, red and orange bell peppers, garlic, onion, apples, oranges, lemons, peaches and mushrooms.

"No, babe. Just sit and relax. I'll let you know if I need something. By the way, how was your day?"

"Enlightening."

"How so?" Taylor asked as he continued to take items out of the bags.

Sonja rounded the breakfast island and sat on

a stool. It seemed so natural to have a man in her kitchen as Taylor opened the freezer to store the gelato. "I don't know who MS is, but I found receipts indicating she was the recipient of ninety thousand dollars' worth of jewelry between 1906 and 1914."

Taylor whistled. "That's a lot of money to spend on jewelry during that time."

"It would be equivalent to two million today."

"Maybe MS was Charles Bainbridge's wife?"

"Or his mistress."

Taylor turned and stared at her. "Are you certain of that?"

"No, I'm not. I only found one article written about Charles Garland Bainbridge saying that he'd been prevented from building his summer cottage in Newport, Rhode Island, because there were rumors that his wife may have been a mulatto."

"So you haven't uncovered whether MS is his wife?"

Sonja shook her head. "Not yet."

"Maybe she was his daughter."

"I doubt that, Taylor. Daughters usually inherit jewelry from their mothers or grandmothers."

"What else did you find?" Taylor asked.

"There were ten trips to world's fairs between 1881 to 1915. Did you father ever reveal how his family amassed their fortune?"

He paused for several seconds, seemingly in thought. "I do remember him mentioning railroads, steamships, real estate, theaters and electricity."

Sonja gave herself a mental check when she recalled the number of world's fairs someone had attended with a focus on electricity. "That confirms what I found. There were hundreds of stubs for plays, concerts and films, and receipts for cross-country train trips and transatlantic sailing to Europe for the fairs."

"Judging from the amount of paper in the trunks, it looks as if the Bainbridges were hoarders. Nowadays everything can be saved electronically."

"Once I go through every piece of paper I am going to enter the information on spreadsheets and charts to generate a written history of your family's eminent ancestors."

"They may not be so eminent if you uncover something scandalous."

"No family, regardless of their income or status, is ever scandal-free."

"I suppose you are right, sweetheart."

"You suppose, Taylor? I'm certain your family has its share of secrets."

"I'm certain they do, but aren't families entitled to privacy? Or is it incumbent on them to air their dirty linen just for public consumption?"

Sonja was slightly taken aback by his queries and sharp tone, wondering what he was hiding. Did he know more about his ancestors than he was willing to admit? Or, if she did uncover something immoral or reprehensible, would he demand she not include it in her written report. She recalled him telling her about the clause in his modeling contract prohibiting the agency from disclosing anything about his personal life. What, she mused, was he hiding?

"No, it's not," she answered. "I believe everyone is entitled to a modicum of privacy."

"I believe people are entitled to more than a modicum. Public figures or personalities would fall into the category of the exception. I met a young woman from a very wealthy family, but you wouldn't have known it if she hadn't mentioned it. I don't know whether it was because she feared being preyed upon by those asking for a handout or whether she didn't want to become a target for someone seeking to abduct her for ransom. Whatever her reason, I respected her stance."

"I think you misunderstand me, Taylor. I'm not a newshound looking for dirt on your family to sell to a tabloid. Your hotel will become a living museum, and your guests will want to know about the lives of the people who lived in Bainbridge House."

Taylor halted placing the fruit and vegetables in the sink. "Are you asking me for permission to write a book about the Bainbridge family?"

Sonja hadn't thought about writing a book about his family, but now that he'd mentioned it she suddenly warmed to the idea. "Yes. Depending upon how much I can glean from the trunks, it can be a five-by-eight hardcover with a jacket of Bainbridge House and filled with narratives and photographs of the artifacts. And if I can find photographs of family members it would make it even more factual. Of course, you would have to approve everything before it could be published." She held up a hand when he opened his mouth. "The book could be sold in the museum shop."

Reaching for the retractable sink nozzle, Taylor rinsed the fruit and vegetables. "Did anyone ever tell you that you have a gift for gab?"

She flashed a bright smile. "Yes, but only when I believe in something." It was the second time that day that she'd talked to someone about writing a book. First her mother, and now she was attempting to convince Taylor she wanted to write about his family.

"I'm not going to promise anything at this time, but continue your research, and after you write up your findings we'll go over it together. And I'm warning you that before a single word gets into print, my sister and brothers will have the final say. The decision will have to be unanimous because I have no intention of becoming embroiled in a family feud. When my mother told us about Dad leaving us the property, everyone but Viola decided to get directly involved. The rest of us respected her decision without pointing fingers or trying to strong-arm her to change her mind. My parents raised us to be independent, but to always have one another's backs. If Viola decides she doesn't want to become the executive chef for Bainbridge House then I'm not going to hold that against her. She's her own woman and in control of her destiny."

Sonja didn't know why, but she felt as if Taylor had just chastised her for something she hadn't done. She'd merely mentioned the possibility of uncovering something sordid about his family, and he had taken it out of context. In other words, he was protesting prematurely. In that instant she made herself a promise that she would not bring up the subject again.

She slipped off the stool. "I'm going to set the table."

Taylor knew Sonja was upset and realized he was responsible for the change in her mood. He knew she was excited about what she'd found in the trunks, yet he wasn't the one with the final word as to what the public would be allowed to know about Conrad's family. That responsibility lay with Elise Williamson. She was Conrad's widow, and he'd willed her the property that she in turn had given to her children. Scandal or no scandal, Taylor refused to tarnish the reputation of the family of the man who had become his father and protector in every sense of the word.

"Do you have a glass pitcher or a large carafe?" he asked Sonja as she opened a drawer to remove flatware.

"I have a pitcher, but it's plastic."

"That will have to do. I'm going to need it for the sangria."

"Taylor, you're going to have to let me help with

something because as much as I enjoy looking at you I feel so helpless."

A slow smile parted his lips. "I got you beat there, because there are times when I can't take my eyes off you. Viola never told me what you looked like, so the first time I saw you approach my table at The Cellar I couldn't believe you were real. And when I saw men at other tables sneaking glances at you I wanted to tell them they could look, but I was the lucky dude that night. Then when I met you the next day I was shocked by your transformation. That's when I realized that you're a chameleon and I'd never know what to expect because you manage to look different each time we get together. It could be your hair or makeup or even what you choose to wear."

"Are you saying I keep you off balance?"

"Totally."

"Good."

His smile faded. "Why good?"

"That way you won't take me for granted."

"Is that what you think, Sonja?"

Her eyelids fluttered. "I don't know, but I'm hoping you won't."

Taylor dried his hands on a towel, took a step and rested his hands on her shoulders. "I am not your ex-husband or any of the other men in your life, sweetheart. I'm not perfect, but I've never been accused of taking advantage of a woman, and what I don't want is a relationship with you that will become a power struggle. Yes, I have the power to keep you on the project or let you go, but I hope and pray it will never come to that."

"Are you saying we make a good team?"

Lowering his head, he pressed his mouth to her ear. "We make an incredible team."

"In and out of bed?"

Taylor froze. He'd admitted Sonja kept him off balance, and she had done it again. "Before we go any further, you need to tell me what you want from me."

Easing back, Sonja met his eyes. "Whatever you propose I will let you know without question whether I'm willing to accept or reject it."

"You have to know I'm attracted to you."

"It's the same with me," Sonja admitted. "But how attracted are you? Enough to want to sleep with me?"

Taylor knew it was useless to lie. He had known he was physically attracted to Sonja the instant she'd introduced herself. He'd had no idea whether she was married or engaged, despite not wearing any rings. She could've been in a relationship, but that hadn't stopped him fantasizing about her as an incredibly beautiful and intelligent woman.

"Yes. Enough to sleep with you, Sonja Rios-Martin."

"Wow! You must be serious to mention my entire government name."

Taylor laughed despite the seriousness of their conversation. "That's because I am serious." He sobered quickly. "I need to know if you feel the same about me, however, I don't want to put any pressure on—"

"Not to worry," Sonja interrupted. "I will not succumb to pressure from you or any man to sleep with him. You know that I like you, Taylor—a lot. But I must figure out if history is going to repeat itself if I decide to sleep with you. What I didn't tell you was that my ex had been one of my professors. Something told me it was wrong to get involved with him, yet I refused to listen to my inner voice."

Taylor brushed a light kiss over her parted lips. "This time I want you to listen to your inner voice. If it tells you not to sleep with me, then don't do it. And if we do share a bed, then that decision will have to be yours and yours alone."

Sonja wondered why she hadn't met Taylor earlier in her life, when she could've had a relationship with him rather than a man that treated her more like an object than his wife. "You know if I'd met you when I was twenty, my life would've turned out drastically different."

Attractive lines fanned out around Taylor's large dark eyes when he smiled. "I doubt we would've crossed paths because my life revolved around modeling and I had little time to devote to a girlfriend or even have a lasting relationship. And marriage wasn't even on my radar."

"Has it ever been on your radar, Taylor?"

"Only when my mother tells me I'm going to wind

up an angry, lonely old man because I'm too selfish to share my life with a woman."

"Do you agree with her?"

'No. I try and tell her that when the right woman comes along, I'm certain she will be the one I'd want to spend the rest of my life with."

"So, you are open to marriage."

"Of course I am," Taylor said adamantly. "What gave you the impression I wasn't?"

"I don't know. You're thirty-five, unencumbered, and I just thought you were quite satisfied with your status and lifestyle."

"I am unencumbered and comfortable with, as you say, my status and lifestyle, but that doesn't mean I can't change it whenever I choose. What about you, Sonja? Do you think you'll ever remarry?"

It took several seconds for her to say, "I don't know. There were times when I told myself *once burned, twice shy*, and never again. However, lately things in my life have changed."

"How so?"

"This is the first time since leaving home to attend college that I've felt like an independent adult. I had a college roommate, then I married Hugh, and after leaving him I stayed with my parents until my divorce was finalized. Then when I reenrolled in college to get my degree I lived with my aunt and uncle. And I was still living with them until two days ago when I moved here."

"Why did you continue to live with them after you graduated?"

"I was staying with them rent-free because I was saving money to buy a house or condo. But that wasn't happening, because most of my jobs were either as a substitute teacher or part-time."

Taylor smiled again. "Until now."

She returned his smile with a bright one of her own. "Yes. Until now."

"You could buy this condo if you want."

Sonja stared at Taylor as if he had taken leave of his senses. First he told her the units were overpriced, and now he was saying she could buy it. "I suppose I could if I rob a bank," she quipped.

"Even though you look incredible in the color, I don't want to see you wearing an orange jumpsuit."

Sonja landed a soft punch on his chest. "I was just joking."

"And I wasn't joking about you buying this condo. That's something we can discuss once the lease expires."

Sonja was aware that the lease on the condo, her SUV and the credit card Taylor had given her, were all charged to Bainbridge House Trust, Inc., and at the end of her two-year contract she would not only have a history of steady employment, she also would've saved enough money to put down on a house or condo.

"I'm going to get that pitcher for you."

Taylor released her. "If you want you can cut up

the fruit for the sangria while I make the dressing for the salad."

"Do you need an apron?" she asked him. "After all, you are wearing white."

He glanced down at his shirt. "I'll take one as long as it doesn't have ruffles."

Sonja made a sucking sound with her tongue and teeth. "Sexist." Turning on her heel she went to the pantry to get one of several aprons she'd bought. She wore an apron when cooking because it was something her mother said every woman in her family always did whenever they cooked.

"This one is a little large for me, so I double it up and tie it twice around my waist."

Taylor unfolded the apron and smiled when he saw what was printed on the bib. "Kiss the Cook?"

Sonja rolled her eyes upward. "Yeah. It was the only one left, so I was forced to buy it."

He slipped it over his head, secured the ties and beckoned to her. "Come here, babe, and kiss the cook."

She took a step back. "Stop it!"

"Not until you kiss the cook," he crooned.

Sonja rested her hands at her waist. "And if I don't?"

Taylor stalked her like a large cat. "You don't want to know."

Then with a motion too quick for her to follow, she found herself in his arms, her feet several inches above the floor and her mouth covered in a kiss that stole the very breath from her lungs. Her arms went around Taylor's neck to keep her balance, and she found herself kissing him back, her tongue as busy as his as she tried to get even closer. It had been so long, much too long since the passion that lay dormant had flared to life. She heard a deep moan, not realizing it had come from her. She was on fire—everywhere, and Sonja knew Taylor was the only one to extinguish it.

It did not matter that she worked for his family and that her career and the next two years of her life depended on the man with whom she had fallen inexorably in love. Sonja had known Taylor was someone she never should have become involved with once she recognized him as T.E. Willis. Although he had left the world of modeling where he'd become an icon, she'd had second thoughts about working for Taylor Williamson, the engineer.

At first she thought her attraction was because of his gorgeous face and perfect masculine body, and then she chided herself for acting like an adolescent obsessing over her favorite actor or performer. After all, she was a woman in her midthirties who had been married and now was mature enough not to go, as her mother said, gaga over a man who had made a name for himself in his chosen field.

The more time she spent with Taylor the more she liked what he presented. He hadn't come on to her like some men she'd worked with or who had come into the gallery. He was the perfect gentleman that she was certain her mother would approve of. And she'd never had a man ask permission to kiss her. Hugh thought it was his right to kiss her when she wasn't expecting or even ready for the gesture the first time they were alone together at his house. He'd believed because she'd agreed to come to his home that she would agree to anything. She had come close to punching his lights out when he saw her expression and apologized profusely. His apology had been enough for her to agree to see him again, unknowingly to her detriment.

But it was so different with the man holding her to his heart. He respected and treated her as an equal, for which she was grateful. Sonja had lost count of the times she'd told herself that she liked Taylor as a friend, but that inner voice told her she was a liar, that there was nothing friendly about her thoughts. In fact, they bordered on erotic fantasies, and that when she'd told herself she was sex-starved it was because it had been almost ten years since she'd slept with a man.

Taylor had been forthcoming when he admitted he wanted to sleep with her and had given her the option of acting or not acting on it. What he hadn't known was the second time she saw him she'd wanted to jump his bones.

"Taylor."

"What is it?" he whispered against her mouth.

Sonja felt the runaway pumping of his heart against her breasts and knew if he didn't let her go she would shame herself when begging him to take her upstairs and make love to her. "You have to let me go."

"What if I don't want to?" He'd released her mouth and pressed his mouth against the column of her neck.

"You have to, because I'm not ready for this." Her statement must have gotten through to him. He loosened his hold on her body and lowered her until her feet touched the floor.

His eyes appeared abnormally large under the recessed lights as his chest rose and fell heavily as if he'd run a grueling race.

"Do you think you'll ever be ready?"

Sonja knew it was time for honesty if she hoped to have an open and uncomplicated relationship with him. "Yes. Please give me time to get my head and heart together."

Taylor stared at her from under lowered lids. "Take all of the time you need, sweetheart. After all, we have two years to get it right."

"You're right." He was giving her more time than she needed.

"I don't know about you, *muñeca*, but I'm hungry as a horse, so let's get to cooking."

Sonja couldn't believe she had eaten so much. The stuffed clams were the best she'd ever had, and there had been more than a few in her life when there were more bread crumbs than chopped clams. Taylor had cooked bacon until crisp and then crumbled it and set it aside while he sautéed onion, pepper and garlic until tender. He had then combined bread crumbs, oregano, grated parmesan cheese and the sautéed vegetables with the fresh chopped clams he'd gotten from the supermarket's fish department. He filled the shells with the mixture, sprinkled them with parsley and paprika and, after drizzling them with virgin olive oil, placed them in the hot oven until the tops were browned and the mixture bubbly. The Caesar salad with homemade dressing, warm buttered Italian bread and the delicious penne with ground sausage rounded out an incredible dinner, comparable to those served in restaurants.

She dabbed the corners of her mouth after swallowing a mouthful of sangria. "Who in the world taught you how to cook like this?"

"My mama."

Sonja slumped back in her chair. "You're kidding?"

"Nope. My mother made breakfast, lunch and dinner for us Monday through Friday. On the weekends it was either brunch and a light dinner or we went out to restaurants. Brunch was always a family affair with everyone cooking what they wanted to eat. The menu included omelets, waffles, pancakes, bacon, sausage, ham and cheese grits. We had live-in help that cleaned and did laundry, but Mom insisted on cooking for her children. We accused her of being paranoid, afraid someone would poison her kids."

"What did she say?"

"She completely ignored us. Mom had dozens of cookbooks and she planned her meals the same as she did her lesson plans. Each of us was assigned a week to watch and assist her preparing dinner. She was harder on her boys because she claimed she didn't want us hooking up with the wrong woman just because she could cook, and we couldn't."

"I have to assume her cooking lessons were successful because you are an incredible cook."

"Tariq and Patrick are even better than I am. They've mastered Asian and Middle Eastern cuisine. Joaquin and I are about equal, but it's our baby sister who surprised and surpassed everyone. That's why she's a professional chef."

"What about your father?"

"Dad was completely clueless in the kitchen. During the week, he usually got home too late to eat with the family, and that's why he devoted the entire weekend to us. His office was in Manhattan and he was up and out of the house to take the early train into Penn Station. There were nights when he didn't leave the office until late and had a car service on call to bring him home because a few times he'd overslept on the train and missed his stop. His edict to his employees was never to call him at home on weekends. That was his time for his family, and he couldn't be bothered with what he called minutiae that could wait for Monday morning. He'd called it minutiae, but there were a few times he substituted an expletive when he thought we were out of earshot. My parents were very free thinkers and proud to be labeled liberals, and although not ultrareligious, we did attend church services. They would not allow cursing in their home. It wasn't until I went to college that I was given a crash course in cuss words."

Sonja laughed. "I forget you were homeschooled until you left for college. Did you have to wait until then to date?"

"No. Once I got my driver's license, I hung out at the spots where many of the local high school kids gathered. Although many viewed me as an outsider I did manage to make a few friends."

"If you had children, would you consider having them homeschooled?" Sonja asked.

"That would all depend on their mother. My mother was certified to teach grades K through twelve and was also a reading specialist. She'd converted the library into a one-room schoolhouse, and floor-to-ceiling bookshelves were packed with books she'd inherited from her mother and grandmother. During the school year, we rarely watched television or played video games because we spent most of our free time reading or hanging out in the game room putting together thousand-piece puzzles, competing with one another playing pool, Ping-Pong or teaming up for board games. Summers were spent outdoors playing tennis and basketball, and swimming."

Sonja neatly folded her napkin and placed it next to her plate. Again, she envied Taylor and his siblings for their closeness. As the eldest, Taylor was seven years older than his youngest sibling, while her brother was ten years her senior. It wasn't that she and her brother did not love each other. However, it was the difference in their ages that had made it difficult for them to share a lot of the same activities.

"Oh! I forgot to tell you that I went online to look up companies in Italy that manufacture the windows you need to replace the ones in the château. I've also compiled a listing of Vermont quarries for the roof tiles. I'll send both to your email."

"I need to order two hundred forty-two windows. If we're not able to get them from Italy in time to install them before the winter, then they will be replaced with custom-made duplicates. What I will need from you is the name or names of faux bois specialists to restore the walls and moldings."

Sonja nodded and made a mental note to call someone she knew who owned an art restoration service. "I'll try and get that information for you. I'm going to spend one more day going through the trunks before heading over to the house to start with the crates."

"I'll have the caretaker give you a remote device to operate the front gates, and that way you won't have to call him in advance. My Thursday schedule is filled with back-to-back interviews, so I doubt whether I'll get to see you. I'll also make certain some of the crates are brought up from the cellar and into in the library."

"Thank you," she said, and then quickly covered her mouth with her hand to smother a yawn. "Sorry about that. Red wine always makes me sleepy." Even when traveling through Europe she'd made certain not to drink red wine if she'd planned to stay up for any appreciable amount of time.

"Why don't you go into the family room and chill. I'll clean up here."

"You don't have to, Taylor. You cooked, so I'll clean up."

He stood. "Not tonight, babe."

Sonja knew it was useless to debate the issue when Taylor rounded the table and scooped her up in his arms. He carried her into the family and lowered her to the love seat. She smiled up at him when he leaned over her. "I'm just going to rest my eyes for a few minutes."

She had no idea that resting her eyes for a few minutes would translate into falling asleep, and when she awoke she discovered she was in her own bed. Apparently, she had not woken up when Taylor carried her up the staircase. Rising on an elbow, she glanced at the clock on the bedside table. It was after ten. Sonja did not want to believe she'd been asleep for nearly two hours.

She closed her eyes while fantasizing about how much she'd wanted to wake up with Taylor in bed with her. He was everything she wanted in a man, yet old fears would not let her acknowledge what she'd been feeling for a while. She was falling in love with her friend's brother. They'd talked about marriage and children, and perhaps if Hugh had not turned into a monster she would be more receptive to a man's attention. It had taken years for the emotional scars fade, but she did not know if they would ever completely disappear.

Sonja opened her eyes and moaned at the same time she rolled her head on her neck. Her shoulders were achy from sitting on the floor hunched over for hours earlier in the day. She knew it was time to use the table doubling as a desk to do her work. Slipping off the bed, she headed for the bathroom to brush her teeth and wash her face. After changing out of her clothes into a cotton nightgown, she got back into bed and fell asleep for the second time that night.

Chapter Twelve

"I can't believe you came all this way for a pool cue."

Taylor dropped a kiss on his mother's hair when she closed the book she'd been reading and rose from the rocker where she'd sat awaiting his arrival. "Don't get up, Mom."

Elise sat down once Taylor took the rocker opposite her. "You didn't answer my question, Taylor." Her sapphire-blue eyes narrowed. "What's bothering you son?"

Stretching out long legs, Taylor crossed his feet at the ankles and stared at the scuffed toes of his running shoes. He'd made a mental note to throw them away a long time ago but was loath to part with them because one of his pet peeves was trying on shoes. In fact, he didn't like shopping and trying on clothes because of the years he'd spent standing motionless while designers and tailors adjusted an inseam or the length of jacket sleeve. Then there were the fashion shows where, within seconds of leaving the runway, he was stripped of whatever he was wearing for a new outfit while a makeup artist fussed over his face.

"What makes you think something is bothering me?"

"When are you going to accept that I probably know you better than you know yourself, Taylor? Call it a mother's intuition, but I know when my children are happy, angry and troubled. And right now, something is troubling you, and I hope it's because of a woman."

Taylor gave his mother an incredulous stare. Either he was that transparent or she that intuitive. He knew it was useless to lie her because it was something he rarely did. "I did come to get my pool cues."

"Who is she?" Elise asked.

He frowned. "Now I know where Viola gets her tenacity—you're both like dogs fighting over a bone when you think you're onto something."

Elise smiled as a network of fine lines appeared around her eyes. "Well, after all she is my daughter." Her smile faded. "Talk to me, Taylor, about this woman that probably has been keeping you up nights."

"I did meet someone."

"Is she a nice girl?"

Taylor closed his eyes and shook his head. Whenever any of his brothers talked about dating a woman, Elise always asked if she was a nice girl. "Yes, Mom. She's a very, very nice girl." He wanted to tell his mother that Sonja wasn't a girl but a woman.

"Tell me about her."

He told her everything, beginning with Sonja walking into the restaurant to their sharing dinner the night before. He did not tell his mother that he'd wanted to make love to Sonja and would have if she'd given him permission. "She's so different from the other women I've known that it's scary."

"That's because you're in love with her, Taylor. You may have liked the other women you dated, but I'm willing to bet you weren't in love with them."

"I don't know. Maybe I don't know what love is. I know I love you, my sister and my brothers, but that's different from what I feel for Sonja."

Elise rested her head against the back cushion and closed her eyes for several seconds. "I know what you're feeling, son, because I felt the same way when I met your father for the first time. He was one of the best-looking boys on campus. However, it wasn't his looks that made me fall in love with him—it was his charm and sensitivity. Whenever we were together I felt as if I were only woman in the world because he treated me like a princess. It took me a long time to admit I'd fallen in love with him, and once he asked me to marry him I knew I wanted to spend the rest of my life with him. That's what you must ask your-self. Can you see yourself spending the rest of your life with this woman?"

Taylor had asked himself the same question, and the answer was surprisingly yes. "Yes, I can. But what I find so strange is that I really don't know her. I met her for the first time about six weeks ago, and since then I can't get her out of my head."

"You don't want her in your head?" Elise asked.

Taylor wanted to tell Elise that he wanted Sonja in his bed, and then perhaps he'd be able to get her out of his head. When he'd spied her approaching his table, his initial attraction to her had been wholly physical, and that hadn't waned. "I don't know what I want at this point in time."

"Why are you measuring your relationship within segments of time, Taylor? Some couples meet and fall in love at first sight, marry right away and then go on to have a long and happy life together. Others take longer because the timing isn't right. Your father and I dated for two years because we were young and had goals to accomplish. You're exactly where you want to be in your career. You don't have to concern yourself with not having enough money because you were a millionaire even before you celebrated your twenty-fifth birthday. Now, what's holding you back from telling this woman that you love her?"

Taylor realized he wasn't telling mother every-thing about Sonja. "She was married to a man that was a lot older than she was. I think it scarred her, and she really doesn't trust men."

Elise sat straight. "Had he physically abused her?"

"I don't think so. If there was abuse, then it had to be either emotional or even psychological. In any event, she said she'd felt smothered and had to get out. And whenever we talk about marriage, she claims she never wants to marry again."

"Maybe you can get her to change her mind."

"I don't want to change her mind, Mom. That decision must be hers. And what I refuse to do is shack up with a woman. If we're going to live together, then she has to be my wife."

Elise glared at Taylor. "Sonja is not your mother, Taylor. She made the mistake of living with a man that deserted her when she needed him most. It's different with you and Sonja because you are *not* living together. If you love the woman, then let her know and wait for her to come around. If she does tell you that she loves you, then don't put any pressure on her to marry. That must be her decision."

"Are you saying we should live together?"

"There are worse things in this lifetime." She crossed her arms under her breasts. "Wake up, Taylor. This is not the forties, fifties or even the early sixties, when living together was akin to living in sin." Elise waved a hand. "I can't believe I raised someone with such antiquated views of life."

"I'm not that old-fashioned," Taylor mumbled under his breath.

"Enough talk about your love life, now tell why you want your pool cues."

"I have a little wager with Dom Shaw that I can beat him. And if I lose then I must hand over a bottle of aged scotch. I need to go through Dad's liquor cabinet and find a bottle." Conrad was also a collector of aged brandy, whisky and scotch.

"Take whatever you need because you know I won't touch the stuff."

"Maybe the next time I come I'll box them up, take them to the house and store them in the cellar with the wine."

"If you're shooting pool with Dom, then you'd better be careful."

"Why would you say that?" Taylor asked Elise.

"Because his father was a pool shark, and Conrad said he remembered him conning some of the household help."

"Well, Dad, was no slouch, and I learned from the best."

Elise laughed softly. "You're right about that. I used to accuse him of turning our kids into pool hustlers."

"Thankfully he didn't, and we all turned out all right."

"I suppose I should take some credit for that. How is everything going at the house?"

"Slow, Mom. I've interviewed a few candidates, and right now I'm considering hiring one. I have to see a few more tomorrow and hopefully before the end of the month I will have everyone onboard."

Elise nodded. "What's good is that you've given yourself a realistic timeline in which to complete everything."

Taylor agreed with her. There was nothing worse than pressuring workers to fast-track a construction project, which sometime resulted in on-site accidents and possible violations.

"Do you know where you'll live once the hotel is open for business?"

"I'd like to move into one of the cottages."

"That's a good choice. I was really surprised to find the rooms were much larger than they appeared from the outside. And three bedrooms is perfect for a couple with a one or two children."

"Maybe you can convince Patrick to move back east and live in one with his new bride"

A scowl distorted Elise's normally pleasant visage. "If he moves back, then I prefer he be alone."

Taylor could not understand his mother's disdain for his brother's fiancée. It was true that Andrea was spoiled and used to having her way, but that was Patrick's problem. "No comment."

"You say no comment when you should be the one warning him that he's going to ruin his life if marries that brat."

"I'm not going to interfere with my brother's love life. When he's had enough, he'll do what he must to extricate himself from what you see as a toxic relationship. Meanwhile, I suggest you don't bring it up with him because Patrick will only resent your interference."

"It's amazing how you always take up for him," Elise said angrily.

Taylor didn't want to get into it with his mother about his brother. As the eldest he'd been the one to protect his younger siblings, something he'd felt duty-bound to do even as an adult. Pushing to his feet, he forced a smile. "I'm going inside to get my cues and a bottle of scotch."

Elise reached out and caught his hand. "I'm sorry for what I said about you taking up for Patrick."

Leaning down, he kissed Elise's forehead. "No harm done, Mom. I know you love Patrick and only want the best for him."

"I want the best for all my children."

"We know that." He kissed her again, this time on her cheek.

Taylor left Belleville, his head full of what he'd admitted to his mother about falling in love with a woman who was more a stranger than he'd realized. If anyone had told him he would find himself in love with a woman he was beginning to think of as his counterpart, and, more importantly, a woman with whom he could be himself, he probably would've laughed.

He knew if he told Sonja that he'd fallen in love with her she'd probably believe he was crazy, or she would run in the opposite direction. She would remind him of the fact they were strangers and hadn't known each other long enough to profess an emotion as strong as love. And while he was ready to marry and have children, she wasn't. That had become his reality.

Taylor realized he had it all, but there was something missing. He'd been adopted into a warm, loving family; had found fame and fortune as a top male model; realized his boyhood dream to become an engineer, and now claimed one-fifth of a mansion appraised at 150 million dollars.

Ten minutes into his drive, Sonja's number appeared on the navigation screen. Smiling, Taylor answered the call. "What's up, sleepyhead?" Her sultry laugh came through the speakers.

"Please don't remind me of that. That's the last time I'm going to drink red wine when I'm with you."

"If you do, then there's one thing you'll know."

"And what's that?"

"That I'll never take advantage of you." There came a pause, and Taylor waited a full ten seconds before he said, "Sonja? Are you still there?"

"Yes, I am. And I want to thank you."

"For what?"

"For not taking advantage of me."

It was his turn to pause. Just what did she think he was? Some pervert who would take advantage of a woman under the influence? "I would never do that, especially with you or any other woman."

"Why me, Taylor? Is it because I'm your sister's friend?"

"My sister has nothing to do with what goes on between you and me. I told you before that I wouldn't discuss you with Viola, because she knows not to get into my personal life."

"Point taken."

"Is it, Sonja? Because you keep bringing up Viola."

"Okay, Taylor. I won't bring her up again."

Taylor heard the slight edge in her voice and hoped he hadn't come on too strong. "Look, babe, I'm sorry if you—"

"There's no need for you to apologize, *papi*."

Taylor grinned from ear to ear when he registered the endearment. *"Gracias, muñeca."*

Sonja laughed again. "Look at you speaking Spanish."

"I'm trying, sweetheart. I figure if we're going to hang out together for the next few years I could become fluent."

"How many years of French did you have?"

"Three, maybe four."

"You told me your mother spoke fluent French, yet you don't speak the language."

"I understand and read it better than I can speak it."

"Well, if you want to learn Spanish, then you have to speak it."

"Can I hire you to become my tutor?" he teased.

"I doubt if we're going to spend that much time together once you really get involved in the restoration."

"How about weekends?"

"Weekends are fine, Taylor, if I'm not working."

"No one will work weekends, and that includes you, Sonja."

"Is that an order?"

"No. That's the company policy."

"I thought you told me you're an easygoing boss."

"I am. But there are certain rules that must be followed, and no-work weekends is one of them. Weekends are for families. During the months of July and August, contractors will be given Fridays off. After the Labor Day weekend, they will resume their Monday through Friday schedules."

"Isn't it different for me, Taylor because after all I am a contract worker, and I can make my own hours."

"That's true. But wouldn't you want to spend some time with your parents, or aunt and uncle?"

"I hadn't thought of that."

"Well, I have. I can't have you burned-out before we have our grand opening."

Taylor wanted to tell Sonja it was something he also was looking forward to. He wanted to schedule the grand opening for late spring when the trees and flowers were in bloom, and host a reception in one of the ballrooms for the press, local, state and national politicians.

"That's something I don't intend to miss. Thankfully, that's quite a way off because I estimate it's going to take me a long time to catalogue everything, and especially now that you tell me there's even more crates than the ones I saw."

Taylor chuckled. "Maybe I shouldn't have mentioned that to you."

"I'm glad you did because I don't like surprises, Taylor."

He sobered. "I'll try and remember that." He wondered if Sonja would be surprised or even shocked if he told her he was in love with her.

"I just sent you an email with the information you asked for. The guy that owns the restoration company is a doll. I told him what you needed, and he said he'll get back to me and let me when someone can come out and view the damage. Of course, I'll check with you to see when you're available."

"Thanks, sweetheart."

"I'm going to hang up now because I want to finish what I'm working on. Then I'm going downstairs to heat up some of your delicious leftovers."

"Okay. I'll probably see you tomorrow at the house."

"That's a bet. Later, Taylor."

"Later, love."

Love, he thought. How had the single word slipped out so easily when he had made a concerted effort during their conversation not to tell Sonja that not only had he fallen in love with her?

Taylor drove along the paved path to Dominic Shaw's cottage. His mother's warning that Dom's father had been a pool shark only served to heighten his competitiveness. And if the son was anything like his father, then Taylor wanted to warn the caretaker he didn't intend to be that easily maneuvered into handing over a bottle of aged single malt scotch whisky.

Dom opened the door at the same time Taylor alighted from the SUV. Reaching for the case with the cue sticks, Taylor grasped the velvet bag with the bottle and handed it to Dom. "Careful with the prize."

Dom opened the bag and smiled. "This Balvenie Caribbean Cask 14-year-old single malt whisky will go nicely with my collection."

"Nah, son."

"Who are you calling son? I bet I'm older than you."

"You," Taylor countered, smiling.

"Nah, Taylor. I just celebrated my thirty-fifth birthday."

"I'll be thirty-six in November, so I've got a few months on you." When meeting Dominic for the first time, Taylor realized despite the fact he was graying there wasn't a single line on his face or around the brilliant dark green eyes. Tall and almost rawboned, there wasn't an ounce of fat on his lean body. "What I'm going to do is beat the hell out of you, and then I'm going to crack open that bottle and have a few shots and you're going to join me rather than sit back and admire it on your shelf."

Dom laughed loudly. "You talk a lot of shit, old man. Let's go inside and have a go at it. Better yet, why don't we crack open this baby and sample it while we play?"

Taylor gave him a direct stare. "I thought you wanted to add it to your collection. Could it be that you're afraid I'm going to beat you?"

"Not really. I'm more than confident that I can hold my own, but when I saw that you brought your own cue sticks I realized you're no novice."

"In other words, you realized you couldn't hustle me."

A flush darkened Dom's face under his tan. "I don't hustle folks. I've lost some games and won many more."

"Okay. Let's go inside and find out if you're going to win some and lose many."

Taylor had to admit that Dom just wasn't good. He was an expert. In fact, his eye-hand coordination was comparable to that of Joaquin, who could've turned pro if he hadn't chosen to become a landscape architect.

They played the best of five, and Dom won three and Taylor two. After each game they took a shot of whisky, and Taylor knew he had to stop; otherwise, he wouldn't be able to get behind the wheel and drive. "I'm done."

"Don't you want to play one more?" Dom asked.

"No. What I need to do is sober up before I leave."

"I have two extra bedrooms where you could crash."

"I don't want to impose."

"You won't be imposing, Taylor. After all, you do own this cottage."

"My family owns it," Taylor said, correcting him. "I'm going to sit here for a while."

"I'm going to the kitchen to make some coffee. You're not the only one feeling the effects of the whisky. This is the first time I've tasted The Balvenie. It definitely lives up to its reputation, and drinking it is a lot more enjoyable than staring at the bottle."

"I agree," Taylor drawled. He rarely drank hard liquor, but when he did it was only from his father's bar. The soft and lingering notes of toffee and vanilla with a hint of fruit on his palate made the single malt whisky exceptional.

Dom returned with two mugs of steaming black coffee. He handed one to Taylor. "Drink up, old man. I added a couple of shots of espresso to yours."

Taylor smiled. "Don't push it, son." He took a sip of the hot brew, grimacing when it burned his tongue. Staring at Dom while waiting for his coffee to cool somewhat, he wondered what had made a supposedly healthy thirtysomething-year-old man live alone on an abandoned estate.

"I forgot to ask if you wanted milk in your coffee."

"No, thanks." A beat passed. "Do you like living here?"

Dom stared at Taylor over the rim of his mug. "Yes, because it's all I know. I was born here, and I'll probably die here. The only time I left was when I enlisted in the service and then attended college, but like a homing pigeon I came back."

Taylor knew very little about the caretaker. "What did you study in college?"

"I have a master's in Business."

Taylor was surprised by Dom's revelation. He did not want to believe the man was licensed plumber and had earned a graduate degree yet was content to live on an estate in the role as a glorified maintenance man. It was obvious Dom had his reasons for wanting to live out his life on the Bainbridge property.

He managed to finish the coffee, and the extra caffeine was enough to clear his head and jolt him into alertness. "Thanks for the coffee," he said, pushing off the sofa and coming to his feet.

Dom also stood. "Are you sure you're okay to drive?"

"I'm good."

"Aren't you going to take your cue case?" Dom asked as Taylor walked to the door.

"No. I'm going to leave it here for when we play again."

Dom followed Taylor to the door and opened it. "I'm looking forward to it."

"No shots," Taylor said.

"No shots," Dom repeated, laughing loudly.

Taylor paused. "Oh, before I forget. The architectural historian is coming tomorrow, and I want you to give her one of the remote devices for the front gates. Her name is Sonja Rios-Martin, and she has no set work hours. My schedule is filled with back-to-back interviews, so I doubt I'll get to see her."

"No problem."

Taylor made it home and once he opened the door to his mother's condo he cursed himself for engaging in what he thought of an as asinine frat boys' game. He did not want to believe that he'd waited until thirty-five to do shots.

Never again, he mused. It would be the first and last time, he vowed as he brushed his teeth and rinsed with a peppermint mouthwash. He stripped off his clothes, leaving them in the hamper, and stepped into the shower stall. Ice-cold water rained down on his head and body before Taylor adjusted the temperature to lukewarm.

After drying off, he walked in the direction of the guest bedroom and fell across the bed. His last thoughts before Morpheus claimed him were of Sonja as he stood beside her bed, watching her sleep.

Chapter Thirteen

Decelerating, Sonja turned onto the private road leading to Bainbridge House. Some of the older trees that had been still bare the last time she'd come to the estate were now resplendently covered with bright green leaves. She drove through the open gates and seconds later they automatically closed behind her. She wanted to get to the house by eight and work nonstop until midafternoon. Maneuvering into the driveway behind Taylor's car, she shut off the engine. It was obvious she wasn't the only one planning to begin early.

Scooping up the tote with her camera, legal pads and felt-tipped pens, and the insulated bag with her lunch in glass containers filled with salad, fruit and bottles of water she got out of the SUV. She climbed the six steps, opened the front door and came face-to-face with a tall, slender man dressed entirely in black: shirt, jeans and boots. Sonja forced a smile she didn't quite feel because there was something about him that made her uncomfortable. The dark green eyes the exact shade of peridot had deepened to a dark emerald the longer he stared at her. She wanted to ask him if he'd been taught it was impolite to stare.

"I'm Sonja Rios-Martin," she said, shattering the soporific spell.

The man inclined his head. "Dominic Shaw." He reached into the back pocket of his jeans. "Taylor wanted me to give this to you. It's the remote device for the front gate. The first button opens the gate. It will close automatically once you drive over the metal plate, but if you want to keep it from closing, then tap on the left."

Sonja took the remote device. "Thank you."

Dom ran a hand over raven-black hair. "I brought up some crates and put them in the library."

She smiled. "Thank you again."

"Taylor's in the back checking the foundation. Do you want me to get him for you?"

"Please don't bother him. I'll see him later."

"I'm going to be in the cellar for most of this morning. So, if you need anything and Taylor's not available, then just come down."

Sonja wanted to tell the man she doubted whether she would need him for anything. He wasn't what she thought of as handsome, but attractive. There were too many sharp angles in his lean face. "Okay."

She walked in the direction of the library, curbing the urge to look over her shoulder to see if Dominic was still staring at her retreating back. There was something about him that was creepy. Taylor had told her that Dom, as he called him, was the only one living on the property, and Sonja deduced that the man had spent so much time alone that he probably resented having to share what had become his private lair. She could not imagine living on a 350-plus-acre property year-round with only sporadic human interaction.

Sonja entered the library. There were eight crates lining one wall. Unfortunately, none of the crates were labeled with their contents, which meant a guessing game as to what she would find. Setting the tote on a small round table, Sonja took out the materials she needed to begin identifying and cataloguing.

"Yes," she said softly after she'd removed the top of the first one. She took out a crystal wineglass protected by Bubble Wrap. Sonja recalled Taylor telling her the late-nineteenth-century mansion was abandoned in the 1960s when the last Bainbridge died at the age of ninety-four, and his father was the last surviving direct descendant of the original owner. She knew bubble wrap hadn't been invented until 1960.

She emptied the crate, lining fragile glassware on an oak Mission-style table. One by one she photographed a liqueur glass with transparent enameling, circa 1900; a Daum Frères cameo glass vase, circa 1890; E. Bakalowits & Söhne floral glasses; four Bohemian drinking glasses with purple and gold medallions on the base and two more Bohemian liqueur glasses in a rich ruby color. The minutes stretched into hours as she took pictures of the glassware, listed them on pads, and then carefully rewrapped them and returned them to the crate. Sonja found it odd that there were no complete sets, leaving her to wonder if someone had packed them away without regard to whether they matched. She marked the crate with the date and its contents, and then moved onto another one.

This one was filled with large flannel bags of velvet boxes she knew contained jewelry. There was a gold, pearl and amethyst brooch; another with parrots bejeweled with diamonds, sapphires, rubies, emeralds and onyx. Her breath caught in her throat when she held a Cartier brooch with large bloodred rubies, diamonds and sapphires. There were more brooches, rings, necklaces, earrings and bracelets with priceless stones set in gold and platinum.

"How's it going, *muñeca*?"

Sonja turned on her chair to find Taylor in the doorway. She smiled at him. "One down and who knows how many more to go."

Pulling over a chair, Taylor sat and brushed a light kiss on her mouth, increasing the pressure until her lips parted. "You look and smell delicious." He didn't think he would ever tire of kissing Sonja, inhaling the sensual fragrance of the perfume that was perfect for her hypnotic feminine scent.

"That's because you're biased," Sonja whispered.

"Hell, yeah." He reached out and picked up a pin with a large blue stone surrounded with gold leaves topped with rubies and stems dotted with diamonds. "Someone really liked bling."

"Someone was really partial to brooches." Sonja handed him one completely covered in diamonds designed with an arrow attached at the back of a heart. "This is an amatory brooch."

"Amatory as in love?"

Sonja nodded. "They were jewels representing sentiment and love, common from the seventeenth to the late nineteenth century. Early symbols included the true lover's knot, and Cupid shooting arrows and flaming hearts like this one."

Taylor set the brooch on the table and picked up a diamond-and-sapphire ring. "This must be worth quite a bit."

Sonja met his eyes. "I've seen enough jewelry to make a rough estimate as to carat weight. The diamond looks to be around two carats and the sapphires flanking the center stone approximately a half carat each, while the platinum setting increases the ring's value exponentially."

Taylor balanced the ring on his palm. "Whoever wore this had a small finger."

Sonja took the ring from him and slipped it on her left hand. "It's a five," she said, taking it off and giving it back to him.

"The diamond is not like any I've ever seen."

"It's known as an Asscher cut."

Taylor peered closely at the ring. "It's exquisite."

"It's beyond exquisite," Sonja agreed. "I'm not going to repack the jewelry. I'll give everything to you for safekeeping until I take them to a gemologist I trust who will give you an honest appraisal."

"You can hold on to them for now."

She blinked slowly. "Are you sure, Taylor?"

"Of course I'm sure. I trust you with my life."

"That's a lot of trusting."

Taylor couldn't pull his gaze away from the large brown eyes with lashes that had touched the ridge of high cheekbones as she slept. "It is for me, because I equate trusting to loving."

A hint of a smile curved the corners of her mouth upward. "And I believe trust is more important than love because people can fall in and out of love. I'd rather trust you than love you."

Sonja had just given Taylor the opening he needed. "Can you love me?"

"I'm sure I can."

Her response was both indifferent and evasive. Do you love me, Sonja?" Taylor saw indecision in her eyes, and that was enough to give him hope that what he felt for her could be reciprocated.

"Why are you asking me this?"

"I'm asking, sweetheart, because I need to know."

Sonja's gaze did not waver as she gave him a long, penetrating stare. "If I tell you that I do, it's not going to change anything between us. Whether you know or admit it, Taylor, you're a traditionalist. You want a wife, two or three kids, a cat and dog, along with a house in the suburbs with the white picket fence."

He struggled not to laugh. "I'm really not crazy about cats."

"I'm serious, Taylor."

"So am I, Sonja. I admit I'm a traditionalist because I don't believe in living with a woman unless I'm married to her."

"That's where we differ, Taylor. I lived with a man to whom I was married, and I realized later that if I'd lived with him I never would've married him."

If she does tell you that she loves you, then don't put any pressure on her to marry. That must be her decision. Taylor recalled his mother's words as if she were whispering in his ear.

"Did you love him, Sonja?"

She closed her eyes and shook her head, and Taylor felt her vulnerability as surely as if it was his own, because falling in love with Sonja Rios-Martin had allowed him to open his heart to love a woman beyond those in his family.

"Good."

"Good?" Sonja repeated.

"Yes. Because he didn't deserve your love."

"And you do?"

"I should hope I do. Remember I told you if we do share a bed, then that decision will have to be yours and yours alone. And it will be the same if you want more."

Sonja rested her head on his shoulder. "Should

I assume you mean living together and then marriage?"

"Yes."

"I need time, Taylor."

"Take all the time you need, sweetheart. You're not going anywhere, and neither am I."

There came a light tapping on the door, and Taylor and Sonja sprang apart. He glanced over his shoulder. "Yes, Dom?"

"Your next interviewee just arrived."

"Thank you, Dom." Pushing back his chair, he stood and rested a hand on Sonja's shoulder. "How long do you plan to hang out here?"

Sonja picked up her cell phone. "I want to leave around three."

"I'll be here much later than that." Robbie had called to say he was coming to New Jersey to spend the weekend with his sister and her family in Hackettstown and wanted to set up a time when they could meet. "I'm going to be tied up for the next few days. Is it all right if I come over Sunday morning to let you sample my chicken and waffles?"

"Of course."

Leaning down, Taylor kissed the bridge of her nose. "I love you."

"Love you back."

"Did I really say that?" Sonja whispered aloud. She did not want to believe she'd admitted to Taylor that she loved him and entertained the possibility of them living together.

She wasn't the twenty-year-old coed with stars in her eyes, and she wouldn't lose her head just because a former top male model and successful engineer had shown an interest in her. At thirty-four, she knew exactly what she wanted and what she would or would not do. In the years following her divorce, Sonja had not had a relationship with a man because she did not trust them not to go from Dr. Jekyll to Mr. Hyde when she least expected. She had dated a few, and those expressing a sincere interest in her were made aware that she wasn't looking for anything serious, and for her *serious* meant sleeping together or seeing each other exclusively.

Taylor said she should take all the time she needed to decide whether they would live together and eventually marry. They had two years, and that was more than enough time for Sonja to know if she'd want to share her life and future with Taylor Williamson.

"I'm sorry to bother you, but is there anything you need, because I'm leaving."

Sonja glanced over her shoulder at Dom. "I don't think so. Thank you for everything."

"Are you coming tomorrow?"

"Yes."

Dom smiled, the expression softening his features to where he appeared almost boyish. "If you need me to move something just send me a text."

"I would if I had your number."

Dom walked into the library, scooped her phone off the table and entered his cell number. "Now you have it."

She returned his smile. "Thank you." Dom left, closing the door behind him, and Sonja shifted her chair to face the door. She didn't want any more walk-in surprises.

Taylor gave his former coworker a rough hug. "You look incredible." Robinson had shaved off his beard and his nut-brown face radiated good health.

"I'm trying, Williamson. Let's go because I'm anxious to see what you're working with."

Taylor unlocked the doors to the Infiniti. "Let's ride, brother."

Twenty-five minutes later, Taylor tapped the remote attached to the visor, and the gates protecting Bainbridge House opened smoothly. The trees lining the path to the property were in full bloom, and dappled sunlight filtered through the foliage like the brilliant diamonds in the priceless jewels that had been packed away for decades. He'd purposely kept busy to keep his mind off Sonja. The interviews had yielded results with positive prospects to fill the positions for his restoration team.

"You've got to be kidding me."

Taylor gave Robbie a sidelong glance. "What's the matter?"

With wide eyes, Robbie stared straight ahead. "Why does this château look as if someone picked it up from the French countryside and set it down in Jersey?"

"That's because someone did, Robbie. I found the

original plans and discovered the château was disassembled stone by stone, stored on ships sailing across the Atlantic, then hauled up here by wagon where it was rebuilt."

"It is magnificent."

Taylor nodded, smiling. "That it is. The interior is even more impressive."

Robbie slowly shook his head. "I can see why you quit working for the firm. I would've done the same if someone left me this place."

"This isn't mine alone. I share the property with my brothers and sister."

"From what I see, you have enough to share with dozens of brothers and sisters."

"What's the expression, Robbie? Too many cooks spoil the broth. Right now it's just me. Two years from now it will be Joaquin, and then Tariq, and finally Viola." Taylor had said *finally* when he wanted to say *hopefully*. "I'm going to take you around the grounds before we go inside."

He led Robbie to the stables and barn. "We have paddocks for six horses."

"Do you plan to house horses on the property?"

"Yes. My brother Tariq is a vet, and his specialty is horses."

"What are you going to do with the barn?" Robbie asked.

Taylor glanced up at the rotting crossbeams. "I'm seriously thinking of demolishing and rebuilding it. There's too much rot. I'd like your expertise when I put up another building."

"What do you plan to use it for?"

"I'm going to need an additional entertainment venue. There are two ballrooms in the main house for weddings and private parties, but after I show you the blueprints, you can suggest how to reconfigure them for meeting rooms and an on-site restaurant. The new structure can be used for larger banquets."

"Where do you plan to rebuild it?" Robbie asked.

"Behind the main house with an enclosed walkway connecting the two structures."

"Will the design conform to the château?"

"Yes. I want it to look as if it is a part of the original design. Will that pose a problem?"

Robbie ran a hand over his shaved pate. "Not at all. But I have to admit it will be my first time designing a château. How large do you want it?"

"Between five- and six-thousand square feet."

Robbie nodded. "That's enough room for almost two hundred people."

"That's sounds about right. Let's go inside and you'll see what awaits you."

Taylor showed Robbie original copies of floor plans and blueprints of the entire property spread out on a banquet table in the larger ballroom. Robbie listened intently when he showed him his blueprint and what he'd planned for the vineyard, orchards, gardens and the golf course. He was forthcoming when voicing reservations about whether to refurbish the golf course.

"I'd keep it, Williamson, because it's only nine holes. If it were eighteen holes then I'd say scrap it.

If you're going to have guests come for a week or even a long weekend, some may want to play a couple of rounds."

Taylor smiled. "True, but if they want to exercise they can always use the health center with a workout room and the indoor pool."

Over the next three hours he showed Robbie the bedroom suites on the second and third floors. He explained the structural modifications he'd planned to make when removing walls and expanding more than half the suites to accommodate four to six guests in each suite. Taylor also told Robbie that he wanted to install two more elevators, bringing the total number to four.

"What do you plan to do with the turrets?"

"I'm still up in the air about the space. I have to confer with my brothers and sister whether they would want live up there or take up residence in the cottages."

"Where do you plan to live?"

"I've claimed one of the cottages."

"Nice, Williamson," Robbie drawled. He extended his hand. "If you want an architectural engineer, then I'm your man."

Taylor shook the proffered hand. "Thanks for joining the team." He had his two architectural experts: Sonja Rios-Martin and Robinson Harris.

Chapter Fourteen

Taylor brushed a kiss over Sonja's mouth when she opened the door. As promised, he'd planned to make chicken and waffles for their first Sunday brunch. "Hey, beautiful."

She flushed with the compliment. "Hey yourself, handsome."

He'd stopped by the night before and left a container of marinating chicken. He did not ask to stay over and for that Sonja was grateful. She wasn't quite ready to take their relationship to the next level. After all, they had two years in which to get to know each other in and out of bed.

Not having dinner together for several days had allowed her more time to devote to the contents of the trunks. She had anticipated spending hours on the project so she'd planned slow cooker meals. Beef stew and chili accompanied with salad fortified her for lunch and dinner.

"I've set out the cast-iron pot and waffle iron for you."

"Good." Taylor held up a small shopping bag. "I have all I need in here to make red velvet waffles."

Sonja moaned, smiling. "I am addicted to anything red velvet."

Taylor winked at her. "And I'm addicted to what I'm looking at."

She waved at him. "Flattery will get you nowhere."

"It's not flattery, *muñeca*. It is the truth."

Sonja looped her arm through his free one. "Come and feed me. I'm starved."

Hours later, Sonja reclined against Taylor on the sofa in the family room, her back resting against his chest. "I have a confession to make."

He pressed a kiss on her hair. "And that is?"

"You were right about your chicken and waffles. They were the best I've ever eaten." The chicken, drizzled with melted butter and honey, was the perfect complement to the fluffy red-hued Belgian waffles. They'd opted for freshly squeezed orange juice sans champagne as an accompanying beverage.

"Does this mean we can do this again?"

Tilting her chin, she smiled up at him staring

down at her. "Yes. We can do this again and again for a long time to come."

"How long, darling?"

"For a very long time, *papi*. I've spent the past three days thinking about what we talked about in the château's library. You are so different from Hugh that it's frightening, and that's why I wouldn't allow myself to get close to you. But, in spite of that, I couldn't help falling in love with you."

"Or I you, Sonja," he whispered. "You just don't know how easy it is to love you."

Sonja closed her eyes, realizing that what she was about to tell Taylor would change her, change them forever. "I want to know what love is, Taylor. I need you to make love to me."

Sonja remembered Taylor carrying her out of the family room and up the staircase to her bedroom. He took his time undressing her and then himself. She closed her eyes after he'd slipped on a condom and before she welcomed him into her embrace for their introductory dance of shared passion.

She bit her lower lip to stop the moans of pleasure rippling through her body like currents of electricity, shocking every nerve ending as she experienced la petite mort for the first time in her life. The orgasms kept coming, overlapping one another until Sonja feared fainting.

"I love you. I love you," she repeated over and over until it'd become a litany. "I love you, Taylor Edward Williamson, and I will marry you and have your babies."

* * *

Taylor thought he was hallucinating. Passion had clouded his mind to the point that he did not know where he began or ended.

"When, babe?"

Sonja rubbed her leg over the back of his. "Christmas. I want a Christmas wedding at Bainbridge House in the small ballroom with just friends and family in attendance."

"My mother can't be there because she'll still be on her cruise."

"Then it will have to be the following Christmas."

Taylor supported his greater weight on his forearms as he loathed pulling out of her body. "Are you sure? We could marry before she leaves for her cruise in August."

"No, Taylor. I want to wait. There's no need for us to rush anything. Didn't you say you're not going anywhere?"

"Yes, I did."

"I'm also not going anywhere. I'm going to be here today, tomorrow and all the days thereafter. And the day I marry you I want us to start baby making. Meanwhile I'm going to go on birth control because I don't want to become a baby mama before we're married."

Taylor wanted to tell Sonja he had no intention of fathering a child and deserting her, married or not. He did not want to repeat the scenario of his biological parents' fractured relationship.

"I will protect you until then."

He pulled out, left the bed and went into the bathroom to discard the condom. Sonja wanted to marry the following Christmas, and that meant an eighteenth-month engagement. By that time, the extension to the château would be completed and they could hold the ceremony and reception there. Taylor returned to the bedroom and got into bed beside Sonja, who'd turned on her side. She moaned softly when he pressed his groin against her rounded hips. Resting his arm over her waist, Taylor pulled her even closer. His breathing slowed until he fell into a slumber reserved for sated lovers.

Sonja felt as if she was existing in an alternative universe as spring gave way to summer. She and Taylor were now living together. His mother had finally sold the house where she'd raised her children and moved into her condo. Days later, she flew out to the West Coast for a reunion of her college sorority sisters, and Taylor packed up his clothes and stored them in the closet in the smaller bedroom.

She went to Bainbridge House on Mondays, Wednesdays and Fridays, and worked from home on Tuesday and Thursdays. Cloistered behind the door in the château's library she heard but rarely saw the workmen going about their tasks. Pickup trucks and vans lined the driveway, and several dumpsters were positioned around the house.

Her condo's backyard had undergone a metamorphosis with all-weather furniture, umbrellas, portable lighting, a gas grill and fire pit, and Sonja found herself, weather permitting, eating breakfast and dinner outdoors. She and Taylor grilled chicken, steak, fish, veggies, and fruit, leaving little or no cleanup in the kitchen.

She was halfway through emptying one trunk when she found a batch of letters wrapped with a red ribbon and finally discovered who MS was. Melanie Shaw had been Charles Bainbridge's mistress, and also a house servant and the mother of his love child. Why, she mused, were a mistress's love letters stored with possessions where anyone might discover them?

"Oh, my word," she gasped when realization dawned. The property's caretaker was a Shaw, and Sonja wondered if there was connection between Melanie and Dominic. She did not want to invade his privacy, yet the historian in her wanted and needed to uncover the truth.

Reaching for her cell phone, she sent Dom a text asking if she could talk to him. She didn't have to wait for his reply, and he said he would available later that afternoon to meet in the library.

Taylor walked in the direction of the small ballroom that he'd set up as a temporary office and stopped when he heard Sonja's voice coming from the library. The door was slightly ajar, and he was caught completely off guard when he saw Sonja in Dom's arms. Not only wasn't it her scheduled day to work outside the condo, but he hadn't expected to see her embracing the caretaker.

Taking long strides, he made his way to the ballroom and closed the pocket doors as scalding fury gripped him and he struggled to draw a normal breath. Taylor did not want to believe the woman with whom he'd fallen in love, slept beside every night and made love to was having an affair with another man. When she came in on Mondays, Wednesdays and Fridays he rarely saw her because she tended to work behind closed doors. However, he was aware that after she'd completed several crates Dom would return them to the cellar and bring up more.

He paced the length of the ballroom, pounding his fist into his hand when he'd wanted to punch something hard to make him forget about the emotional pain threatening to explode into unrestrained anger. Taylor sat on the stool near the drafting table, staring at the plans he and Robbie had designed on the computer and revised several times before they were finalized and printed. He lost track of time, then stood and walked out of the ballroom to talk to Dom.

He saw Dom kneeling near a flower bed, pulling out weeds. "We need to talk."

Dom rose and met his eyes. "What about?"

"I want you to stay away from Sonja."

The green eyes narrowed like a cat ready to attack. "What the hell are you talking about?"

Taylor chose his words carefully. "I don't want you anywhere around her when she's working in the library. Meanwhile, I'll have someone else move the crates."

Dom crossed his arms over his chest in a gesture mirroring defiance. "Have you forgotten that you're not my boss? You don't pay my salary, therefore I don't have to take orders from you. But if you want me to stay away from Sonja, then I will. Not because you say so, but because I don't want to make trouble for her." Turning on his heel, he walked away, leaving Taylor staring at his back.

Taylor cursed to himself—raw, ugly, frustrated curses because Dom was right. He wasn't his boss, and it wasn't incumbent upon him to pay the man's wages, therefore he couldn't fire him. However, he did pay Sonja; he decided to wait until later to confront her.

Sonja couldn't believe what she was hearing. The man she'd pledged her future to had accused her of cheating on him with another man. It was history repeating itself. "You saw something you probably shouldn't have seen and jumped to the conclusion that I was seeing another man. Maybe you should have come into the library instead of accusing an innocent man. What happened to trust, Taylor!" She was screaming but no longer cared. "Remember I told you that I value trust over love? I believed once we agreed to live and sleep together that we would trust each other." She threw up both hands. "You're no different from Hugh because he, too, didn't trust me." The tears she'd held at bay fell, and she backed away when Taylor attempted to touch her. "Don't! I have to get away. Even if it is just for a few days." She swiped angrily at the tears streaming down her face and walked over to the closet to take out a suitcase.

"Where are you going, Sonja?"

"I don't know. I'll find out when I get there."

There weren't that many places she could go aside from her parents', and her aunt and uncle's. She thought about Viola and quickly changed her mind. Taylor was her brother, and there was no doubt she would side with him.

She opened drawers and threw clothes in haphazardly before going into the bathroom to gather a number of personal items and products. Sonja closed the bag, grabbed her tote off the chair and went downstairs. She didn't know if Taylor was following her as she opened the door and walked out into the late-afternoon warmth. It wasn't until she'd left the complex that she decided to drive to her parents' house and spend time there to clear her head.

Sonja knew they were away, but she had the keys and the code to the house's security system. It was almost laughable. When she left Hugh she'd run to her mother. And now she was doing it again. There was something about sitting on the porch and staring at the lake that she found therapeutic. She planned to spend the weekend there, and when she returned she would continue with her project. Once it ended she would move on to the next one.

* * *

Taylor sat in the family room staring at the flickering images on the flat screen. Night had fallen and he hadn't turned on any lights. If it hadn't been for the sound of the television the house would've been as quiet as a tomb. He'd blown it. Jealousy had reared its ugly head, and he'd accused the woman he loved passionately of sleeping with another man. It had taken her almost two minutes to reply to his accusation, and during that time he'd felt triumphant because she hadn't thought he knew. His victory was short-lived when she told him there was nothing going on between her and Dominic, and what he'd witnessed was a friendly hug between friends. It was when she told him he was the same as her ex-husband that it was apparent he'd done something that made her distrust him. Taylor decided to give Sonja a few days to cool off before calling her. After all, she hadn't put enough clothes in the bag to last more than that.

Taylor counted off the days: Wednesday, Thursday, Friday and Saturday. It was now Sunday and Sonja hadn't come back or returned any of his calls, but he didn't want to believe he'd lost her. His apprehension increased knowing it wasn't the first time she'd walked away from a relationship.

He'd become a detective when he accessed the credit card he'd given her and discovered she hadn't used it for gas, food or lodging. He thought about calling her uncle before realizing that wasn't a good idea. If Nelson didn't know where she was and he had to explain what had happened, the situation could possibly turn hostile between him and the retired police officer.

Taking the cell phone off the bedside table, he called the one person he could talk to without prejudice. "What's up, Taylor?"

"You don't want to know, Viola."

"What's the matter?"

He registered the apprehension in his sister's voice. "I need to talk to you about Sonja."

"What did you do to her?"

"Is she there with you?"

"No. I spoke to her a couple of days ago to let her know I'm planning to leave The Cellar at the end of the summer and then hang out with you until the mansion's kitchen is up and running."

The news rendered Taylor speechless. "When were you going to tell me?" he asked, recovering his voice.

"I just told you."

"Stop playing games."

"And don't take that tone with me, Taylor Williamson. I am not responsible for what went down between you and Sonja."

Taylor knew he had to tell his sister about his relationship with her friend; he had no one else to talk to. "We had a disagreement and she left, and I haven't seen or heard from her since Thursday."

"What did you do to her?"

"It wasn't what I did but what I said."

"Tell me everything, Taylor, and don't leave anything out."

Taylor was forthcoming when he told his sister about his relationship with Sonja and their agreement to live together and the importance of trust. "I violated that trust when I saw her with another man and accused her of being unfaithful. That's when she told me I was just like her ex-husband."

"She's right, Taylor. The only difference is your ages. Her ex was more than twenty years older than Sonja and a predator. He loved younger women, and as a college professor he preyed on his female students. Sonja told me he was handsome, charming and erudite, and she fell hard for him. When he noticed younger men staring at her he suspected she was flirting with them. The one time he spotted her hugging one of his male students he went into a jealous rage and accused her of sleeping with the innocent boy. She denied it, and he begged her to forgive him and that it would never happen again. But it did happen again over and over, and that's when Sonja knew she'd made a mistake marrying Hugh Davies.

"She moved out of their bedroom and refused to host his parties. He turned on her. He placed a tracking device on her car and stopped giving her money. She looked so ashamed, Taylor, when she admitted to me that she'd begun stealing from her husband whenever he put down his wallet. Two dollars here and five dollars at another time. After a while she had enough money to buy a prepaid phone and hid it where she knew he would never find it.

"Then the monster made her a prisoner in her own home after he changed the locks on the doors in the house and refused to give her a set of keys. It was a double cylinder lock where you needed a key to unlock the door from the inside to get out. She waited two months before she began pilfering again. This time it was tens and twenties because she was planning to escape. She gave the SOB four years of her life because she'd hoped it would get better, but it never got better.

"There were times when she wanted to call her father to tell him what she had been going through but knew he would've murdered Hugh. She finally was able to escape after she found a second set of keys. She walked away when he went out of town for a conference. She never asked her husband to love her. All she wanted was for him to trust her. I was the only one who knew what her ex did to her, and now you know."

Taylor felt an icy shiver eddy down his back as if doused by cold water. Sonja had told him about feeling smothered but hadn't given him any details of what she'd endured with her ex-husband. Now he knew why she'd insisted he trust her. "I'm sorry, Viola."

"Don't tell me, Taylor! Tell your girlfriend."

"I've called and left voice mail messages for her to call me. She hasn't returned any of them."

"I'm going to do this one favor for you, brother, and if you mess it up then you're on your own. I'm going to call her and let her know I've spoken to you. I'm also going to tell her to send you a text to let you know she's safe. And you're going to text her back that you're willing to give her as much time as she needs to get her head straight. That can be either two days, two weeks or even two months. I'm warning you, Taylor. If you put pressure on her to come back, you *will* lose her—for good."

"Okay, Viola."

"Say it like you mean it, Taylor."

"I promise not to put any pressure on her."

"That's better, brother love. I'll talk to you at another time about why I've decided to become executive chef for Bainbridge House."

"Thank you, baby sis."

"You're welcome. I'm on vacation for the next two weeks, so if you need a shoulder I'll rent a car, drive up and hang out with you."

Taylor smiled for the first time in days. "I'd like that. We've just begun working on the house and I'd like to show you the plans for the restoration."

"That's a bet. I'll contact you before I come. Now hang up so I can call my friend."

Taylor ended the call and pressed his head against a mound of pillows under his back and shoulders. His conversation with Viola had left him shaken.

He could not imagine a young woman becoming so intimidated that she feared telling her parents that her husband had made her a virtual prisoner in her own home.

It was like a rerun with Sonja and Dom. He'd asked the caretaker to stay away from Sonja. However, it was obvious Dom had misconstrued it as a threat, not a request. Taylor hadn't said anything to Sonja once he'd noticed Dom lingering outside the library waiting for her to open the door. It wasn't until he spied them embracing that he began to wonder if it wasn't the first time Sonja and Dom had been together whenever the door was closed. He sucked in a lungful of air and held it for several seconds before he exhaled an audible sigh. Viola had asked him to wait and he would.

Sonja was sitting on a rocker on the porch, enjoying her second cup of coffee, when her cell phone rang. Taylor had left several voice mail messages asking her to call him. She wasn't ready to listen to anything he had to say. And she was going through her own self-examination once she realized she'd waited almost ten years to become involved with a man who had the same personality trait as the one she'd married: distrust.

The phone continued to ring and when she reached over to silence it she saw the name and number on the screen. The caller wasn't Taylor.

"Hi, Viola."

"How are you doing?"

Sonja smiled. "I'm better."

"Good. I'm calling to let you know I spoke to my brother. I don't want you to bite my head off, but I had to tell him everything you'd gone through with your ex-husband."

Sonja closed her eyes. "It's okay, Viola. It doesn't matter anymore."

"Yes, it does matter because my brother is in love with you. I'm not going to interfere any more, but I want you to text him that you're okay. Will you please do that for me?"

"Yes, Viola."

"Yes, what?"

"I'll text him." Sonja stared at the calm surface of the lake. "I love Taylor."

"You love Taylor, and he loves you. As two mature adults you should be able to work through your differences because I've always wanted a sister."

Sonja shook her head, smiling. "What you want is a sister-in-law."

"That, too," Viola drawled. "Since graduating culinary school, I've always wanted to run my own kitchen and prepare a wedding banquet. That definitely can become a reality if you marry my brother at Bainbridge House."

Sonja wanted to tell her friend that wasn't going to happen. Not when the man she had fallen for did not trust her to be a faithful wife. "I'm going to text Taylor to let him know I'm okay," she said instead.

"I'm not going to ask where you are, because if Taylor asks me I don't want to lie to him. When are you going back?"

"Probably in a couple of days. Originally I'd planned to spend the weekend here, but when I got up this morning I knew I needed more time to get my head together." What she didn't tell her friend was that she had to decide whether to move out of the condo, lease a car in her name and find a rental within the vicinity of Bainbridge House or stay where she was. She had no intention of living with Taylor after their breakup.

"Good. I'll call you again in a couple of days."

"Okay, Viola." Sonja ended the call and sent a text to Taylor.

Viola: I'm okay. Need some time to myself. Will be in touch.

She did not have to wait for his reply.

Taylor: Take all the time you need. I'll be here if or when you decide to come back.

If or when. The three words were branded into her head. Had he believed she would walk away from her work? That she was so unprofessional that she would abandon a project she'd sought since becoming an architectural historian? Bainbridge House wasn't just a structure some celebrity had erected because they were obsessed with all things French. Not only was it listed on National Register of Historic Places, it was originally commissioned in 1803 by a French nobleman who had fled to France during the Haitian Revolution as a gift to his new bride. And it wasn't until 1883 that Charles Bainbridge spotted the château and offered to purchase it from the then-impoverished owners who were hard-pressed to make the necessary repairs to the mansion. The Bainbridge House had an illustrious history, and Sonja wanted her name included in the restoration narrative once she listed it on her résumé. And she would follow Taylor's advice and take the time needed to sort out the next phase of her life.

Sonja was still at the lake house when her parents returned two weeks later, and she told them she was on holiday and needed a place to stay because she'd been working nonstop on the project. She knew her mother didn't believe her when she motioned with her head that they should go outside where James Martin couldn't overhear their conversation.

Rather than sit, she suggested they walk. Then Sonja told her mother everything from the time she'd gone out with Hugh for the first time, what he'd accused her of and why she'd had to plan her escape. She felt as if she'd been stabbed in the heart when she saw Maria cry.

"Why didn't you say something, *chica*?"

Sonja bit her lip in attempt not to lose her composure. It had been a long time since her mother had called her *little girl*, and in that instant she felt like an innocent, trusting little girl who had surrendered her will to someone so undeserving. "I didn't say anything because I didn't want Dad to kill him. And you know your husband would've done it, Mami."

"No, he wouldn't. He would've told your brother to get one of his buddies to take him out and make it look like an accident."

"See! That's why I didn't say anything."

"I know you didn't come here because of your psycho ex. Should I assume you've fallen in love with someone and you need your mama's advice as to how to proceed?"

"How did you know?"

Maria shook her head. "I don't know why kids believe their parents are oblivious. The last time we spoke I could hear something in your voice that told me you were happy, and that joy had come from you being in love. When you didn't tell me who he was I decided not to pry. But that was then, and this is now because I want to know everything."

Sonja was forthcoming about her relationship with Taylor. She admitted she was in love with him and wanted to marry him, yet that wasn't possible if he did not trust her.

They stopped in front of a boathouse and Maria turned to face her. "Can you put yourself in his situation and imagine you saw him hugging another woman. Wouldn't your first impulse be to accuse him of cheating on you?"

Sonja stomped her foot. "Why are you taking his side?"

Maria glared at her. "I'm not taking sides, Sonja. I

just want you to think about what this man has done for you. You claim he doesn't want to live with a woman unless he is married to her, yet he's done just that. Did you ask him why? There must be good reason why he doesn't believe in shacking up. The man appears to be everything that good-for-nothing you married wasn't for you to walk away without listening to him. He's jealous because he loves you, *chica*. And you've told me he's willing to give you all the time you need to get your head together."

Sonja nodded. "Yes."

"How long have you been here?"

"A little more than two weeks."

"That's more than enough time. Now, when we get back to the house I want you to pack your stuff and be ready to leave in the morning."

"Mami!"

"Don't Mami me, Sonja Mariana Rios-Martin! You're a thirty-four-year-old woman not a little girl running to her parents when things don't work out the way you want. Then you must ask yourself when you need to stop running and deal with your problems head-on. Your Taylor may not be perfect, but neither are you."

"What went on between me and Dominic was innocent, Mami. He'd disclosed something to me that I'd promised never to tell anyone, and he'd hugged me in appreciation."

"Wouldn't a handshake have been better?"

"I suppose it would, but what's done can't be un-done."

"What's going to be done is you leaving my house tomorrow morning and going back to Jersey to handle your business."

Sonja knew by Maria's expression and tone that she was serious about her not staying. "Okay. I'll leave in the morning."

Chapter Fifteen

Taylor waited for the arm to go up to drive into the gated community. It had been more than two weeks since Sonja left, and he hadn't realized how much he missed her until it was time for him to come home. As promised, Viola had driven up to spend two days with him, and it was the distraction he'd needed not to dwell on Sonja.

Viola had toured the kitchen, jotting down notes as to what she needed to update the space. She hadn't told anyone she was leaving The Cellar in mid-September and vacating her Greenwich Village apartment at the same time. She'd planned to move back to New Jersey and stay in their mother's condo while Elise was away. His sister did not bring up the topic of Sonja and for that he was grateful.

His foot hit the brake hard, causing the SUV to screech to a stop when he spied Sonja's vehicle parked in the driveway. Taylor wondered if she'd come back to pick up the rest of her clothes because she always parked in the garage.

Maneuvering in behind her car, he got out and opened the outer door. He smiled. Sonja always left that door unlocked to save him having to open two. He unlocked the inner one and walked in. Then he saw her. She looked the same, yet there was something different about her, and it wasn't only the curly hair falling over her shoulders. And it wasn't that she'd lost weight. It was her eyes when she stared at him.

"Hello, Sonja."

Her impassive expression did not change. "Hello, Taylor."

"Why didn't you tell me you were coming back?"

She blinked once. "I wanted to surprise you."

"I must say I am shocked and surprised."

"We have to talk."

Taylor did not want to believe they were talking to each other like strangers. "Okay. Have you eaten?"

"No."

"Then we'll talk in the kitchen while I put something together."

Taylor tossed his keys in a straw basket on the table in the entryway. He waited for Sonja to precede him and then followed her into the kitchen. She sat at the breakfast bar as he washed his hands in the half bath off the kitchen. He stared at his reflection in the mirror over the sink. He hadn't shaved in over a week, and there were tiny gray hairs in the stubble.

He returned to the kitchen and opened the fridge. "I made meat loaf using your recipe, so I hope you don't mind eating leftovers. I'll bake some potatoes and put together a salad to go with it."

Sonja wanted to scream at Taylor to stop, stop acting as if she was someone he'd met a few days ago and didn't know what she'd like. "I don't mind. What I do mind is you being overly polite and acting as if you don't know what I like to eat."

Taylor rested both hands, palms down, on the countertop. "I've been trying to be polite and patient while you got, as you said, your head together. Well, my head is totally together, and I want and need to know what you want from me."

Sonja closed her eyes and sighed. "I need you to be honest with me, Taylor."

"What about trust, Sonja? Weren't you the one who declared that trust is more important than love, or maybe even honesty?"

"Yes. And I'm being honest when I tell you that nothing happened between me and Dominic. I went to Bainbridge House to ask him about something I'd discovered in one of the trunks. He told me what I needed to know, and then made me promise never to tell anyone. It's when I promised him his secret was safe with me that he hugged me. End of story.

It had been more than ten years since I'd allowed a man to touch my body or make love to me because I didn't trust them not to go from Dr. Jekyll to Mr. Hyde. You were that man, Taylor, and when you accused me of cheating on you with Dominic it was as if I were reliving what I'd gone through with my ex. He accused me of sleeping with any and every man that glanced at me, so many that I lost count after the four or fifth one. And that was something I did not want to experience with you."

Taylor rounded the bar and eased her off the stool. "I'm so sorry, darling. I've been a fool and it was only after you'd left me, and Viola told me what you'd gone through with your ex that I had to apologize to Dom."

With wide eyes, Sonja stared at him not daring to believe what she'd just heard. "You approached him about me?"

"I did."

"To tell him to stay away from you."

"You didn't!"

"Yes, I did because I was jealous, Sonja. And angry. I saw how he'd linger outside the library door, waiting for you to open it."

"You're a fool, Taylor. I'd text him to come and pick up a crate I'd finished to take back to the cellar. He'd wait until I opened the door to come in. It was more than I could say for you when you'd walk in without bothering to knock and lock the door behind you."

She turned her head to hide a smile when his expression became sheepish. It was during those times when he'd come in to massage her back and shoulders and they'd end up kissing and touching each other, stopping short of making love.

Taylor rested his hands on her shoulders. "You enjoyed those impromptu visits as much as I did."

"I did. What did Dominic say when you accused him of fooling around with me?"

"He told me in no uncertain words that I wasn't his boss and couldn't tell him what to do. But he did promise to stay away from you because he didn't want to cause any trouble between us."

"Wouldn't it have been easier to tell him that I'm your fiancée?"

"But you weren't, Sonja. I know we talked about marriage, but we hadn't made a formal announcement."

"You're right about that. Maybe if I'd been wearing an engagement ring Dominic would've reacted differently to my agreeing to keep his promise."

Taylor's hand went to her waist, pulling her close. "I'm so sorry for not trusting you. Will you forgive me?"

"I'll think about it." Sonja wasn't going to let him off that easily.

"You said you wanted honesty, and I'm going to tell you something about myself because I love you and want to spend the rest of my life with you."

"Is it something most people don't know about?"

He nodded. "Yes."

Sonja cradled his face, her eyes making love to

it. Talking with her mother had made her look at life differently, that as a thirtysomething woman she couldn't continue to run away when she had to stand and work out her problems. Spending time away from Taylor had made her realize how much she loved and missed him, and the next time he proposed marriage she would give him a resounding yes without any attached stipulations.

"What's said in this house will remain in this house."

She rested her forehead against his chest, holding back tears when he told her he never knew the man that fathered him because he'd deserted his mother when she told him she was carrying his child. And he didn't remember his mother, who'd died from kidney disease when he was three. He had gone to live with an aunt who neglected him, and it wasn't until he'd entered the first grade that the school social worker intervened and he was placed in the home of Conrad and Elise Williamson as their first foster child.

"It took a while to adjust to wearing clean clothes, sleeping in my own bed, having enough to eat and calling a woman that looked nothing like me Mom. It took me a while to trust her when she said I could live with her for as long as I wanted. That's when I told her I never wanted to leave, and I would always be her son. She was able to convince Conrad to apply for more foster children, and that's how I ended up with a sister and three brothers. The day we were all legally adopted we promised one another not tell folks we weren't biological brothers and sister even though we don't all look alike."

Tilting her chin, Sonja smiled up at Taylor. "Your parents were truly remarkable people."

"My Dad was, and mother is," he said proudly.

"And they raised a remarkable son and daughter."

"My other three brothers are also remarkable."

"I can't wait to meet them."

Taylor's inky-black eyebrows lifted. "Are you saying you want to join my remarkable family?"

Sonja couldn't help smiling because she was so happy she feared her heart would burst. "If it means becoming your wife, then my answer is yes." Tightening his grip on her waist, Taylor lifted her off her feet and kissed her until she struggled to breathe. "Taylor, stop before I pass out."

"Now that we're engaged, you need a ring. I'm going upstairs to look at your jewelry stash to see if I can find one Conrad Williamson would want to pass along to his future daughter-in-law."

Sonja sat on the stool, waiting for Taylor to return. She'd brought all the jewelry home and stored it in a portable safe in the closet in the spare bedroom until it could be appraised. She estimated the rings, bracelets, necklaces, brooches, watches, hair and tie clips were worth millions and told Taylor he should confer with his mother and siblings which estate pieces they wanted to keep or sell.

Sonja covered her mouth with her right hand when Taylor returned holding the Asscher diamond ring between his thumb and forefinger. Her eyes widened when he went down on one knee and grasped her left hand.

"Miss Sonja Rios-Martin, will you do me the honor of becoming my wife?"

She had accused of him being traditional and he was playing the part. "Yes, Mr. Taylor Edward Williamson, I will marry you."

Taylor slipped the priceless ring on her finger, rose and kissed her mouth. "Thank you, *muñeca*. And thank you for trusting me enough to accept me as your future husband."

"I love you for being you and for trusting me with your family's secret."

He eased back, meeting her eyes. "You have no idea how much I love you, Sonja."

"I think I do," she said shyly when she saw lust shimmering in the dark eyes. "Dinner will have wait until you show me, *papi*."

Taylor scooped her off the stool, took the stairs two at a time and walked into the bedroom. No words were spoken because their bodies communicated wordlessly how much they had come to love each other. They fell asleep, their limbs entwined, and it was much later when they left the bed to shower together before returning to the kitchen to eat and make plans for their future and establish a new foundation for Bainbridge House.

* * * * *

MILLS & BOON

Coming next month

TUSCAN SUMMER WITH THE BILLIONAIRE
Susan Meier

It wasn't right. He was feeling things he wasn't allowed to feel, definitely mixing business with pleasure, when he knew better.

He shook his head. "I could virtually run our multi-billion-dollar conglomerate in my sleep, and your simple family business is breaking all my rules, making me crazy."

She shrugged. Her lips turned up into a smile that stole his breath and made his blood race.

He still held her hand. They stood only a few inches apart. The full moon smiled down on them while the vineyard that was at the center of their problems rustled in the breeze.

But she was smiling. Amused by him.

The humor of it struck him and his own lips rose. "This is crazy."

"There's that word again. You use crazy a lot...especially about yourself."

She really was funny. Fun. He felt like he was getting a glimpse of her as she really was, maybe as she had been before their employee embezzled.

With their gazes locked, everything inside him slowed to a crawl. Warmth suffused him, along with a yearning so pure he couldn't fight it. He inched closer.

The connection between them rose, swelling around him, urging him even closer.

"I think I'm going to kiss you."

Her eyes didn't even flicker with surprise. And why would they? They'd been attracted since the second they'd laid eyes on each other.

"You shouldn't."

Her voice was a soft whisper that skipped along his spine, but she didn't move. Didn't step back. Held his gaze.

Expectantly.

The hum of whatever it was that buzzed between them drowned out his common sense and reasoning. Simple curiosity filled him, as desire surged in his blood and temptation promised fulfillment, pleasure enough to make it worth the risk.

He lowered his head and kissed her.

Continue reading
TUSCAN SUMMER WITH THE BILLIONAIRE
Susan Meier

Available next month
www.millsandboon.co.uk

COMING SOON!

We really hope you enjoyed reading this book.
If you're looking for more romance, be sure to
head to the shops when new books are
available on

Thursday 1st April

To see which titles are coming soon, please visit
millsandboon.co.uk/nextmonth

MILLS & BOON

LET'S TALK

Romance

For exclusive extracts, competitions
and special offers, find us online:

 facebook.com/millsandboon

🐦 @MillsandBoon

📷 @MillsandBoonUK

Get in touch on 01413 063232

For all the latest titles coming soon, visit
millsandboon.co.uk/nextmonth

MILLS & BOON

THE HEART OF ROMANCE

A ROMANCE FOR EVERY READER

MODERN

Prepare to be swept off your feet by sophisticated, sexy and seductive heroes, in some of the world's most glamourous and romanti locations, where power and passion collide.

HISTORICAL

Escape with historical heroes from time gone by. Whether your passion for wicked Regency Rakes, muscled Vikings or rugged Highlanders, aw the romance of the past.

MEDICAL

Set your pulse racing with dedicated, delectable doctors in the high-pre sure world of medicine, where emotions run high and passion, comfort love are the best medicine.

True Love

Celebrate true love with tender stories of heartfelt romance, from the rush of falling in love to the joy a new baby can bring, and a focus on t emotional heart of a relationship.

Desire

Indulge in secrets and scandal, intense drama and plenty of sizzling ho action with powerful and passionate heroes who have it all: wealth, stat good looks…everything but the right woman.

HEROES

Experience all the excitement of a gripping thriller, with an intense ro mance at its heart. Resourceful, true-to-life women and strong, fearless face danger and desire - a killer combination!

To see which titles are coming soon, please visit

millsandboon.co.uk/nextmonth

JOIN US ON SOCIAL MEDIA!

Stay up to date with our latest releases, author
news and gossip, special offers and discounts, and
all the behind-the-scenes action
from Mills & Boon...

 millsandboon

 millsandboonuk

millsandboon

it might just be true love...

MILLS & BOON

HEROES

At Your Service

Experience all the excitement of a gripping thriller, with an intense romance at its heart. Resourceful, true-to-life women and strong, fearless men face danger and desire - a killer combination!

MILLS & BOON
MEDICAL
Pulse-Racing Passion

Set your pulse racing with dedicated, delectable doctors in the high-pressure world of medicine, where emotions run high and passion, comfort and love are the best medicine.